Virgin Princess

An historic novel of Mewar (Udaipur, India) — the world's oldest dynasty

Jane Richardson

Virgin Princess

An historic novel of Mewar (Udaipur, India) — the world's oldest dynasty

Jane Richardson

Published by:

 Thistle Publishing
11985 Cherokee Circle
Shelby Township, MI 48315

All rights reserved. No part of this book may be reproduced or transmitted in any form or by any means, electronic or mechanical, including photocopying, recording or by any information storage and retrieval system without written permission from the publisher, except for the inclusion of brief quotations in a review.

Printed in the United States of America.

© 1991, Jane P. Richardson.

Publisher's Cataloging in Publication Data
(Prepared by Quality Books Inc.)

Richardson, Jane P., 1919-
    Virgin Princess : an historic novel of Mewar (Udaipur, India) — the world's oldest dynasty / Jane P. Richardson. —
443 p. 21 cm.
    Includes bibliographical references.
    ISBN 1-879403-09-9

    1. Udaipur (India) – History — Fiction. I. Title.

PS3568.I27   813'.54
                                             90-90395

Preface

Virgin Princess, an historic novel (which incorporates a few fictional characters) reconstructs documented events in the 1200 year history of the feudal kingdom of Mewar. The setting is in northwest India, in the state of Rajasthan, frequently referred to as Rajputana. This oldest dynasty in the world was ruled by one family until India gained her independence in 1947.

The author became one of the most widely traveled persons throughout the Asian sub-continent, commencing in 1969, as attested to by late President of India, V. V. Giri and late Prime Minister Indira Gandhi, both personal friends. She was adopted as a sister into this Mewar family in 1970, an extremely treasured rite. Living in various parts of India and her constant travels brought her in contact with civic leaders of national governments as well as heads of the princely states on the fringes of Mewar (Udaipur). Much time was spent acquainting herself with persons in all walks of life, creating a deep love for and insight of things present and for the last millennium.

The author has lectured on this extensively in the United States and India. She formed a company which designed specialized tours to the sub-continent, frequently taking her tours into the homes of presidents, prime ministers, the Maharana and maharajas.

With Jane's intensified love of colorful Rajasthan she felt compelled to acquaint the world of the rich lives of an ancient and little known area. While the thrust of the book takes place in 1770s through mid 1800s, with the reign of Maharana Bhim Singh, it includes many bizarre, intriguing, documented stories of his illustrious predecessors of 1000 years. It created for

Bhim Singh an urge to keep alive their vanishing past and his curious treatment of his beloved daughter, nicknamed the *Virgin Princess.*

The cover photograph depicts the main City Palace in the lower right, Jag Niwas Palace (now Lake Palace Hotel) in Lake Pichola and the Monsoon Palace atop the Aravalli Mountains in the center.

All photographs taken and copyrighted by the author.

Any similarity between fictional characters and real persons, living or dead, is purely coincidental.

Acknowledgements

With allegiant thanks to Shriji Arvind Singh Mewar, Maharana of Udaipur, for setting my course to his spectacular kingdom, and his introduction to his father, late Shriji Bhagwat Singh Mewar, Maharana of Udaipur.

Overwhelming thanks to late Highness, Maharana Bhagwat Singhji, for his gracious and lengthy hospitality and creation of my deep-seated love of his kingdom.

To his younger brother Narendra, who, with brotherly affection, adopted me and was responsible in large part for my lengthy travels within Mewar and Marwar, and for whom I have named one of my heroes. (No similarity between my brother and fictional characters is intended.)

To Narayan Singh of Pali, recipient of the prestigious Padma Shri award by the President of India for his august contribution to his country in the fight against dacoity. Without his limitless descriptions and background on dacoits and dacoity I could not have understood or described such crimes.

To Thakur Sahib, Amar Singh of Sardargarh for his enlightening rendition of his forebears outwitting of the Mughal Emperor.

To the many other heads of feudal estates within the kingdom.

To Mr. K. B. Saolapurkur and to the vicarious merchants, professionals, farmers and others who rendered their recollections of earlier times as told them by their ancestors.

To those who accompanied me throughout the kingdom.

An especial thanks to Ramnathji, past acting curator of the old Palace Museum, who proudly explained countless historic pictures within the palace, which, in many cases documented their ancient history.

To the palace librarian who tirelessly brought me books, maps and documents from their archives, translating those not in English.

To Shabha Kanwar Bai-ji, granddaughter of late Highness Maharaja Partab Singh, Jodhpur, for escorting me to Mandore, to the old fort and places of historic interest and relating inspiring stories of Jodhpur.

To members of the families of Jaiselmer and Jaipur, all of whom helped balance my viewpoints.

To A. Sanjiv Rao of New Delhi and Houston who continuously prodded me to write on India.

To my husband Arch for his constant encouragement and support during the numerous travels to and around India.

To my son Bob for his tireless efforts in editing this book.

And to all those too numerous to mention, but whose help was equally appreciated and required.

To Narendra

my esteemed adopted brother

Prince Narendra Singhji, younger brother of late Highness Maharana Bhagwat Singhji, uncle of present Maharana Arvind Singhji, adopted brother of the author, shown standing atop the Main Palace overlooking Jag Niwas Palace (now Lake Palace Hotel) in Lake Pichola, Udaipur.

Contents

Chapter 1 11
Chapter 2 43
Chapter 3 71
Chapter 4 101
Chapter 5 121
Chapter 6 137
Chapter 7 151
Chapter 8 167
Chapter 9 183
Chapter 10 191
Chapter 11 207
Chapter 12 233
Chapter 13 255
Chapter 14 273
Chapter 15 303
Chapter 16 317
Chapter 17 339
Chapter 18 353
Chapter 19 369
Chapter 20 395
Chapter 21 417
Epilogue 427
Bibliography 429
Glossary 431

Chapter 1

Narendra stood motionless in the solemnity spreading to the four horizons as if he was God looking from heaven on unspoiled handiwork. An unfettered view from the fort was awesome, the advantage tactical. Predestined time formed the massive solid rock high above sprawling brown desert. Foreordained, Maharajas lived luxuriously for centuries atop the rock, their palaces built with the sweat of thousands of laborers over countless years.

Time had stood still here for the thirteen centuries of Jodhpur's existence. A strong six mile stone wall encircled the old city and fort, pierced with five huge gates. Beyond, unseen at this vantage point, toylike villages remained stubbornly unchanged, dotted only with parched water holes. The air was the same through all this vanished time, an occasional desultory breeze lifting crisply clear voices from the ancient city below. Narendra had bristled at his host's gruesome story of the man Banhi Rajia who had been interred alive in the foundation, thus making the fort impregnable and invoking good fortune for those who would dwell here. Helping the cause of security, the wall in strategic places was built seventy feet thick, the substantial masonry of heavy cut stone cemented and pinned with iron spikes.

Voices below addressed themselves to thousands of yesterdays and a pivotal tomorrow — expectantly little different. One cackling woman joked of His Highness's newest folly, the concubine from the Oswal tribe. If the conversation disturbed the Maharaja standing beside Narendra it did not show. Narendra's towering Rajput frame stepped away from the king to the edge of the immense ramparts, glancing steeply down to the melancholy city glimmering a mystical pale grey in the moonlight, a green water tank the only splash of color. The year was 1777.

His Highness the Maharaja strolled over sumptuous oriental rugs carried to the ramparts for an impromptu late dinner in Narendra's honor. India was growing hotter each day prior to the monsoons and the breezy ramparts dispensed temporary comfort. Though the party was small and informal, all the men were in full dress: churidar trousers, knee-length aachkan coats, colorful turbans, and their ever-present tulwar, the curved sword of Rajasthan. Rajputs were handsome men, tall, stately, frequently sporting heavy black beards and massive moustaches.

His Highness drew Narendra aside listening indulgently to the sweet sounds of a crinkled old man's flute. At his side a youngster sang a gay old Rajasthani folk song while a troupe of Lagha musicians awaited their turn. "It is amazing, is it not, the talents which lie dormant in our desert villages or jungles ... but everyone wishes to play for his king."

Rajasthan, a northwestern state in India, is regularly referred to as Rajputana, consisting of thirty-six kingdoms. Jodphur had been founded in 459, the largest of these princely states. Unfortunately the land is basically waste, covered with sand and hills. All of the northern sections of this kingdom is desert and one would think the 400 foot rock had been strategically placed there for the express purpose of building a fort upon it — one of the most impressive in the world.

Narendra's kingdom of Mewar, on the other hand, was founded two and a half centuries later, in the 700s, boasting a straight line of family rule — if one takes into consideration childless rulers adopting nephews or cousins, blood worthy of the title of "Rana," king. Only Mewar uses the title "rana" instead of "raja," Maharana meaning literally "king of the Maharajas."

For centuries Rajasthan was regarded as a stronghold of chivalry and valor. Endless centuries brought everything from skirmishes to full scale wars, sprinkled with indolent years of peace. Mughal emperors fought Hindu princes. Boundaries changed — but little else. Buildings, ancient customs, clothing, myriad languages and dialects, these remained the same as did court intrigue; brothers and sons slaying kin for gaddi or throne. Hindu rulers gave their princesses to Muslim would-be invaders for another year of dishonorable peace.

Yet in all this timeless misery there was one kingdom alone which cherished its valorous past and the glory of her chivalrous deeds. Mewar. More than all else the pure Hindu royal blood of the princesses remained forever all-important to Mewar's succession of rulers, under no circumstances to be compromised. Narendra was of this kingdom, and as ardent a believer in this cause as his need for air to breathe.

Today Narendra was 350 kilometers from home, relaxing as guest of his friend, His Highness Vijai Singh, Maharaja of Jodhpur. Twice before he had accepted this illustrious man's invitations. Ardently he admired the expansive fort with its incredibly impressive palaces pierced with screens of red sandstone and the view from the ramparts of barren beige slowly sifting sands of the vast countryside. It was Jodhpur's coup de grace. Warriors astride elephants and camels found it impossible to hide en masse, and unwasted acoustics offered up to the fort the most meager of sounds.

Beyond this, should invaders manage their way through city walls by virtue of sheer strength and tenacity, their elephants would have found it impossible to charge the fort. Once inside the main darwaza or door, the incline becomes significantly steeper. More darwazas and lanes bend sharply and again steeper. A charge would be impossible. Added to this, each door is impregnated with lengthy spikes strategically placed to impale an elephant.

Of course there was the case of the mahut in Mewar who slipped his body down over the head of his beloved elephant, ordering the beast to charge. These pachyderms have generally grown up with only one mahut and fearlessly obey each command. He charged, as ordered, and his mahut was left dangling on the spikes with the desired outcome, the gate had been successfully rammed open and the young rider's master sitting behind him on the elephant had gained entry. Mewar is still singing the honor and praises of this mahut.

"The hour is growing late. Let us dine," Vijai Singh directed Narendra out of an intoxicating fantasy. Words barely out of his mouth, they were met with distant discordant sounds, something of a muted cacophony. Everyone on the ramparts stood motionless, then suddenly a small bright spot of light appeared in the distance, quickly growing in intensity. A force gripped Narendra and he turned, speeding down the ramp, twisting and turning down another beneath magnificently carved stone windows of the zenana, the ladies palace.

"Where are you going? It's probably only village huts ablaze," the ruler called loudly after Narendra, leaning over a low wall, following his descent. But Narendra was too fleet of foot, his mind filled with a gut hunch of hideous disaster. He could perhaps help.

Rushing downhill, fright added speed to his feet, nearly toppling his bulky frame headlong. He wondered what he would use for a horse when he would reach the outer gate. His would have been fed and bedded down for the night. He had no time to wait, even for a moment.

Through many gates he fled, an added shiver as he raced through Loha Pol only newly completed. He knew the munitions of war were stored here but there was no time to beg His Highness for support. Here too, the handmarks of the Satis seemed especially to show themselves, the women who left the fort through this gate to join their husbands on blazing funeral pyres. Were their prints an omen?

Reaching the last or main exit, a gateman squatted with his friend who had earlier arrived at the fort on camelback. They jumped to their feet, issuing deep salaams. Narendra, without asking permission, threw his bulk upon the humped back. He was off in a gallop in the direction of the furtive sounds and ominous red glare.

The silent-footed creature carried his burden quickly as the fire grew brighter and the offending human sounds quieter, in itself a disquieting thought. Was it his kismet or karma, his fate, which was racing him to what must surely be a very small village? He wondered what it was that forced him instantly from the luxury of the palace across these flowing sands. He knew no one here except the royal family.

In recent years Narendra felt he was living at half speed, wandering aimlessly, searching for a meaningful existence. He was born into one of the families serving the Maharana of Mewar. There were many such families, for the ruler of that kingdom of 10,000 towns and villages had within his feudal state sixteen first-class nobles and thirty-two second-class. Each had his own fort, military and judicial system and Narendra's father was one of the honored nobles, ruling over the estate of Jagatpur. Each personally served his master for specific periods of time throughout each year. This young man usually accompanied his father and lived on the palace grounds in Udaipur for the duration of his father's session at court. Thus it was he came to be learned in the arts of protocol and the wiles of court intrigue.

Still at a gallop, past years and questions of the future played hopscotch across his mind, now interrupted by what lay immediately ahead. Everyone had been hearing the tales of Motilal and his band of dacoits rumored to be in the vicinity of Jodhpur. Could it be true? The increasing spread of flames could be nothing less than the sacking of a village. Narendra could see no others. Was no one coming to the assistance of the villagers? Or had others arrived and been killed? If Motilal was as despicable as suggested, others might shy away from assisting these people. True, the Rajputs were fierce warriors but their battles had been organized. Narendra had given no heed to his safety, for if the problem was dacoits, the villagers would need all the help they could get.

Dacoity is the commission of a crime: robbery, rape or murder by a group. Those committing such crimes are called dacoits, commonly kidnapping for ransom, though rarely kidnapping girls. Narendra had seen by now enough of the terrain to consider this a breeding place for dacoits with good hiding in its sands and deep ravines. He had raced many kilometers and now he rushed into the center of an ill-fated village.

Crackling fires of grass huts and voiceless bodies surrounded him. Devastation was unbelievable and his arrival took Motilal by surprise. He rose from the ground, half clothed, jerking upwards with him the raped body of a grief stricken young woman, naked from the breasts down, her little bodice tied in the back, pushed around her throat like a cloth necklace. Faster than lightning Narendra was beside the dacoit, but in that same flash Motilal grasped his dagger severing the heavily silver-adorned arm of the girl.

This flagitiously revolting sight nauseated Narendra and he too brandished his ever-present sword of the Rajput. Two slashes did their job and this intensely angry man neatly removed both hands of the bandit, the one still clutching the jeweled severed arm of the hapless maiden. Even in separation Motilal's hand resisted parting with the silver bangles which would bring a fine price on the market. Here in Rajputana it is custom to wear one's wealth. Scattered throughout all of India there is to be found surprising age-old wealth, for often these bangles have remained in families countless generations.

There are those who would argue one hand was enough for being caught at this night's horror, but instinct told Narendra of the countless misdeeds here alone: rape by others in the band, pillaging, mass murder — it appeared from precursory glances no one else was alive. Motilal fell stunned, disbelieving, as the newcomer turned his attention to the hapless girl. Apparently the loss of honor and arm so incalculably shocked the maiden that before Narendra could grab her she had thrown herself into the largest of the roaring bonfires. Not a grass hut remained, all of which had stood in a large protective circle.

Pernicious misery filled Narendra's being, gasping at the girl whose life was already snuffed out with intense heat and suffocating flames. Swinging full circle he stared at dead bodies of men, women and children. No one breathed except Motilal. How many had it taken to reek this havoc? All the other dacoits had already fled, leaving their leader with his final conquest. In the distance could be seen just the barest glimpse of camels over the horizon, five he thought, and it would serve no purpose now to give chase. In all the nullahs or ravines of the encompassing desert and with their head start, chances of catching them were extremely slim, and what could one man do?

With deleterious precision Narendra turned, staring hostiley into the murderer's agonized face. Motilal had not moved since losing his two hands, his cadaverous eyes glaring back at his assailant. Minutes seemed to slide by with neither man stirring when, with a sudden move and one vengeful thrust, Narendra drew his sword high above his head and sped it savagely into the heart of the dacoit.

Narendra checked carefully those persons who lay beyond the fires. He could not know whether any villagers had safely fled this holocaust though it was unlikely. All those visible were dead. Wearily he threw his tremulous body onto the borrowed camel and let it slowly walk back in the direction of the huge rock fort of Jodhpur.

"My God, I've killed a man." Reality had finally set in. Nausea once more overtook him and he slid from the camel, retching into the parched sand. Delineations of their evil and his performance brought desolation and it was still dark with just a hint of light beyond the fort, outlining the top of the ramparts' crenels. The four silent hooves beneath him continued at a slow and steady pace. Inside the walls of the city the orange glow of the morning sun overtook the horizon and there started the low rhythmic beat of the dhobis at their morning laundry chores, beating brilliant colored clothes of the desert against the steps of the city's ghat.

The gateman's friend had spent the night awaiting his camel's return. Throwing his leg across the body and sliding onto the ground, Narendra wearily thanked him with random rupees thrust into his hand.

Stumbling upward that long, long series of zigzagging cobblestone paths he dropped exhausted at the steps of the palace, oblivious of the pink and brown splendor of carved stone doors and windows surrounding him. He shrugged off a servant offering assistance, falling into a nightmare violated sleep on the refreshingly still cool stone step. He could go no further.

Several comfortless hours later, the Maharaja, having completed morning devotions, issued urgent orders to bring Narendra to the Diwan-i-Khas, the Hall of Private Audience. There Narendra was requested to reveal every graphic detail of the previous night. He had wondered why His Highness had not sent reinforcements to back up his efforts, but in a foreign kingdom it was not wise to verbalize his annoyance. Narendra's description of the dacoit left no doubt in the minds of His Highness Jodhpur and his Prime Minister that this was indeed Motilal.

Orders were peremptorily given to arrange for cremations of the dead.

His Highness turned to yet another subject. "What of Motilal's mistress? He was known to have one. Was there no sign of her? She could be lying dead amongst the others. Some of these women occasionally join their men in such raids."

The thought of such a woman lying there with the victimized unfortunates made Narendra bristle. "By God, I hope she didn't die there." His teeth were clenched but his words were clear. "I wouldn't want her ashes sanctified with those of the poor villagers. I'd <u>bury</u> her body before I'd have her cremated with the others." This burly man was, to say the very least, a devout Hindu — just how unceasingly devout even he did not yet realize.

Repetition of details became burdensome and Narendra suffered a scathing anguish unrealized by the Maharaja or his Prime Minister. "I beg your leave." He tried to explain his weariness of mind and body but it was his soul which was strangled by anguish beyond all understanding. Could he live with himself after vengefully murdering a man? Would he be made to atone? While he was of immense proportions and brought up in the Rajput tradition of bravery, chivalry and valor, still ... "Oh dear God, erase that bewildered look on Motilal's face before I <u>killed</u> him. How can I ever have peace?"

There was only one thing to do — see his father who had always been his mainstay. Yes, father would know what to say and do. His Highness, compassionately understanding, ordered Narendra's belongings packed and a packet of fruit, chapatis and some of the orange colored jellabies wrapped for the trip, for he knew of his guest's sweet tooth.

"Everything will be fine, maré dhost, you will see. God is great. When you are ready come back to us at Jodhpur and we shall have the visit which was cut so short. Namasté."

"Namasté." Narendra, palms touching each other before his forehead, bowed low in reverence to his friend's high station in life.

Although offered a royal escort Narendra declined the offer thinking it to be faster. Vapid conversation taxed him greatly, lasting far longer than he had liked. It was by now late afternoon and Narendra chose the route which would take him beside the legendary but defunct kingdom of Mandore. In its quiescent atmosphere perhaps he could regroup his thoughts. His horse Chetak, named after Mewar's greatest animal hero, was condemned to a thunderous gallop until suddenly the rider came to his senses. Slowing to a more leisurely pace he reached the ancient cenotaphs. In the remnants of Mandore's once alluring garden surrounding the cremation sites of its rulers, stood the tallest, statuesque monuments. So greatly did they differ from all others in Rajputana, they appeared to have been designed by the architects of India's deep south, of heavy gray carved stone. Those cenotaphs of the many northwestern kingdoms were usually of white stone or marble, gracefully arched in Persian style.

As Narendra walked among them he wondered what really had drawn him here, having been in such a rush to reach his father. The sun was beginning to set and there could be no real distance put between last night's tragedy and his troubled spirit. Sandy roadways would not be visible in the dark of the night, and he was fearful of losing his way and wasting more time.

Continuing across parched ground, the sky hinted of the vivid color it would soon become. A muted, plaintive sound of partridge carried through the air. "Tee-tree. Tee-tree." It took a sharp and delicate ear to hear it — only one of Narendra's diverse attributes. He wandered eight or ten minutes in the direction of the sound, climbing a barren hill, leading Chetak by the reins. At the top of the hill he saw an amazing sight, unnoticeable from the road on which he had first traveled. Sprawled ahead of him another 400 meters were the exquisite white marble cenotaphs of the recent queens and princesses of Jodhpur. He'd heard strange rumors of these structures spread across this open pathless sea of sand-cum-soil. Rarely seen was this graceful charm of Mandore's and Jodhpur's relics. Between the pillars and lovely chhatris or domes the sun slid its vibrant tones. And now at dusk the sounds which first attracted Narendra were more vocal. "Tee-tree, tee-tree."

"Partridge," Narendra rang out aloud as if to waken the spirits which must abound here. He'd learned to hunt partridge and quail as a youngster with his father, graduating to bluebull, then tiger and leopard. The latter skins are lovely, especially when spread across marble palace floors throughout Rajputana, but it had taken him a long time to become accustomed to killing these gorgeous animals. And now that thought brought back vividly last night's horrors. "Partridge," he quietly quavered.

At his first raucous outburst there had been a definable rustling of feathers. Was it only fowl he frightened? Could there be something more? Some one? Cautiously he stepped forward with the cunning instincts of a hunter. His formidable body was proportioned for fitness and he possessed the feline agility of the cats he had come to love. Now he stalked a possible unseen prey, grimly. Not forgotten were the dacoits who escaped last night's carnage. They'd be vicious and quick to kill.

Narendra firmly grasped a dagger, crouching close to the ground, surveying the dangerous territory spread before him. Steps and massive plinths on which the cenotaphs were constructed marred the view of surrounding ground giving undisturbed hiding places. The structures were built high enough to make it impossible to see inside from this now semi-prone position. Were they harboring criminals? Creeping forward he stretched his bulk upward slowly at the side of one of the larger monuments. Marble groins of the domes were supported by heavy pillars. He glanced inside at emptiness, and through as many others as his vantage point allowed. The red heaven burned deeper toward the horizon offering an awesome view, but there came an ominous breath on the air.

There's more here tonight than partridge, he sensed. Quail joined in the continuous evening song-ritual. He could afford to be patient only as long as the dusk remained, after which would follow a tactical disadvantage. On shikars he would necessarily sit motionless, impressively silent for two, three or even four hours before the beaters skillfully maneuvered the prey in the direction of waiting hunters.

Now the dark rushed in. He could not remember it ever before happening this fast. If Motilal's escaped cohorts were indeed hiding here they were clearly at an advantage for they'd have heard his boisterous arrival in the open vastness of the desert between Mandore's cenotaphs below and those of the queens at this higher level. They would have followed his every vulnerable move.

Could the dacoits indeed be here, he wondered, his heart beating faster. It would be an ideal meeting place, pre-arranged, for distribution of their newly acquired riches, however little or much that might be. They could have waited through the day for the return of Motilal; now they could be waiting for blessed darkness to again escape. It had been known widely that otherwise honest men unable to find work would join a band of dacoits. It was also common knowledge that the money and jewels acquired by looting is shared equally with the band. They would have arranged a rendezvous. Without their leader the task of distribution would become disjointed.

Narendra slithered to yet another cenotaph when suddenly there fell a shadow. Dagger still in hand, he leaped onto the raised square chabutra turned pink in reflected sunset and grasped fanatically the arm of a female, bedraggled even in this left-over light. Her knees buckled under his grasp. "A woman," he moaned, a deep scowl crossing his face, her full red and green gagra continuously swirling back and forth across her hips from the force with which he grabbed and spun her around to him.

"What in hell are you doing here? Who are you?" Narendra asked in a voice which struck terror in her marrow. There were no villages within a convenient walk of the cenotaphs, nor had he spotted any horse or camel she may have ridden. Confused thoughts rushed through his mind, apprehensiveness savored of fear. But if she was with the dacoits, if they were hiding here, they would have kept their camels hidden in a nullah or ravine. Dacoits? It was more than uneasy apprehension which gripped him now. A pall of foreboding would be more accurate. Any of the dacoits could have seen him last night as he seized upon Motilal raping the girl. They'd recognize him, even in this fast fading light. They'd have their revenge for their murdered despotic leader. And again those cadaverous eyes of the dying Motilal haunted Narendra. The gruesomeness must be pushed from this moment and instantly replaced with life-saving thoughts. This was burdensome, for the last twenty four hours had bred an ugly discontent for evil doings and all things remotely associated with dacoity. "Lord, am I doomed to a pattern of running into dacoits?" he wondered.

He would be cunning and intimidating, for he had seen it work wonders by his father's treatment of unruly chaprasis. This would be his strategy. To the girl his clasping fingers grew rigid creating rankling pain, her already large black eyes widened with alarm. He looked into them long and quietly, watching them change to a vague anxiety. He repeated his unanswered questions. "Who are you?"

There was a wistful droop to her mouth and she replied simply, "My name is Nina," her throat tight with unshed tears.

"Where are you from, Nina?" he continued, holding her fast.

Words came in a monotone, yet there appeared to be a faint lifting of weight from her heart. "My village is past Alwar. But my ancestors long ago were from the Punjab."

"You're a long way from home. What are you doing here?"

She again took her time in replying, hopelessness losing itself in tears, and an incoherent outburst of words. He would automatically carry a burden of doubt for any reply she would make; still, he had to ask. "Are you one of the dacoits? Are you by any chance the mistress of Motilal?"

"Your words are more accurate than you can imagine. It indeed was by a terrible chance I became his mistress. I did not want ..."

"Tell me about it girl. Tell me everything, but do not lie. Don't ever lie to me. But first, are there others here?"

"We are alone. I swear it." There was a cold sea of impersonality about this conversation and Nina had succumbed, even before Narendra's arrival, to a fatalistic indifference to life. Most men or women would have cowered from this gruff, fearsome Narendra but Nina's life had been a sad one for such a long time and nothing any longer seemed to matter. "About a year ago I was kidnapped from my village by dacoits."

"Motilal?" he interrupted.

"Yes, Motilal was one of them, and when the leader died soon after, Motilal took his place. I became his woman. I didn't want to," she raised her voice, eyes widening as if to convince him.

"Are you quite certain none of them are with you? If you're lying to me I'll kill you where you stand." He tried hard to sound persuasive.

"It would not matter. I might even welcome it, but I assure you there is no one here except you and I and all those partridges to whom you called."

"How did you come to be here? Were you on the raid last night? You're waiting for the band if they're not already here, aren't you? You're waiting for your cut."

The night before Nina had walked many kilometers from the planned meeting place to have followed the raid in an attempt to escape Motilal and his band. Clever and vicious, he would probably find her in due course, but the valiant effort had to be made, however unavailing it might end. She tried to explain her fears, and feeble attempt to escape.

"But you're his woman, by your own admission."

"I told you. He is vicious." She started perceptibly shivering. "I tried to escape for almost a year but there were always too many spies among us. I could never trust anyone. I could never forget how they killed my parents."

"You can relax now," he loosened his grip. "Motilal is dead." He hoped he had read this girl correctly.

Good fortune dispenses her gifts at random and Nina, as a recipient, could not easily comprehend this stroke of luck. "How do you know? Are you sure?"

"I was there. I ought to know," Narendra replied. "When did you last see him? Did you go to that village last night?"

"Yes, he would always make me go, I think so I wouldn't try to escape during his absence, but he mostly would make me hold the camels as he would quietly slip into some village and take them by surprise. Last night I watched in horror behind bushes as they ravaged the women and children and stole any money and jewels they could find. Then they burned the straw huts. Some village men were beaten and stabbed by the dacoits and if they tried to run, our men would kill them. We started with nine men besides Motilal. The element of surprise is strong and the whole village was at a disadvantage. They never had a chance."

"And when did you run away?" Narendra wondered if she had seen him in the bright firelight, though she never indicated any recognition. But could he believe her stories? Earlier today he indicated his intense feeling of hatred for Motilal's mistress. The words he spoke to His Highness Jodhpur came back to him now, that he'd rather bury her than have her cremated if she had been found among the dead and identified. As a Hindu this would have been horrific.

He thought too of discussions with his beloved father who tried to teach him the meaning of ahimsa. He'd explain it is the greatest love and charity and if you truly believe in ahimsa and live it, all people in your life must be treated the same by you. If a raja and a lowly sudra do the same misdeed to you, you must treat the raja and the sudra the same, ideally speaking. Surely his father must be right, if he said this, and just as surely in life this would be a difficult task to put into practice. He looked down from his two meter frame into the face of Nina, only three quarters his size.

"I walked our camels behind a barn full of animals — some camels and some cows I think — and I saw Pancy, one of the dacoits, set it afire. From the glow I saw Motilal tear the clothes off a girl and start to rape her. She was so petrified and he was so forceful. So brutal." Nina started again to softly cry. I knew I was not the only one, his only woman. I never cared for I loathed and despised him. I knew he'd go to the cities and be with nautch girls, but last night was different. His lust suddenly was much more loathsome. As he started to rape her I started running.

"After a while I stayed in a ravine and then when I was sure no one else was leaving the village and all sounds had stopped except the crackling of the embers I walked and walked until I came here. By then it was daylight and I hid behind these cenotaphs until it would get dark again and I could walk some more."

Ahimsa. Father would probably want me to believe her, Narendra considered. More accurately he chose neither to disbelieve or dispute the story. It was clear each of them was emotionally exhausted. "To what place do you walk?" he asked.

"All my family was killed when Motilal kidnapped me. Even my aunts and uncles were unfortunately visiting us then and they too were killed. No one was left. I have no one to go to, and have only the clothes which I now wear. Our village was destroyed, but even if it wasn't I could never go back. I have been dreadfully shamed. I shall have to beg for my food and try to find work ... but not until I reach a place large enough that no one will ask questions. Perhaps somewhere there is someone who will let me work in their household."

"We'll talk about it tomorrow," was his dictum, a man suddenly filled with compassion for a young woman he just hours ago had pledged a dishonorable burial and a resultant life after death of a fiendish hell. They sat on the edge of the cenotaph, now in darkness before the rising moon, legs dangling over the side. He unwrapped the little bundle of food from the palace, eating the chapatis, fresh fruit, and gooey jellabies. She had not eaten in over twenty four hours; famished, she was grateful he happened upon this place. "We'll talk tomorrow," he repeated. "You'll be safe with me. We'll think of someplace for you to go. Not to worry. Right now I am much too exhausted to think."

Gripped by the magnetism of his words, the young girl crossed to the opposite side of the cenotaph and curled up. Sleep would come easier with the knowledge she was safe from any vengeance of her captor of more than a year ago. Meanwhile her newfound hero tended and tethered his horse for the night.

Desperately Narendra tried through the night to force himself from consciousness, a priceless balm, but Motilal's eyes were ever with him, haunting, taunting. Even before any suggestion of the morning's radiance Nina stirred to find Narendra awake, stretching, jumping from the platform and moving none too exhilaratingly in the direction of Chetak. Yesterday afternoon he fled from the inevitableness of a puzzling confrontation with his father by riding first to the cenotaphs. His confusion was a smoke screen to his baffled mind. He needed a frank talk with his father to sort out his deeds or misdeeds. His procrastination here brought only more aggravating confusion.

There was a subtleness about Nina which made her different. No, not her misfortunes but a quality which he could not yet pin down. It was nothing sensual for she was neither particularly pretty nor distractingly plain. She was void of the regal bearing to which he was accustomed, for though Narendra had never explored the thought, there is indeed something elegant and graceful about the women of the courts which he had visited, an inbred regal bearing. She was neither fearfully shy nor truculently aggressive. He was allowing himself to be saddled with her and what was to be her fate? For that matter, what was his? Fate is stronger than any cult. His procrastination must end and he must get on with the immutable laws of living, a reorientation of thought and deed.

Nina for her part had lived what seemed an entire lifetime in this last year in an ugly webwork of evil. She awakened this day with a deepening sense of the gravity of her situation. Free of Motilal's shackles she should have relaxed, but would this stranger assist her in finding a new way of life? He certainly was not obligated. Seeing through his outer layer she was not oblivious of his deep thoughts and troubled countenance. He, like herself, had launched into the pathetic aloneness one feels following unimaginable tragedy. The barren emptiness of life without family or friends enshrouded her. But Nina was so proud. Her miseries were not of her doing but cast upon her with unremitting force. Wallowing in this dense sadness was not to be tolerated nor would she indulge in what might have been. At this very moment she would commence a new life. It would have to be this way and had no energy for regret. She would make herself believe that Narendra Singh would help her find herself and a place in which to exist. He was kind last night; he would be even more helpful today.

Narendra knew the role he must play. He once more thought of his father's lessons on ahimsa. He therefore could not judge this woman, nor did it matter whether or not he truly believed her story. If indeed her life had been servile, as a fellow human he owed it to her to find a new existence. "Oh hell," he shouted over his back as he untethered his docile horse, "you'll come with me and somewhere we shall find a place for you to stay." The dictum issued, he shrugged the first of many weights.

Now the immediate need was to be at the feet of his father. Everything else paled by comparison — even this girl's future. Narendra felt his soul in jeopardy, his sanity at stake. An animal could kill, but could a man? He could watch the extermination of brindled tigers, then walk barefoot over their beautiful coats. How elegantly they enhanced marble floors of sumptuous homes. He even learned to hit them where a bullet hole would not show in the skin. But thrust a sword into a man you first mercilessly maimed, a man whose eyes stared up into yours in helpless misery, even though Motilal's atrocities made him worse than a beast. Those thoughts were no better than cheap whitewash on pukka desert houses before the monsoons — easily washed away.

The last chapati was unwrapped and shared with his charge. With Rajput chivalry he helped her atop Chetak and commenced a lengthy walk. The better part of an hour elapsed before reaching a roadside hut. Beside it squat a man old with ageless dignity. At his feet a water kettle atop a smouldering dung fire sent a misty steam upwards.

Throughout all awakening India, as night gives birth to day, these little dung fires glow, the steam from each reaching out in every direction trying to mingle with that of the next, however distant. India is heaven's closest neighbor. In this ever changing country with eighty percent of the population living in villages there are literally millions rising to this daily spectacle. Imaginary silken grey veils slowly, silently lift and dissolve until finally one can see past trees, bushes and huts to far flung fields. Sleepy dwellers leave their homes for morning obligations of nature outdoors. Soon ladies in yards of cloth below their waists, gracing every movement of their unhurried bodies, wind down dirt paths to village wells. Brass water pots glisten atop heads in slightly more affluent towns but here in poorer villages of the northern desert, sun-dried red clay pots are in use. Easily patted into shape with little wooden paddles, rapidly dried in the heat of the desert sun, they are gratifyingly inexpensive.

"Do chay," Narendra ordered, firmly seating himself against a stumpy gnarled tree. Nina covered her face with the orange scarf of the Rajasthani women. Head slightly bowed she sat a little behind her newly acquired backer waiting for tea to brew. They spoke but few words this morning and she began to hope he could be trusted to take her well beyond this region where she would feel safe. The escaped dacoits could be anywhere. "Slow and easy wins the race" was always heard throughout Rajasthan. She'd make it her new credo.

To reach his father in the next week he'd need another horse if he was to take Nina very far. A horse not too old and certainly not lame. Where to find one such in the desert where camels were in greater number? He enquired of the chay walla, not too hopefully. Coincidentally the old man knew of a couple horses which might be purchased and pointed in the direction of the farm no more than a kilometer down the road. Narendra urged Nina to drink her tea quickly as he gulped his.

Nina was beside herself with glee for why would a man, a stranger, buy a horse for her to ride if he shortly intended to drop her off someplace. There was hope she could ride well away from the territory of the dacoits who knew her.

Bargaining was brisk for a mare. Narendra was an excellent judge of horseflesh and a gallant horseman. He teethed on it. It took only minutes before Nina was on its back. More accustomed to riding camels, she found this horse a rather gentle creature and certainly a much smoother ride. They took to each other easily. Another obstacle in Narendra's fast arrival home was now unshackled.

They got themselves quickly onto the road to Pali vowing not to stop for a bite until Rohat. Narendra loved this desert land wide swept with dunes, winds crinkling the waves of sand into artistic ridges. They passed villagers who would daily sweep sand from the roadway lest the path be lost forever. Nina had never seen this done and thought of it as friends strewing flower petals before a bride on her way to her wedding. She had taught herself to see her world more glamorously than its reality, something of a game to make a sad life more beautiful.

Narendra was compressed in thought. Yet from his shroud he could step momentarily into something beautiful before again returning to his meditation. Beauty to Narendra was something different than the beauty beheld by others. Had he been asked if Nina was beautiful he would first have to look. Never had he looked at her with a thought of beauty or ugliness. It was more like never looking at all. Yet at a moment galloping down the road to Robat he stopped suddenly, slid from his horse to examine the low-cropped fuzzy white bush of the desert, a plant not seen in his area. Now this was beautiful. It had a sweetness and serenity. A foot and a half of rounded loveliness slightly swaying over the changeless shade of beige sand spreading in every direction. Villages were far apart as were the semi-dried palms. Narendra ran his fingers across the feathery fine white bush so majestic in this massive openness, moving with sanctified authority. In its blissful realm it lives on unmolested even by camels for it has no food value.

"Who can figure God?" Narendra reverently spoke. Here was a lovely mystery of the universe but conversely the sight of the armless raped young woman flinging herself into the hottest of the flames flashed before him. Everything he did, everything he saw brought back the events of two nights ago. In one graceful motion he was atop Chetak and off to a steady canter. Nina managed to stay close behind and he became almost oblivious to her presence. The sun stung at the riders and they were soon compelled to allow their horses to move at their slowest gait. Tomorrow they'd start earlier and stop before the intense heat of the day.

From a ridge Narendra noticed a small stone house with richly carved arches and the shimmer of a little lake. Veering slightly off course they pulled rein and found the building stood empty. "What is this?" Nina asked.

"Perhaps it's a little palace of a queen who wanted to live away from court. They did things like that sometimes, you know."

"I know nothing about kings and queens or how they live but if I were a queen I would want to live forever in the biggest and finest palace of all. I would never move away, not even to a pretty little place like this," she replied.

"You are an idealist. Things are not always as grand as one suspects."

"I don't know, but I'd be willing to find out."

Narendra chuckled at her humor. By this time he was down at the water's edge, giving drink to Chetak and motioning Nina to do likewise.

"What's that?" she questioned. "Some strange kind of lotus blossom?"

Dipping his hands into the cooling pool he brought up several water chestnuts, the outer shell falling easily away from the nut. "Go ahead, eat. You'll like them. You should be hungry." The crunchiness was a surprising delight and of course she was very hungry. He shelled more, carefully wrapping them in cloth and packing them away until another hungry moment.

A few hours later at a branch of the slowly rippling Luni River they stopped again to water their horses. A signpost indicated several more kilometers to the center of Rohat. Taking tiffin of cooling buttermilk they were eager to continue their journey to Pali. They simply had to put more kilometers behind them.

"Just how far do you think you should go with me?" he broached a difficult subject with a degree of pity.

"To where do you ride?"

"My father's home is well past Udaipur. Much farther south."

"I'd be safe there. No one would recognize me. Could I go with you all the way? I would work very hard there. I can cook Rajasthani and I do some stitching." Her eyes grew wide with enthusiasm.

He answered halfheartedly, "I had thought I could leave you at a city somewhere a little farther on. You could sell this horse I shall give to you and with that money you could buy food for quite a while."

She did not answer but cast her eyes to the ground, swallowing hard to choke back the sudden hurt. Seeing the evident sadness, more tumultuous was his boggled mind, the murder, the blood on his head and in his heart.

Pali yielded a rest stop and both were tired enough to eat early and sleep reasonably well.

In the dark of the early morning, with no desire to dawdle, Narendra urged Nina to ready herself for a five minute departure. The narrow, seldom-used road to Sadri was lined with green trees moving to a pianissimo breeze. The Aravalli Hills lay ahead yet out of sight and the windswept soft sands of the Jodhpur district were now conspicuous by their absence. Reaching Sadri by noon was a goal, and, with luck, into the walls of Udaipur by nightfall if they could ride reasonably hard.

Nina's face lit up like a big city on Diwali hearing her traveling companion discuss the best way to Udaipur. Thoughts of Sadri and its nearby famous temple of Ranakpur did nothing for her though she had often heard of its unimaginable beauty, built in the last century. But it was Udaipur that brought life to her being. Udaipur. The city of her childhood dreams. A fairy land. The people of Persia could have their mystical magical carpets. She wanted just once before she died to see Udaipur, and Narendra was planning to go home by way of it.

Now in the early morning he once more brought mixed emotions to the young girl. "You can come as far as my parents' home," he said. However he added, "we'll sleep within Udaipur's walls, God willing, but we'll be off at first light from there to my home. That will take several days longer."

Would she not get a glimpse of the palaces? In the face of this new smarting disappointment Nina found the unsettled world a little sadder. There had always been those rays of hope and always they were smothered. Well, almost always. Wasn't Narendra leading her to safety, but oh, how she'd love to spend some time strolling around near the palace and its famous city. Now it would occur only in fantasy?

Narendra explained to her that the Mewar kingdom had its origin somewhere well into the 500s. This was now 1777. She knew because the dacoit Motilal used to speak of it. And she recalled something Narendra had told her about the Great Bappa Rawal in the 700s, but that was only history and she could not be bothered with it. The subject held no interest for her and she was not even of that kingdom. To farmers and laborers history and years meant very little. But Narendra knew that India is of all times, changeless yet ever changing. He knew of the British East India Tea Company, their sahibs and memsahibs, but it was a vague villainy, obscure and dim.

Nina was from an entirely different background. Her parents had raised wheat on a tiny plot owned by ancestors, through the years broken down into smaller plots for all the sons and the sons of sons. An uncle east of Delhi near Mathura raised mustard but that family branch had died out years ago from a deadly pestilence. If there were other relatives she did not know them. She had loved to bathe and dress for the holidays, Diwali, Dussehra, and dance in the fields with neighbors and friends, and to throw colored powders on Holi. What more was there to life?

But what of the Rajkumaris and Ranis? Surely the lives of these princesses and queens would be full of excitement in spite of what Narendra had said the other day. They were reputedly beautiful. She knew because people often told her about the loveliest of them all, Padmini; how the Emperor Khilji wanted to just set his gaze upon her gorgeous face after he lost a battle against her husband. Nina broke another long silence, catching up to Narendra's horse asking, "It is true, isn't it Narendra Singhji? Padmini really was, wasn't she? She isn't just a pretend fairy tale?"

"She's a fairy tale, alright. But yes, she was real. Someday you must go to Chittorgarh and you can stand right where Padmini stood."

"Oh," she yelped, chagrinned, "I couldn't do that. It would be sacrilege."

Narendra laughed hard at her innocence. "Well, in that case you can stand where Khilji stood to look upon her reflection. Would that be better?"

The suggestion was pondered for a moment before deciding yes, it would be permissible. After all, he had been merely a Muslim Emperor over a vast domain — but Padmini was a royal Hindu Queen, the fairest of the fair. That made her superior. Besides she was the first woman in history to...

"Sadri," Narendra shouted. "There it is ahead," as the two rounded a turn in the road. They let the horses slow down to a walk. An old man, nose and mouth covered with a snowy white cloth tied behind his ears squatted in front of a wooden wheel, seemingly impossible to repair. Next to him a younger man lifted the leg of a swayback horse to check its hoof. Everyone else seemed oblivious to the intruders. "Jains," he said very quietly to Nina.

"What?"

"Jains. Do you know any Jains?"

"I have no friends. Who are they? Why the white cloth?"

"As I understand it the Jains believe that anything living was created by God and must therefore have a soul. If this is so they cannot then purposely kill any living object and so the orthodox Jain will cover his nose and mouth so as not to breathe in any insects."

"I wish I could believe in something that much," was her reply.

"But you do," he laughed.

"No. I think not. I am most grateful to you for taking me to a safe place. Beyond that I cannot believe in anyone. My parents and all the good people I knew were killed by dacoits and I was forced to live that awful life with Motilal. The good are killed and the bad just go on doing terrible things. What is there to believe in?"

"You believe in the sanctity of the spirit and the goodness of Padmini. You have just now indicated that. It shows you have good feelings toward others. I predict one day you will find a place to live in serenity. Wait. You will see."

"And you, Narendra Singhji, will you live again with peace in your heart?"

They had approached an outer wall of spotlessly whitewashed pukka houses made of dirt from the nearby river bed, dried long in the sun, lasting many years. Down the lane he chose a little place to eat, being ravenous, and hired a lad to feed and water the horses. A cloth had been stretched overhead, tacked to poles at its four corners. In the mottled shade of this awning at a crude little table with rickety benches, Narendra's sweaty body hoped for a semblance of breeze. Too hot for heavy food, he ordered a mixture of cream of corn and buttermilk into which had been mixed salt, cumin and onions.

The short rest was comforting, listening with momentous interest as the waiter talked to Narendra, Nina's eyes all the while on the colorful ladies in their wide, gaudy swaying gagras, bright kanchukis and pastel colored head scarfs edged in shiny silver. The town was not too large but there was more obvious affluence here in Sadri than she had seen since leaving Jodhpur. Silver bangles were plentiful.

At the edge of friendly little Sadri they crossed the narrow Sukari river, not much more than a trickle awaiting summer's monsoons. Trees were far more abundant and in just one kilometer they rode a narrow winding path through semi-dense woods. Ground rose slowly but the rested horses cantered much of the way until a sudden clearing. They had stumbled upon magnificent Ranakpur, the fabled marble Jain temple.

"Aiyayeji," Nina urged courteously. "Come, we are beckoned to go inside." Not waiting for his decision she galloped toward the main entrance, jumped from her horse, tied the reins to a ragged tree and raced across a small clearing. Kicking off her chappals in honor of the Gods she bolted up the steps only to stand reverently back from the entry to stare at an awesome ten foot tall marble carved casement. Voluptuous human figures stood out in graceful pose as if some mystical goddess had spun a lace web of marble tracery around the door. Above, in the center, a small figure sat as sentry and above that two dozen more in erotic poses coaxed the viewer inside. It was this inner temple which would captivate visitors, regardless of faith, who would discover this fairyland of crystalline stone and her enduring beauty seemingly so far from civilization.

Inside they stood beneath an electrifying dome circled with row after row of deeply carved figures, hundreds and hundreds of them. No wonder it took sixty years to complete as their Sadri waiter had told them. Countless lotus blossoms were crocheted of this flawless snowy white marble until not an inch of the dome was left untouched. And there were many such domes.

The pair climbed the stairs to the rooftop and the steps built laterally over rounded domes, then sat on a ledge upon which are placed six pillars holding the heaven-pointing roof cradled in all her glory. The magnificence was so intense, the discovery so unexpected they stood in mystic reverence. Three hours they stayed in this temple of a religion foreign to theirs, Narendra very much aware of a divine scheme of the universe.

"Don't you sometimes wonder, Narendra Singhji, why this place is not even near a city, much less a village. It is a couple hour walk just one way to get here from Sadri, and just imagine how much longer from all the other villages."

"I personally believe when one has a need to talk with God he will find a way to do so and if it is preferable in a temple, then the walk will be as nothing." But to himself he added, "but why did God not aid me now in my deepest need? I asked and asked his help but he didn't even answer."

"Remember the man at the restaurant," Nina said. "He told us those are not gods whose images are enshrined at Ranakpur but teachers."

"I believe the Christians had a teacher too. They called him Jesus and they go to churches and pray to him. What is the difference? It would seem we reach up to God in various ways but I am sure of one thing. He is always up there somewhere to hear each one of us, whether we are Hindu, Jain, Muslim, Christian, whatever." But there remained the confusion of God not answering him.

Eventually they crossed the border into the kingdom of Mewar. Ranakpur temple had been at times in Mewar and other years, after various wars, within the kingdom of Marwar. The land had been given by the Hindu Mewar Maharana to the Jains in honor and respect; sixty years later they had completed the awesome structure.

Instantly the jungle was thick with deep greens and hills suddenly steep, inhabited by tigers and leopards. Riding was necessarily much slower and Narendra wanted to reach a village or possibly Kankroli, a fair sized city, before dark. His calculations on reaching Udaipur had been far amiss. He dared not sleep in the open with Nina in his benign protective custody. Vegetation was extremely dense, the nocturnal creatures sure to be surrounding and watching the riders. Some of them would be making their kills tonight.

"Who would build such a splendid place so far from anything?" Nina still could not get over the magnificence.

"It is a strange thing, Nina, but it was our Rana Kumbha who gave the land, Rana Kumbha who once held the place of Mandore where I discovered you hiding. For seven years he held it while they fought with Jodhpur and at last he had to ask for peace and in doing so gave up Mandore to his foe."

"What kind of man was he really?"

"It was said that when he learned the Muslims began to kill cows he became extremely angry. You are a Hindu and you understand what that means to us, to kill cows. So angry was he that he amassed 50,000 horsemen and attacked the Muslims, killing thousands.

"Nina, they had a custom which is done a little bit less today, still, it is there. Do you know the word 'Charan'? They are people who write and sing to the many grand and glorious things that the rulers and Rajputs do and it was the custom to have these people attend upon their Highnesses. It is said that once an astrologer told Maharana Kumbha that he would be killed by a charan. When the Rana's son became aware of the story he decided he would find the charan and aid and abet him in this crime, even though it was his father. But the Rana knew of this and he banished the prince and all the others."

"So his life was saved," satisfied that she was right.

"On the contrary. Another son lived to kill his father, stabbing him. You will learn of these things and all these people one day if you come to live in Mewar, for to live within its borders is to hear its tales through song and word, and there is no place on earth, I'm sure, where stories are more glorious. They have said of Kumbha that he was so militarily clever he could have conquered far more than he did but it was his idea that people should respect humanity. Just to go up to a man and kill him on the battlefield was not his way of doing things if there was no tremendous cause for it."

"But you said he killed thousands for slaying cows."

"That was sacrilege. He felt justified in that case. But to gain a little more property if it meant killing thousands, then it was not worth it to his way of thinking. He did not enjoy bloodshed for the sake of bloodshed. He did in fact conquer many places and defeat many enemies, but that was all different.

"It is all these things and thousands more that make up the rulers and feudal lords of Mewar like my father, past and present."

Weary of riding, talking, eyes strained from superb beauty mixed with the sands of air, Narendra lay restless that night on a charpoy rented at a small wayside inn beyond Kankroli. Thoughts reverted back to his mission and the need to confess the murder of the dacoit to his father. Strangely, visiting the temple created a different outlook for this man. Thoughts were not easily fathomed. In the midst of the temple at Ranakpur he knew he was standing in the presence of the Almighty. Though he was Hindu and the temple in honor of Jain "teachers," there was today an evidence of the oneness of God. God did not seem displeased with him at Ranakpur for if it had been so He would have made it evident. Or would He? <u>How</u> could He? The more deliberation the more confused he became until finally drifting off to an uneasy sleep. Now he could tolerate no further delays though he felt the last one strangely preplanned.

There was little discussion all the following day. Nina had sensed his preoccupation. Scenery from the temple had been ecstatic. Coming down out of the hills later she watched the most colorful clothing she had ever seen — even brighter than around Jodhpur. Faces were smilingly happy, but as the day wore on peasants were less in evidence with the intense heat of the desert. Midday approached 50°C in the open, the soothing coolness of the forested jungle trees now left behind.

The pair crossed the ridge of the Aravalli Hills and were now very close to the city of Udaipur, capital of the Mewar kingdom. She still wondered if she'd catch a glimpse of the palaces but did not. Narendra knew this territory exceedingly well from attending court with his father, from riding with the late Highness, Maharana Ari Singh II. Now Ari's young son Hamir II sat on the throne and the Queen Mother acted as regent until such time as her child would come of age and take over the copious duties of ruler.

It was unavoidably late when the dispirited travelers reached Jagatpur a few days later, the dipping sun broadening the horizon. The two had not stopped riding except to feed and water their horses as they themselves drank refreshing buttermilk, made daily. Narendra became oblivious to the noiseless presence of Nina, thoughts dwelling on his father and the blessed panacea he was sure to find for his raging guilt.

At the entry to his father's feudal estate Narendra slipped from his saddle, coarse sandy loam scattering at his tremulous step. In his renewed gloom there was only darkness and confusion. Unlike the goddess Kali, he could not exult in the carnage reaped many nights before. The red blood of the hapless and the tainted blood of ravaging dacoits had long been swallowed into the parched earth, but there remained the blood of Narendra's heart and mind. Is there a justice, he continuously wondered. The sensitivity of this young Rajput nobleman could not support the horror of his act, killing in a time of peace within the kingdom. A storm of anguish filled his burnished body. Misty eyes blotted his father's house as he staggered to a courtyard neem tree, stomach benumbed with cramps. Body tremors increased convulsively — and then it was no longer fear nor passion which rocked him back and forth but the veined and withering hands of his beloved embracing parent.

"My son, you are ill." Unseeing eyes looked down at his father. "Speak to me son; what is it? You are sick?"

Narendra slowly emerged from a hideous phantasmagoria, all 250 pounds slumping to the ground beneath the tree which he had climbed as a youth. His frame cut to half size, resting elbows on bended knees, digging clenched fists into bronzed cheeks. His weight was well placed and firm upon large bones and he was much admired among the men of the principality. One of six children, they were a close and happy family, and though he had one sister it was Narendra who was the light of his father's life.

Crude definiteness of sorrow crept from the younger to the elder Singh. He stood woebegone over his son, gently reaching a trembling hand to his shoulder. "What has happened? Can you tell me now?"

"Biteaye," he invited his father to sit, remaining quiet until he had regained complete composure. "My father, I have killed a man. What shall I do?"

If there was any sense of horror or chagrin the old man's actions did not betray it. "Tell me everything which happened," he requested simply. "Start from the very first."

His woeful tale commenced with the small banquet party atop the ramparts of Jodhpur. His father knew this rival kingdom and terrain better than he. There had been royal weddings and occasional durbars there. He could clearly envision all that had happened. As Narendra described the mysterious pull which had taken hold, delivering him to the pathetic village, his ensuing rage raised his voice in metered tempo bringing his mother to the courtyard. She was quickly waved off and in dutiful Indian tradition acquiesced to her husband's wish.

"Father, I must tell you," he said, "the dacoit looked so fierce and grotesque as he finished raping her, as he slashed her arm from her body. Why did he do that? She did not even seem to resist him, not when I saw her. Yet, you know father, it was a look of wonderment on his face, almost unfeeling, uncaring as he watched me raise my sword later to kill him. Maybe because I cut off his hands. I don't know. It was as if he pleaded with me to kill him. He just did not seem to care. There was no fight left in him. Can this be, father? And now his eyes haunt me at night and it is almost impossible to sleep. Will I ever find peace in my soul? Father, you have always taught me what it is I must do in life. And now in this crisis I come, for only you can help me."

"You are wrong. It is you who will help yourself..." the older man started, but Narendra interrupted.

"We stopped in Ranakpur temple and there I stood before a Jain god. I heard your voice saying to me as you have all my life, 'God is great,' and for the first time I felt a oneness in God. I asked him, 'Was I wrong to kill Motilal? How do I live with myself?'"

"And did you get an answer my son?"

"No. None. Perhaps He will speak to me through you now, father. I think that is possible. I think that is what I have been expecting."

"On earth many things are possible. You said before that you asked God if you did wrong. Narendra, you have already answered your own question. I believe that you knew instinctively that morally you were bound to try to save that poor woman. Unfortunately she made it to the pyre before you could grab her. You have learned that a Rajput must sometimes swiftly mete out justice. You are a Rajput first and foremost. You acted as you would have on any other battleground. This was your own private Haldi Ghat. You were courageous and valorous. Is it not that which is expected of every Rajput male? To have ignored Motilal would have been cowardice.

"Listen," the elder Singh continued firmly. "You know now the cruelty inherent in dacoits. For centuries we have had a history of bravery and chivalry, and you were born of this nobleman's house. It is only fitting and proper that you too be brave and fearless. There has never been doubt. No, you have not committed a sin. Dacoits are a heinous band and for the sake of the innocent people they must be dealt with in the best possible manner. To catch someone stealing an apple from an apple walla is one thing. In the case of dacoits the penalty must of necessity be much more severe. You cannot cure the itch by scratching off the skin.

"You look upon this as some dastardly deed of yours. Why not turn the picture upside down? I think you could not hear God speak to you because you were not really listening. I think He spoke to you from atop the ramparts. Who else would have told you to dash off to the village? No one on earth told you; you said so yourself. I think God has summoned you to serve humanity.

"Go now and speak to your mother. I wish to think on this longer. We shall talk more of it tomorrow."

Narendra walked into the house embracing the woman who had so gently and firmly raised him. She in turn pointed out the door to the gate across the courtyard. "That woman has been standing there since you arrived over an hour ago. Who is she? Why does she just stand there?"

Nina had been completely forgotten and for the moment he passed her off as merely an unfortunate who had escaped the band of dacoits, which in its way was, of course, true. Having no family he felt obliged to bring her home until they could discuss her future. Thus she was removed to tomorrow's agenda. She took a meal then quickly excused herself to sleep in a servant's vacant room arranged by the household mistress.

Very weary but relieved emotionally, the young Rajput laid his head down trusting sleep would quickly overcome him, with his father's soulful words ringing over and over in his ears — "God has summoned you to serve humanity."

Chapter 2

For the first time in days Narendra awakened fresh and renewed. There must have been a little sense of peace for Nina also, the two standing discreetly apart. One could already hear the early morning sounds beyond the stone walls of Narendra's home. Cobblestone lanes flow in a neatly organized rhythmic pattern in front of homes and shops of countless families who pay homage to their liege lord, the Rawal, Arjun Singh. Perimeter of lanes dip into open earth sewers against stuccoed walls. Seasonably warm temperatures of pre-monsoons bring an unpleasant urine stench and the weak stomached long for heavy rains to drain both odors and dirt. Shopkeepers and capricious customers move slowly in the lazy early summer days.

Today brought its urgencies to Nina with the infinite abysses of the unknown. She called quietly to Narendra, "What of me? Can we talk of it today?" But Narendra's mother, Bhadra Singh, called the two to breakfast, her dark grey eyes deep-set in aging sockets. Nina refused to dine inside, not fitting her lowly station, and took her meal outdoors. It allowed Narendra a little longer to disentangle the provocative puzzle of the girl. Father had left instructions that he would be busy for several hours with urgent business matters. His mother had been born with the Asian patience long ago admired by the western world; she knew in due course a story of the girl and her surprising arrival would unfold.

Slowly the situation spelled itself out to Narendra. Here was a girl, not much more than a child, of a lower caste. But it was not the caste which loomed before him. She had been defiled. There would be no one to marry her after living a sinful life with Motilal — should anyone come to know of it. Also, she would have no dowry. He had come to believe her story and felt poignant stings of pity. Left to her own devices she could do nothing more than sit on the streets with other beggars anticipating a lifetime of undesirable indolence. If not for himself, who would there be to speak on her behalf? Morally he felt an obligation. Would his parents be too devout to go against Hindu law? Would they unjustly look past the circumstances which created her metaphysical problems? Would she then be forced to go out into the world a wastrel? He could not take that chance. He must concoct with her a plausible story, not too far afield from the truth. This much she deserved.

He came up with a plan and after breakfast called Nina to join him in a far corner of the inner fort where an ancient shrine now lay in partial ruin. Here he had done his daydreaming as a youngster. Paths to it were completely covered with brambles. He chose it to be far from listening ears of servants or brothers. Narendra carefully unfolded his tale for her approval, the basics being that she had been married and lived with her in-laws back in that little village beyond Alwar. Its name was to be of no importance. Alwar was far enough away that the probability of anyone knowing its neighboring hamlets or their inhabitants was judiciously remote.

Exemplary conscientiousness forbade him saying she was unmarried, having lived that life of sin with Motilal. Yet he could not make her admit the full truth, taxing her overburdened life with yet more grief and shame. His version was simple and forthright. There would be an honorable place in the world for a "widow" and Nina accepted the fabrication with a broad and lively impact. There was an undistinguishable grandeur in this new reality. She was. She could shed her shrouds and live with dignity.

Feeling giddy, she looked at Narendra as if through a pair of someone else's spectacles and for the first time saw a giant with the face of a god, a bronze statue. He appealed to her lustered heart. They had until now been as abjectly impersonal to each other as any two people could be. Now amazingly there was a love in her heart. She did not fool herself that he too could share this rapture. She would always be the lowly chaprasi. Caste alone would dictate she keep her place. Yet there was an unspeakable bond which would always tie them together. Some day she would hopefully find a way to repay him.

Words of thanksgiving came hard to her now for the things which chance passed her way. He fluffed off any suggestion of gratitude and helped her across a few crags down the pathway to the main house and a talk with his mother. Could there be a place for Nina in this household? Bhadra Singh felt dreadfully overstaffed. Some of the servants long in their employ had married and now even their youngsters worked for them.

Then Narendra remembered Nina's lifelong desire to see the fairyland palaces of Udaipur. "Mataji," he came more alive, "what of Queen Mother? Could we arrange for Nina to work there?" Nina's face glowed.

"What impertinence!" his mother argued and the girl's glow died quickly. Narendra took little stock in his mother's reply for it was still father who would have the final say. As the queen's rawal perhaps he could arrange it.

The same story and pleas were laid before Arjun Singh when he returned from his business affairs, Narendra spinning the story as woefully as the best of weavers. There was no immediate answer. Arjun Singh had had quite a hold on the thinking of the late Highness but his wife, now the regent for the last several years, was a little more difficult to handle. She would not be forced into things and the idea would have to be broached at the proper time and in the proper way.

"Then can we not keep Nina here in our household until you go to durbar? Perhaps then a place can be found for her within the palace walls?" the son coaxed.

"Oh, I would do anything, anything at all," Nina begged. "I can even stitch." She had become terribly torn between two loves — the new one she felt for the man championing her cause and the lifelong desire to see the story tale palaces of Udaipur. My, she thought, a possible chance to live in one of them... even if it was in the servants' quarters. She could try from time to time to see Narendra, this man so far beyond her reach. She dared hope. It must be left to the gods to decide and she strolled to another far corner of the fort.

"Narendra, my son," the father began, "I have been thinking through the night of what we talked. I told you God had summoned you to do a job. I truly think this is so. Dacoits have attacked our villages more frequently of late. They should be dealt with. We must protect our people. For this our police force is not adequate and it should not be the job of the army. These dacoits are worse than man eating tigers for they attack many. I met with some of the elders this morning and it is agreed that we should send you out and see what can be done. Think on it. You would be required to carefully pick each man to work with you. They would be organized as you see fit, well trained, for we do not wish harm to come to our own men."

"I know just the person to teach me the ways of the dacoits," Narendra replied, "but I must have free rein. I think you are right, father. We will show these men they can no longer get away with their fiendish crimes. Let's put a stop to it, once and for all. We will wipe them out, I promise." Narendra had not stopped to realize that dacoits had been around for centuries. How then was it possible to wipe them out in a year, or even in a lifetime?

When next he saw Nina he made arrangements to meet at the same little shrine after dark, each attempting to reach it in the shadows, for at this most important meeting he wanted no audience nor anyone to learn of the girl's background. The project was at least temporarily to be kept secret from the general public. He suggested she think about all the things she knew about dacoits and their ways, not only Motilal's gang of hideous men but any they might have discussed in her presence; dacoits both past and present.

Narendra then took off to find several old friends to determine whether they'd harbor the same interests as did Narendra and his father. Ramesh was the first he came upon, sitting listlessly at the door of his home outside Arjun Singh's main gates. The two men greeted each other affably. Ramesh was remarkably handsome in a clean-shaven way, a masterpiece of subtle grooming, ever impeccable. His eyes were a strange mixture of blue and grey, rare in Rajasthan, and as round as the full moon. He was considerably shorter than Narendra, about one hundred eighty centimeters, but with an impressive build, and never shied from a fight.

Narendra told Ramesh merely that he had encountered some dacoits in the north beyond Jodhpur, that he and his father thought something should be done to curb their appetite for silver bangles and their lust for the traditionally beautiful women of Rajputana. Ramesh was something of a gentleman farmer, leaving the chores to the peasants and doing a slip-shod job of overseeing. He had endless time on his hands as did Narendra, yet Narendra knew that under his tutelage Ramesh would be a game fighter and someone on whom he could depend in the midst of mortal combat.

They agreed Pandu and Ran could also be relied upon to not only support the cause but shoulder the sense of burden one must feel in protecting his teammates. They were eventually found together sipping tea of all things. Narendra was glad they were not, as sometimes, semi-stuporous after the effects of bhang, a cheap drink offering euphoric dreams. But while Narendra was aware they frequently enjoyed this evening pastime, he also knew they could prudently refrain from it and remain level headed when necessary.

Pandu was of a different build, muscles bulging out into space, his only physical defect the silly little hairs standing straight out from his ears. Ran on the other hand was usually quiet and straight-faced, so different from Ramesh whose wide white-toothed smile would light up a street at total eclipse. Ran's body, however, was proportioned for fitness and he was sure to make a reliably excellent addition to the team.

They each contemplatively meditated about what others might be recruited for this sobering, thankless job. They wished to keep the program quiet until the multitude of details could be worked out. Arjun Singh desired to take his son to durbar in the next ten days to discuss these ideas with Queen Mother, although he would implement the plans in his district with or without her consent. After all, the villagers in his domain were his unending responsibility and it was to his advantage to keep peace in and well beyond his fort.

In the velvety magic of night Nina stole to the shrine waiting in its shadows. Narendra was a ferment of anxiety when he joined her with no time for preliminaries. She was destined to be of great help in his study of the situations for in the fourteen months in Motilal's grasp she had never been sheltered from discussions of up-coming dacoities or comparisons to other gangs, either current or those of the historic past. To be of any help to the man she was spontaneously coming to love kindled her spirit anew; how else could she show her love. It would not be for her to hold him in her tender arms at night, stroke his body, abide in his love. That she would never have. Being his lover would come only in her private dreams. While such fantasies can serve to put a woman into a beguiling sleep, they do not serve the innermost needs of a woman of great fiber. Such a woman must do for her man. She must be there when he needs her — not only her body but to listen indulgently, to let him know she also understands. Though not well schooled, a clever woman can be all things to her man. But most of all she must be needed. Nina was aware that without being needed she was nothing to Narendra.

It had been beyond her fondest dreams that he should suddenly require what little knowledge she possessed. That would bring them closer together. In spite of her past clandestine lifestyle she could help whatever cause he championed.

Narendra had moments when he wondered why he brought her to Jagatpur. He could have dropped her off at Kankroli, a city large enough that she could have lost herself in the crowds. In moments of annoyance he had told himself he was not responsible for her; only by accident had he stumbled upon Nina. What if he had not gone to Mandore. Now that he was about to embark on a new adventure came the realization he desperately needed her knowledge.

"Tell me everything there is to know about dacoits," he commanded. "I shall take you trustingly into my confidence. My father has ordered me to clean up this part of Mewar and rid ourselves once and for all of the ruthless evils of dacoity. I go with father to the durbar in Udaipur in ten days time and I shall want everything organized, at least in my mind. With your help I can do it."

Nina was to impress upon him that dacoits are fierce, not necessarily brave. Yelling loudly they might swoop upon alarmed prey, brandishing knives, oblivious of the possibility they too might be killed. All is madness and confusion. This element of surprise is of great import to the dacoits. This advantage allows for them to kill the strongest first, and in their madness, they frequently followed up with the maiming or death of youngsters and women.

Nina went on to caution him to be ever alert. "And it is not enough for you to learn their ways and habits, Narendra Singhji," she had added. "All must work and train with you until you think as one. Nothing less will do.

"There is no second-best in a fight with dacoits," Nina continued. "Their most common offenses are kidnapping for ransom and though they claim to rarely kidnap girls I am, as you can see, a girl, and he did kidnap me. There is murder, sometimes for enmity. Some of the dacoits have only hate in their hearts and they kill even relatives of the victims or anyone who gets in their way, as you yourself saw in Jodhpur."

Narendra listened attentively.

"Then of course there is always the informer. If a citizen is brave enough to inform a nearby police force and tell when someone can be found, it is frequently the case that the informer is killed. Sometimes they will even kill all the informers' relatives, and this is why they are so feared. People are afraid to inform, if not for their own safety, then for the safety of their wives, children or parents. So now you can see why sometimes entire families have been wiped out."

They remained quiet for a while until she again took up the conversation. "I know that there are many, many bands of dacoits here in Rajasthan and Uttar Pradesh and Madhya Pradesh. Motilal would say that where the river Chambal merges with the Jumna River in Uttar Pradesh it has created great ravines wherever it flows. He'd say, 'The water of the Chambal creates dacoits, for this type of terrain makes a good breeding and hiding place.' Commonly they take shelter in this area. What will make it difficult for you, Narendra Singhji, is that in such places dacoits are virtually worshipped. They call him 'baghi.' This hero worship makes foolish people wish to become dacoits just for the attention. It's not right, yet I can almost understand it, but I think that the high-born cannot understand."

Narendra had not thought of hero-worship as an aspect and suddenly realized what an unpolished gem he had in Nina. He strangely thought at this moment of his mother's two-inch wide band of uncut diamonds worn high around her arm on very special occasions. They did not shimmer like the other more refined diamonds and emeralds she possessed; she had told him they were worth far more money, and now Nina was just such an uncut jewel.

Intensively appreciative, he was unaware what great good his vocal thanks would be to her. Any scrap would be appetizingly savored by this girl who had absolutely nothing in the world except the ragged clothes she had worn since picked up at Mandore. She felt like a newborn babe, unclothed. Now to be needed by someone for even a few hours for her knowledge of dacoits, this was sadly all she felt she had to offer.

Narendra had clung to every word. "We're just touching the surface," she went on. "Disputes over small parcels of land have also created dacoits. For centuries the farms have been divided down and down. Now there is barely enough space to raise an adequate crop. And if the farmer has sons, it again will be divided when they marry. True, he himself will die one day, but if he had two sons, it will be cut in half, will it not? With tiny parcels it's hard to feed all the mouths, and one must search elsewhere for food or money."

On rides through picturesque countryside he had seen this; all the neat rows of cactus which delineated such acreage although it had always meant little to him. Narendra's stomach had always been filled and never did he have to sleep in the rain, all his needs cared for. Miseries of other less fortunate were for the first time coming alive. Nina forcefully brought this home in her next statement.

"You have never had to work for money, have you, Narendra Singhji? I am sure it is as difficult for you to know the ways of the chaprasi as it is for us to know the ways of court life. There are those who continuously hate the lords for their wealth and plenty, yet we do not know what all trouble you may have. By the same token you must realize what difficulty there is sometimes in earning honest money. When work is non-existent then one must think of other means to feed his family. A man cannot easily watch those he loves starve.

"It is also well known that money acquired by looting is shared by the bands. You will recall you asked me if I was at the cenotaphs of the queens to divide the loot.

"And there is something more plausible. Imagine yourself married and some dacoit comes and snatches your wife. Being a clever man, you'd find a way to rescue her, maybe by gaining the confidence of the gang. After that you could always reek revenge on them.

"So you see there are three main reasons for becoming a dacoit: jar, jamin, jaoru — the money, the land and the wife.

"If the jagirs and rawals would band together and fight the dacoits perhaps you could rid the countryside of them. It's well worth the effort. But always remember one thing, they do become animalistic."

As the summer moon reached the other side of the little temple/shrine Narendra left Nina behind and sped back to his house, anxious to speak with his father. The two men drew together with a calm and quiet consciousness of the new role which was to become Narendra's karma.

Buoyant days rushed by and it was time to leave the fort for the long ride to Udaipur and the durbar. The men left at four in the morning and were well past the nearest villages by sun up. Each lived in his own thoughts: Narendra on ridding the countryside of dacoits, hopefully with the blessing of the Queen Mother. Arjun Singh was devoured with thoughts of the many subjects likely to be brought up at the durbar. This great meeting at the palace is attended by nobles representing all portions of this feudal kingdom, each trying to win the favor of Maharana Hamir II's mother, the regent. Sometimes it was a great nuisance, he thought, having a mother run the country. If she was weak then she could be talked into your viewpoints. But this regent was strong-willed, clever. Things could be far more difficult.

By noon two days later they stopped beneath a well-branched tree in the district of the ancient Zawar zinc mines, the first in the world. Hills were roly and semi-green and there was a steam in the air. Seven meters from a tree stretched a lengthy row of ancient crucibles, piled ten high, like an elongated magnified honeycomb. Its hard grey mass resisted the great heat necessary for melting and calcinating the zinc, silver, copper and lead mined nearby. Today their only heat was derived from scorching sun.

It is said when Emperor Akbar caused the Maharana and family to flee Udaipur that the ever faithful Bhils, Mewar's aboriginal tribespeople, carried their babies in baskets to these Zawar mines where they were hidden and cared for. Arjun and son stood looking at the places on the trees from which the baskets had been hung.

This was no season to be riding to court but the urgency of the Queen Mother's could not be dismissed. When a durbar is called one must go. Water supplies on this year were already dangerously low. They must have a good monsoon this year or many crops would be ruined and wells dried.

The elder Singh chose to nap through the heat of the afternoon, servants rushing about setting up a makeshift awning, capturing for him any degree of cooler air they could manipulate. Narendra rested his back against the trunk of a tree, dozing intermittently, more anxious to reach the palace than wile away the hours. They would not resume travel until late afternoon.

It was just before midnight when they reached the palace. The city's gates had been closed at ten o'clock as customary and Arjun had some fast talking to do to get the gatekeepers to open the massive doors, rigidly forbidden after the nightly closing. These darwazas had been set up in strategic points and everyone arriving after that hour had to wait outside the walls of the city until morning. Luckily the gatekeeper knew Arjun well, believed him when he said it was imperative he be at the palace in time for a morning durbar. Afraid for his job, the gatekeeper quickly permitted access, just as rapidly closing the great doors behind the small select group.

Udaipur and its surrounding countryside were even more charming than Jagatpur, the short cropped trees, the distant hill with "monsoon palace" fitting into the roof of the little mountain. They passed the 120 year old Jagdish Temple. The Lord of the Universe, Jagannath, looked down on the small parade from his temple built at the cost of 15 lakhs of rupees. The Singhs were now within the shadows of the massive white palace. Other nobles had already arrived. Arjun caught sight of the parties from Salumbar and Durgarpur. But the day had been far too stifling for such travel and they took themselves wearily to bed.

Narendra was restless the following morning, necessarily waiting outside the durbar hall. Queen Mother had made a late appearance and her various matters regarding Mahrattas, taxes and other essential business took the better part of the day to conclude, the desert heat making everyone argumentative.

It was not until after a much needed tea break that Arjun Singh had requested a private audience with the Rani. She gave him ten minutes. Narendra was immediately hailed and they came right to the point.

"Your Highness, you are aware of the centuries of intermittent fighting of dacoits. I believe my son and I have stumbled upon a plan to rid Mewar of these troublesome people. We owe it to our subjects to protect them. If many of the dacoit bands grouped together they could be as bad as any small Mughal or Mahratta invading army."

"I don't think it would ever come to that," argued the regent in sober abstraction. She sat on her throne clad in a somber sari, jeweled fingers and arms adding an extra dimension to attractive facial features. Narendra wondered why she still adorned herself with jewels when all other widows cast them forever aside at the moment of their husband's death. In front of her on the floor squat the two men, each searching his mind for a way to buttress their desire for her support in this new idea.

"Your Highness," Narendra spoke, "I have seen the devastation firsthand. I was visiting His Highness, Maharaja of Jodhpur, when dacoits wiped out an entire village. I rode to it. I saw with my own eyes and I have since studied their methods..."

The queen interrupted, "How could you study?"

"I have a source, Your Highness, a friend who was forced to live with them, and I have learned how it is they think and how they act. I believe I can be successful. I know I <u>must</u> do this thing. Surely you would want nothing less for the rest within the kingdom?"

"Perhaps you are right, Narendra Singhji. You are brave to start such a mission and I wish you luck with it. You and your father must remain a few days to tell what all you are planning. Perhaps other rawals can implement the same system." But when the next day came the Queen Mother busied herself with other domestic problems and a decision to take off for the monsoon palace.

"You must excuse me now," she said to the men who dutifully came to bid her goodbye. "Things are in a constant mess here. I'll be glad when my son is grown and I need no longer look after affairs of State. Politics takes all one's time. Household staff can be awful. I can't even find a suitable woman to stitch properly for me."

"Your Highness, we know of a young woman who can stitch," Narendra succumbed to the first jab of fate regarding Nina. He had in fact forgotten her these last two days.

"Bring her to me one day, Narendra. Perhaps I can use her. Has she stitched for another royal house?"

"Will our recommendation suffice?" Narendra asked. So many things crossed his mind this inspired moment. Could she indeed sew? Luscious embroidery on the finest of fabrics? Even placing jewels onto cloth? Or could she only mend the tears in farmer's clothing? Perhaps he had better arrange for Nina to work for his mother until they were sure her talent was sufficient for the royal household. They could not afford to risk their standing by sending a mediocre craftsman. "She is busy with other jobs at the moment, but perhaps she can come to you after two or three months, Your Highness?"

"Since when must a Queen wait for an order to be obeyed?" she chided, but in actuality it was much too warm to think of new clothes or articles for the home. All she wanted now was the bliss of a pungent breeze high atop the Aravalli Hill in the shade of Sajjangarh Palace's white walls. On return the royal family would reside for the balance of the summer at Jag Niwas, the gorgeous white marble palace floating gracefully in the midst of cooling Lake Pichola, forest-bosomed on its south side. They'd not return to the biggest of their homes, a five minute ride on the Maharana's royal yacht, until the sunbaked tide of the year had ebbed.

The two men abhorred the time wasted rattling back across the miles. Nothing had been accomplished with regard to a sanction or a specific manner of handling the dacoits. Narendra would have to employ his own tactics, overwhelmed by the manner in which his queen passed it off in the end. The light had left the eyes of Arjun and Narendra, dampened by the regent's disinterest. In fact, the whole trip seemed a waste... except of course for Nina's potential employment.

Nina was vigorously overcome with explosive joy at the news. "You shower me with great gifts," she addressed Narendra even through her twinge of sadness in the thought he would be distant from her. But the idea of perhaps living in the palace was profoundly unfathomable. "How can I thank you?"

In a serious tone he said, "First, you have already thanked me with advice on dacoits and dacoity. However, and this is extremely important, you must behave very well when you are in the esteemed household of the queen. You must not dishonor our family by doing anything other than your best work and behaving in a manner befitting the ancestral house of our unbroken dynasty. Anything bad would reflect directly on us."

"What is meant by the world's oldest dynasty?" She was not concerned with bad reflections.

"You did not know? Mewar is the oldest kingdom on earth which is headed by a direct line of descendants. You would do well to learn to read and write and study all the history you can of our great kingdom. It may one day stand you in good stead with the regent. How, I do not know, but one must never cease learning. Mewar is filled with the lives of great people. Oh yes, the world knew many others to be sure, Genghis Khan, Alexander the Great, and I do not know who all. But we are proud of our heritage, our ancestors who fought so bravely to keep honor among our women."

"But where can I learn all this? Can I be taught to read and write at the palace? How could that be?"

"To begin with," Narendra wanted to keep the record straight, "Queen Mother has not said she will definitely employ you. You will only be on trial if she even likes you first. If during your probationary period you do well I am sure she will keep you. She had told us it is difficult to get someone to stitch nicely. She is a perfectionist and you therefore must become one too.

"As for your questions about lessons, I don't know, but you must be wisely sharp and keep your eyes and ears cautiously open and surely a way will present itself. I think you are wise enough to perhaps make this happen. It is important she is pleased with you and your work for without her help you will be as nothing there. Show her that you are anxious to do her bidding. Surely there in such pretentious circumstances you will have a life of goodness as few ever could. But do not get lost in the shuffle of all the others. You would then be almost as a prisoner."

Nina sat in rapt attention, as if a little child listening to her first fairytale.

"Nina, I have bought some time from the queen. I have already spoken with my mother. She will see that you learn by doing things for her with silks and brocades. But if the first thing you sew for Her Highness is not perfection I will lose favor with her, and you will be sent immediately from the palace. Sumje?"

"I understand. You'll be proud of me, you'll see, Narendra Singhji. I will <u>make</u> good things happen." How could she go into her next life without first pleasing her protector?

Bhadra Singh personally saw to the sewing lessons, although she could not imagine why the big fuss created by her husband and son. Surely there could be no romance involved. Once in Udaipur the Singhs would see very little, if anything more, of her. There had to be sufficient reason for this treatment, but what? And as for Narendra, it was time they found him a suitable bride. She would speak to Arjun about that tonight.

Weeks and months went by with Nina showing a great aptitude toward the needle and cloth. She easily picked up the art of embroidering around little mirrors worn in the heavy winter cottons. She was being readied for the arduous position of seamstress in the regal household, and busily contemplating a breathing world she had never known.

In these same weeks Narendra abided in portentous meditation. Down there somewhere beyond the fort, beyond his father's city, lived gangs of licentious dacoits in what he felt was the buttocks of the world. These were people he must round up and jail to make the world a safer, better place. Only to Ramesh, Pandu and Ran, the closest of his fleet of fighters, was it apparent that Narendra was fast becoming an extremely complex man. They had always known him as a carefree soul who loved to hunt. He was always good for a laugh, occasionally drinking bhang with his boyfriends in the nights with nothing better to do. As an excellent horseman, when the weather was not too warm he loved challenging his friends to a good race. Or they would take long trips visiting Rajasamand or Jaisamand Lakes.

But by now Narendra developed a larger grain of uneasiness. His spirit was clearly troubled. Suddenly it was no longer possible to meet him until late mornings. Narendra had sought the help of one mightier than family or friends. He knew in the deepest recesses of his being that he could not do this new job without God's guidance. Strange, for until his recent visit to the Jain temple of Ranakpur, Narendra paid little heed to his Hindu religion. It was not that he didn't believe in Hinduism but rather that he let his mother faithfully attend to morning pujas. The prayers were being said by her and the religious duties attended, therefore no urgent need for him to enter into it.

Ever since his father's prophetic words, "God has summoned you to serve humanity," he realized how necessary his life had finally become. He would have to deal with the worst of the offenders harshly, capturing them when he could. If it was necessary to save his henchmen he might again be forced to kill.

But now each morning Narendra was conspicuous by his hours of absence. After immaculately bathing Narendra would enter his explicitly defined prayer room. His puja would last no less than three hours, smoke of incense spiraling the air around his head like a halo. Before his white-draped body hung the images of his gods, ever present in time of need and time of thanks. A coconut would rest on the marble floor beside a stone idol. He felt here God would more intently listen and indulge his fervent wishes. Thus he came to believe his pious reverence would culminate in fulfillment of his father's dreams. In his ears would ring his father's words, "God does not give us end results, He gives us the means to achieve them."

By the time his puja ended, in this season the day would be approaching 38°C. Queen Mother was probably parenthetically correct in stating the dacoits would do little in the heat. Escapes could be hazardous with monsoon swollen rivers and washed out roadways. Perhaps when the rains had subsided in mid-September the human vultures known as dacoits would resume their despotism.

Narendra and his men were flauntingly lazy until late August, but he never lost his awareness of being custodian of the lives of those who would serve with him, the need to develop a buoyant instinct for danger, and shielding them to the best of his ability.

They formed two teams simulating raids and defenses. They'd frequently meet at seven in the morning, Narendra forcing himself to arise no later than four A.M. for puja. Never could he be satisfied until each knew what the other would do in any of countless situations Narendra devised. A stickler for detail, he worried endlessly that they would never be truly ready.

By noon it would be again too hot to train, leaving their afternoons and evenings in idle anticipation.

Seldom did Narendra give a thought of Nina. But Nina's extraordinary workmanship pleased Bhadra Singh. The light had been bad for stitching after dusk and she'd rise early, taking advantage of the morning light and cooler air, awaiting rains which broke the incessant warmth. There were times when she would spin fantasies of the man with whom she had unwittingly fallen in love. She could close her eyes and hold him close. "If he were mine it would be hard to let go, those moments which would be ours alone." She would wonder what it would be like to be kissed by Narendra. Motilal had been nothing less than an insatiable monster. A kiss was never something gentle, tender and loving. It was rapacious. Always she would cringe when she would see it coming, whenever the spirit moved him. She had no way of knowing what a kiss really was, but with Narendra's face of swaggering masculine beauty she knew it could not possibly be the same as with Motilal.

In her acute reflections of Narendra she knew she would have to love him from afar; of this earthborn dream she could never be robbed. He was locked securely in her affection-starved heart and none other could ever gain entry. Nor did she believe that sex with her ideal would even vaguely resemble the body movements of Motilal for all his contortions and persuasion. In those many months she never lost her fear of Motilal. He ridiculed everything about her until even she believed she had few favorable features, if any. Yet he allowed none of his men anywhere near her.

Then came the long awaited day she would leave for service at Udaipur. Narendra had staunchly taken it upon himself to personally deliver his charge to the regent. By this time his mother had grown extremely fond of this winsome creature who justified her life at Jagatpur in many ways. Nina had walked in the fields picking flowers, the few which existed, brightening the living quarters of the Arjun Singhs.

Nina had always known her place and kept it, yet there were times when the elder woman would draw her aside to chat informally. The young girl's allure was poignantly difficult to resist. Clearly she would be missed here in Jagatpur. Arjun had guessed Narendra's source of knowledge of dacoits. It could be none other than Nina, but he asked no explanation of his son. Surely in due course all would be told.

Nina packed the few hand-me-downs collected from Bhadra Singh and the two women embraced, unheard of in employer/employee relations. Bending low Nina touched the feet of the older woman in humble obeisance, leaving her at the door of the main house. In the courtyard she walked slowly to Arjun Singh, now also much respected by Nina. They had been aristocratically benevolent to her and exceptionally so in a country not tolerant of castes lower than their own, a country where a mere shadow cast upon another by an untouchable brings unjustifiable fear. Nina climbed atop the same waiting horse which had delivered her to Jagatpur four months earlier. Narendra was already astride Chetak and they started their journey to Udaipur's palace.

Riding for hours at a reasonable pace they stopped at a small village for tea. The two accompanying servants were at a loss to understand why Nina dared sit with their master when they, as always, remained at a discreet distance. Nina sensed their amazement but cast aside any secret concerns driven by carefree imaginings.

Monsoons had been particularly hard on certain areas of Rajasthan the summer just ending and one of the popular roadways between Jagatpur and the capital of Mewar was in bad straits. Local government officials had already set about having them repaired. Mothers with wee ones sat on their haunches near the roadbed while little boys carried to them whatever rocks they could find in the fields nearby. Resignedly, young girls and women of all ages toiled with heavy hammers rhythmically breaking the rocks for the new roadbed, faces crimson with scorching midday heat, dusted with finest powders of the stone. Nina watched them, sighing in deep relief that her new life, though servile, was to be infinitely easier than those poor people wracked with each shuddering beat.

Turning from the main route Narendra chose an unserviceably narrow path leading to the home of an old friend. There they could bed down for the night. He could renew old friendships and might even be able to recruit Ashok as a dacoit-fighter. There was no specific day he had to have Nina at the palace and he may as well make this trip as pleasurable as possible.

An orange sun still moved in the cloudless heavens when they arrived at Ashok's, the meeting one of great jubilation. Ashok, a few local friends and Narendra found a restful spot in which to savor each other's gossip. But it was not until Narendra was alone with Ashok several hours later that he eagerly discussed his plans to capture as many existing dacoits as humanly possible. Ashok had heard of Ali, a despicable and elusive dacoit, and the rumor that he was heading in the direction of Mewar. There was something else perennially rumored which detestably bothered both of these men... Ali's preference for young boys in his sex life. Narendra quickly appointed Ashok a committee of one to persistently scout around and learn what he could of Ali's present whereabouts and hopefully his future plans.

"There will be no other way but for me to join him," Ashok stated with a fixed determination, so quickly was he imbued with his friend's psychic need to eliminate the appalling scourge.

"But what if he should choose you for a lover?" Narendra scowled.

"He won't. I hear he likes boys much younger. I shall hope that he will come to trust me. When I learn anything important I shall get word to you."

Narendra pondered, "You will not be able to take anyone into your confidence. You must be extremely careful, Ashok. Plans shall have to be carefully laid. I don't want you hurt, my friend."

"The fortunes of war, Narendra Singhji. Are there not spies in every war? They may make their plans at the last minute or do things strictly on impulse. Then it would not be possible to get any word to you, and I would probably have to join in the raid."

"Your best is all we can ask, maré dhost." With this Narendra asked to be shown to his charpoy for the night.

The next morning the four well-assorted travelers started on yet another narrow but exciting pathway to Udaipur, Narendra anxious to acquaint himself with every inch of Mewari terrain. By late afternoon they passed through a wee village of Jagat, indicated by a crude little sign. They jested about the similarity of name, the only thing which in any way resembled the fair sized fort from which their journey began. The road now came to look like a dry river bed. Here rocks were of every size imaginable and the desert rose and fell at will, then just as suddenly flattened itself. There were very few houses, all kutcha, made of mud and appearing easily destructible. And across from the houses stood the lovely temple to Durga.

Nina jumped from her horse, stepping over an exquisite lintel. Frame, pillars and sturdy dome embraced this young girl. For eight centuries the gods, goddesses and horses have held their magnificently carved bodies out to the elements and withstood all that nature had wrought. Today the sun highlighted well-rounded breasts and curved limbs. Shadows of leaves from overhanging neem trees danced playfully across their bodies with a tender caress. Narendra admired Nina's inquisitiveness, and was it not he himself who first instructed her to learn all she could about anything "Mewar?"

But the terrain was equally exciting. Cactus was of a softer grey-green and the earth was of another hue and color. People were not as numerous here, but those who appeared, poor and simple as they were, added unsurpassed color to the scene. Men's small pugris wound tightly around their heads rivaled the brilliance of blues, greens, yellows and reds of the very full gagras of the women. Golden earrings flopped from the lobes of men as they turned to watch the tiny parade of four. Women stopped their chores of pulling water from ancient Persian wells. Walls of jagged cactus, unbroken along both sides of the path which served as roadway, became so narrow the riders had to continue single file.

In their circuitous path to Udaipur Narendra chose Jaisamand Lake as his next stopover. There in the midst of sparkling water were small man-made islands inhabited by aborigines. Leading up away from the crystalline water at the head of the ghat or steps stood three spotless white marble chhatris reminding Nina of the Mandore cenotaphs where she had been discovered. Elephant statues played sentinel. At the top of a steep emerald hill stood a melancholy palace. Would you want to live up there" Narendra inquired.

"Much rather live in the big one in Udaipur." she answered perceptively. There was Queen Mother to meet and maybe if she was lucky she might even get to know the Maharana, Hamir II. To be sure, she would be confined in tiny quarters with other servants, but hopefully she would get into other sections for the queen's work.

Once in Udaipur it would be difficult to travel for there would be no transportation. And where would there be to go? Did she dare visit the Singhs in Jagatpur in a year or so? How would she reach it? It might just be that she could never leave Udaipur, in which case she had better enjoy each moment of this trip. She did another 360° circle, encompassing the tremendously large lake, its islands, the encroaching jungle beyond the backside of the ghats and the little primeval palace. The scenery was magnetic, spellbinding.

"It wouldn't be too bad up there after all," she conceded.

Narendra had with him his hunting rifle, a necessary adjunct when traversing Indian jungles. While lions were many kilometers south in the Gir forest, tigers, leopards and cheetah were prevalent here near Jaisamand Lake. They would come to drink at night, disappearing quickly, their soft pads taking them deep into the underbrush and trees.

With a speculative impulse he lead the group into the thickness which laid before them, cautioning each not to speak, instructing them to step single file, into his footsteps, avoiding needless crackling of twigs or anything which might lay in the path. It would soon be dark and he knew he must hurry. Close to the ghats he had seen a small goat, captured it and now held it quietly in his arms, along with his rifle. It was about 15 minutes before they reached a small hunting box which he had used on various occasions.

Handing the goat to one of his servants, Narendra gave explicit instructions to tie his legs firmly to the four corners of a large object which appeared like a too-tall table. This, he explained to Nina, would make the goat bleat, attracting any tiger or leopard hungry for a new kill. It seemed unsparingly cruel to the girl, but hers was not to reason. As they crept up the steep flight of darkened steps inside the hunting box, Nina caressed the walls with her hands and silently spoke a prayer that all nearby animals had had their fill recently and would not come on this night.

Once atop the hunting box they crouched, afraid to sneeze or cough, scaring the predator. They watched out the slanted holes made for aiming rifles down toward the goat. Someone must have heard her prayers for it was finally too dark to see anything, and while the bleating continued throughout the night, she did manage a bit of sleep from time to time. Playful monkeys awakened them in the morning and Narendra sent one of his servants to untie the weakened goat which had been left unmolested by the tigers.

"Your puja...." Nina spoke with the suggestion of dawn.

"I'll have to make it twice as long tomorrow, won't I?" It was rare Narendra would allow anything to interfere with morning prayers. And on this day they took off with great haste in the direction of Udaipur. The jungle was heavy and dark with underbrush reaching up to the lower tree limbs. The air held a unique morning freshness while all knew that somewhere beneath this greenery would be those elusive tigers of last night. A huge cluster of spotted deer stopped to watch the foursome, tails aloft, eyes as big as plates, ears straight up. There was sambhar too, and a bluebull with his funny hump back and Nina could not help but hope that somewhere, but not too close, they would come upon a spotted panther, India's lovely leopard. Soon there was nothing left in their path but one little bunny and the wriggle of a cobra.

"You're sure to have good luck now, Nina. What an auspicious day for you," Narendra spoke from the heart.

"Why do you say that?"

"Did you not know that it is an auspicious omen — when a cobra crosses your path?"

Now only thoughts of the palace and Queen Mother occupied Nina's mind. Was Narendra right? Would she have good luck there? Nightfall again came before they could reach the outskirts of Udaipur's walls.

Restlessness overtook Narendra. He'd be glad when tomorrow was over. Tonight he felt inferior, breathing the same air exhaled by Hamir's sixty five predecessors. They had lived and died valorously, bravely, viciously, but mainly with a deep sense of honor and pride. With their respect for womanhood, their centuries old vow that none of their queens or princesses would ever be conquered or sold to the barbarous Mughals, how could one tread lightly on the soil devoutly hallowed for 1000 years? As for refusing subjugation, about the only others to join Mewar were the Mahrattas. Before Narendra's birth their government fell to shreds. Many little people here and there came forward to collect taxes claiming to be rightfully theirs and the Mahrattas' original dreams of a beautiful Hindu empire washed away as easily as a leaf on a swollen river.

Narendra strained in his half sleep-half wake to <u>feel</u> what all this meant to his kingdom. One day he would rule in his father's vast estate of fort and many villages and hamlets. At one point in time, nobles and peasants alike were forced to fight. Many of the Mewaris fled to their fortresses, causing an economic collapse. Everything stood still. With no wealth there came no trade and all around the villages outside Arjun Singh's fortress the fields were left uncultivated. Countless families came to dwell within the walls of the fort.

Narendra was old enough to recall that in the days which followed, Jagat Singh II formed a triple alliance with himself in paramount power. He represented his Mewar with its capitol in Udaipur, Amber with its in Jaipur and Marwar with its capitol in Jodhpur, the kingdom which Narendra last visited. There had followed much juggling of names, power and power-plays.

Narendra and Nina had each slept fitfully outside Udaipur's walls until the first rays of day expressed themselves. Gypsies in wooden carts were stirring down the road and Narendra scuffled to a low thorny shrub for brief morning worship; only one hour on this day and hardly any at all yesterday. He began to feel guilty for relaxing his self-imposed restrictions.

Tea was all the sustenance they had this morning with little talking, his head still full of the slow march of history which invaded his sleep. This morning his mind took up where it earlier left off.

Knowing the Mahrattas had become very powerful, it was amazing none of the Mewar territory had been lost to them. Only eight years ago, in 1770, the city of Udaipur was held by the Mahrattas. He did not know how much it cost the kingdom in money but he had been made clearly aware that the then Maharana Ari Singh was forced to come up with cash any way he could to save their kingdom, and especially their capitol. Ari could not have afforded a war. Luckily he could sell jewels and other items to make the necessary payments to the Mahrattas and ensure at least a temporary peace.

Then more misfortune. In 1773 Maharana Ari Singh died, leaving two babies: Hamir, the present child Maharana, and his little brother Bhim Singh. What a chore for their mother, the regent. Hers was an arduous position, not only as regent, but the task, however illustrious, of her son being Maharana, literally "King of the Maharajas," was in itself cumbersome. It struck Narendra with painful clarity for the first time.

Would the Mahrattas ever invade again? Could she handle all the details of running the kingdom? No wonder she called durbars at odd times. No wonder his father and all the other nobles rushed off to them eagerly, for there was so much business to be covered. Little wonder the question of the dacoits did not seem of paramount importance to her, as it did to him. Sleeping out in the fresh air these last nights seemed to clear away all fuzzy illusions. Queen Mother had already lived through so much.

Vowing to do whatever he could to help bring the kingdom of Mewar to its one-time brilliance and prominence, he would offer to help the Maharani, Queen Mother, in every conceivable way, as well as aiding his own father. There now was within Narendra the feeling of just being born, not as an infant but rather as a responsible adult.

The little foursome left the Gypsy band far behind. It was still many miles to the palace. The hills which had risen slowly and gently were now spreading farther away. The level ground which stretched for miles before them found the ordinary morning delicate mechanism of civilization. Heritage was richly allotted to these Mewaris and their pride showed in the very sway of a woman's body, heads caressing four or five shiny brass pots of water, swinging gagras singing quietly to the movement of delicate limbs. Children scampered bare-bottomed near crudely constructed huts. Stately men with full moustaches curling to their brilliant colored saffas tied massively around heads, dipping behind to their waists, walked for unknown reasons down the roadway. Families worked together in wheat fields and a bend in the road produced another man-made lake. At its shore several dozen water wheels squeakily churned, while overhead pretty little grey-blue birds sang in accompaniment.

To this rhythm of a dawning world Nina wondered anew of her fresh start in life. So many intimidating questions, but spaced between were these lovely sights and sounds of Udaipur.

Only the faintest echoes of the last of the dhobis charmed her ears, mixed with laughter of the little ones. At another turn there spread a little city square and standing in its midst a young lady. Her very full skirt sank below a plump round navel. The tomato red cloth had been tie-and-died in geometric patterns, a major trade of this city. Her ankles blazed with thick silver bangles covered heavily with clinking bells. Begrimed hands loosely grasped a round wooden pole. Tied to it was an immense pile of hay resting atop jet black uncombed hair.

Soon Nina shouted, "The palace!" Not too far distant was the magnificent outline of its very top. Horse drawn tongas and the multiple sights ignored. Tremendously increasing her gait she'd bend down over her horse, pushing aside water buffalo or cows which intruded her pathway.

They reached the first of the palace gates. Entering, Narendra almost expected Nina to kiss his feet for having arranged the whole thing. Fortunately discretion took hold and Nina muffled as best she could some of the joy produced by the unimaginable good luck and the awesome size of this home.

"Will I meet Queen Mother today?" she inquired.

"One cannot know, my little one. Perhaps you will never meet her. Perhaps she will just send all her work to you."

She looked up at the man with whom she was in love. "My little one" he had called her. This couldn't be a term of affection. In this decorous society, levity could not be thinkable. But the sulphurous words would be shelved until she could quietly sort out their meaning.

The palace was no longer make believe for it cast its shadows on her young body. It engulfed her in the glory of its veil. Whether it would become her pall or her refuge mattered not in this first moment. She had attained the utmost of her dreams. Her fairytale palace rose a hundred feet above her in welcome. The mighty structure which had invaded the rays of the sun verged its shade upon her. To Nina it was an auspicious omen. This shadow was there for her. The magnificent building was touching her, this proxy of outstretched arm of Queen Mother.

Narendra looked down at her with a new set of values. He had respected her, but was there creeping into his soul something more?

This little waif before him would surely never marry; she had no family, not one rupee for dowry, "widowed," or so their manufactured lie would impart. He has organizing her life. He could now forget her and go about his business. Why then did he suddenly feel sad that she would be far from him?

Nina wanted to drink in all the alluring beauty, to savor it, anointing her as with the ambrosial fragrance of a lovely flower. Off to one side of the granite palace a silver grey monkey swung his body from parapet, to wall, to gate in cynical mockery. Nina stepped backward in the shade little by little, taking in the magnitude of this structure Maharana Udai Singh came to build after the last sacking of the famous fort of Chittor. Still farther back she moved, tripping, sprawling on her rump with a thud, both legs spread apart, pointing skyward. Then sideways she slid down a cement incline. Exploding with laughter the men stood, hands on hips, as Nina struggled to regain her foothold in the soil at the base of the cement incline, turning to look at the queer forms on which she had just lain.

"So those are slides for youngsters," Narendra teased. "All along I thought they were for elephants."

"Elephants indeed," she glowered up to the mass of laughing manhood.

"Sahee, really." Narendra pointed to a long two foot high stretch of concrete wall explaining, "That's where the elephants fight, and this is where they rest."

"You are teasing me again, Narendra Singhji."

"No. He's not," said one of the servants, convulsed with mirth. "They do have elephant fights and from up there Their Highnesses watch." He pointed high above to pretty colored windows in a recessed part of the structure. Queen Mother was looking down upon them, laughing just as hard as they.

Instantly the servants bent extremely low, almost to the ground, hands with palms together, whipping them up and down feverishly, grins erased. The men looked like woodcutters chopping away at a low lying prone piece of a tree. She wondered whether she should even dare glance upward again at Her Highness and looked instead at Narendra. He motioned her to do as they. Narendra was then beckoned to come up.

"You will perhaps have a lifetime to enjoy this beauty, Nina," he said somewhat somberly. "Come. I cannot know whether Queen Mother will wish to meet you now or just place you into her employ —or perhaps send you abroad to a circus after your acrobatics."

"It is best that we say goodbye here outside her portals. I wish you all the best. Take care of yourself. Make us proud of you, no matter how menial and insignificant the work. And I shall personally put in a very good word for you."

Nina nodded, keeping her head slightly turned. Tears had started to well as she began suffering pangs of parting's grief. Narendra stepped up his pace under the hanging marriage symbol at the top of the doorway. Two huge wooden gates had been swung back, their massive elephant spikes placed high.

A message quickly arrived from Her Highness to meet the girl who so violently sprawled below. Through all this Nina's poignant allure shone through, the queen finding it hard to resist. They chatted about her abilities and the Queen's needs. Now it was quite clear to Narendra that she would be well looked after. It was quite evident too, that Nina's clumsiness was outdone only by her eagerness to serve.

How wise Narendra had been to say his goodbyes before entering the palace. Would they ever meet again? How cloistered would be her life? There was a loud thud heard only by Nina like the closing forever of a prison door. On which side of it was she?

Chapter 3

Queen Mother withdrew temporarily from the struggling world, calling on Nina to brush her silken tresses. These two women were far different from each other, yet strangely drawn together. Nina respectfully seldom spoke in the Rani's presence, yet was an avid listener. However, when asked for advice, old beyond her years, Nina's judgement was sound. Not even the queen knew why she felt able to express herself to this young girl, unversed in politics, devoid of protocol, a lone and lonely soul. Perhaps this very lack made her the ideal sounding board and confidante. More and more Nina was called upon to listen to the Rani's decisions. She became in ceaseless demand in the proud zenana with less and less time for stitching.

Nina was in a quandary over this position. The role put her in bad stead with the jealous servants with whom she had to live. They were unable to fathom such a close relationship. Nina necessarily grew more aloof with them, choosing to take her meals across the room from the more cantankerous who spoke in her presence in semi-audible tones. To amuse herself during idle time Nina would theorize what made each of them so unjust. Some few she thought were inflamed to a morbid degree by inferiority complexes, others suffering from pressures of inhibitions and lacking an intelligent foundation. As they came aware of her greater foothold in the palace they were more livid.

Here solely to serve the Rani Nina felt withdrawn from the world. With no friends, her only recreation was the walks through the old city or on the backside of the palace through wonderfully dense woods. Through Narendra she had, perhaps unwisely, lost her fear of wild animals. As for snakes, the one she had seen en route to Udaipur had portended good luck rather than bad and in retrospect it would seem the omen was correct. Who would possibly have imagined her good fortune in becoming closer to the regent than anyone else?

Unfortunately her walks did nothing to pacify her mind which seemed day by day to require enormous reinforcement. Through Queen Mother she was quickly acquiring an appetite for the aesthetic. A deeper knowledge should certainly appeal to the Rani's visionary sense but first Nina should learn to read and write. Exceedingly patient with Nina, perhaps the Rani would agree to Nina joining lessons with her children. The youngest boy had not yet commenced his formal education.

Jumping headlong into her presumptuous plans the teenager asked Her Highness a tremendous favor — to be allowed the unheard-of privilege of receiving lessons alongside little Bhim Singh when his studies would commence. Nina feared the reply to her spoken request, remaining with hands pressed together before her forehead in salute, her body bowed low, knees on the floor, her butt on her heels. Only after a short pause she raced on, explaining how Mewar captivated her soul.

Completely nonplussed the regent remained silent. Nina dared peek. She quickly added it was a shameful request, being of such a lowly caste unworthy of even being near her sons. She appealed to the fact that surely Queen Mother did not condone illiteracy.

"Beat me if you will," Nina stated without a quiver in her voice, "but I definitely had to ask. If there is just the tiniest chance I can learn about Mewar, then I had to risk it. Somehow I must study, I must. Somewhere. I cannot go through life this dumb. Until I came here I did not know how dumb I am."

"You are not dumb, Nina, nor shall I strike you. Although you took me off guard, I am manifestly pleased with your eagerness. You often startle me with your ideas and suggestions. I never know what to expect of you... ever since you splattered yourself on the elephant slabs. But you have already brought me pleasure and I shall think on your request. Of course you may not sit alongside my sons. Certainly you are smart enough to know that. But...who knows... perhaps there is a way." The Rani knew she could use someone in the zenana with a greater appreciation and understanding of things current and past and it was not too long before the request was granted. Little Bhim Singh should have started his lessons on his heritage before this.

The seamstress pondered her good fortune as it continued to multiply. The domestic staff isolated themselves from Nina. Only the sentries remained quietly courteous.

Of late the Rani felt a faint twinge of uneasiness. These days would have been difficult for any ruler what with border skirmishes, high-wrought feelings on taxes, the British rumbles stirring throughout India. Five years earlier her husband had prematurely died, leaving the gaddi to her elder son, Hamir II. And now at 18 his mother strongly feared for him too.

Normally the widow of Maharana Ari Singh would have joined her husband on the funeral pyre, but sati was not for her. With sons so young the Rani's duty was clearly to watch over and mold the boys to fit her plans. She felt betrayed and abandoned by Rana Ari but she did have powerplay ambitions. She thought of Ari now and his ungovernable temper and his meager twelve years on the throne. Never had she been overly proud to be his Maharani, unable to rise above the fact he was merely a second-class noble before taking the throne. His predecessor had been Rana Raj Singh II who sadly had done little for his people and his land. In the 1000 year old kingdom of Mewar, so rich with dazzling history, unsurpassed in valor and chivalry, these two men who preceded her eldest son paled in the rosy glow of the dozens before them. On the death of Raj Singh II the order of succession retrograded to his Uncle Ari, the man this Queen Mother had married.

She reminisced on her husband's rule, forced to somewhat forgive his lack of ability or accomplishment. There had been the famine a decade earlier, beyond his control. He'd sit in a courtyard resting his outthrust chin on a rail, staring sullenly out over the throbbing white city of Udaipur and his pitiably hungry subjects. But little or nothing was done to help it, save for the ever changing tide of nature and passing time.

Five years later a siege in Udaipur neither helped Maharana Ari's temper nor the populace. Perhaps his ill humor stemmed from his originally having had that seat below the sixteen chief nobles, the umraos or first-class nobles. Although being one of the thirty-two second class nobles held some distinction he was of the genre who desired being on top. His wife felt even more strongly about it. Attaining the illustrious throne of Mewar should have erased all the evils which preceded this moment, but for Ari there was little in life which enthralled him. Aware of his unsuccessful career there was little or nothing he could seem to do about it. It was while out on a boar hunt that he had been stabbed to death by the heir to the Bundi throne, leaving his son Hamir Singh II to take Mewar's seat of power.

Queen Mother left her reverie, suffering a quixotic expectancy. "Strange Nina, but I feel cold all over. I am sure that something is about to happen."

"Are you having fever or chills, Your Highness? Come, I shall see you are put to bed." Nina rose to her bare feet, standing at the side of her mistress.

"It is not that, Nina. I had long ago forgotten but I had these same strange premonitions when my husband went boar hunting, and the terrifying reality when the hunting party came home with his dead body. It is the same now..."

"You must not think such terrible thoughts, Highness. All is well. I am sure that it is."

The rani had acquired a well deserved suspicious nature. For a terrifyingly brief moment it crossed her mind that Nina could be an implement of a plot against her. But no. She quickly discarded that possibility. To be a plant for court intrigue or murder was out of the question. Recommended by the royal house of Arjun Singh was the only proof Queen Mother needed to trust Nina. Arjun's family for generations had loyally addressed themselves to the needs of the court, had offered sage advice, attended durbars more faithfully than most other feudal families, had fought at the side of Their Highness. Serving in this manner was to dwell in the towering fabric of honor. In no way could Narendra or Arjun ever have planted a decoy in the main palace. Of this the Rani was sure. Besides, she had to put her trust in someone.

Beyond all that, she thought, Nina was not sufficiently schooled nor wily enough to contrive court intrigue, yet aware she possessed a more level head than her other aides. During such times as Queen Mother requested Nina's thoughts on various matters, her ideas and suggestions were sound, rarely dealing in the realms of vagueness. The Rani would keep Nina under her wing.

"If you do not wish to lay down and rest perhaps you would like to stroll the gardens of Jag Niwas, Your Highness. It might be a nice change of scenery. Possibly there you can dispel this cloudy obsession which has poured down upon you."

Once again the regent accepted the girl's advice. Walking several paces before her down to the little dock the two boarded a small barge for the short glide across lovely Lake Pichola. Nina welcomed the chance to accompany her on a visit to this loveliest of all structures, seemingly straight from the most misty, alluring fairytale. Extensive travel was not easy in these centuries and it therefore had been decreed by Maharana Jagat Singh a new palace would be built below the main palace, on a huge rock jutting above low ground. Of Indian/Persian design with graceful chhatris, windows of vivid colors capturing southern sunlight of early afternoon, and bays of blue glass windows to the west giving illusion of sunny skies in midst of cloudy days, it is magnificent. The ultimate in sumptuous splendor was made even greater when, on completion, the surrounding area was flooded, giving birth to tranquil Lake Pichola.

Today the regally imperial barge slipped serenely to a wide stone platform butting against three massive doors graced on either side with white marble elephants, their exquisitely embellished trunks of golden garlands raised eternally in formal welcome. Jag Niwas was occupied mainly in the heat of summer, but the queen occasionally came to it as a change of pace.

The women walked to Dhola Mahal made of white stone serving as the dining hall for the chiefs and nobles while on duty.

Leaving the Maharani in solitude, Nina walked through the inner courtyard with its diaphanous crystal fountain. Above it an upper terrace bordered by delicate lacy marble railing led to the far end of the palace. Beside it the late **Maharana** would sit in his adjustable "moon-gazing chair" so that as the moon moved through its normal sky-route an attendant would change the angle of the chair.

Nina never ceased to wonder at the beauty and man-made comforts: the minute fountain-heads in ceiling and floor of Virka Niwas, spraying the finest mist of scented water to cool the room. Beds, tables and mirrors of crystal defied description.

Nina waited with great patience for Queen Mother on the heavy brass swing, over a meter and a quarter square. Chains of brass elephants tinkled merrily with their little bells. Here she sat staring across the mirrored walls delivered from Bohemia. Meanwhile the queen sought answers to her increasing woes. Problems were excessively heavy and even in this exhilarating atmosphere she found it difficult to mentally sedate herself. It seemed impossible for an idea to germinate, a plan in which she could enrich Mewar in her name. She sat longer, awed by the past, taunted by the present.

Meanwhile, creeping into Nina's thoughts were Narendra and the ill-considered beauty of loving him, but he was already shackled to her heart. In his absence she eagerly added to her life the haunting awareness of the natural and material beauties of Udaipur and God's chosen form of blessing her: the friendship of Queen Mother. Being thus accepted was genuinely baffling and Nina hastened to develop her own honor code, resigning her life to bow readily to the exigencies of whatever fate lay ahead.

Four hours had passed before Queen Mother chose to return to the main palace. Earlier today the new fear in the regent's heart manifested itself in hypocritical meekness, contrary to her true self.

Haunting dusk descended with Jagdish temple bells drowning other sounds. Where the palace stands its highest Nina surveyed the city, those who chose to worship, and some who ambled lazily through Udaipur's winding streets. Staring through soft tinted oblong glass the world was painted a prismatic hue. Often Nina would think about how much of her life was real and what portion was a self-imposed delusion.

Breaking the day dream, a dappled horse entered the main palace gates below where she stood. There was no doubt this easily recognizable animal came from Jagatpur. Nina instantly raced through the upper large courtyard, down all those flights of narrow steep steps until reaching the main staircase of the palace, arriving in time to hear the rider request an audience with His Highness. "Is everyone well at Jagatpur?" she blurted to Kaushik, the solitary horseman. It had been the Rani who earlier in the day sensed doom. Now it was the inharmonies of fear-consciousness which gripped Nina. What horrible news could he be bringing?

"Everyone is well," he replied, half smiling. He had often seen Nina in the grounds of Jagatpur's fort and could understand her concern. She sat with him until three-quarters of an hour later Hamir Singh and his mother received Kaushik, Nina dismissed from their presence. She was transfixed with apprehension, returning to her quarters, unaware of the meaning of the spun gold envelope the rider presented to Their Highnesses.

The palace had become ghostly quiet, silence shattering Nina who found it possible to only fitfully sleep. The spasm of anxiety lasted through the following morning. Kaushik was nowhere to be seen. It was not until after the Rani's midday rest period that Nina was summoned to her chambers. Incoherent by this time with morbid worry and wonder Nina spat out a barrage of questions. "Is Na... is everyone really alright in Jagatpur. Has something awful happened? Why did they send a messenger? Oh, Your Highness, please tell me. Please tell me." Nina had managed to say all this in one long breath, shrinking two inches as her lungs gave out.

The two women were alone, the elder gesturing the other to sit at her feet. "Nina, there is good news. I have been thinking how to tell you. I am sure you love Narendra Singhji very deeply..." Nina in trying to refute this statement was quickly silenced. "It is no use to try to hide this fact from another woman for this can be easily read in your eyes. I saw it unmistakably when he brought you to me the first time. I have come to feel very close to you and trust you perhaps more than any other, Nina, so do not try to hide something from me which I already know."

She continued, "If you do truly love Narendra then you surely want the very best for him. He is a healthy, vigorous young man and will one day be the rawal of Jagatpur. His father and uncle have gone to Jaiselmer to arrange final plans for his marriage. They have sent my son and me invitations to the wedding, to take place in Jaiselmer, of course, in a little over a months time. She is one of the Kumaris."

Dark eyes poured their sadness without tears, heart bruised with violent impact. Even Queen Mother ached with poignant pathos for this young girl who had clearly been destined never to attain fulfillment of her love. "Is she beautiful, Your Highness?" It was such an obvious and expected question.

"I do not know the princess, Nina, but I am sure she is very lovely. It would certainly be one of the conditions of marriage. Arjun Singh would see to that. She will naturally offer a very large dowry and we would hope one day make a fine lady for the house of a feudal lord. Let us hope they will be blessed with healthy sons to continue the line."

Someone else in Narendra's arms? Nina never knew this wondrous feeling with Narendra, and today's news brought one more closed door in her corridor of life. Nina adored his father and knew in her heart that Arjun Singh would settle only for a very fine and pretty girl. She would have great attributes. It was true, Nina would want nothing less than the best for her heart's love. She must give up intermittent desperate thoughts that he was to one day be hers alone. How very, very strange. Give him up, even in thoughts? In dreams? Queen Mother had been indulgently kind to her; Nina thrilled at life is such a magnificent palace, yet her happiest moments were those when she lay in dark silence, holding in fantasy the man of her life.

Nina knew it highly unlikely anyone would ask for her as a mate and certainly not a titled person. As for another servant as a husband, it was a tossup: loving Narendra as she did, living with another man would be painfully difficult. It offered only one joy — the prospect of one day bearing her own child, a little human being to fondle and caress.

Both ladies were silent for a seemingly long time when the regent again spoke. "There is other news, too. Narendra

Singhji has been fighting dacoits. But do not worry, my child, he is safe. Everything is fine."

"Do I have your leave, Your Highness? Oh please, I must go hear it from Kaushik."

Queen Mother's countenance changed sharply. "How is it you worry about dacoits?"

Nina answered cleverly, "My parents were killed by dacoits. You will remember Narendra told you of this." It sufficiently satisfied the regent's curiosity. The girl was dismissed, rushing to Kaushik, found sitting with his tired back against a wall. Nina quickly pressed him into relating all news of Narendra and dacoits.

"Well, it all happened quite unexpectedly," he started. Narendra Singhji and his friends, Ramesh, Pandu and Ranjit, I believe Narendra Singhji calls him Ran, had been out riding horses one afternoon, They had traveled some distance from the fort when suddenly Ramesh said to Narendra, 'There is a man sitting up in that tree we just rode under'. Narendra Singhji answered 'You silly Rajput; why would a man be sitting up in the tree? Ramesh said it most certainly was a man.

"By this time they were farther down the road where they'd have to cross a nullah. It was here in the dip of the road they discovered a dozen camels all standing around drinking water. But the man in the tree had made strange sounds like the mating of quail as a signal to the others. A dozen men who had been resting under more trees twenty meters from the camels hastily jumped to their feet, racing after the beasts.

"Across the river and directly into the midst of a small village they rode, my master directly behind. The dacoits jumped from their camels, rushing into various little huts screaming 'kill, kill.'

"Narendra Singhji spotted an elder and asked if he knew who these twelve were. Luckily the old man recognized several of the dozen and knew them definitely to be dacoits. Four against twelve. What to do? It was the ladies and children's good fortune that they were down at a well getting water for that evening and the next morning's tea. By a stroke of luck there were a few men in several huts who had overpowered some of the dacoits, bringing them outside. Narendra is said to have ordered Ranjit to hold them all at bay or kill any who made a move to escape. It is said the dacoits were not excessively brave. My master, Ramesh and Pandu then went into each of the huts, fighting furiously until they had rounded up all twelve. Ropes tied around them, they were hauled off to the jail in Jagatpur. There is soon to be a trial to determine their sentences. And now the whole fort is calling our four men great heroes."

Nina now had a new fear, that the ease with which this all happened would create in Narendra and his men a false sense of security. She thanked Kaushik for the rendition and asked if he would deliver a message to Narendra, though realizing he might wonder how she could know about dacoits. She was just learning the first strokes of her writing lessons. Her message would have to be verbal. It must be brief and cleverly worded.

"Kaushik," she spoke, "please be sure to tell Narendra Singhji that I wish for him the best in his coming marriage and hope to hear from him personally the very unusual story of capturing the dacoits. Be sure to use my words exactly." She could only pray that Narendra would catch the word "unusual" and attach great importance to it.

No stranger to travel was Nina. A little more than two weeks had passed since the announcement of the wedding in Jaiselmer. Queen Mother had been in a quandary regarding Nina, for to take her along might be more cruel than leaving her behind. The young Rana Hamir would attend out of necessity and little eight year old Bhim Singh would be left at the palace with a bevy of servants and numerous rawals and rawats. The overland trip would be long, Jaiselmer being quite distant from Jodhpur, in a region called the Thar. But so accustomed had Queen Mother become to the presence of Nina that it was decided to include her in the travels.

Nina had developed a special plate of armor against the cruelties of her peers who by this time were afraid not to follow her instructions. She would be in charge of some of them on the trip. Like her superior, Nina was filled with mixed emotions.

No time was lost in preparations. There would be innumerable tents; the royal family would demand incredible comfort. Palanquins must be carried for their Highnesses. The traveling party would be many in number. Cooking pots and food would be cumbersome. Many water jugs were filled. Clothing was neatly arranged in immense boxes, carried by elephants. Jewel cases would be well guarded. There would be hunters with them who could trap or shoot quail, doves or partridge as well as something bigger, an occasional bluebull or sambhar. Blankets would be required against desert night chills. There would be portable bath tubs and toilets for the royal family only, tanks to heat water, piles of wood and cow dung for fires, many lamps and oil to burn in them.

The Rani however could seldom rely on instructions to most servants. While they smiled toothy white grins at every request, and while the men appeared to comprehend, that was no criterion for having directions followed. It was not that they intended to disobey, they simply found it difficult to remember everything told them, or to move at a reasonable speed. In the East what does not get done today may just possibly tomorrow. The regent, therefore, took it upon herself to call in several Rawals and jagirs now serving on duty at the palace. They were to aid her in overseeing the myriad of details.

Nina packed her few clothes. Local women wear no undergarments and often walk barefoot. Nina did have, however, a pair of chappals for her tiny feet, her unobtrusive luxury. They had been handmade by young lads not more than a kilometer beyond the palace gates for a meager rupee and were her most treasured possession, the first thing she was ever to buy and pay for, herself.

With small scraps of cotton cloth left over from her stitching chores she made herself a few of the little bodices, small colorful bands of material cut to fit the bosom, held together in the rear by slender straps crossing an otherwise bare back. About half the female population wear these bodices only across the upper half of their breasts, exposing their nipples. Handy for breast-feeding mothers, but she herself suffered from a delicate womanly modesty. Atop this slight garment she wore the customary odhni, a rather straight blouse-piece which somewhat flattened her youthful bosom.

Realization of the upcoming slow travel finally settled upon Nina. Alone with Narendra from Mandore to Jagatpur they were able to move speedily with the two fine horses. This upcoming junket would be tedious. The men would tire quickly, carrying Her Royal Highness plus the weight of the gaudy mirrored palanquin. Bearers would change at regular intervals and the party would necessarily stop early each day, other bearers racing ahead to pitch tents and build fires in the sand to commence the lengthy procedure of cooking rites.

Abruptly upon them was departure day, Nina a prey to shadowed misgivings. Though she longed for the sight of her beloved, to see him wed another was beyond endurance, coming to think of herself as being punished for some past sin. The journey dragged. Was Narendra already up in Jaiselmer? Lord, they weren't even near Jodhpur yet. It was well over a year since running away from the northern desert in the care and security of Narendra and now she was painstakingly backtracking. When and if she should meet Narendra alone, however briefly, she would of necessity surround herself in a cold atmosphere of impersonality. Queen Mother had guessed of Nina's love. Would Narendra also guess? She should not let him.

One day the party came upon a magnificent oasis, stopping for an extra day of rest. Limpid pools reflected barely swaying date palms behind which nature piled massive rocks. Soft clouds ripened to the perfection of heaven. A bearer was ordered to ride quickly to the nearest hamlet, announce their royal presence, and command the whole village to join and entertain them.

Dinner that evening had been especially opulent. Appropriately early the same morning several hunters had come upon two extraordinarily large rabbits which were immediately skinned and readied for the fires. The cooks were radiantly happy with the decision to camp early for their delicacy could not be rushed. Quickly they made a pit in the soft warm sand, hastening to build a fire. Others painstakingly created a piquant mixture of rice, peas, herbs and spices lovingly stuffed into each of the rabbits. They were moistened with ghee, a clarified butter, and wrapped with dampened cloths. Next came an outer wrapping of heavier fabric, then covered with earth, before placing them into a hole to steam. They remained thus for six hours, destined to be the tastiest meal of the entire trip.

Queen Mother later sat in the entrance of her tent. Inside were three luxurious oriental rugs spread on calloused ground, a table beside Her Highness's bed. A gaudy colored bidri wall hanging screened off a section of the tent serving as a dressing room. The beige and brown tent itself was of double thickness, the inner portion of handblocked stencilled print in geometric pattern. To the rear a three foot flap allowed entry into a smaller ante room containing a crude commode. Immediately behind the potty chair was a much smaller flap set low to the ground, sufficiently large for a servant to reach in and remove the pot, keeping it fresh and clean at all times. This same bathroom held a big tin portable bathtub placed there each morning. Near it stood a crude two-tiered wooden table with a ceramic washbowl and toilet articles neatly laid out each day by Nina. She had come a long way from merely stitching.

"Garum panni, garum panni," a bearer would call each morning, entering at the rear with his hot bath water. At the same time, Malaam, her Highness's current favorite, would make his presence known outside the front flap. "Garum chay, garum chay," he would call, preparing to serve his hot tea. Placing the silver tray on a table pulled beside her bed he'd roll back the mosquito netting, tying it overhead. Stonefaced, he'd carefully pour the morning bed tea, add hot milk and sugar, bow extremely low while backing through the room until exiting.

The sight of such refined luxury in the midst of a melancholy desert intrigued Nina, now sitting at the feet of her Rani awaiting the evening's entertainment. Although she herself came from a village background, customs of Rajputana and beyond varied greatly.

The ancillary group appeared over the rise of drifting sand. Tall village males wore tan colored dhotis and long coatlike blouses, closed at the neck, with very tight sleeves. Atop their heads were pink rumpled turbans, somewhere between the size of the small pugris worn at the palace by most of the male staff, and the immense saffas of other regions of Rajasthan. One man carried a hand made drum, its dried gazelle skin pulled tightly across its top. Others held long narrow flutes. Women and children tailed behind, seating themselves discreetly distant from the royal family, heads somewhat bowed but huge dark eyes always on their Highnesses. Unschooled musicians struck up a danceable tempo, clearly enjoying themselves. Flutes became haunting and meditative and soon the bright flames of the bonfire rejoiced, mocking the music makers. The balance of the men surrounded the fire in a circle, dancing their quaint step, step, step - hop; step, step, step - hop. The circle closed until the men were shoulder to shoulder at which point others leapt deftly atop, first jumping onto hips, then shoulders. The second tier joined arms unafraid of falling into unresting flames, or perhaps willing to brave it for the chance of showing off in front of their rulers. The cleverly adroit villagers dragged out their performance, now three tiers high.

That day and evening had been another precious interval in the arduous journey but now in the followed hush Nina could think only of Narendra. She dared to pray they would not pass the site of the little village near Jodhpur where Motilal had been killed or the lovely cenotaphs of the queens where first she encountered Narendra. Whims of fate were strange and vivid memories would burn still deeper when next she would lay eyes on him; picturing Narendra in the arms of that other woman was yielding to a formless fatality.

Camp was being broken two days later when to the south a screen of sand rose several feet from the ground, quiet desert resounding with pounding echoes of animal hooves and human voices. It was the first contingent from Arjun Singh's entourage and the proud groom. They had unknowingly been camped so close to the royal family in recent days. Fewer in number, they had moved faster, catching up with Queen Mother. The two groups would now be travelling together.

Nina's heart pounded when realizing her beloved was so close. It continued to frighten her. Could she avoid him? She'd have to have a long talk with herself. Today, she said, is a beautiful day. There are no storm clouds, no war. People are happy. I am lucky and I'm healthy so I should be happy in this day. Tomorrow is not here yet and it will look after itself. I will rejoice in today. It will not come again.

In the morning Nina stood near five decorative zal trees, a camel stretching its distended neck to eat its thorny leaves. A herd of graceful chinkara sped near a thicket, their funny stubby white tails raised in the air, saluting her presence. She prayed the hunters would not kill one for dinner.

Making herself as inconspicuous as possible, luck remained with her another day. Her Highness chose to make a side trip to the nearby temple at Pokharan frequented by pilgrims. The Arjun Singhs accompanied her and the party took off on horseback leaving Nina and others to rest. She took a left over paratha from one of the cooks and walked a short way in the opposite direction, away from all others.

Many years ago the region surrounding their camp site had been a popular trade route when Jaiselmer had created an important marketplace for the 35,000 living in and around the fort, but some fifty years ago a new seaport opened far to the south, called Bombay, and now the long and arduous camel caravan routes gave way to cloth sails and whimsical ocean winds. People of the Thar region began to move elsewhere as the economy diminished.

The two parties were now within several days of their destination, everyone anxious for the sight Arjun Singh exclaimed as indescribable. Nina had been sitting near the door of Queen Mother's tent when Narendra made an unscheduled appearance much later the same evening. They smiled but Nina, in her awkwardness, sputtered, "Narendra Singhji, do not think all dacoit fights will be as simple and easy as your last." This worry obsessed her. Instantly she was ashamed. She had forgotten to offer marriage congratulations.

"Nina, I am on my way to my wedding," he scolded rather harshly. "I cannot be bothered with thoughts of dacoits at this time. Let us not think of it." Embarrassed, she walked to a far corner of the tent, having not been dismissed from the queen's presence.

The groom spoke briefly to his regent telling of the senior bearer working for Arjun Singh who had been born and raised in Jaiselmer, the kingdom beyond Jodhpur to which they headed. Queen Mother felt this a fine opportunity for a good briefing on Jaiselmer's background and protocol required it. While there had been many wars and battles between the two kingdoms through the centuries, she actually knew little of its historic features. The old man was summoned. Everyone within range could listen to his insatiate story of the birth and life of Jaiselmer.

"There was once a prince by the name of Jaisel who lived in the twelfth century," his tale started. "Even in those times there were marauders and he felt his capital of Lodurva unsafe for his people. He spent considerable time trying to find just the right spot to resettle until he came upon a hermit.

"The hermit took him to a hillock. He told him that in the sacred epic, Mahabharata, Lord Krishna had arrived at this spot. He was the head of the Yadav clan and knew the clan to be doomed by a dreadful curse. 'Some day,' he said, 'another Yadav will find this place and when he settles here it will thrive. This I prophesy.' And so it was that all those centuries later Jaisel, considering himself and his people Yadavs, did come and he founded Jaiselmer in 1156, second in age in Rajasthan only to Mewar's fort of Chittorgarh.

"Soon you will see how unique it is, It's nothing like the upward movement of Jodhpur's fort, nor is it in any state of ruin as your beloved Chittorgarh. There are few trees. Convex mounds bevel in and out constantly around its massive perimeter, shining in the sunlight like gold poured by the gods from heaven. Jaisel named this new oasis after himself. The funny thing is, it's only 16 kilometers from where he first lived and ruled. Can you imagine that?"

The old man was allowed to continue uninterrupted. "Jaisel's faith had been rewarded. All enemies found it too difficult to come across the pathless wild and sandy incontrovertible ground, unmarked in any manner. And so the people of Jaiselmer were happy and peace loving. They became prosperous and soon joined the important trade routes. But now it is losing importance because they say there are great ships with big sails which come from everywhere to that place far south. It is sad. Now the sands with wind and time have erased most trails, but still there is some semblance of wealth and beauty and the remnants of the great palaces of once rich merchant princes."

Days were becoming increasingly warmer but the nights held a chill. Natives from the area, what few could be seen, wore at night the scratchy wide long shawls made of their own carded, dyed and spun camel wool. So large were the shawls they showed only heads and feet of those persons they were wrapped around. Of earth tones, they blended into the scenery as one would camouflage himself on a tiger hunt, these human chameleons.

Now grass inverted-funnel-shaped huts dotted the landscape but little was seen of the inhabitants. Little hamlets were farther apart and compactly smaller. Nina spotted some of that short scrubby inedible white bush Narendra had stopped to admire when they first met. It had been her first hint of his gentleness, often hidden in his massive frame.

Then one day came the first glimpse of the awesome structure, Jaiselmer fort. It was far more noble than described. Narendra raced to the side of the covered palanquin. "Your Highness, please stop to look. I never thought it to be so ... what can I call it — fearsome. No wonder it was never besieged."

The Rani stepped gracefully out from her carriage, the four bearers setting it gently onto the sand. Neither spoke further for a buoyantly long time. Then the Rani said, "If the beauty of your bride corresponds with this grandeur ... Oh, my dear Narendra. Your father will have done well by you in this marriage agreement."

There was a sense of relief within this man that the wedding would not be until two days hence, permitting plenty of time to swagger through the fort. Never in his life had he ever imagined anything so grim, so foreboding, so awesome and so spectacularly gorgeous. The trip was worth it for this alone, not to mention his prize of a wife. Still, he had not yet let the excitement of a wedding impinge upon his rights as a free and unencumbered man. He lost himself in a fantasy of romance, not physical, but the traditional chivalry and honorable sword-fighting, swash-buckling legends with which he had been brought up, living and loving with a passion unknown to the outside world.

Both groups camped outside the fort for the night. Trumpeters heralded their coming, a red carpet rolled out to the palanquins of Their Highnesses. Chairs resembling thrones faced each other, ready for the initial meeting of the important parties. Campsites had been swept clean daily. Special sentries with new wedding uniforms were on the alert for the auspicious arrival of not only the Queen Mother and her son, the Maharana of Mewar, but equally for the happy bridegroom.

Queen Mother's advance group had already rammed the stakes into the ground, erected tents, secured guy-wires. Fresh water was brought to the travelers daily for neither the Singhs nor the royal family would meet with the Jaiselmer royal family until they were refreshed, cleansed and properly dressed for the occasion. In its own way this grand occurrence would vie in elegance with the actual wedding preliminaries and ceremony. It was difficult at this moment to know which rite took precedence.

Left far behind were the scraggly light green trees. Here amidst the brown sand and nutritious sewan grass. Gadisar Lake reaped the harvest of the last good monsoon, for all too frequently it would become a completely dry bed. Rainfall ranged from a horrendously pitiful two or three centimeters to an occasional 30 centimeters per year. Luckily they had this time reached the peak.

Narendra had been sorry for snapping at Nina the other evening, seeking in some manner to make it up to her. Perhaps they could enjoy together some of the richness of this territory, so enamored was she of nature's bountiful goodness. He asked Her Highness' permission to allow Nina to accompany him on a stroll.

They walked silently for a considerable distance before stopping near the haveli or mansion of one of the past prime ministers. So intricate was the jali, the stone work of the screens which were in fact the walls and windows of the house that it defied verbal description. Through very narrow cobblestoned streets they came to another palace built in the finest tradition possible. On completion it was graciously presented by its rich merchant prince to the Rawal, the ruler of Jaiselmer. The Rawal appreciated the gesture so greatly that with magnanimous and deferential courtesy he handed it back. Of such unusual quality are some of the Rajputs made.

All the lanes outside the fort were unbelievably narrow and picturesque, and nowhere on earth are homes and buildings more lavishly ornamented, intricately cut in wide dimensions around doors and windows. Entrances are low, repelling some of the sand and wind of the desert. Balconies protrude delicately overhead, sometimes without window or door, merely an exquisite ornamentation.

There was not much conversation between the duo in the midst of all this newness. But there was on the part of each an all-absorbing gratification in their togetherness. Nina was amazingly at ease with her love, whereas Narendra's emotions were an enticing phenomenon completely foreign to him and enchantingly pleasant. He was never more comfortable with anyone than with this girl. He realized this as soon as he placed her in the queen's care and peculiarly missed her ever since. While he was now absolutely sure that move had been the best for Nina, he could not understand his strange fixation.

By now everyone had become thoroughly enthralled with this contagious fantasy called Jaiselmer and the outstanding story of Salim Singh, the most infamous of the Rawal's Prime Ministers. Salim Singh was a despot, a hated and feared man who unleashed terror on subjects as well as the Rawal. His word was so absolute that no one could do anything without his stringent agreement. How it could be so is not to be understood, but for his superior, the Rawal, to buy the least little thing, it was necessary to ask Salim's permission. So exorbitant were his levied taxes that one of the groups living near Jaiselmer, the Paliwals, could stand it no more. They had chosen one particular moment and each one of them from their eighty villages fled, leaving everything behind. If Salim Singh wanted what was left, it was his — the hot tea on their fires, their sun-parched fields, their unpretentious abodes. This was about fifty years ago. It took its toll on a once flourishing city. Whispers around camp were that the Paliwals did leave one other thing behind. A curse on anyone who would steal anything which had been theirs... inside or out of the huts.

Dawn brought echoing gongs and chants of worshippers from the small temple down at Gadisar Lake, a favorite of many a nearby villager because of the legend that the temple arose from the midst of the lake. Finally the pangs of curiosity reached Narendra and he began really wondering what his new bride would look like, whether she would be receptive to his husbandly advances, someone with whom he could come to share laughter. He was getting no younger and would want a large family, as did his parents.

Narendra retreated to a quiet spot, settling himself for today's worship, extraordinarily important on this day before his wedding. Puja lasted three and a half hours in front of portable pictures of Lord Siva, his incense, and the minute brass oil burner, immersed in inaudible hallowed prayer and concentration.

Meantime his father departed for the fort and the home of the bride-to-be. When the groom finally arose and looked up toward the mighty fortress, he once again felt the overwhelming awe and wonder of yesterday. Four camel drivers and three hundred fifty beasts had angled to the calm lake in their weeklong search for water. So silently had their pads touched the warm sands, Narendra had been oblivious to them when they first passed and now they were on their way back.

He chatted informally with the camel drivers asking all manner of questions. On what did they feed in this seeming wasteland? "Too," they told him, a bitter melon, growing wild, feeding them well and satisfying their thirst. Far more gratifying is the water from the tank when possible. Work is no longer abundant as in the times of their fathers. It was as explained by the old man previously. But camels were still their mainstay and they have much pride in and care for their animals. Besides, when they grow old their hair is used in the making of those scratchy blankets which become the warm wraps for cold desert nights.

Once more Narendra started for the fort, and once more he was stopped by its strange appeal; that long hill on which it was built, encircled by high wall of solid stone and absolute perfection of contours. Bastions and high turrets form a complete defensive system. And the walls took on a different hue in this morning sun, a brighter burnished gold, a contrast to last night's orange tint in the setting sun.

There would be pre-marriage ceremonies which he must attend. For the first time in his mainly untroubled life he longed for his mother. She had traditionally stayed behind in their own much smaller fort. Narendra, the oldest son, would be the first of the seven children to marry and hopefully the first to present them with a grandchild. Narendra loved his mother very deeply although it was his father who had been more a pal. Mother was always busy seeing to the household and the upbringing of each of the children, leaving little time for lengthy individual play.

It was lunch time before Arjun Singh returned to the campsite, followed by a horde of people: cousins, nieces and nephews of the bride, all with large tallis atop their heads. These silver platters held sumptuous foods, luscious as the wedding feast would be. This was one time the Jaiselmer bearers strode past the tent of the Queen Mother to that of the bridegroom in deference to his big day. A long line of individual tallis were placed on cloths stretched onto the ground. The Rani and her young son Hamir II joined the group, beautifully attired for this auspicious occasion. Narendra and Arjun Singh sat at her side. The balance of the guests, friends of Narendra who numbered more than 500, sat in long lines facing the royal family and the man they had traveled so many miles and weeks to honor.

Commemorating the festivity, food consisted of vegetable cutlets so cunningly blended in flavor one might think they contained meat. There were fresh vegetables grown just beyond the fort, relatively close to the border of Afghanistan. The curries were countless, some hot and others devilishly hotter. Rice was plentiful. There were chapatis and deep fried puri, swelling into balls.

Though the honored guests had been served on sterling silver tallis the remainder of the groom's party ate from the carefully molded plates of peepul leaves called pata, held together with fine slivers of wood, hygienic and easily discarded.

Fruits are perplexedly difficult to acquire in this hintermost corner of the world, but dessert was definitely not omitted. Among goodies was the favorite of Rajasthan, gulab jamun. Tedious to make, the dough requires a specially prepared milk and flour rolled into small balls, deep fried in ghee and soaked for hours in a sugar syrup to which has been added an abundant mixture of exotic rose essence.

The bridegroom had another sweet favorite, barfi, each piece carefully covered with edible silver. This, his mother used to tell him, took longer than anything to prepare. The mava, or special milk, was boiled slowly until it seemed that nothing was left but an almond colored goo. Sugar was added to the mava plus cardamon for a delightful taste and, dependent on availability, either flavored with almonds or pistachios. When it set the candy was covered with finely beaten sheets of silver to enhance its beauty and give a happy feeling, for to some there is a belief that the silver is extremely healthy.

There was much rejoicing, the permissive mood becoming lighter with every passing hour. Nina ate, as always, after all the guests had been served, and in the presence of the other countless servants, becoming increasingly sullen. They continued to distrust her friendliness with their queen, the Rani, and now it was reported she spent several hours strolling with the bridegroom. Just who was she to live like this? It was bad enough they had to obey her orders, which were becoming more frequent.

Queen Mother was busy with state matters, this wedding especially pleasing to her. Narendra remained intimately close to his father, brothers and sister, every few hours bringing another Hindu ritual. Bleak hours without Narendra brought Nina a longing to fly some magic carpet to those naive free and easy days of her earliest youth when all she had to do was lay about the fields, eat or sleep. The realism of this man's life with another woman was something to which she had become a slave. She mired in the rich confusion of wanting his happiness, yet jealously wanting him for herself. Her eyes carried a helpless vagueness seeking a healing panacea. She knew that in no way could she live her whole life like this, the skein of her very being unraveling itself until soon there would be nothing left of mind or body. What could she do? Then her name was spoken by one of Arjun Singh's bearers, beckoning her to follow.

Arjun Singh and his betrothed son shared the same tent. While very large and comfortable, it lacked luxurious appointments. Arjun motioned to her to be seated on the floor in front of him explaining that he and Narendra were most grateful for her having won the respect and solicitude of the Rani without her having placed the Singhs in an uncomfortable position with their regent. Their faith in Nina had been rewarded. It was their understanding that she had become a favorite which made them exceedingly proud. They had also taken an opportunity to ask the queen's permission to allow Nina to view some of the major wedding ceremonies.

She was jubilant to the point of unrestrained tears for though she dreaded the moment he would truly be married, she was sufficiently curious and eager to see the bride's face. Besides, she had never been to a wedding of such high social standing. In spite of being a servant they promised her a good vantage point behind the guests.

Arjun Singh had left them alone briefly. There was a subtle compulsion for Nina to defend herself against the awkwardness which could develop. "Narendra Singhji," she addressed herself to him, "I wish for you enduring good luck. If ever I can be of use to you I would want to. Not just with the matter of the dacoits. Oh Narendra, I do not know what I mean except I would want to be there if you ever need me."

It so suddenly struck him from the tone of her voice and the look on her bewildered face that she really was in love with him. Not just a fleeting fancy or gratefulness for having placed her in the palace of her fairytale dreams, nor a childish infatuation.. She was suddenly very much a woman and really loved him! He took her small featured face into his hands and turned it upwards. He found her, in spite of cheap cotton clothes and lacking any jewels, to be as alluring as a sapphire, and delicately soft as the moonlight.

They stared long into each other's eyes. Now all of a sudden she <u>wanted</u> him to know. "I wish for you only happy times, Narendra Singhji, but always rain falls from the skies and if you should ever need me please come to me. I shall dry you. I'll always await you."

Now there could not be the slightest doubt of her feelings the way she so carefully phrased her words, the undercurrent of anguish in her tone. The meaning was clear. "I shall come to you ... if ever the rains fall on my life, Nina. I know you will be there to comfort me, as I am told you often comfort our Queen."

"Always," she said, leaving his tent, the last time she would speak to him as an unmarried man. Well beyond her sleeping quarters she had noted an ancient lingam, a religious relic of the past. To it she walked, squatting in front and reciting silently, over and over, "Make him happy, but don't let him forget me. Oh please make him happy, but don't let him forget me." She returned to the campsite thinking, "... maybe ... one day ... who knows. God is great."

On the auspicious day of Narendra's wedding he was carefully prepared for the rite by his sister and an assortment of brothers, all bustling about, chatting, teasing, laughing. Gleeful sounds carried triumphantly throughout the camp. To Nina it was a day not as heavy hearted as she had anticipated. She had skillfully imparted her message to Narendra and she had already unctuously asked God to look after him.

New earthen pots were purchased early this morning from the vendors up near the fort. The scarce clay was pounded out with big wooden paddles, until they were so uniformly round they appeared to have been thrown on a potter's wheel. Left to dry in the fierce sun they became an inexpensive item for those who could ill afford brass. For this festive occasion family tradition demanded the use of earthen pots.

Narendra was seated on a low stool, his family rubbing his feet and legs with turmeric, his shirt splattered with the same dye. Bathing was yet another preparatory formality and slowly, oh so slowly, he was dressed, garment at a time. Intermittently, his sister and several aunts poured out the water from the new pots. Narendra was at a loss to know what it all meant. Customs had been handed down for centuries, performed from memory. Then came the churidars, his brand new white pants which fit so tightly on the calves, crinkling at the ankles. Over this hung a very long skirt, heavily pleated, the ankle crinkles visible. His blouse buttoned at the neck, with long sleeves. And over this his father lovingly placed a string of evenly matched pearls. Around his waist was a wide sash of brilliant orange silk woven with strands of solid gold thread.

Then he returned to the low stool. Arjun Singh stood over his first born winding a new orange turban, the small pugri of their area, edges tinged in more gold thread. Onto this crown of cloth they fitted a panache, a feathery ornament. And covering this they placed the wedding piece twined with white flowers smothering his face. Orange and gold slippers covered his huge agile feet, turning up at the toes into a semi-circle. He proudly held his tulwar sheathed in velvet and was led by hand outdoors to his waiting horse. It was not his beloved Chetak this time but instead a pure white stallion, as required for a groom.

Nimbupanni made of lime juice and water was passed to arriving guests at the Singh tent, the mood of happiness an added extract of heaven.

At a little distance futily waiting for this moment stood Nina. Narendra's little boy cousin was placed in front of him on a horse in accordance with Hindu tradition and the merrymakers started in full blast. Revelry continued effortlessly, dancing around the groom's horse in large circles, a phenomenon of happy spirits. Queen Mother sat majestically nearby. Hamir, however, observed his regal prerogative, jumping wildly as musicians stepped up their beat. Then from a signal by Arjun Singh they turned and made their way through the crowd until in the clear. Once more they struck up a rhythm, Narendra's horse led by a brother to a spot immediately behind the musicians. He was surrounded by his family and the best of his many, many friends, Ramesh, Pandu, Ranjit and all the others of his boyhood.

Strangely, the tempo had changed, now sounding more like a funeral dirge than a wedding procession. Several people ran around to the front barring the musicians' way, as declared by custom. Although the music continued, no one would move until those stopping the procession were handed coins by the groom's father or his aides. Every ten or twenty feet this went on and while the whole crowd lapped it up, Nina felt like screaming. Couldn't they get this damn wedding over with? She had to be near her queen in the event her services were needed; that meant she was too close to Narendra for comfort. Other servants were sitting nearby with her palanquin until such time as she would want to sit in it, making an historic and ceremonious entrance, eminently prepared to meet the bride's immediate family.

The party had reached the narrow streets of the town surrounding the main fort entrance necessitating the processioners to elongate their formation. The pompous parade became even slower for many of the city-folk had run from their homes to join the hundreds of others in ardent revelry. Such fantastic events were not an everyday occurrence.

Wide open was the decorated gateway to the fort and at the entrance stood a select group from the bride's family: father, uncles and assorted male relatives. First the two fathers embraced, exchanging garlands of marigolds, the auspicious flower of India.

The group reached the small palace of the bride's parents where the string of freshly cut neem leaves swayed gently, a sign of a religious ceremony. Lead through several rooms they reached a great hall, large enough for a sizeable durbar. At the far end stood a magnificently arrayed mandapam, the place at which the bride, groom and parents would solemnly sit for the wedding ceremony. To its right were two massive chairs for Their Highnesses, in front of which stretched a lengthy piece of red carpet.

Nina and a few select servants were given the peculiar privilege of standing near the door, across the room from the mandapam and when the crowd finally seated itself Nina had a rather broad view of the room. This semi-royal ceremony would be dramatic. Two young men came to stand before the child Rana and his mother, attended by youthful members of the bride's family. Gleaming silver trays were held before the men, each taking an ornamented bottle of chased silver from which they poured hauntingly exotic perfumes. The next trays held sweetmeats and shredded betel nuts.

Priests in snowy white clothes arranged and rearranged the customary coconuts and other symbols of marriage as in a dress rehearsal.

With the bride's chin scraping her chest, head covered in filmy scarf, she entered from the far end, red and gold wedding garments throwing glittering sparkles across the room, reflecting from flickering flames of pungent oil lamps. Nina's heart almost stopped beating. She strained for a look at the face so far down the way but it would be a long time before anyone could see it. She wondered if Narendra's heart beat as wildly as hers. Narendra's head remained bowed low before the priests and woman. No. Wait a minute. Now he was getting up, assisted by his attendants. Could he see her through all those flowers hanging over his face? And how wispy was her traditional scarf when close?

"Oh, dear God, let her be beautiful so he will be happy — but not too beautiful."

The wedding couple met for the first time, faces still gently veiled in cloth and flowers. Next came the first ceremonial act, the exchange of their beautiful garlands. Was this the very moment they became husband and wife? Nina could not be sure.

They bound the hands of the bridal couple together, his left hand placed into one of hers along with coins. A new cloth was wrapped around them to the accompaniment of prayers too silent to be heard across the room. Then Narendra stood again and held a part of her wedding garment as they walked around the sacred fire at the altar five times, invoking the blessings of the god. Once more they sat and in another fifteen minutes the bridal party stood ready to leave the mandapam, walking slowly through the lengthy room and passed Nina at the door.

Her eyes caught Narendra's. By now his facial flowers had been thrown back and he paused so briefly that no one else would have noticed, issuing to his "little one" a magnetic smile.

"Be happy for me," he whispered, brushing his face past her, pretending to trip. Nina dared not answer, the movement was so swift and unexpected.

The emotional strain was too much for Nina who raced downhill through the sloping cobbled streets of Jaiselmer fort, through the outer city and well past the area where she was to bed. Off at a safe distance from all other humans she crouched in sadness. The newly unveiled flawless face of the bride and her classic beauty had been made evident. There was a statuesque composure to her lissome body. She looked a flower swaying on a stem and exhibiting such comeliness, how could Narendra do anything but fall in love with her instantly

The regent had offered the bridal couple use of Laxmi Vilas Palace, the royal guest house in Udaipur, as a retreat after the wedding. Thus it was both the royal family and the Arjun Singh group journeyed back to Udaipur together, adding safety with its preponderant numbers.

Her magnanimous gesture was well taken for Laxmi Vilas was a structure only twenty four years old within a lovely bowered setting. To reach it one climbed the exposed terraced hillside. From it was a swelling view.

Nina meanwhile settled down to a lethargy of depression. Queen Mother quickly tired of her alien emptiness, allowing Nina a grace period in which to rid herself of her aching heart. It was still 1778 and the lives of everyone were to again change swiftly.

From the moment Narendra first looked into Kala's jet black eyes he was gripped by their magnetism, and an alluring quality. Each time she appeared before him she furthered his connubial happiness. Kala's spirits were light and girlishly gay, the transition accomplished easily from her sheltered childhood life to a married woman, living with a man she had never seen until exchanging garlands at the mandapam in Jaiselmer. Her parents had considered Narendra worthy of her and that was all the proof she required. They were older and wiser than she and it would never have occurred to Kala to question the reasoning and decision of her elders. Her dowry had been a huge one with lakhs of rupees and many material gifts.

This whole marriage package was a supreme benefit to Narendra.

Happy days solemnized the marriage and often they walked to new places holding hands when they thought no one watched. Kala had grown up with considerable luxury but her new life with Narendra surpassed anything which she had heretofore known. As all young girls are accustomed to doing, she had dreamed of her future prince charming and the joyful life he would take her into. Her dream surely had come true.

Narendra had learned much of the early days of Jaiselmer from the old man near the fort. Now it was time to tell his bride of the beginnings of the kingdom in which he lived, Mewar. Though Narendra was born of a high station, he had a peculiar fondness for the Bhils, the aboriginal tribespeople. These "children of the forest," as they had come to be known, were great hunters and descendants of the people who comprised a portion of Rajasthan long before history was recorded. They had all quietly moved about in their jungle with bows and arrows, dressed in loin cloths.

Far back in 524 A.D. the northern barbarians slew a prince and his clansmen. Only his queen who was absent from the slaughter was spared. Soon after she gave birth to a boy whom they called "cave-born." Not long after that she too died but her son was kept by a Bhil family, hidden from the public. The child proved to be a difficult person to handle and the foster parents felt it was because of his royal blood. History has recorded that he entered into wild sports with the Bhils and through an odd circumstance was chosen as their chief. A Bhil cut his finger and pressed its blood onto the forehead of the young lad, proclaiming him their chief. And so it came to be that in the identical manner a Bhil will mark the forehead of succeeding rulers of this Mewar dynasty.

These aborigines continued their simple life, choosing to govern themselves in preference to being ruled by a prince who would of course come from a different background. In the eighth century history repeated itself and the Bhils hunted and killed the prince, leaving his family to escape however they could manage. Then very strangely, by an exciting twist of fate, a child of the prince's family was saved by another friendly Bhil.

This time the three year old was taken to the home of a Brahman girl in the very sacred town of Nagindra in a spot six kilometers north of the present city of Udaipur. They simply called him "child" or "Bappa." The girl and her family kept Bappa well hidden and safe until 734 A.D. when he began to rule his little kingdom until his death eighteen years later. "Bappa the Brave" was the eighth ruler in this oldest dynasty in the world. And until 973 peace prevailed in the land. Now eight hundred years had passed.

    Finally it was time to return to Jagatpur and Narendra's mother. He and Kala were living in the laps of the gods.

Chapter 4

estiny masqueraded its doom to the regent for three and a half months, the doom of which she had often spoken so clearly to Nina. That whimsically vague feeling had never left and quite suddenly errant fantasy became oppressive reality. Hamir II was dead.

First the Rani had lost her husband and now her elder son. Little Bhim Singh would take the gaddi in his brother's place and once more would come the tortuous task of raising a son to be king of the mighty Kingdom of Mewar. He was so much younger, just little over nine years. "Oh God," she pleaded, "help me."

She sent immediately for all of the lords, the rawals and jagirs, though most could not reach the noble city until long after the funeral pyre had lost its glow. But as always there were those lords within the feudal system who lived temporarily at the palace, in homage and service to their master and mistress, the little Rana and his mother. Once more Queen Mother, as regent, faced an awesome task.

Grandiose plans were immediately made for the funeral procession from the palace to the Maha-Sati, site of the cenotaphs of most of the rulers since quitting the fort of Chittor a hundred fifty years earlier. Other than Udaipur's founder who died in the Aravalli Hills, successive Ranas had been brought here. The exact sacred spot within the Maha-Sati would have to be chosen for the cremation and all must be made in astonishingly rapid readiness.

Queen Mother had been the wife of a Maharana, then the mother of a very young king, and now god had willed that she would again act as regent until little Bhim Singh came of age.

"If you had made mistakes with the upbringing of Hamir they can be rectified in this second chance you are given," Nina desperately tried to reassure her queen who kept blaming herself for having a son who left nothing to Mewar's history. "I am sure you did everything just right, Your Highness," Nina added hastily.

There was so much to think about, the awesome task requiring unweeping solitude. It grew late but sleep would not come to the Queen Mother nor could she abandon her irremediable grief with contrite tears. Had she been to Hamir a prudent and circumspect mother? Need she ameliorate failure? She thought of all the glorious stories she knew of the fabulous first Hamir, so much more daring than her first-born child, Hamir II. She tried the ministration of clumsily consoling herself that her offspring had not been able to sit on the throne for forty years as did Hamir I. How then could he, still a teenager, accomplish anything for the annals of history? Yet deep in her heart she realized her son had not the spirit of which the truest heroes are made.

The Rani once had an elderly grandmother who would sit telling over and over the tales of the girl she had come to admire immensely, tales carried by word of mouth through the years and written into Mewar's history books. This girl was a charming and consummately clever person. She had a father who was governor of a fair sized area and resided in the Chittor fort. He wished to marry his daughter to the Rana who had a deep desire to regain his lost fort. Though the governor thought his wish manifestly impossible, nonetheless he determined to try to make this match. An entourage was sent to Hamir I offering him the daughter of the imperial governor as a wife. Hamir had just beaten back the Mughal ruler who had ravaged the lowlands once his. He vowed he would continue his campaign to one day retake Chittorgarh. Now all of a sudden an offer to marry the daughter of the man who governed there? Was this a plot to trick him?

It is said the Mewar rawals and thakurs, not trusting the barbarians, had pleaded with Hamir to refuse the offer, but the Rana's adventurous spirit prevailed. He would be on the lookout for any trickery. If it appeared none existed he felt having such a wife would help in his future endeavors to regain his precious Chittor. This offered a superb chance to revisit the fort. No better opportunity would arise. He soon rode to the fort to claim his bride.

While the young girl had nothing to do with the marriage arrangement she was not particularly fond of her father, and being of sound mind she reasoned why her parent would plan such a wedding. What an outrage against the Rana Hamir when he would come to know the truth. It left the poor girl in an awkward position and she, determined to avenge this act, prepared to discuss it thoroughly with her husband when the right time would come.

On the morning of the wedding the bridegroom must have been as anxious as any man. A painter of ideas, illimitable heavens were spreading before him, the fort his canvas. He approached it feverishly, unable to conceal his anxious happiness. But it was not until he reached the entrance to the palace that he had to know something was desperately wrong. It was then it hit him there was no wedding emblem he was to break at the door. There was no revelry; no music; no people; no indication of any jubilation or festivity.

Inside the bride regretted all that was happening to the Rana. If he were to turn and run the bride's father would nefariously capture him. But the girl knew the Rana's reputation of fearing nothing. The bride's father finally arrived with a welcoming smirk which Hamir I graciously chose to ignore.

In time the wedding couple came face to face, hers heavily covered in traditional fashion. The harshness of the quiet was offensive and there was no proper paraphernalia to perform the sacred rites. The whole ceremony, or lack of it, which followed was unthinkable...yet it was being done. As soon as it was over she asked her new husband to her private rooms, looking at the man with deep pity through heavy veils. A corner of the Rana's dress had been tied to the bride's long veil, consecrating the marriage.

"Why is there no feast, woman?" Hamir asked. She could not speak. "Why was there no proper wedding ceremony?" He raised the veil covering her face finding her astonishingly pretty, anything but what he expected. His voice softened. "Speak up. I shall not beat you. Of what are you afraid?"

In sympathetic communion she uttered the words "You have been tricked and shamed. Your bride is a widow." Devouring such horrendous words took an agonizingly long while, an unmitigable disgrace for a Rajput to be married to a widow. He slowly untied the knot that bound them together, morally and physically, pondering his next move. But it was his wife who took over the conversation.

She explained prefatorily that she had been married as the tiniest of little girls, living in the home of her mother and father. Never had she seen her bridegroom and while he himself was still rather young he was slain in battle. "My lord," she continued, "I have thought long and continuously about what it is we should do to avenge this act, ever since learning I was to be your bride. My father was unpardonably wrong and since I am not to blame for the major events of my life I have worked out a plan of action to vindicate me. Let me explain." She felt certain the Rana would embark upon her clever scheme.

"I am sure you would like to win back this very fort which is rightly yours, and in my heart I feel my idea can work, given the necessary time." She felt the gods would allow her the privilege of bearing a child and when it should become a year old she would want to return to the shrine in Chittor to show it to her gods. Certainly doing such a thing would not arouse the suspicions of her father or anyone else. She would pretend to be traveling alone but the Rana would follow close behind with some of his men so that he too could visit the temple with his child.

The woman's scheme did work out, the Rana Hamir I grateful that his wife possessed both wisdom and courage. When the day came, the girl's devious father was actually out of the fort, her brother in charge. The Rana's long wait of two years was about to end. When the old man returned to Chittor he was aghast to find Hamir's flag flying over the fort, the Rana's men now once more occupying it. He had in the short span of that marriage amassed a vast army. A mere "widow" had played a supreme part in Mewar's overall picture.

Now Hamir II was dead and his mother in these long sleepless hours of tossing and half-wake conjured up that large building in Chittorgarh, the fort which Hamir I had regained and which she visited often. She loved the palaces of Udaipur, so delicately lovely, none of them laid in ruin and those in the fort, yet she longed to nestle deeply into the ghosts and shadows of a reverent past. She would have preferred her home there, though now all lay in idleness. In that huge building within the fortress she often climbed a steep stairway of rounded stone, thick, tan, strong, into the former treasury where all the jewels of the kings and queens had been stored during the centuries they ruled there. Great wealth was enjoyed by the sovereigns who loved showering their women with precious gems set into dangling earrings, wide bangles, superb necklaces of immense emeralds from India and Ceylon, rubies from Burma, pearls and diamonds from near Agra.

When the Mughal Emperor Allaudin came from Delhi and took the fort all this was stolen. That which he did not want was destroyed including sumptuous buildings, so furious was he. In all this confusion there was one lost object, an heirloom which Hamir I sought for long and hard — the two-edged sword of Viswakarma with which Bappa Rawal way back in the 8th century had been ceremoniously made ruler.

Hamir could not dismiss the lingering thought that Bappa's mother had been so cautious to keep him alive to continue his bloodline, surely somehow she would have arranged for the safe keeping of this royal sword, so implicitly and historically important to Mewar. Yet its whereabouts were not known these last 600 years. Of such tremendous pride and significance to Bappa and to future generations, Hamir I determined not to die until it was found. It became a cramping obsession.

Palace archives held many accounts of what followed, the Rani having read them all countless times. It is said his search was tedious and long throughout the countryside, following any lead and any wild story ever told. Generations would have embellished tales and his task was near impossible; still he would not give up. For withering months he searched. Everything to him became a possible hiding place: ruins of old buildings in and out of the fort; old villages or what remained of them; dilapidated temples, shrines and lingams, of which there are many hundreds in Mewar. The torturing obsession continued to pour down on him like the worst of the heavy monsoons.

Born on the wind a suggestion came to him that he look deep into the bowels of one of the oldest buildings in the fort. Jubilantly he emerged with the sword holding it high for everyone to view. It is still raised high in the hearts of the Mewaris, worshipped yearly by the faithful. Hamir I would have braved all odds to retrieve it. Hamir II had accomplished nothing of value.

Queen Mother had sent for the sword from its special place, holding it in her trembling hands for inspiration. Perhaps from it and the spirit which had been Hamir I she could be inspired on toward greatness.

Perhaps little nine year old Bhim Singh would bring greater joy to his mother than Hamir II. This was her overriding desire. The funeral procession and cremation had taken place on schedule with Bhim Singh dutifully filling the role of the little king-about-to-be. Some of the theatrical glamor was already beginning to fade from the lives of the Mewar royal family. No longer did they distribute coins to the people of the city through the open window on the day of coronation as they had for many generations. The Queen Mother sat upon the royal marble seat up the dozen marble steps near the large vat hollowed out from a single slab. Into this vat had been placed a hundred thousand rupees, ever since the time of Maharana Udai Singh and through the time of Jagat. But now this ceremony of Lakhu gokra was no more. The marble window was destined to be filled in with stone, another illustrious page of Mewar history closed forever.

The complexity of teaching a little king the administrative history and dazzling life of his land was not new to Queen Mother, yet Bhim seemed such a babe compared to his older brother. The task would be more arduous. He had been too young to sit in on Hamir's lessons and the thought had never occurred to Queen Mother that he might one day live to rule. The Rani could not know that this second son would be Maharana for fifty years.

To the palace among all the other nobles came Arjun Singh, his son Narendra and new daughter-in-law Kala who was insistent on paying personal respects to Queen Mother after her generosity with the honeymoon offer of Laxmi Vilas. Perhaps there was a way she could help ease the pain of the boy's death. The group had left Jagatpur instantly on learning the sad unexpected news.

"I beg to attend you if I can be of service," she addressed Queen Mother when given the opportunity of a private though extremely short audience. The regent was reservedly kind although deeply engrossed in more pressing matters. Kala had no status in the zenana and with absolutely nothing to do all day she quickly wearied of this life. At least in Jagatpur she had people with whom she could talk. None of the other nobles had brought their women. It was not their place. Kala begged Narendra to let her return to their home.

But it was during this same time that Nina got to know her just a little bit. On the regent's request Nina had taken Kala to see some of the gorgeous palace, stopping first at spectacular Dil Kushal, a room with an exquisitely shaped mirror dome. The floor was also solid clear mirror with walls of mirrors set into geometric patterns of brilliant reds, greens and blues, a room now a hundred years old. Nina had often slipped through many narrow staircases to this her favorite room only to stand at its entrance staring at its sophisticated glamour. Today she was compelled to share its romance. What discordant irony. Here stood Kala, silently envisioning a night of rapturously wild passions, reflected and magnified a thousand times through surrounding mirrors.

Nina was enveloped in the same voluptuous raptures but only one of the women could have Narendra truly within her beguiling grasp. Into these same mirrors Nina stared at the sobering reflection of the woman she expected to envy and hate. Envy, yes. Hate, no. There was too gentle and genuine an air of conjugal devotion encircling the bride. "Nina, you are the girl who worked for my mother-in-law?" Kala asked.

Nina replied briefly and ushered Kala through the next room lined with miniature paintings of Mewar's most famous wars and heroes. From them Nina had learned of elephant fights, battles, tiger hunts and durbars, She learned from them of the jewels and clothing worn in days long gone, exactly the same as worn now. And oh how she longed to know much more. The more she could pick up from the pictures the more she realized she knew nothing at all. Oh, if only she could study with little Maharana Bhim Singh.

The door at the far end opened into a high airy courtyard, walls paved with blue and white tiles from Canton, China. Through the arches on the eastern side of the courtyard one could see the old city of Udaipur, and to the west placid Lake Pichola. They enjoyed the high-swung breezes before touring more of the spectacular rooms, Nina always standing respectfully a few steps behind the woman she envied. Pointing Kala down a narrow flight of steps she directed her to Narendra's rooms. Quieter than a whisper she turned, speeding to her tiny room before her absence was noticed. Nina's world confused her unless she could lay undisturbed, remote from the hollowness of reality.

Days of Nina's careless dreaming came to an abrupt end after the Jagatpur party left for home. With the end of the important one-month death anniversary of the late Maharana and the rigors of a coronation, the Queen Mother lunged into the serious business of having her next son pedagogically taught the important facts of Mewar life, starting with the basics.

Nina was again presumptuous enough to ask if she too could join the valuable lessons. The wrath of the kingdom flew upon her young head this time, Queen Mother threatening to banish her forever from the kingdom. Pondering the girls viewpoint, she came to a prudent settlement. Being worlds apart in life's stations the servant could not sit in the same room with the boy, but there could be a compromise. Nina could sit outside the door, picking up any remnants of discussions. So far Nina had made everything work for her. She remained in good standing with the queen, she had a fantastic place to live and super food, she and little Bhim were comfortable in each other's company, and now she could be taught some history and other things. She had almost everything.

One vapory morning found little Bhim Singh frolicking in the stoney courtyard of the zenana. He frequently enjoyed coming to this spot, not yet weaned from the presence of his mother. Nina sat stitching beneath a neem tree, watching the child playing jacks. Small stones were jacks and for the bouncing ball he had discovered a somewhat rounded pebble which he would bounce with force and remarkable skill.

"That game is for girls, Your Highness," taunted Nina. She had recently dared to speak to him. They were fast striking a semblance of friendship, extremely odd under the circumstances of divergent breeding, sex and age.

"Just remember Nina," the little Rana answered unhesitatingly, "I am His Highness, and if I wish to play jacks it is jacks I shall play. And for that you shall sit here and play with me," be ordered, ever anxious to exert his authority.

Later that day a pandit came to teach many things.

"Oh my mother, it's all so boring," he spoke.

"Boring indeed. This only goes to show you know nothing of our history. Many things you may call it: valorous, chivalrous days of the past; bloody and full of fighting, intrigue and sadness. But boring? No. Never boring. There indeed is much you must learn and the sooner we get to this business the better it shall be."

Bhim Singh started out of the room quickly to be called back. "I did not dismiss you Bhim Singh," she scolded shrewishly.

"Mataji, it is I who am Maharana and I who dismiss."

"Not me you don't, my boy," she answered sternly. "You may rightly have achieved the gaddi but I am the regent. You have much to learn before you really become Maharana. Are you fit to rule? What do you know of life? What do you know of history? What do you know of organizing armies? Of keeping your men in line? Of handling the nobles, the thakurs, the sardars? What will you do about all the taxes? What do you do next about the Mahrattas? And the Pathans? My son, you know nothing. You may be excused to go sit in your rooms and contemplate what a precarious and ennobling time you have ahead of you."

Bhim Singh left the zenana without another word. His mother remained in one of her rooms deeply yearning for her son to become illustrious, to be looked upon with envy. Twelve hundred years of brave, bizarre and daring deeds and preposterous mythology preceded them. Which of his ancestors would he emulate? Would her life-ruling ambitions ever become fruitful? And for whom did she honestly want this? Her son, their kingdom, or herself?

Somehow she and Bhim would bring back the glory. This was her last chance and she dared not stumble.

At last the tutor, Hari Lal arrived. He learned of the regent's acquiescence and was pleased to have Nina as an additional pupil. Anyone anxious to learn was due his respect and effort, regardless of rank. He had become learned through tenacious endeavor; so could Nina.

"I am ready master," Bhim Singh spoke a bit impatiently to the guru, in a manner older than his years. Hari Lal began his first lesson.

"Thank you Your Highness," bowing his head down as close to the floor as his aging body allowed. "Many centuries ago," the teacher started a little nervously, not caring to have the Queen Mother in his presence, a matter over which he held no sway. "Many centuries ago when the first Muslims invaded upper India they found mighty cities. Time and time again the Rajputs have beaten them back. Wherever we lived, in the Aravallis, in the desert or in the plains, we would like to have lived in peace. But of course there were always wars, not only with the Mughals but also with Marwar and other Hindu kingdoms. We will cover all that in time, but what I want to tell now is that it was the Muslim invaders we hated the most. The Princes of all royal Hindu races had to fight valiantly to keep the Mughals or Muslims out but of course it did not always turn out too good." He tried to speak in simple terms.

"Am I the ruler of the greatest of the races?" Bhim asked excitedly, wanting confirmation of something he had always been told of their family.

"We like to think so, Your Highness. You we held above all the other Rajput Princes because as you know, I'm sure, from Rama the tribes are termed the Suryavansa, the Race of the Sun. It was Rama's oldest son Lava from which you are descended. So it is that you rightfully claim your seat on the chair of Rama."

"How big is my kingdom?"

"Mewar contains 10,000 towns and villages. The largest of our districts of Mewar is that of Mandalgarh. In it are 360 villages and in it many lovely ancient structures may be found."

"I wish to see them. Why must I sit here and listen to lectures when I could go out and see these things for myself," Bhim Singh grew more restless and excited.

With assimilable wisdom of the ages and a soft hushed voice the guru continued. "All in due time, Highness; all in due time. There is yet much to be learned here. Why in this palace alone one can spend a lifetime studying, for in it are stored countless relics of the glorious past. And you must learn to deal with all of your subjects."

"I can handle them," the child answered defiantly. First it was his mother and now Hari Lal. "They must obey whatever I say for I am Maharana, their king."

"Can you handle them indeed, Highness? Well, in that case let us suppose someone comes to you for help. How would you handle this case," he asked, calling his bluff. "If a Brahman accidentally kills one of your aides, what is it you will do?"

"That is easy. I should fine him."

"Quite right, Highness. But how much would you fine him?"

"Well, uh... I guess I don't know," but he hurriedly went on to add, "but I have my mother and my nobles at my side and if

I did not know what fine, they would," then in not quite so sure a tone, "wouldn't they?"

"Perhaps they would, but Highness, who is to run this country when you are older? You or your mother or the nobles?"

"Teaghi. How much would be the fine?" he asked dejectedly.

"Mund-kati or compensation for the Brahman is four times the value of a soldier, eight times that of the merchant and sixteen times that of the Sudra. Now do you understand?" Gently Hari Lal tried to show him the complexities of his life.

"Yes. No. You still didn't tell me how much he would have to pay."

Sitting outside the door, Nina could not believe Hari Lal's words. What superior injustice. Though she was born into this caste system, accepting it as the normal way of life, for the first time she could not accept its snobbery, at any level. She heard Hari Lal's reply.

"Patience, my dear Bhim Singh. Patient waiting to attain great knowledge may be the highest way of doing God's will." He meant this to apply to Nina too.

Queen Mother felt she would be satisfied with Hari Lal and his exemplary lessons. Finally her youngest would have a calculable chance to stand preeminently against the confounding odds. She sat remarkably quiet listening to the smooth flowing balance of the first days salutary session, touching lightly on many subjects.

As the tutor was about to ask his leave Bhim Singh interrupted. "What is the story about Bappa Rawal and our temple at Eklingji?" The boy remembered elusive words he had heard spoken in years past, unmindful of their prophetic meaning.

"Ah, yes. I shall conclude today's class with this story. It is perhaps the tale I like the best to tell because it gets down to our very roots." Hari Lal settled himself more comfortably on the cool floor at the feet of his young master. The Rana's father Ari

Singh and Hari Lal had long been friends and whenever the pandit wished to learn more of this fantastic dynasty the Rana allowed him full use of palace archives. It was thus he read the many papers, books, documents by countless authors and considered himself something of an authority on the thousand years prior to his birth. The long-lost resonance of his voice cracked through the hushed atmosphere and he started:

"In the early eighth century there was a fine town in our Mewar kingdom called Nagda. It was scenically beautiful, surrounded with mountains, lakes and a very thick forest. Now in this town lived a well-to-do Brahman. There was abundant agriculture and many cattle and he had lots of servants who carefully managed his affairs. Among these helpers was a little lad like yourself, of ten years, who was entrusted with the job of taking the cowherd to forest in the morning for grazing and bringing them home in the evening. After the cows returned home they would be milked and the milk given to the Brahman, the owner of the cows.

"The boy did his job well for a long period of time, feeding the cows in the fields and taking them to the nearby lake for water, then back home in the evening. This routine went on for many months. The master was pleased with the boy's work until it so happened that one particular cow at milking time would have none to give. The master was very much angry and scolded the boy, thinking that he must be stealing it. He started to hit him soundly every day.

"The boy knowing the milk problem was through no fault of his was annoyed and pondered often on why this thing should happen. He could not understand the mystery of the milk any more than could his master. The boy started keeping a better vigilance over this particular cow.

"One day it happened at midnoon exactly — at 12 hours — this cow left the herd and started running towards the thick forest. This boy sharply chased the cow and was stunned to see that it suddenly came to a halt at a certain spot in that thick wood. It stood erect, stretching her hind legs wide apart and let her milk flow on that spot. She moved from the place only when her supply of milk was exhausted. The little boy staring at that sight could now obviously know the reason as to why this cow was not giving her milk at home. But he started trying to imagine why she should do this. He had never seen such a thing in his life. Who would believe him?

"When he was returning home one certain day, grossly engaged in the mystery, he noticed a Tapwasi seated in meditation with closed eyes. The boy stood there folding his hands. When the saint opened his eyes and saw the little boy watching him, he asked what he wanted. The boy narrated to the Yogi the whole story and requested his help.

"The saint told him he was doing meditation on this place 100 years and now his work was nearly finished. He would soon leave for heaven and he ordered the boy to come to him daily and help him in the collection of flowers for his puja. The lad readily agreed. Pleased with the boy's services, he told him that on a particular day in that week he would be leaving for heaven at twelve noon and requested the lad to be present at that time. He said he would reveal the mystery of the cow dropping the milk at that special spot and also wanted to give the boy his blessings because he had been so pleased with the child.

"The day came and the Yogi began his journey upwards but the boy was not to be seen. The Yogi went higher and higher in the sky and from there observed the lad coming running towards him. With his super power he made himself stand still in the sky and asked the boy why he came so late. The child told the Tapwasi he regretted it but that it was not his fault. However the saint told him 'regardless I am pleased with what you have done for me in the past and I want to give you prasad and blessings. Before I do that I would like to tell you why the cow is dropping her milk at that spot.'

"The youngster listened spellbound to the Yogi who continued, 'This is a place where God Shiva lives on the earth. At this particular spot if you dig you will find big Shiva Murti and the cow being a big disciple of Shiva goes there and bathes God Shiva with her milk.'

"The lad was speechlessly amazed. And then the Yogi said, 'Boy, open your mouth'. He did so and the Yogi spit. Taken aback by what the boy thought a dirty thing he shut his mouth but the spit had fallen on the toe of his right foot.

"The Yogi shouted, 'You fool. What you have done? Had you gulped this Amrut which you thought as dirty spit, you would have been the Emperor whom nobody could best. However, now that it has fallen on the toe of your right foot, all this territory in and around you will be under your thumb. You will be a brave king.'

"The Yogi disappeared and his blessings came true. This little boy came to be known as a hero and with his strength and might, became the Maharana of Mewar. As you have probably guessed by now, Your Highness, he was your predecessor known as Bappa Rawal, founder of the dynasty which has lasted all these many centuries."

"And the temple?'" the young Rana asked.

"After a big victory he unearthed the Shiva Shrine and built over it a big temple which you now visit for your darshan at your weekly worship service. As you perhaps are aware, Highness, each family has its own worshipping deity. You, as the ruler of this State of Mewar, worship faithfully and weekly at Shri Eklingji. Actually I should say, Your Highness, that the deity, the beautiful four-faced image of lord Shiva carved of black marble is really the ruler of Mewar and you, with all due respect, are merely the Prime Minister."

Inspired, Bhim Singh firmly ordered "Take me tonight. I'll attend arti at seven, and you are to definitely come with me.

"Respectfully Highness, I would suggest you make it another time. Even tomorrow would be better. You are but a child and have had a grueling day and the way is long," the tutor stated forcefully.

Queen Mother was abundantly pleased with her son's enthusiasm. If this guru could retain it within him for the next several years she would be more than satisfied. Hari Lal was released until time for darshan the next evening. Bhim Singh could prepare his mind for the most sobering ceremony of his life as ruler, a reverence of Eklingji.

Morning brought an unwanted idleness to the little Rana and he roamed the massive palace looking for something different to occupy his time. When he reached the room of the sun window he thought to himself, "why not?" Glancing around to make sure he was not followed too closely he rushed to the little platform a bare half meter above the floor, stepping onto it cautiously and seating himself cross-legged before the round window of wood. Inside it was covered with gold leaf and the little hinges which held it shut squeaked as he slowly pushed it open. Looking him squarely in the eye now was a circular golden sun with the painted eye and moustache of a man, an image of the Maharana himself, for was he not the descendant of the sun? He peered outside ready to smile upon anyone who might be looking up at him, the sun, but there was no one. Sadly he closed the window; it seemed to his little mind that there was no one who paid any heed to him and his rank in life, ostensibly so high. There was no one who came rushing to him in dutiful reverence. No one who stood bowing before him at every room he entered, touching his royal feet, garlanding him with small marigolds or the pretty rose leis which he loved to smell. Not even the children with whom he played seemed to hold him in awe. They were, in truth, accustomed to his being only the younger brother of the Rana. Now that he himself held the title he did not seem any different to his friends. This lack of respect was disquieting. He'd have to somehow change that.

Much later in the afternoon when Hari Lal arrived Bhim Singh went running to him. "Today you will sit with me in the temple and explain everything to me. That is an order."

"I have definitely come to accompany you, Your Highness, but as for sitting with you, even your mother is not allowed at the seat of the ruler of Mewar. It is for you alone. It is the most sacred and revered spot on which you shall ever sit ... anywhere. Nor can I sit behind you; that place is reserved only for the family," said Hari Lal emphatically and soberly.

"Tonight I issue a command that you attend with me; you are to sit behind me and answer my questions. How else can I know what is going on and what to do?"

"It is the revered priest who will best answer your questions, for he and he alone knows well the Vedas by which the service is conducted. You would do well to pay close attention to him. You may not realize sire, but to our knowledge Eklingji is the only temple remaining in these lands of India where the worship is done according to the sacred book. Our priests are well versed on the Vedas. Our other Hindu temples are fine too, but it is better to hear the sacred Vedas from the mouth of one who knows them so well. If you learn the Vedas you could one day conduct your own service, since your rank supersedes that of the priests. But you must study very hard, Highness, for every offering of a flower, everything that is done within the confines of the temple is done with proper chanting, proper respect and the saying of proper words."

"Some day all the Vedas I will learn," Bhim Singh said as if to reassure himself. Then he added sheepishly and in a bare whisper, "What does Veda mean?"

Hari Lal suppressed a smile, "There are four Vedas, Highness. The oldest is the Rigveda which was composed somewhere in the period between B.C. 1200 and 900. To some the learning of the Vedas is a tedious task, but it is something most interesting. These were the first spoken words of the Aryan man. The Vedas, Your Highness, are not only a history of your land but a history of the world."

The instructor continued: "Our priests observe celibacy. They must remain bachelors. They observe all four darshans each day at Shri Eklingji and live right there on the premises. They are some of the most highly educated men in the field of worship."

An hour later mother, son and teacher left for darshan with an assortment of guards on horseback. As fitting and proper the child had a servant wrap a new unworn pugri around his head, white aachkan and white churidar trousers. He appeared a midget in fine appropriate clothes.

Twenty one kilometers into desert and up winding softly rising hills they rode, past the Sas Bahu temples, Queen Mother's personal favorite. Though the party did not pause, the regent's mind took her from the main road across a narrow river, through open land, until she would come to stand in her mind's eye before the two small architectural beauties. Sas and Bahu were built by jealous queen and daughter-in-law, each having her own temple, canceling the need of sharing.

The ride had been hot and dusty, past sparsely dotted huts, the small ancestral parcels of farmland edged in cactus fences strewn across hillsides. Cactus holds back precious topsoil during forceful monsoons.

Inside Eklingji's grounds Bhim Singh stood beseechingly at the image of the Yogi floating into eternity and below it the image of Bappa Rawal,the founder of Bhim Singh's dynasty. Of course he had seen it many times before. He had to pass it to enter the sanctuary. But after Hari Lal's graphic portrayal yesterday it indelibly imprinted its mythical meaning and he was at once justly proud to be the successor of a dynamic country. His head and chest swelled. He descended from Bappa Rawal. There would be no other on earth to compare, thought Bhim. Little did he realize that history would, in fact, find him lackluster in comparison to dozens of his predecessors.

Many men and women were attending the evening darshan, chanting repetitiously. They moved quickly aside when His Highness arrived, passing the crowd with a swagger, dignity and air befitting his high station. It would seem to the pandit that this was surely an inbred trait and though Bhim Singh was lacking in demeanor in other respects, when it came to parading before his subjects, his bearing was quite satisfactory.

In his proper place, close to the sparkling silver wall and altar reserved for the royal family, he watched the balance of the darshan which lasted a full hour. Two priests tolled the pair of huge brass bells to the right of him, on the outer side of the temple. Ringing for the entire recitation of the Vedas they make certain that their god is ever mindful of the observance of worship. Frantically their ears pained and arms ached from constant and lengthy tolling.

Young Bhim Singh sat dutifully motionless. At this darshan he could watch the image of Lord Shiva being fed his nightly meal, food placed on all four sides of the deity after a suitable table setting was made. Prayers and Vedas were eloquently recited. When completed, a curtain was drawn around the image shielding him from public view. The lord was then prepared for his night's sleep.

Through none of this did the Rana move. Then having lifted up his heart to his lord he quickly rose and departed for the palace after stopping briefly at the temple of Mira Bai where his mother had strolled. Queen Mother could never forget this outstanding songstress.

The evening had been tremendously heavy for the child. He honestly paid strict attention for the first time in his life. These last two days would firmly imprint the spectral past in the Rana's young developing mind.

Chapter 5

Time did little to heal death's stiffening wounds for the queen. Hari Lal, a scholarly and devout Hindu interested in other religions, brought to his queen a translation of one of Lord Buddha's teachings, originally quoted in the language called Pali, the spoken language derived from Sanskrit. The reading was neatly etched in black India ink on a delicate parchment. His suggestion upon handing it to the regent was to read it herself each day, Buddha having pronounced this a way to reflect on the death of a dear one, admonishing that we not agonize over a death.

It forcefully brought to her mind the religious songs of her husband's ancestor, Mira Bai. Offtimes the Rani would kneel at Mira Bai's temples, either within Eklingji's grounds or near Kumbha's palace in the old fort at Chittor.

Mira Bai had been the granddaughter of Rao Jodha, founder of Jodhpur. History and old cultures are so thoroughly mixed it is difficult to separate one from the other, but it is said that one day a wedding party was passing the palace where lived Mira Bai and her mother. Mira Bai became excited and asked her mother where her bridegroom was. It seems the mother was at this moment worshiping their family deity, Krishna. She pointed to the idol and said, "Here is your bridegroom." And so it is believed the girl took her mother literally, the reason for her lifelong religious devotion to Lord Krishna.

Mira Bai was married in 1516 to a son of Mewar's Rana Sanga. It was presumed he would follow his father as ruler of Mewar. Unfortunately he left Mira Bai a widow who was forced to live a difficult life under her brother-in-law's rule after he, Vikramaditya, had taken the gaddi. Though she could not have been a threat to the Rana, Vikramaditya nonetheless tried various ways of killing her. He once sent a box with a poisonous snake and another time she actually was poisoned but her life was spared. A devotee of Lord Krishna, she moved about with mendicants, finally making a pilgrimage to Brindavan where Krishna spent much of his time many centuries ago.

Throughout her songs she speaks of her search for god and asks why he had forsaken her. At that same time Emperor Akbar was besieging Chittor fort and the whole kingdom was in grave danger. There were those who blamed the troubles onto Mira Bai who had left the palace, saying it had incurred the wrath of the gods. So it was that paradoxically the Rana wanted Mira Bai back and sent many people to try to retrieve her.

When Mira Bai finally was found she refused to obey Vikramaditya's command and literally disappeared into the temple. Vikramaditya vented his volcanic wrath upon his men for the inability to bring back one impertinent female. Queen Mother spent much time in recent days searching desperately for an inner healing from a higher realm. She expected the same omnipotent powers as did Mira Bai. The Rani felt there was no other female on earth who so divinely found a spiritual way to attain salvation. She must pray to live a minimum of another fifteen years, manipulating and conniving. It was a never-ending struggle.

She reflected further on the time Mira Bai mysteriously disappeared from the sight of everyone forever, singing her last songs:

> Take me, if you thinkest me to be pure,
> excepting thee I know none else,
> Oh, lord have mercy on me![1]

The regent added her own prayer, "Oh Lord have mercy on me and Bhim Singh. Visit upon us no further trouble, that I

---

[1] From: *Mirabai, Saint and Singer of India* by Anath Nath Basu, George Allen & Unwin, Ltd., Museum St., London

might raise him well, that he may serve thee and our kingdom with equal force and vigor and with clear vision."

Perhaps the Rani could find some scant solace in these fervent prayers and hymns, but Hari Lal asked for a private audience. With the seemingly good progress he was making with his young charge and the favor he found in his regent he could be forthright and speak openly.

"Your Highness, I humbly beseech you to get away for a while. Can you not visit one of your sisters? Do you not have one in Bundi and Baroda? It would do you good to draw yourself away from court. As for your son, our little Rana, I can assure you he will be kept within the confines of the palace until your return. Your physician agrees with this plan."

"Well, you seem to have things arranged, haven't you?" Her depressed mood turned quickly affable. "Yes. It would be good to see my sister. Yes, I shall think on it a while longer."

When next the Queen Mother saw Nina she told of her plans to visit abroad offering her a leave also, to visit Jagatpur or any place of her choice until Her Highness might be expected back at Udaipur, which would probably be some months. Nina herself had long been at the palace and well past due for a leave.

It took several weeks before the Rani was confident that all would be in order at her capitol so that she might depart. Arjun Singh had arrived for a tour of duty at the palace.

After the Rani's departure Nina strolled the grounds beyond the zenana courtyard, away from whispering servants where the breeze could overtake her, unhampered. Arjun Singh had the same idea and they greeted each other in traditional "namasté," genuinely happy to see each other.

"All is well in Jagatpur?" she asked.

"Everyone is fine. And you?"

"I am keeping well, And is there anything that is new which I should hear?" She looked for a way of learning whether Kala was yet with child.

Arjun Singh was something of a reader of minds, and Nina's eyes had always betrayed her feelings before the elder Singh. "There is nothing new, Nina; no sickness, praises to God. Nothing."

"Kala is well?" she inquired.

"Kala is quite well. No babies yet on the way." That should satisfy her curiosity, he thought; and it did.

"Any problems with dacoits?"

"Nina, there has been gossip of a band on the outskirts of my area and Narendra has been talking with the jagadir about help in the capture of the gang. He's been scurrying around to learn their exact whereabouts. Just about the time they seem to be getting somewhere the group disappears well beyond Rajputana. Narendra fears they will one day soon return."

As long as one dacoit lived her numbing fears would never be allayed. She preferred keeping Narendra in half-awake dreams. She would slither one leg up and down the other, tickling him with her toes, breathing deeply as she imagined him almost crushing the breath from her body, adding lyric notes of ecstasy. In these moments of rampant fervor Nina would drop off to an enchanted sleep. There were times when morning brought something close to sadness for she would have enjoyed the fantasy even more had it lasted longer.

But there were the other nights when fearful depths of terror became immeasurable. Although a Hindu, she feared sati and its roaring flames, yet willing to die alongside Narendra if fighting dacoits. And when she thought of <u>johar</u> and the thousands who died together she cringed. Would she have cowered in a corner of the fort of Chittor, unfaithful to the other ladies and to the kingdom? This act of johar she determined to soon learn more about. Hari Lal had not yet covered it in little Bhim Singh's incessant lessons.

Yes, death was something she wished put off for a long period of time. But on her sleepless nights blatantly contradictory feelings took hold. Considering herself responsible for Narendra's dedicatory decision to fight dacoits, it followed that she desired to be with him in major encounters, even to the death — especially to the death.

"I must remain at the palace until Queen Mother returns to the city, Nina," Arjun spoke. "If you wish you may borrow one of my horses and ride to Jagatpur."

"Queen Mother has already offered me leave so long as I'm back by the time she returns to Udaipur." Even the Rani was not sure exactly when that would be. Driven forward by the thought of Narendra and the dacoits she suddenly longed to sit and hear of his efforts firsthand. Since his marriage except for those occasional moments of happy fantasy, there was for Nina no light or dark. There was no smell. No sound. For her everything was nothingness. She did not trust her emotions on seeing him again but the offer of Arjun Singh's horse and her total boredom with the Rani's absence inspired her to leave.

"I accept, sire," she bowed low in acknowledgement. "I am excited to see your wife again and perhaps I can be of some little service. I'd appreciate a servant coming along if that's possible. It would be difficult for a woman to camp out alone."

"The day after tomorrow then," he said.

"Aapke marzi." Of course there was nothing much to prepare. Nina was now wearing several hand-me-down garments, each dawn inveterately washing the one dirtied on the previous day, pounding it on the worn stones at Pichola's edge; spreading it to dry near the door to her meagre quarters in the shadow of the zenana. She thanked Arjun Singh most graciously for the use of his horse and left his side.

Retrieving a single rupee from its hiding place she walked into the outer courtyard. Through the Sarasenic tripolia built in the early part of the century she strolled, braced by the good luck just befallen her. A strong and irresistible hand of destiny and an unknowable urgency made her wish she could leave on the morrow.

Beyond the triple arches her bare feet skimmed across the cobbled roadway, downhill she followed the stones, twisting past sari shops and vegetable stalls, now closing for the night.

Almost running into a hand cart of brilliant orange jellabies she regained her somewhat blemished composure and walked on and on until coming to the newly built clock tower. Turning to the right she followed a narrower lane. Children giggled in the street, a stray water buffalo waddled toward her and at another rutty lane a snowy white bleating goat stood tied to a rusting metal post jammed into the dirt, a cloth wrapped loosely around its nipples; her milk would be reserved for her owners.

It was just beyond this point that Nina remembered the chappal shops. While she was accustomed to bare feet she wished again for a new pair of chappals. Narendra's wife was sophisticated, beautifully drenched in fine perfumes, silks and jewels, and Nina felt herself so antediluvian and frumpy. For just a rupee she hoped she could purchase a lovely pair of shoes of a bright colored velvet sewn onto slippery pointed leather soles. She'd choose a pair trimmed in gold thread and she'd pack carefully the best of her shabby clothing until such time as she would reach the fort. If she tightly covered her hair perhaps she could keep most of the dust from it.

She found bright tomato red chappals with golden flowers embroidered across the toes. The walla wrapped them in a skimpy piece of paper and she carried them triumphantly back to the palace, the biggest, most exciting purchase of her life.

Now if only she had something in the way of jewelry. Everyone had jewelry except for Nina. The poorest little waif had cheap little bangles; not even the cheapest glass ones could she afford. Neither did she own toe rings. There was nothing to enhance whatever comeliness she possessed, but Nina was not one to feel sorry for herself. She had too much to be thankful for: meeting Narendra at the cenotaphs beyond Mandore; taking charge, finding her pleasant employment at the magnificent palace, undoubtedly in the greatest kingdom ever known on earth. Who else could boast such fortuitous good luck. What a unique life she lived.

A labyrinth of perplexing thoughts kept the next day tiresomely long. Nina went to bed before the sky was completely dark. Resplendent daybreak brought Nina and the servant Kaushik together. The twosome were to take the shortest possible route to Jagatpur with as little strain on the horses as possible. They were, after all, only servants.

When they arrived at the fort a few days later the sky was still clothed in sunshine. Nina reached her soft hand upward to her silky black hair; smoothing it back, combing it with nimble fingers, readjusting the scarf over her head, loosening it to show her cheeks.

Heretofore she had been thinking mainly of Narendra. Strangely at this moment she conjured up an image of his delightful mother. Bending over she removed the precious new chappals she had just placed onto her feet, rewrapping them with a new desire to give them to Bhadra Singh, so badly had she wanted to offer the woman some little token of love and affection.

They reached the inner gate of the Arjun Singh mansion. Narendra was not to be seen, or anyone else of the family. At the main door Nina asked to be announced to the mistress and would wait in her old servants' quarters. It was late that evening before she was received. Narendra's mother chatted with Nina but briefly, embracing each other as sisters rather than servant and elder superior. No mention was made of Narendra or Kala. Nina handed a letter to the elder woman written by her husband and turned, taking her leave.

Prayers occupied the customary three hours of Narendra's early day and it was 10:30 before he had completed his morning meal and walked into the courtyard. Under a distant babul tree squat Nina and something about her caught Narendra's eye. Nervously he hurried to her. Her heart and mind raced; her body remained still. "You are here?" he put it questioningly as if not to believe his eyes.

"Your revered father has loaned me one of his horses. Queen Mother suggested I take leave and revisit my friends here at Jagatpur."

"You traveled alone?" He would not put it past her.

"Your father released Kaushik for the trip. We shall return together after a short visit."

"You are learning much of Mewar?" he asked hopefully.

"Hari Lal is a most amazing person, Narendra Singhji. He makes everything an exciting adventure. I am allowed to sit beyond the open door and Hari Lal knows of my presence there and speaks in loud clear tones. I do not miss a thing. One day I shall become an expert on Mewar, just as he is," she giggled.

"Enough about me," she continued. "Now let us talk of you. You are happy? And your wife? Is she keeping well? And what of all the dacoits? Is there anything you can tell me of your progress."

"You ask many questions, my little one."

Her heart raced at the sound of those words again, "my little one," as if they were meant only for her and she was something extremely special to him. She was now vicariously associated with two low castes, that of a servant, and the farmers to which she had been born, not to mention the atrocity of sinning with a dacoit. Each category was worlds apart from the kysatrias or warrior class of which the Arjun Singhs were hereditary members.

He answered, "Yes, I am very happy. I think never as much as now. It is because of Kala, and secondly I have found a place in life, an honorable job to do," He hesitated but a moment and went on, "We are very much in love, Kala and I."

The two friends soon separated.

Nina offered her services to Narendra's mother but nothing was required of her. "Just relax while you are here, Nina. Rest, for I'm sure you must be keeping extremely busy in the palace. Certainly this leave must be well earned. You are welcome for as long as you are able to stay."

Bhadra Singh was so deeply touched with the gift of new chappals. She was wearing them on this day, choosing clothing which complemented the color of the shoes. She could not know that all but the last couple very small coins had gone toward their purchase. Nina in the meantime was far happier offering them to this kindly woman who befriended her so graciously. She regarded her as nothing less than her mother.

Nina was also wise enough to know she must not inflict herself on the Singh family. Walking through the streets of Jagatpur she stared at the food stalls; not unlike those of the palace town. Time was more abundant here and her gait became slower. For the chapatis there were the various flours and grains: wheat, barley, maize or millet, townspeople choosing according to their income. There were the customary vegetables: carrots, potatoes, onions and her favorite garnish, the bright green coriander that tasted so good snipped over fresh vegetables. She wished, too, that the mangoes could be in season.

It would be a long time before another meal; the two of the day being breakfast somewhere around ten A.M. and the main meal at the fort/home served about seven in the evening to the family, servants eating the remains about an hour later. Afternoon tea or tiffin was hours away so Nina continued to cavalierly stroll to the edge of the fort and beyond. It was not as wild here as the southwestern spurs of the Aravallis, the "hilly tracts of Mewar." Nor was it as flat as the raised plateau of the northeast sloping off to the plains of Malwa. Nina enjoyed this intermediary geography. She walked aimlessly, passed small houses and more marketable vegetables strewn on sack-cloth, covered by protective umbrellas of dried and woven palm fronds.

Fascinating to Nina were the sights of bamboo jungles which covered some of the Aravalli hills. Here on the outskirts of the fort the trees were stunted, many chopped and loped for firewood by the families in and outside the fort.

By the time she returned she had missed her tiffin and settled for the cold wet of the well water. Shortly it would be time for her evening meal. She sat in the kitchen awaiting the remains to be spread before the help, today 24 in number. Kaushik was there too and all the others she had come to know during her lessons as a stitcher of fine cloth.

Then the wait for deeper nightfall.

"You are here?" Narendra called softly in the shadows of the bushes and trees. Inside the battered temple sat Nina on a stone step up to what must have once been the altar, the idol stolen long ago.

"I am here, Narendra Singhji."

He took her hands softly in his. This meeting seemed more planned than chance, it was so instinctive for each of them, though anything but clandestine. He spoke at not too great length about the inexorable scourge of more dacoits. And as he might have expected, she again pointed out the fact that any roundups of gangs were relatively easy thus far. One day he would surely meet fiercer gangs.

"Remember what I've said in the past, Narendra Singhji. You must think as the dacoits think. Be wary of possible informers. It would be easy for someone to set a trap against you."

Nina changed the subject. "Has Kala adapted well to her new surroundings? Is she happy here aside from not yet getting pregnant?"

"Our family has been fabulous with her. They think it's fun having another female around; and especially mataji. When Kala and I argue it's about my work. She hates the idea of my leaving home to fight dacoits. She insists it's far beneath my station and I should consider how it looks to others."

"<u>Others</u> would think you a brave hero. I imagine her real concern is the same as mine, your safety, not how it looks to others. Do not worry unduly about Kala, Narendra. She will come to realize you will take great care."

Narendra realized in this moment that with Nina he could quietly talk out their difference of opinion or their innermost feelings. With Kala it always erupted into something volcanic, neither one totally willing to give in to the other. Nor had they yet learned to achieve a judicious compromise.

He looked down at Nina. By this time the moon had risen sufficiently to make out the lovely outline of her profile.

Strange that before this he had thought of her so drearily plain. How was it that now standing near the entrance to the dilapidated temple she acquired an ethereal aura. Could it be some heavenly spirits visited themselves upon her? Why in front of him? He was married and was not to look in any covetous way at the face or body of another. He wiped it from his mind. Perhaps it was just the shadow of a cloud which passed in front of the moon. He sent Nina along on the private pathway which was hers alone. He'd take another route to his wife.

As for Nina, to stand near and not hold him was to touch her heart with aching pity. But she could not betray herself. She'd spend more time with Bhadra Singh, telling her stories and making herself useful while remaining careful not to disclose personal or secret matters. She regarded as sacred the intimacy of her position with the regent.

Nina had seen little of Narendra after their temple meeting. There were still those suppressed rumblings of dacoits within two days hard travel which he had sent others to check on. He gathered around him his trusted friends, setting off in the direction of Kokala-ki-Dhani after receiving more unconfirmed reports.

On the third of the month eight dacoits on four camels had looted one dhani of the village of Kokala-ki-Dhani and stole one thousand rupees worth of property. On the fourth, seven dacoits on four camels looted another nearby village of five hundred rupees in cash taking four camels and gold from three persons. The value of the earrings was in itself worth more than the cash.

The dacoits continued their mischief in neighboring districts taking another camel and a pair of earrings from the village of Sarli, plus a saddle and camel as they left the town and roared down a dirt road. It was to these places that Narendra now traveled to investigate the procedures, and to learn whatever he could about the mannerisms of the small band.

Narendra felt a small sense of relief, for everything he learned was far from the despicable villainies of that Jodhpur encounter when he killed his first man. Still, they were crimes, and no police.

By the next day Narendra and his men reached the village of Kawas when he dismounted his horse and studied the footprints of a man accused by a villager as being a dacoit. The day wore on slowly yet Narendra felt he found a very weak pulse of the gang itself. His men had followed the footprints until it became too dark to go further, not wanting to destroy other prints. It was considered wise to send Ran and a man of his choice to further interrogate other villagers. Anything would be helpful in this subjective cause.

The morning of the sixth broke and it was nigh impossible to follow the footprints, the ground had become extremely hard. Another seven neighboring villages had been checked thoroughly. Still there was no trace of the dacoits.

Then a surprising thing happened. Two camels which had been stolen had somehow broken away in the night. Markings on them were verifiable. Narendra's men were spurred to search harder for more footprints and there were enough to make the hunters suspicious. But once again darkness fell. They had tediously checked many miles since leaving Jagatpur, tired and dirty each night, fed by villagers anxious for the dacoits' apprehension.

The morning of the seventh started with a serious discussion. They deputized four sawars they had come upon to join the original party. In frustration they had not found a single clue. Sadly their leader decided to head back toward Jagatpur, morbidly overcome by his temporary setback. It was in the next few hours that they came to yet another small village where Narendra was informed the dacoits had been seen. Now it was necessary that they track them through the jungle village of Zabli. But once again night came.

The morning of the eighth the men divided into two parties including the deputized sawars who stayed on with them, plus a few residents picked from the last village. Fortunately they were again able to track. It was only six A.M. and Narendra had instructed the second party to stick as close to the first as possible. At 2 P.M. they passed through a section where a few people ran from a dhani of a Sindhi. Two of them appeared to be women but were in fact men covering themselves in disguise, attempting to run away. With the sudden suspicious movements Narendra instantaneously accelerated his horse. In moments he was upon the "women" in a flat and open plain and at a distance of a hundred yards Narendra's party suddenly was shot at unexpectedly. One bullet passed through the turban of Pandu who was close on Narendra's heels, miraculously missing his head.

Narendra ordered his men down from their horses, motioning them to slip nearer the dacoits on foot and continue firing. When everyone was in a good location he called to the dacoits to stop their shooting, throw their arms over their heads and surrender. Expectedly, they paid no heed. Unfortunately one of the dacoits had an excellent position, determined to kill Narendra and his force, stepping up his attack. Pandu and two others took a dangerous flank action to the side. Before much longer the fighting stopped with three dacoits killed. They appeared either Muslims or Hurs with exceedingly strong and beautiful physiques. From these dacoits they recovered not only rifles but a big supply of ammunition and two camels.

Nina was still at the fort when the men returned, but it was Kala who stood in the doorway to their home. Nina kept her distance. No one could accuse her of not knowing her place. With a sigh she watched until he walked to Kala, arms outstretched, leading her into the secret confines of their private rooms. At least he is safe, she thought. Thank God he is safe.

Nina could see how a true Rajput warrior such as Narendra would certainly be willing to give his life. A Rajput is a chivalrous, proud man with a distinctive lineage. Certainly if the women could die for their men, await their arrival in heaven the men could die for their country in whatever manner destiny prescribed.

Kala, on the other hand, born of a Rajput ruling class, did not share this viewpoint. She welcomed her husband's return with open arms, disappearing quickly with him into their private sanctuary and while the loving, tender moments turned into hours, they ended in heated argument. "I hope you have worked this silly notion of yours out of your system," she had started amicably enough.

"It's not a silly notion, Kala. Something has to be done." He called a halt to the discussion.

Again on this night Kala took up the same exhaustive argument, "It's like prostitution, my husband. Such things went on from the beginning of time. Nor will dacoity come to an end because you wish it would. Why are you so blind? You are nothing more than a policeman. Why do you stoop so low when you were born so high?"

"Is a policeman really so much lower than I, Kala? Does he not breathe and eat and raise his family? Is there something so wrong in being lower caste? I find that rather offensive." He tried to walk out of the room but she followed.

"Just who is there to thank you when it is all ended? Will the regent make you Rana? Will you rule the world?"

"Would you love me more if I was ruler of the whole world?" Narendra bellowed. "Just look at my father. He rules this jagir and he does it well. The people all love and admire him, regardless of their caste. They touch his feet when he comes to their homes. He is a great man and some day I shall walk in his shoes. Is not that good enough for you? We may as well stop fighting right now. I am going out."

"Narendra..."

"Not another word." His voice was loud, words distinct, face strained in pain with angered brows, lips and still firmly set jaw.

"When will you be back," she defied him by speaking.

"That is for you to find out only when I walk into our rooms," and he stormed out.

Several hours had gone by after Nina arrived at what she now considered her own private piece of the world, the battered temple. About to leave, there was a slight crackling of brush. Remaining silent she heard it again. Then,"Little one, you are here?" Little one. He said it again. If only he could mean it tenderly, passionately instead of a reference to her stature,

"I am here," she replied wistfully.

He was weary enough from all the reports he had had to fill out all day and horribly disgusted with his marital fight. But he had a need to talk with someone who understood him. After a while he asked, "Have you talked with Kala these last days?" His problems with Kala were justifiably serious; he needed help.

"We have spoken but briefly in the courtyard a few times. I do know my place, Narendra Singhji. I don't expect her to converse with me, although I have offered to assist her in anything at all if I am needed."

"Mother speaks with you. I speak with you. Why wouldn't Kala?"

"That is different, Narendra. And it is alright. There is nothing wrong, is there?"

"We have just had a dreadful fight. I discussed with her about going to a doctor. She wanted only to see a midwife but I have convinced her she should see the doctor too. You know how it is, I suppose. A woman, a wife, cannot bear the thought of another man looking at her body. I personally do not like the idea either. For my sake she finally relented. Kala is a good wife, Nina."

"Then she has already seen the doctor?"

"Yes; he said she is a healthy woman and should have no problems in bearing a child. She saw him today only. He is to perform some religious ceremonies tomorrow, after which it is hoped she will be able to become pregnant. Mother is to prepare the sacred tray with the help of a priest she has called. The doctor will also be there and together they shall do the ceremony. We will do anything anyone suggests so that my Kala can have my child."

Nina felt all his urgencies, all his desires of masculinity. She could imagine the great joy and pleasure he would bring to his children for he loved life with a full measure. "I pray it will be so," Nina responded quietly. "And now you shall not see me for a while, I shall tell Kaushik that we must leave for the palace as soon as he is able to ready our horses."

Nina turned to leave through the tiny doorway, over the stone lintel and onto the narrow path, now brush covered. "Go with God," he called after her.

Kala adhered to the burdensome rituals of which she understood nothing. She had been instructed to wear one of her most beautiful red saris after carefully bathing and to omit breakfast. A silver thali had been brought into the puja room. On it were a few varieties of spices, a coconut, the inevitable little oil lamp and wick of twisted cotton. Shrimati Bhadra Singh and her unmarried daughter joined Nina as well as Narendra, the priest, and the doctor. Chanting was mainly in Sanskrit, not understood by the others, nor did they understand the ministerial functions. Fifteen minutes later it was over, Narendra whispered to his beloved wife, "If it be God's will that we be parents then it will now be so. Not to worry, Kala. We will not be forsaken."

Several months later Kala made the joyful announcement to her husband that she was indeed pregnant; and word spread contagiously through the household.

By the time she was in her fifth month word even reached Queen Mother, long since resettled at the palace. She in turn informed Nina.

Then came another word: miscarriage. How could fate be so cruel? Nina's heart pounded in fury for the suffering she knew her Narendra would be bearing.

Chapter 6

As day bent gently, happiness followed upon the heels of sorrow. Nina strode near the outer palace walls. She had forgotten today was Holi. Everybody was happy in the streets. Powders of blues, greens, pinks and yellows were flying through the air. Laughing crowds swarmed past her, nudging and shoving to get into the palace grounds. Oh lord, she had forgotten to place colored powders upon the feet of her revered Queen Mother. She should do this before another moment went by.

Nina rushed past the crowd as best she could. Grabbing some gaudy powder from the tiny bag of a woman in the mob, she sidled up to the Rani and the young Bhim Singh, rubbing the powder onto the bare feet of the two Highnesses. Mother and son blessed her with an enormous red tika on her forehead and Nina regretted she did not have a garland of auspicious marigolds. Between son and mother stood the aide d'camp taking from each the garlands of peasants as fast as they were placed around the necks of Their Highnesses. Was it not an insult, to receive a garland from a subject only to have it instantly removed? "Not at all," a servant explained. "They have displayed their homage and the rulers have acknowledged the act."

This was the second year Nina had observed Holi here at the palace, a non-religious festival. Last year she completely enjoyed the indignities allowed during this festival, but Narendra's sadness was too heavy upon her this day. The streets were a mad place until early afternoon, when they became even worse with the "playing of water." Best she remain in the more sombre confines of the palace, where crowds dare not enter. Thousands of jovial subjects danced in the courtyard. Nina picked a place out of the warming sun above where she had fallen on her seat during her original arrival. From here she could watch the dancing and the great array of clothing.

In Northern India, on the full moon of the month of Phalgun, in all the ravishing garb of spring, comes this least dignified of all festivals where men and women mix more freely than at any other time. Buffoons abound and all classes or castes mix for these few hours they are allotted each year. In every household mothers receive the tilak powder dot on their foreheads from their Hindu servants. In earlier days, Nina had been told, only red powder was used for it symbolized the blood of the demons which Lord Krishna had slain along the banks of the Jumna near her native Brindavan. It had been said that these powders brought immunity against the many rampant diseases. At this moment it would seem there were only robust, healthy men, women and children with a driving devotion to their rulers and an infinite hunger for a mirthful life.

Although Holi would last only one day in other cities, here in the palace grounds it would be celebrated for a full week with peasants walking for many days or being pulled in bullock carts to honor their rulers. They would stand in interminably long lines outside the palace gates until such time as there would be a clearing in the large courtyard and they could be received by their Rana and queen. This could take from hours to days. Each wanted to dance. Sometimes there would be a half dozen little groups energetically performing uncaring that Their Highnesses would not remain to see each of them. Yet they ingeniously danced and fervidly played their hand-made instruments, the music endless. For seven days and nights this would go on.

Surreptitiously Nina tried to pick out the individual villages or area from which each little group had come. There were those with the small white pugri with the small navy blue print wound around their heads. Other men wore a gold dangling earring from their right lobe. There was the odd looking batch of men who sat playing their squeaky violins with dhotis wrapped around their lower bodies, loose short blouses and fresh green sprigs of some tree pushing into each of their headdresses.

Ladies in heavy cotton tie and dye gagras, the winter dress of the colder regions, brought their babies in rough baskets carried atop their heads, deep beet red dyes bleeding onto their skins. In the shadow of a wall they would separate and each would go into their crude dances, hundreds of tinkling silver ankle bells jangling to the tantalizing rhythm pounded onto the dirt pavement. Furtively heads would bow to the centers of their little circles, silver arms of peasant-family wealth rising and falling as the circles moved clockwise to the beat of anyone's music. Some brought their local drummer who kept in motion all who had entered this outer courtyard. Their Highnesses, wearying of the ordeal, took themselves into the sanctuary of their inviolably private rooms. Nina, however, stayed on to watch.

As each group was rushed back through the gate making room for still others to enter they were fed a small snack and given a refreshing drink of juice. Nina remembered the previous year Queen Mother explained since there is far less money after the ravishing era of the Mahrattas they no longer can feed each of the subjects a banquet as had been done for centuries. For this the Rani felt a sense of tyrannic guilt. Or perhaps it was a sense of betrayal of her loyal subjects, yet her advisors had insisted the coffers could allow nothing different.

Young Bhim Singh had again appeared on the scene ready to start the playing of waters, a raucous ribaldry which had become his favorite once-a-year sport. A galvanized metal tub had been placed in another smaller courtyard at one extreme end and filled with water. Tankards were handed each of the participants, His Highness and the feudal lords and the male members who were spending their allotted time in service at Udaipur.

Their tankards were of tin, formed with a projecting lip opposite the handle. Once filled, the men could dash water harshly against anyone he wished to drench. Experienced men could do it with such precision and skill they could rip clothing from the bodies of their friends. The little king was not subjected to such suffering force but rather a more gentle tossing while he himself tried with all his might to be something of a little rogue. Women stayed away from this encounter for they would not be spared the horrible thrashing if they came within range. And

Nina had picked the most distant spot in this little arena, near a doorway, should it be necessary to escape a sudden barrage.

Late afternoon tiffin was especially delicious on this day, even for the servants. Caught up in the fun Nina turned once more to watching the astonishing dancers who portrayed those wars in which queens accompanied their husbands onto the battlefields, often to their deaths. Today men dressed as women scampering with their bow and arrow around the "villain" they were to "kill." Long ago there had been the Queen Mother by name Jawahar Bai. She had armed herself, went into the battlefield and was killed. She could have remained safe in her palace but that was not her choice.

There were men in costumes tied at their middle which made them look as if they were riding horseback, proud of their home-made costumes. With boundless energy they danced until forced out of the way by other merrymakers.

Women from warmer regions of Mewar showed up in sheer pale pastel trimmed in silver or gold, shawls fluttering flamboyantly in breezes created by their own dancing.

Nina took herself to bed unusually early only to arise soon after to literally follow the plaintive sounds of a flute. Safely moored beyond the triple arch sat a bewhiskered old man playing joyously in the evening of his days. His tempo to begin was slow, picking up speed much as a rider whose gait starts with a metered walk, proceeds to a slow trot, to an easy canter, then to a roaring gallop. The tablas were of his own improvisation. He could not have been schooled but there was a fluid continuity.

One melody was soulful and romantic reminding Nina of her childhood in the hills of Punjab when she'd visit her grandparents. As the flute trilled she imagined a lover calling softly to his love. Nina closed her eyes. She could clearly see a maiden shyly move toward her man, mutely embrace and voluntarily submit. Nina wondered if this was what the old man had in mind, surely once himself a lover.

A musician without peer, the tapestry he wove welded her attention. Once more she surrendered to the idea that greatness in any field was not reserved for the higher born. Nina hoped she too one day could add to the joys of others. Some day perhaps a way would come.

Narendra arrived unexpectedly two weeks after Holi. Queen Mother sent for him and a full report on his work thus far against dacoits. Now there were rumblings of other small bands. It was time she join the Singh family in the idea of ridding the country of this cancer.

Narendra had long discussions with his regent, some of which included little Bhim Singh. As he was now approaching his teens he must become aware of all major problems of the kingdom. The Rani was astute enough to know that time passes swiftly and all too soon would come the year when her son would sit alone on the gaddi making his own tactical decisions. She had come to respect the youngster for his ability to pick up on events of the past and present but had given in to Hari Lal's request not to push him too fast. Pushing meant a jumbled mind and a treacherous frustration. "Slow and easy wins the race." was his favorite observation, yet she could not let Bhim Singh ignore Narendra's work and problems.

Nina remained out of sight. It was not until he had been there for three or four days that he sent a message to her. He brought her the best wishes of his doting parents, and of course Nina's first questions were of Kala. Silently she wondered about Narendra with his deep religious beliefs and if it carried him through the burning grief into which he must have plunged.

"Can we talk somewhere, Nina?" he asked anxiously with barely a whisper. "I need a friend."

"Of course, "Narendra Singhji, whatever you say ... but of course you have many friends, Ran, Pandu, ..."

"True, but somehow I cannot bare my soul to them. It is as if they do not understand, even though they are very sympathetic in their words. I know they are sincere but it is not the same, Nina. It is you I really must talk with."

"I do not think there is any place within the palace walls where we are certain not to be overheard, is it not so?"

"True, but take the back walk and cross over to the hillock to the east of the palace," he said, eyes staring in the direction of which he spoke, and with the slightest nod of his head. "I shall leave by the main gate, through the city, as the sun is sinking across Pichola. I'll double back and I shall find you. Do not fear. Do you remember that bird sound I used to make when we first left Mandore?" She nodded affirmatively. "I shall softly make the same sounds and you can walk in that direction. Perhaps we shall find a good place in which we can meet in the future, if it is ever necessary."

"Necessary," Nina thought to herself. It is good to be needed. Being needed was almost more important to her than being loved. She knew Kala would always be the number one love of his life and she could never attain such a status. Thus to be needed by Narendra was most significant. Nina was eager for nightfall and her meager role in his life.

It was not yet dark when she left the home grounds through an insignificant niche in the wall, across a dirt path beneath verdant trees and up a little dirt roadway she had earlier ridden on trips to Udaipur. Just beyond the hillock she turned to the right, keeping Lake Pichola in sight. Beneath one of the Zal trees she rested her back and started the long wait, so excited at this new prospect of seeing him alone. Her otherwise soaring mind went suddenly blank, supremely content just to wait until Narendra appeared.

Much after dark she heard the trilling bird call, arose and walked in the direction of the contrived sound. They had little trouble finding each other and to her astonishment he voluptuously embraced her. In these lengthy moments of amazement her arms hung limply at her side, but she felt his pulse surge, merging with hers; she felt too the compulsive shaking of his body, now throwing her arms around him, holding him as close as humanly possible.

Looking up into deep non-expressive eyes she pondered this providential circumstance. Both remained silent. His body still shook as a child's with violent fever. They continued clinging to each other, Nina's cheek resting against his breast. The tremors did not stop and Nina lifted her face once more to his. Raising her chin, pecking him on the tip of his nose, she offered with it the suggestion of a smile.

Once more she rested her cheek against his strong quaking body. And once more she looked up at him, planting the second kiss so gently on his lips it could barely be felt by either. She sought an indication of truth in his eyes.

And then he kissed her, so hard and so furtively. Now her body too quivered, aching with intolerable pain. With all the exultant intensity it had never been like this with Motilal. He had been rapacious, rough and cruel, with never a sense of tenderness or longing. Narendra's kisses were neither sterile nor indulgent but passionate and rapturous. She felt naked but somehow it did not matter. How she longed to be his wife, to in fact be naked when he wished.

It was many incredible minutes before their kiss ended and they sat beside each other on the ground, motionless and silent, her left hand resting limply in his. She could not know what it was he had in mind and would not make the first move. After an embarrassed silence he said, "Nina, I do need to talk with you, but can we make it tomorrow?" With that he rose and disappeared in the direction of the palace. She followed at a discreet distance and entered the home grounds at a different point. There was little sleep for either that night.

His tomorrow did not come for several days. Nina had returned to listening to young Highness's lessons, now less exciting, covering mainly mathematics and subjects she considered dull. She had no idea what occupied the time for Narendra but eventually they passed in the palace gateway leading to the city where he took the opportunity to mumble to her, "Same place tonight."

She knew not how to defend herself against this awkward situation, longing more than ever for his potent arms, eager to yield at any request. But would he ever again touch her? Perhaps the other night was an obscure moment in his life, a rare time of weakness. He could be strong enough to overcome any weakness. "Oh lord, Kala is so beautiful, there could be absolutely no reason why he would desire my physical company," the trembling girl tried reasoning. There is nothing so heartbreaking as the realization your desires are impossible.

That night with a sudden pall as bitter as mourning Nina sat in the same spot where she had been kissed. This time when he called to her with his little whistle she did not answer. When he found her even in the dark her eyes glittered abstractly. He sat beside her, not too close, watching her in silence, the curves of her body comfortably inviting.

Nina could not allow him to once again hold and kiss her without an explanation or reason. Her rags and body were a far cry from the silks and sinuousness of his wife. She could not conceive of him as a philanderer. He could have taken advantage of her any number of times.

She could wait no longer. "What is it you wish to speak to me about?"

"You're very formal tonight, Nina. Is it you are angry with me because of the other evening? I could not blame you if it is so."

"I am not angry, Narendra Singhji. I am just baffled. I do not understand."

"What is it you don't understand, little one?"

Nina looked at him in curious fashion. Was that kiss and more-than-ardent embrace after all just a passing fancy, a small desire of the moment? If so, why had he trembled so abnormally? She chose to be blunt. "Why did you kiss me?"

"You do not like to be kissed?"

"Of course I do."

"Then it is *my* kiss you do not like," he teased with a twinkle in his voice.

"Oh Narendra Singhji, you are making fun of me. Because I am lowly and of no proper breeding, because I come from a farmer's home and lived with a dacoit you think of me as nothing..." A lump welled in her throat and she could say no more.

"You are as dear to me, my little one, as my family or anyone could be. Your background means nothing. You should definitely know that by now. Are you trying to hurt me?"

"Hurt you? You must know by now Narendra that I am so fiercely in love with you that at times I cannot see straight. I know no good will come of it. I saw you become a married man and even if you did not marry there is such a chasm between us. It is a matter of great wonder that you should have taken me into your arms and held me so lovingly and kissed me as I have never before been kissed.

"I care about you, Nina. I care a great deal about you and for you. Surely you have seen that. But you must always remember that I love my wife very dearly. I will not pretend otherwise."

"I do realize that, Narendra, and you would be surprised how easy it would have been for me the other night to make love to you; really make love. I would have smothered you with all affection; I wanted to so badly. Oh it would have been so easy..."

"No, Nina. Not easy. For me it would not be easy. I think always of Kala and the way I have loved her. I think all day and night of the torment she feels in wanting to give me a son, of how she tries. She honestly tries — or did. She believes that she had another miscarriage but this time very quickly after conceiving, perhaps just a few months. Oh Nina, that is what I wanted to talk to you about. I have to talk to somebody. I feel her outrage. She is embittered and I can understand that but lately she has become so cold toward me. She seeks the company of the ladies around the house and only comes to our rooms when it is very late, and then she finds excuses to lay across the room from me. I don't know how to cope with this. Such action is a stranger to me."

"You must be patient, Narendra Singhji. I think her impatience has another name — man."

A smile briefly crossed this Rajput's mouth and he answered, "Perhaps you're right, Nina, but I do all I can to make her a good husband. I buy her whatever clothing she wants, and jewels. I had sent for her family when she miscarried and her mother stayed on until just recently. I want her well, Nina. I want my wife back. That wife I married up in Jaiselmer. I want her back," he sighed gaspingly.

"I feel so helpless, my friend. You sought me out as someone to talk to. I can only say one word to you: patience. How unfortunate that I cannot offer wisdom and sage advice. I feel so helpless in your presence, Narendra Singhji. Always be cheerful with her, even though you are shattered inside. It will pay off one day, you'll see."

"I have often told you that you are wise beyond your learning. You have about you an indescribable quality of what is right, and how to find it. You are not letting me down now.

"Nina, I do not know how to say this to you. I came here thinking I would not touch you again, ever. I have told you I love my wife and I mean it. And it is not just that I cannot make love to her very often any more, for her moments of withdrawal are much more frequent all the time. It is not that I seek the company of another woman, but Nina, if you can imagine it, in some ways I know that I love you more than even my wife. Can you understand that?"

"No," she answered only half honestly.

"We must never hurt each other. Whatever we are or become; whatever we do we must never hurt each other nor any of those we love. I did not come here to make love to you, Nina. And if we ever do you must know beyond all doubt that it is in the spirit of caring and tenderness for each other that we would succumb. But I am not sure that will ever happen."

"I would agree with that, Narendra," but now her words were silenced with an inaudible crying by this great hulk of a man. Nina hesitatingly placed her hand gently on his knee. His crying became a wild fit before Nina took hold of both shoulders and forced his head against hers.

He cried long and hard. "Nina, you help to stabilize me. I am grateful for that." They sat very long, mostly silent, and when there were no sounds in the woods or from the city or the birds, they left.

Maharana Bhim Singh's lessons grew tiresome for Nina who had become lost in the mechanics. She was perfectly capable of keeping track of a few rupees, of making correct change on the few occasions she was able to buy a treat for herself. More than this she need not know. The higher the mathematics, the less she cared.

When the little Rana had lessons in reading and writing she could see the large board Hari Lal had faced in the direction of her doorway. It was frustrating learning all those squiggles of the written word. Barely audible sounds were so subtly different. Chhapati; chay. And the written words bore no similarity.

Hari Lal started those lessons with the basic structural patterns of their language and the fundamental grammatical devices. Mewari was not Nina's mother tongue but close enough that she had always been able to understand and converse. Living here at the palace she had a quick ear and readily picked up the spoken language. Reading it was yet another thing. Hari Lal insisted she was smart enough to master it, eventually.

As for grammar? Horrors! Not until the time of these lessons had she realized there was such a thing as good or bad grammar, correct or incorrect grammar. One day Hari Lal said to his student — or was it students? — "About the pronoun apna अपना belonging to self. It has a peculiar use which is important to mention. When in a sentence there is a possessive pronoun belonging to the subject it is expressed by apna. Therefore if you wish to say 'he saw his horse,' 'usne apna ghora dekha.' In that sentence if the possessive (his) belongs to the subject (he) its rendering is apna, but if 'his' means someone else's horse, the rendering should be uska. Understand? It is therefore correct to say 'Main apni pustak parthi hun,' 'I am reading my book.' Or 'Wuh apna pustak partha hai,' 'He is reading his book.'"

Nina felt sorry for the child having to sit through the tedious lessons. It did not matter whether _her_ grammar was flawless. She couldn't possibly care. Poor little Bhim Singh.

Hari Lal also had the grace to shift gears whenever he saw his little charge become too frustrated, injecting a change of pace, a lesson with more appeal. He was aware that it would soon be time for Their Highnesses to attend the great function at Chittorgarh when the ancient ceremony commemorating the death of Padmini and others would be celebrated. Since the new capitol shifted here to Udaipur it had been the custom of the Maharanas to return each year. The long to be cherished memory of Queen Padmini and her meritorious deeds went beyond the threshold of the sublime. The time had come, the pandit knew, when the child should learn properly of this tremendous story, for as ruler he would be in charge of the revered event for the rest of his life.

As regent the Rani would be traveling to the fort of Chittor for this specific ceremony as she had each year since the death of her husband. She agreed that Hari Lal should dramatize it to whatever degree necessary, thereby indelibly imprinting it in the mind of her son. To his way of thinking, however, the tale needed no embellishment for it was undoubtedly one of the most amazing in the history of the world. Certainly it was the most awesome of the true stories of their 1000 year old kingdom.

Political factions were gaining a stronger foothold in Mewar with disruptions and suggestions of sordid court intrigue. Rival clans, the Chondawats and the Suktawuts, tried desperately to get the upper hand with the regent, slowly manipulating themselves into more powerful places. She must keep herself strong and must see to it that her son would learn to do likewise in the hope of returning Mewar to its original heights of glory.

She gathered a few of her nobles around her in the Diwani-khas for discussions on the trip to the abandoned fort. She did not wish to rush this journey. She would require sturdy men to carry the drinking water from Pichola, sufficient tents, food, triumphal palanquins, charpoys on which to sleep, a great number of soldiers in case of attack, suitable arms and ammunition. There were to be many body guards and they must be reverentially trustworthy. There must also be omnipresent spies keeping a sharp ear for malicious rumors, ready to obviate problems. One such person was to be Nina, and she sent for the girl.

Nina never liked the word spy. She felt it demeaning but a bounden duty. She was thrilled with the opportunity to accompany her queen on this auspicious occasion. She had affixed an unswerving loyalty to the regent and was eminently prepared to come to the aid of the woman who befriended her. She also recalled Narendra saying to her one of those first few days they knew each other that perhaps she could one day stand on the spot where Khilji did.

The women's thoughts were along the same line for the Rani confided, "I shall request Narendra Singhji to accompany us and keep a watchful eye for anyone who might do us harm." It was a wise choice inasmuch as he was still in Udaipur and by now adept at handling villains.

It took several days of hectic motion before things were packed and carefully placed upon elephant backs for the cumbersome trip to the fort. The distance was not too great but travel was slow and the Rani gave instructions that she wished a stopover at Nathdwara, though the routing would be circuitous. It had been a long time since she paid respects to the Vaishnava temples of the Vallabhacharya sect. She especially wanted to visit the temple of Shri Nathji dedicated to Lord Krishna. It would add another firsthand lesson to her son's authentic collection, a forerunner to the Padmini feat.

The queen held on to her hypnotic fixation for things old and those things recorded in their precious annals. At this place the image of the lord goes back to the twelfth century B.C. By the end of the fifteenth century the image had been set into a temple in Mathura near the banks where Lord Krishna is known to have played with his gopis, then later it was moved to a holy mount. Muslims prohibiting the worship of idols placed this one in great peril. Emperor Aurangzeb was no traitor to their beliefs. The Hindus who revered it were desirous of preserving the idol and it was taken from place to place where men looked for a safe and protected spot in which to keep it. It was often told that many of the rulers of the Rajasthan States were asked to keep it but they refused to aid the men carrying it around, fearing the wrath of the Mughals.

The bearers asked the last of the kingdoms, Mewar. To their surprise the Maharana not only said that it was welcome in his kingdom but that he'd arrange to have help. The king came, too, to see the idol and have it set in place but the jostling cart which carried it stopped dead in a particular place, sinking down into the ground. It just could not be budged.

Superstition told them that the idol wanted to remain there and the men built a very plain temple around it, hiding the precious idol from view of the Mughals.

When the royal family arrived at the outside of the structure young Bhim Singh sneered, "This temple looks ugly, Mataji."

More patient with him than sometimes, she explained, "It's a well known fact that Muslims viciously desecrate our Hindu temples, my son, for they do not believe in seeing and praising those things which we love such as the statues of our gods and goddesses, our stone elephants, horses or any human or non-human creature. They chisel away all the physical features and leave them standing in ruin."

"How can they be so cruel?" he asked with wrinkled brows.

"It is what they believe, Bhim Singh. We all have a right to our own beliefs and our own way of life, but they desecrate that which we hold sacred. It is for this reason that entrance is forbidden for all but Hindus.

After the day's last darshan the party returned to their campsite. Tomorrow they would continue travel toward Chittor, a fabled fort which had held some of the most stormy and incontrovertible ancient history of the world.

Chapter 7

A nostalgia grips all Rajputs for the glories of the past, the eternal inspiration shed upon them by the very essence of the fort. It rested heavy-laden on the person of Queen Mother. She alighted gracefully from her palanquin, still remarkably handsome with a majestic gait. Little Bhim Singh and Hari Lal remained reverently silent, keeping their distance. A yearning for days that are no more rushed over the Rani like the flow of a mighty ocean's tide. She would not yet enter the illustrious fort. Like the Mughal Emperor Akbar, she would stand back at a distance embracing its prodigious size and admirable historic events.

Rising from near the banks of the Gambhiri River archaeologists trace early man back one hundred thousand years when their enemies were wild animals. Now mortal man is the culprit. But the twist of fate here is the unique manner in which a Mewari accepted his loss. He had the amazing grace to protectively accompany his fallen would-be conqueror away from his palaces, according them full respect. This was but one of the points Queen Mother wished to objectively contemplate. Could she emulate these illustrious predecessors? Determined to make her mark, probably here as no place else in the kingdom she could be shown the way.

It was late afternoon and still warm. Welcome would be the cooling evening breezes. Soft round bolsters were placed strategically on an oriental carpet beneath dhao trees to rest her stiffening back.

Hamir I had brought glory and fame and Maharana Kumbha in the early part of the fourteenth century brought the kingdom its golden era, growing in size geographically. Akbar had sacked it for the third and last time in 1567. Had they been able to save the fort Queen Mother would be ostentatiously housed within its 690 acres today instead of back in Udaipur. Her emotions were mixed, dearly loving the most spacious and unique palace in which she now reigned and the palace in the lake during the hot summer. Nonetheless their history continued to grip her forcefully, most of it made in, around and near Chittor fort.

It was said that when Emperor Akbar came to the foot of this stupendous place he camped here in the plain as the Rani was now doing. Today it lay a silent glory to the past, but in the time of Akbar it was well defended. When Maharana Udai Singh departed to search for a place for his new capitol he left 8,000 Rajput soldiers and a thousand more musketeers within the fort. Their provisions and water, it was said, were sufficient for three years. Moreover it was impossible for the enemy to be camped nearby and get any foodstuffs. Their elephants and horses suffered equally.

Akbar avidly studied the fort for a means to dexterously capture it. Rising 500 feet above the plains, its eight mile perimeter was impressive. From her vantage point rose imposing palaces of an earlier era. The little hillock on the south side once seemed a boon to any invaders. But not always so. Many times the Emperor fought for this seemingly impregnable fort.

Eventually the bastions gave way to marauders, but not without suffering enormous casualties. The Mewaris defended themselves to the final defeat. Queen Mother paid her silent exalted respects at this moment, realizing with emblazoned passion neither their men nor their women surrendered to the Mughal forces.

The fort was grandiose. Looking at a far off break in the crenellated wall meant for her not the break of a Mewari spirit but an opportune chance to look to the uplifting dreams and wavering illusions which surrounded her. As Hamir felt the mystic presence of his historic sword and obstinately struggled through whatever depths to reach it, the Rani grappled now with the perceptions not only of what had been but what could be again. In the air around her came a sobering holiness. Soft breezes brought to her messages of an unparalleled past, and an ardent plea from Padmini herself to keep forever alive her redeeming act. For all generations to come the Rani and successors must keep regenerative Padmini's final love for her beloved kingdom. There were numerous acts of peerless courage within this dynasty but none topped that of Padmini. Queen Mother would let Padmini lead her.

Exhausted both from physical burdens of travel and the peculiarly emotional strain, the regent submitted to a restless night in a tent, flaps facing toward the fort and tied back securely. Her charpoy was placed so that she could lay upon it and stare at the ancient fortifications, the rise of hills within, and the bushy forests fringing the perimeter and continue her dreaming. It was difficult to know where an alert mind stopped and where a semi-conscious and then a fitful dream took over — they blended indistinguishably.

Queen Padmini was married to the Rawal of Mewar, Ratan Singh, for not until his death did they change the title from Rawal to Maharana. Their fort palace was uncommonly large and extremely lovely, joined on one side by a quiet lake. Within exclusive confines of the azure waters stood the even lovelier private zenana of Queen Padmini.

This queen was reputedly the most beautiful of all human creatures with a mellow blending of fervor and softness. With such a valued treasure Ratan Singh could only love her as much as any human can love and adore another. In a different time and place their lives would have intermingled only with bliss and rapture, but hard times had come upon their kingdom. It was 1302 and close upon them was the villainous Emperor Allaudin Khilji.

Bred into the hearts and soul of all Rajputs is a puritanical will of both men and women to protect their honor; an intense impulse to fight to the death, preserving anything or anybody they revere.

Long hard months of fighting had gone by with Khilji outside their fort.

"Is it possible to win this battle?" Padmini asked of her beloved.

"We shall win, my dearest, of this I am sure. Be patient. There is ample food for much longer than the Emperor and his men can hold out. And we have good water here, better than the water of the river below. Each day they are losing many men, 50 to 100 dead on some days.

"Are you watching the Chittori hillock, my master? I have always feared that gentle rise would one day make it possible to enter our fort at that end. Often that which is the weakest spot becomes the strongest and that which is the strongest can become the weakest."

"What a strange thought, my wife," Ratan Singh bemused.

"Not at all. If we think one portion of the fort the safest and too strong for our enemies and allow it to go unguarded and our enemy learns of this, he systematically climbs and climbs until he makes his entry behind our lines. Then has not the strongest become the weakest?"

"Your point is well taken, Padmini, but it would take many more soldiers than they have. We could hold them off if they tried, but as yet they do not seem to consider that possibility. At any rate I shall take your suggestions and post more men there and keep a watchful eye."

In some respects it was almost as if there was no war raging beyond the bastions. The birds still sang in the hundreds of trees. Market stalls remained open each day for the sale of dal, flour, the makings of their daily chapatis and other breads. Women still went about their cooking chores, hopeful that each night their husbands would return to them for a meal and needed rest. When they did not return the silence was a struggle. Invariably more affection was lavished on the sons who were so soon to be old enough to fight alongside their fathers.

Padmini worried too about her husband. But she was a strong person and their combined fortitude made the crucial ordeal of this battle more bearable. There had been many frantic battles in previous centuries and more would undoubtedly follow. But their kingdom had grown, slowly but masterfully, until some day it would ascend to the zenith even Padmini and Ratan Singh could not envision, so imposing would be its grandeur.

"Always be careful for my sake as well as Mewar's, for I have great love for you. More than you can know," she entreated her husband.

"As I love thee, Padmini."

More weeks of fighting had gone by and outside the fort Emperor Khilji grew more sullenly angry. He had long ago become infatuated with the very thought of Queen Padmini and longed to possess her as his prime chattel. "I will have that woman," he would uncontrollably storm at his aides. Losing two personal battles — the capture of Chittorgarh and unable to glimpse this undisputed beauty — was more than Khilji could or would bear.

"That's it," he cried aloud, as if his henchmen could understand what he was thinking. "That's it. I shall ask for a glimpse of her. Then I shall somehow work it out that I shall take her back to Delhi with me. Ah yes, I knew I could arrange it if only I put my mind to it. He knew the Mewari Rawals to be honorable men and certainly they would not refuse another ruler a harmless request.

Self-satisfied, he sat down to compose a message to the Rawal. Offering respects to the ruler, he stated flatly that if he, Khilji, would be allowed to look upon the face of Rawal Ratan Singh's queen with her peerless beauty, it would be sufficient reward and he would thus return with his army to his own capitol in Delhi.

This was a new and unique state of affairs for the Rawal. The behavior of the Mewaris did not countenance an affront to either themselves or their royal enemies. How could he allow a villainous foe to look upon the sweet face of his stainless wife? Could he dare grant such a wish? And to what Mewari purpose? The decision was weighty. He would need judicious help. Ratan Singh summoned his next in command and assorted trusted counsellors.

Hours ran into each other as they contemplated the effects an eventual full scale war would have on their kingdom if the desire was not granted. Though they were winning the battle at the moment, it was unanimously understood that the tide could change at any time, the fort be taken at a cost of the lives of all. Cooler heads prevailed at this tedious meeting and it was agreed that Allaudin Khilji would be granted his wish.

The Mewaris are cunning people, however, and the fact they would accede to his demands did not mean they were either weak or backing down completely. They had decided upon a most clever plan. A courteous reply was delivered to the Emperor. He would be met the day after at the fort gates and could reflect upon the most revered Padmini. Meanwhile the scene would be carefully set by the aides of Ratan Singh.

The Emperor too had his code of ethics, or so he wanted it to appear. He humbly accepted the offer, slowly and deliberately staging the second scene of the next act. When the following day broke, Khilji rose to bathe and dress in the finest he had brought with him from his capitol. He looked dashing, a vain man. Not hurrying, he refused to appear either sensuously excited or at the imperious command of the Rawal's timetable.

Crossing what remained of the plains between his royal tent and the Padan Pol, the initial entrance to the fort, ceremonious words were exchanged between the arriving Mughals and the Hindus of the fort. The sloping mile long stretch with its two zig-zagging curves up to the final gate was taken on horseback, very slowly and deliberately. His heartbeat quickened.

At the topmost portion of the fort Khilji dismounted to be affably received by sub-lords of the fort and taken henceforth to the palace of their king, the Rawal Ratan Singh. There was a considerable distance to walk and he restrained his desire to dash madly for the palace and sinuous body of the object of his affection. Remaining royally discreet he retained a straight undaunted face, looking neither to the right nor left, while being stared at from a safe distance by the inhabitants of the fort. Only a small party was allowed into the fortification with the Emperor.

At the palace entrance he waited, albeit impatiently. At this moment the only thing which amply mattered was the tempting sight of that ravishing woman and the plan to maneuver her into his grasp. He waited still longer until the ruler came to the door.

The two men stared at each other silently. Neither feared the other at this point. It was a period of at least temporary truce. Khilji suppressed a desire to jest about the circumstance which he had brought to bear. He was certain it was extremely painful for Ratan Singh to share his wife in even this meager manner. But Ratan Singh bore no pallor of anxiety for his wife was well protected. Outside its many gates no one would dare start fresh trouble, Khilji's safety being at stake.

As for Padmini, there was an unutterable disgust; she loathed being the subject of such a shameful incident. However, as queen she would raise her head high with immaculate dignity when it would come time to play her part. She would not rush the scene; as queen she would take her own good time.

Through the gateway Khilji was ushered, through an oblong courtyard with simplistically lovely gardens of heavenly sweet jasmine and shade trees, and into a room of quiet elegance. Everyone stood unaccountably still. When many minutes went by the Emperor noticed the Rawal had left the room, and asked, "What is it I am to do?"

"If you would kindly move toward this lone window, sire, and turn your back to it," one of Ratan Singh's thakurs ordered.

Khilji glanced out the opening. "To the zenana."

"Your back to the window," the thakur spoke loudly and unmistakably. The Emperor obeyed.

High up the wall opposite Khilji, almost to the ceiling, there had been placed a mirror for his benefit. So carefully had it been hung that standing in this spot he could see over his reflected head and down beyond himself to the lovely small white home of the queen. From its single wooden door there was a large square platform and from it several steps leading down to the water. This is how he would see the woman? What an affront!

Would she indeed be worth this trouble as all who had beheld her beauty declared? Angered as he was by this unexpected twist to his request he dared not tip his hand. How long must he wait? He tempered his feelings so that he belied his urgency, keeping his eye on the mirror lest she appear but for a second only, quickly disappearing into the confines of the zenana, not to return.

Ah, what impudence. When she would come to be his he would not tolerate such action. He would bring her to her knees and she would obey his every whim and desire, for surely she would be the fairest and loveliest of all his harem. He would tolerate no indifference from any, least of all one of his senior wives.

Still he waited. The news of his arrival had been brought to Padmini, well aware the cards were in her hands. She wanted to play them adventitiously. Being thus looked upon by their adversary brought to Padmini the abomination of desolation. He would wait longer if his desire was so great.

Agony grew with each quarter hour he stood in this position, as if a prisoner. "How long am I to be subjected to this treatment?" he boomed. Then, red-faced with chagrin, he was smitten with awe. The loveliest of the fair stepped gracefully out her door onto the square concrete slab. With a haughty twist of her head and a lissom flex of body she stood in regal pose for a full minute, never glancing up to the window, which would in effect be looking into his eyes. Nor did she stare into the water sullenly. Rather, she looked straight ahead, proud and pleased to be the wife of a man who was according an unprecedented honor to his foe. Just as silently as she had appeared she took herself from the scene. She was indeed a flitting dream.

Depression settled on Khilji like fine dust of the desert. But his day was not over. He knew of the charming traditions of the rulers of Mewar. Ratan Singh's honor would demand he make some lovely gesture of seeing him personally out the gate of his Chittorgarh, and this is precisely what was done.

Virgin Princess 159

Content that their handling of the viewing of Padmini was done with taste and fairness, yet not completely fulfilling the desires of the enemy, the Rawal took the Emperor and his small party from the palace on the straightest route to the gates. Down the remaining kilometer they ambled together, Hindu servants leading the horses of the Mughals. Outside the fort Ratan Singh turned to bow a final goodbye when Allaudin Khilji captured his foe.

"What are you doing?" the Rawal demanded? The few with him were overpowered by the Emperor's men and stood in amazed silence.

"For your life you must give me Padmini," the Emperor raved.

"This is how you honor an agreement?" Ratan Singh would not attempt a useless fight at this moment. He sent word up to the palace of what had taken place and stated he would await their advice.

The Emperor had the Hindu ruler set astride a horse and accompanied him to their campsite a safe distance beyond the fort.

Undoubtedly there is no one who knows a woman better than her husband or lover. Ratan Singh was both to Padmini. He knew her not only to be beautiful, as did the world, but consummately clever as well. If he would be patient he knew that she and her counsellors would come to some ingenious scheme. Padmini, he was certain, would never give herself up to another, and certainly not to a Muslim. This would not only go against the will of herself but the strong tradition of their nation. He could afford to be patient. He was certain that his wife would be very wise and judicious in her handling of the matter.

Up in the fort there were at first for Padmini delineations of desolation in the thought of the current separation of herself and her captive husband. But this would do no good. She prized her honor and would remain ever chaste from the hands and body of any Muslim. She prayed for an answer. She would take as much time as necessary to do the right thing, whatever that might be. Prayer must be deliberate. Padmini reentered her private temple, not emerging until a satisfactory plan had been set firmly in her mind. It was, to say the least, extremely imaginative, ingenious.

It would do Khilji good to think that perhaps Padmini was slowly weakening in the days which would follow. As for her husband, she was sure he would be reasonably well fed and cared for. Khilji would not dishonor his name with anything lacking in virtue. It would not serve his hellish purpose to harm Ratan Singh, at least not until Padmini was safe within his grasp, and that she monastically vowed would never be.

On the morrow she revealed her crafty plan to the thakurs, their jagirs and her counsellors and constructed a message to be sent by horseman to the encamped Emperor.

"I shall, at your request, come to your campsite to free my husband," the message started. "But I can only come in a style and manner befitting my high station in life. I shall therefore be accompanied in due course by 700 of my princesses, friends and maid-servants. We shall arrive in our palanquins, at which time you shall release my husband, His Highness the Rawal Ratan Singh, ruler of Mewar. I trust this will be in complete accord with your thinking. Awaiting your reply."

The Emperor saw no harm in such an arrangement for she was indeed beautiful, a queen of an intriguing kingdom, and certainly entitled to such an entourage. Had she saddled a horse and ridden to him in subjugation, much of Allaudin's desire for her would have dissolved. She remained an admirable adversary, an intelligent woman. Being in love with her husband, as he suspected, she reacted as he expected, save for the huge number of ladies and servants accompanying her. Not to worry. He would quickly dispense with the theatrics.

Padmini wasted no time in having the 700 palanquins readied, each strong and securely covered with lovely cloths. At first the people of the fort thought her mad until the time came that she disclosed the entire story. When a week had passed and it was time to leave for the Emperor's camp Padmini ordered each of the 700 hand-picked men to seat himself inside the conveyance. They were the very staunchest and bravest of all the warriors. Every palanquin was carried by six men, all of whom dressed in disguise and wore their arms well hidden on their persons.

The trek was slow. Padmini was in one of the lead sedan chairs seated with her uncle, as aide and personal protector. When the march was over the envoy/uncle advised in a majestically ceremonious manner that both he and Queen Padmini wished once more to see Ratan Singh to assure themselves he was safe and well and to say a final farewell before she could join the Emperor on the road to Delhi.

Padmini's expected wish was courteously granted. The 700 jumped from their hiding places and with the 4,200 men who had borne them they fought a courageous duel. During the conflict Padmini and her husband made it to the safety of their fort, as did some of the others but the losses were extremely high.

Allaudin Khilji also escaped injury for it would have been the place of no one but the Maharana to slay him. He returned to Delhi an embittered man. Twice he had been foiled. First, he could not closely lay eyes on the woman he was now more than ever determined to own, and secondly, she outwitted him with her clever scheme. True, she was devious, but this he laudably admired in any person, so long as he could control that person. She would be his. He would return with a stronger force and plan of action and whatever the cost, Padmini would accompany him on his triumphant reentry into Delhi. He would have his day.

Tediously the remaining months of the year dragged on. Dipping deeper into his coffers Khilji prepared an army large enough to win this next year. Many more elephants were at his disposal and he ordered thousands more to fight at his side. There would be no thought given to defeat. By January, 1303 he had again come within the shadows of Chittorgarh.

The savage Mughal attack this time was not to be repulsed. It seemed virtually impossible for the Mewaris to retain their fort, valiant as they were. This time the gods seemed to have reversed the pendulum and once again it appeared there was nothing Rani Padmini could do ... or was there?

Months back she refused to be taken by the Emperor, submitting to the will of the Mughals. Nor did she want the other females of her land tainted. She prayed there would never be such submission of bodies whatever the generation or century. If the Emperor and his marauding army gained her precious fort she knew the Mughals would lay waste to all within it and defile the bodies of the females. Padmini was a strong, virtuous woman and the ladies and children of her kingdom always dreamed of following her in whatever footsteps they could. Their divine chance had come.

Padmini devised the bizarre act of johar, ordering the old men and young boys of the fort to bring whatever kindling they could. She then sent word throughout the fort to all ladies and girls to follow her, to bathe and dress in their wedding gowns or finest clothes. To the last female they did as she suggested. As her disciples the wisdom of her plan was unquestionable. They would all retain honor and virtue.

Bodily cleansed, Padmini spiritually left for her private temple and prayed, later to emerge singing hymns of rejoicing, trailed by the women and girls. Triumphantly they marched to the spot where she had the firewood piled high, herself lighting it and throwing her body into the flames to die in this act of self-immolation, and to live in heaven, attaining it first in order to greet her husband when he would soon thereafter arrive. Ten thousand women and girls flung themselves atop this reverential pyre.

While she and the others had been preparing themselves for the hereafter, the men dressed in their saffron death robes, fought fiercely and valiantly until Khilji, on his second arrival into the fort, found nothing but the smoldering ashes of his desired Queen Padmini and the others.

Padmini had won once again!

The gripping legend stirred Queen Mother more deeply now than at any other time. She entered the fort a day later, consumed by the greatness which was a part of her son's heritage. The ceremony which followed in the fortress was meaningful and commemorated not only the johar of Padmini but the subsequent two additional times in Mewar's history this same brave act took place. But now Queen Mother must still come up with her own spectacular event.

Johar was the only subject of discussion in the last two days among all of the members of Bhim Singh and Queen Mother's party. Nina caught sight of Narendra resting beneath a dhao tree among some of the police force brought along to protect the royal family. She walked to him unmindful of speaking in public when the subject was less than personal. In fact it made the pair appear as casual sister/brother.

"What would you have done, Narendra, if I had been your sister or wife in that day long past, and you returned safe from a battle to find that I had not immolated myself with our queen. Would you forgive me? What would truly be your feelings? Think on it."

With a furrowed brow he stared at her for but a brief moment, replying, "No, I could not forgive such a thing. I would disown you. I would probably send you from my house and into the outside world with a few paise for food. You would have to make your own life. You would be a disgrace to me. I could not live with that."

Among this group of men there was but one alone who said he could forgive his wife such a thing. But Narendra was so firm in his immediate reaction to her question that she turned and walked away. He was so gentle at times, so forceful at others.

Once inside the fort Nina was not allowed to attend the sacred ceremony and unable to learn much of what actually took place. But in her own way she could bless the women and children who had been so courageous as to die for their country in this manner, rather than be taken as slaves or concubines into the homes of the invaders. Her feelings on the matter were quite mixed. She would think on it further some other day. Today she wished to forget the johar and bask in the freshness of the warming sun. It was not necessary that her blood remain pure, and she would have no offspring anyway.

As for Bhim Singh, young as he was he knew the story of his country did not end with Padmini's death and he questioned his tutor on this point after the venerable ceremony.

"Picture if you will," Hari Lal started, "a triumphant monarch riding majestically into this magnificent palace after fighting for two years to gain it. He would be tired. He would have had losses. And most of all he would want to collect his biggest prize. To find only her ashes prophetically staring back at him in sardonic mockery must have been a frightful thing for him to bear. Where were his spoils of war?" Hari Lal asked, putting the child's brain to work. "Would you not be violently angry?

"He drew out his sword, slashing at everything and everybody. To have been outwitted was a sobering thing; to be egregiously outwitted now by this same female was a thousand times worse, and just when he thought he had won all.

"He ordered his men to do like him, ravage and avenge. Thirty thousand Hindus were viciously killed. And as if that wasn't enough he ordered all these once lovely buildings around you here to be destroyed."

"I don't understand why he'd ruin the place if it was now his. That doesn't make any sense."

"It made sense to him. His capitol was in Delhi and it was the aim of Muslims for centuries to conquer as much of India as they could and spread their vast holdings to even greater reaches. They wanted to dominate this part of the world and also they wanted to decrease the Hindu population. Besides personal lust there is another reason they wanted all those women. The blood of their offspring would not be true Hindu blood. They would buy or steal as many of the lovely princesses of the royal houses of Rajputana as they could and that is why your ancestors have been so careful not to donate to their cause. To take our women was only one way to drain the strength of us Hindus, but we could not tolerate anything except a pure blood line. So remember always, Your Highness, as you rule Mewar, we have never yet ever sold any of our princesses or queens into the slavery of a Mughal empire. We would never defile our bloodline, for the blood of a Rajput is ever of primal importance. If you forget everything else you have ever learned, never forget this point. Respect and protect your bloodline."

"I will," promised little Bhim Singh, "but you did not tell me. Did Khilji stay here to live without Padmini or not. What happened after that in Chittor?"

"Life for him was temporarily darkened and he let his son Khizara Khan stay. The fort was in his care and he could do with it what he would."

"But we came to rule here again. I don't understand what happened."

"Khizara Khan remained for some years but eventually he too became bored and so he gave it to someone else. When the Rawal and his family had died that strain of your ancestors ended and from then on it stemmed from the Shishoda. Your older brother was named after Hamir I and it was he who took back the fort in 1326. They called him 'Rana' which means 'king' and so we now use the title 'Maharana' which therefore means the 'king of kings.' You must ever be proud of this title, Your Highness.

Chapter 8

Nestling in the cradle of Mewar's history, Hari Lal begged the regent to remain longer at Chittorgarh, the better for little Bhim Singh to absorb his lessons. Once again Nina managed to wangle near the spot where pupil and teacher sat briefly running down the accounts from the time of Padmini until Bhim Singh's own reign.

"I believe you remember the story of Hamir I." Hari Lal commenced early on that sunny day, "When Padmini's husband was desperately fighting for his fort he managed to send Arsi safely through enemy lines to ensure that someone from his family would remain alive to later rule. Arsi was not his own son but that of Laxman. Arsi eventually had a son, our first Hamir.

"After our fort was recaptured it was rebuilt with money which came in part from the Zawar mines of zinc and silver. Maharana Lakha managed that. Today, Your Highness, I do not expect you to remember names and dates of your predecessors, but rather I wish to highlight some of the events which preceded you. Another time we will go over infinite details. Call today's lesson a panoramic picture, if you will.

"Now to get on with it, you'll learn in greater detail some day how a joke was to become a serious matter and the many twists of fate, all due to the very simplest remark. That was during the time of Rana Lakha but the story of his son Chonda is in some respects even more important, and the joke caused the next in line to be Maharana Mokal instead of Chonda. I make a strong point here that you must learn to always curb your tongue. I'll quickly jump past Mokal and Chonda for reason's I'll not go into. Mokal had seven sons, the oldest of which was the illustrious Kumbha who became ruler in 1433. It was his monstrously large palace in which you sat yesterday," Hari Lal continued.

"My favorite," said the child.

"Well, it was this ruler, Kumbha, who was responsible for building other wonderful forts. Kumbhalgarh, with its majestic palaces, temples and chhatris and view of Mewar's desert is the largest and greatest fort; and then the lovely one at Abu. And yesterday you also visited the Victory Tower, Kirti-Stambh. Did you not walk up it?"

"Yes, my legs got tired. It's nine storeys high!" It was obvious he had been paying attention. "But it's very pretty," he added.

"Indeed it is, Your Highness. I've climbed it with your grandfather many times. Not only are the carvings lovely but it tells us in great detail about all the religions in India, not just ours," the tutor explained. "And now when you stand within the temple grounds of Eklingji you have Rana Kumbha to thank for the mandapam in front of the altar, the magnificent wall around it; surely the most beautiful wall in the world. His greatness will long be remembered. Not only did he fight many battles to conquer new places but he brought to our land many works of art, likewise finding time to read and write both plays and poems. Remember him, if you will, for a combination of these many things. I shall become repetitious over the years but I will impress upon you the wonders of your forebears.

"Then, Your Highness, comes one of my personal favorites. I hope he will become one of yours also. In 1509 Maharana Sangram, or Sanga as he was usually called, took the helm." Hari Lal glanced down at his student who was beginning to look lethargic. He was soon to lose him as a listener. Hari Lal opted to become more dramatic.

"You know sire that you have a very definite edge on most other rulers. Some reached their thrones at much older ages, not always knowing they would one day become ruler. Rana Sanga was 27 when he first sat on the gaddi, full of vim and vigor, having been forced in his earlier years to live out in the fields, a far more difficult life than the comforts of a palace."

Kirti-Stambh was built approximately 1000 years ago and dedicated to Adinath, the first Jain Thirthankar. It is 76 feet tall, climbed by a narrow staircase through its delicately carved interior.

"Why did he have to live like that, my teacher?"

"He had a brother by the name of Pritha Raj who wanted him dead. To escape from him it was necessary that he roam year after year through forests and desert trying always to be undetected. He would not want anyone to learn his identity and somehow tell of his presence in fear it would reach his terrible brother. He would dress very plain and eat whatever he could find or he'd take small jobs to earn the money for food."

"But he was a prince," young Bhim Singh roared. "Such things are beneath our station. Why should I not be ashamed of him?" The young child was not certain whether to commend or condemn his ancestor.

"One must learn humility, my son. And besides, when one is hungry one is willing to try almost anything. We all must eat, you know. There is a time when one must stifle one's pride. And absolutely everything is not known of these years but it has been told how he would wander futilely and aimlessly.

"But then came an interesting bit of Mewari mythology when history repeated itself. Sanga was one day sleeping underneath a banyan tree. A large cobra crawled from its resting place near the tree stump and waved its crest back and forth over Sanga's head. And on that snake's head a bird came to perch. A goatherd saw this phenomena and of course you know what that symbolizes."

"It means that he is a king, a Rana," the lad stated unequivocally.

"Yes, the goatherd prophesied that this was to be another ruler and the prophesy came true. Some time later Sanga took the throne of his father. Remember what I told you they called him? The 'lion of battle.'"

"That's a funny name. Is it good or bad?" Deep in his being little Maharana Bhim Singh wanted to admire and revere each of his ancestors although he was constantly made aware by the astute Hari Lal there were those who left much to be desired, Vikramaditya for one.

"As I've told you hundreds of times, there are countless mythological stories written by our Hindu bards all down through the ages and some must be regarded as mythology while many more are factually true. As an example, there is a story of an incarnation of one of the lesser gods who came to Chittor. Rana Sanga knew who he was and welcomed him. He stayed a long time in the fort and when the day came for him to depart he handed Rana Sanga a talisman."

"What is that?"

"A kind of good luck charm. He instructed Sanga to wear it at all times and that it never, never must slip away from the front of his chest. If he would do this always he would have good luck against all his enemies. Over and over he stressed this point to the Rana for he feared the admonition would be taken too lightly and if his instructions were not followed the Rana would forget and his good luck would come to an end. He liked the Rana and he wished for his continuing good fortune and a still better way of life for all the Mewar subjects."

"You spoke sometimes about superstitions, Hari Lalji. How is it we can decide when something is superstition and when it is something real?" The child king was at times like these showing a great maturity growth and his guru thought a moment before replying.

"There is a very fine line between many things in life, child, and I suppose this must be one of them. It is wisely said that even in sanity and insanity one cannot actually tell when another crosses the line from one side to the opposite. Regarding superstition, I do not think we can regard it too lightly for it is extremely unwise to goadingly tempt fate. Fate frivolously maps our destiny and who would like to rattle that which is to carry us through life? Life at best can be quite difficult. No need to make it worse."

The subject was cumbersome for a pre-teen, Hari Lal wisely dropping it as soon as possible and getting back to the story. "It is said further that the old sage allowed the Rana to test him and the talisman, offering ideas which were strange but sure to prove the object's powers. The Rana put the charm to several tests, trying to call the old man's bluff, but always the strange feats would be achieved to the complete amazement of Sanga. There was nothing else to do but believe the old man. The Rana must have thought him something of a magician."

"What happened to the Rana? Can I have the talisman, too? Where is it?" Certainly the child wanted every conceivable way of making his rule and his life easier. If it was good enough for mighty Sanga, surely it was good enough for him.

"We do not know what became of it, Your Highness. There is no talisman available now except for what you yourself make of your life through good deeds and actions. You must become the master of your own destiny and to accomplish this you must learn the ways of many in the past, then pick and choose what is best for you. There is much time spread before you and we trust your foundation is becoming a firm and strong one.

"As for Sanga, we are all extremely proud of him. The talisman continued to protect his life, and apparently in the back of his mind were always those words of the old man that he was never to let the charm move from his breast. But there were many fierce and awful battles in his lifetime. Sultan Ibrahim of Delhi, a viciously cruel monarch, had all his troops in revolt. Rana Sanga knew of him and his misdeeds and would liked to have been his Nemesis. It was a joy to many when mighty Babar came from Kabul and won his victory over Delhi.

"When this happened the Mewaris asked Rana Sanga to rid the Muslims from their midst ... all who remained. They had long been killing our revered cows and desecrating our shrines and temples. They knew Sanga would not run away from trouble or battle and had full faith that he would lead them into a victorious war. We were strong in numbers at that time and records show he took 80,000 with him into the fields, including over a hundred high ranking sub-rulers from our feudal kingdom."

Even Narendra had been sitting in on today's stories, recalling his own grandfather telling of his forebear riding into this battle and returning safely. From generation to generation his story was told with chest-swelling pride. Narendra had always thrilled to the thought of being born into this kingdom. "Five hundred elephants they took into battle," Narendra hesitatingly added from his vivid recollection of his grandfather's tale.

"Yes," answered Hari Lal, "and always the Rana fought hard alongside his men, giving the impetus they needed. At one point the ruler wanted to bathe and rest beside a stream. Possibly he was battle-weary, but it is said that the talisman swung around and when he felt it touch his back a cold calculating sense of doom swept over his frame. Would failure now be his? Was an enfolding death sweeping out toward him on this very day? Why had he forgotten to be more careful?

"The battle that ensued was apparently something to behold. This Babar, the Mughal emperor and descendant of Genghis Khan, was clever in the craftsmanship of warfare. He brought with him gun carriages and wagons, clumping them together to create a tremendously strong front. Trenches were dug, and a horrendous cannon which could shoot perhaps sixteen times in one day. Needless to say this made Babar a formidable foe.

"A king in his own right since the age of 11, he had fought many battles. There were countless things which paralleled the life of Babar and our Rana Sanga. Both men had been exiled from their father's homes. Both had lived with herdsmen. On two different occasions Babar had gained the throne of Samarcand. He was physically strong and exceedingly proud and boastful. He'd run around the grounds carrying strong men under each arm.

"He enjoyed writing and keeping notes of all the things he did. When he came to Hindusthan the land was so strangely different to him. He'd make notes on the types of trees, other vegetation and fruits. He'd try all of them. I wonder sometimes if there was ever anything which did not interest him. Even the 'Infidel' as the Mughals called us. How they hated our so-called idolatry."

But the young Highness was near hysterics picturing this gruesome emperor-foe and two men who must surely be kicking and squealing under his arms as he'd race around the camp. Bhim Singh for the moment could not think of anything else. Laughter had not come easily these last few serious days. "Some day I'll be big and strong, just like Babar," boasted the child when the convulsions subsided.

"I'd personally prefer you'd emulate the strong in heart and body from our bloodline, Your Highness," the teacher scowled. He continued, "Even so, he did have his good qualities, aside from his Herculean strength. He loved fine horses and rode them well. Always he was conscious of others, whether friend or foe, and give verbal recognition to them.

"And certainly there could be no braver or more honorable foe than our Rana Sanga. As Babar looked across the battlefield to his enemy, in spite of Sanga having one eye plus scores of other wounds, he was held in some degree of awe by Babar.

"Now remember, Highness Bhim Singh, this was considered by both sides to be a holy war. The Rana and other Rajputs naturally prayed for victory over those who had previously broken down their temples and defiled their altars. I repeat that through the centuries it was the custom and habit of the Muslims to deface any God or creature within or carved on the outside of temples. Never would they allow such a thing to remain intact. It deeply hurt the souls of all us Rajputs to have our gods and goddesses so dishonored.

"And on the other side of the scale, the Mughals prayed to their god to win over the 'idolaters,' for they could never accept the thought of idolatry."

"You always say that word. What does it mean?" asked the youngster.

"It means worshipping an idol, our statues of gods and goddesses. They believe it is the stone figure we worship and this they cannot believe in, so they deface them," the tutor explained, proceeding, "For almost a fortnight they were camped opposite each other. Babar kept very complete memoirs, as I stated and in it is written that he would repent and give up drinking wine, for the Muslims are not supposed to drink. Some say he had all the wine brought to him and when it came he spilled it onto the parched ground.

"And now, Maharana Bhim Singh, comes the big lesson of the month, something so extremely important that I would like you as a ruler to always remember. Before this time the army of Babar was very dejected. If an army remains in this state or condition it is well nigh impossible for them to win a war or fight well. One day, sire, you may look up the actual words in the voluminous notes Babar recorded from his own pen. The story to his men was to the effect that only God is immortal and that we must all pass away to another life. If this be so, then we must fight our best fight. His speech was apparently far more stirring than my small rendition, for it stirred his men to a brilliant battle. It is said they each had sworn on the holy Koran that they would either conquer or die.

"On Saturday, March 27, 1527, they fought the battle which decided the fate of our beloved Rajasthan. It was fought differently. There was his cannon, of course. But never before had the emperor faced a charge such as had been brought on by our Rajput horsemen.

"I've told you many times that a Rajput fears not death, and astride their horses they rushed down upon their enemy. So many in number were Sanga and his men, and so eager to win, there was little the Emperor's men could do against this onslaught. Probably Sanga wondered at this point whether the warnings about the talisman could be true with things going this well for him. But then the dreaded cannon boomed in their midst, the Rajputs not able to judge where it would hit. Still, their forces were not too bad off.

"But history repeated itself once again. So often through the ages, as in many nations, there was a traitor in Sanga's midst. A Tonwar chief took 35,000 horses and men and quite suddenly, for what reason is not known, and joined the side of the Mughal emperor. With this traitorous act it left the others fighting haphazardly.

"He had fought scores of battles throughout his entire lifetime, some lengthy and a few which were relatively short. The big fight with the Emperor lasted but a few short hours, but was long enough for Sanga to have his left arm cut off with a sword and for an arrow to pierce one of his knees which left him lame. Those were just a few of his eighty wounds.

"Luckily Rana Sanga and some others were able to escape. He swore that he would make the fields in which he had just fought his capitol until he would be able to regain the fort of Chittor. A year later he was found dead and it was questionable by what means his death came, for some said it was through poison and others felt it was a broken heart, not having <u>re</u>gained Chittor after all.

"Meanwhile, Emperor Babar, with much glee and personal pleasure, wrote in his notes how he heaped high the skulls of the 'infidels.'"

The little Bhim Singh had long sat in rapt attention, now not even venturing to take his eyes from the withering face of Hari Lal.

"Rana Sanga died at a time when his wife was pregnant," the teacher continued. "She was thus forbidden to commit sati. When her baby boy, Udai, was born she gave him to another woman to raise and led 13,000 ladies to commit johar, just as Padmini had done. It was the second sacking of Chittorgarh, for as the last of the ladies heaped themselves upon the spreading flames the men opened our gates and battled the enemy to the death. Although we lost the war, our soldiers attained heaven where their wives awaited them."

"And the third sacking?" Bhim Singh was eager for the grizzly news.

"It was much later — in 1568. Another battle had gone on for just short of five months. Food was running short. They could not hold out much longer. The enemy was well fed, had plenty of water, thousands of men, and destined to win. Our ladies remembered their honorable history and sat soberly discussing what it was they should do. This time nine queens, five princesses and over a thousand women ascended the funeral pyre, the third sacred rite of johar and the third sacking of Chittor. And each of these johars we again consecrated with our services here yesterday."

"Will I grow up to be as great as Sanga, Hari Lalji?" the boy whispered to his tutor.

"Only time will tell us. I am not a sage or prophet, but only a teacher. Keep studying what has passed and you will come to know what might one day be. We can never know what the future holds for us nor who our friends and enemies will be. Do remember that even in defeat we have treated our enemies with respect. Rana Sanga is a shining example of this also. In spite of the sometimes vicious and savage deeds, there was a time for man to display his humanity toward other man. After the war with Sultan Mahmud, Rana Sanga and 50,000 of his men managed to capture the Sultan, leaving many men dead on that battlefield. For three months the Rana kept him a prisoner at his fort and at times the men would sit and talk as if the best of friends.

"Never would it have been possible for the Sultan to complain about his treatment as a prisoner. The Rana had been fair and just in these months, acknowledging the Sultan's high station in life. But by now that Rana's wounds were healing and one day he sent a bouquet of flowers to the Sultan. The Sultan roared something to the effect that a man can give a gift as a superior to another superior. He refused to accept the flowers.

"The Rana made light of the incident and told him this was but one of other gifts to follow. The man was appeased and finally accepted them, and was then allowed to return to his kingdom, but only after the Rana extracted from the Sultan the expenses of the costly war. Surprisingly, the Sultan added to this a very costly crown and belt which were covered with numerous precious gems.

"But the Rana felt ill at ease with all this and was not about to be easily tricked. It was decided he would keep the son of the Sultan as a royal hostage to ensure good behavior on the part of the Sultan. Yet, in another act of honor he sent with the Sultan 1000 Rajput soldiers to see that he was safely returned to his throne at Mandu.

"You will read of this generosity in endless books for it never failed to amaze the Muslim historians, story tellers and poets who would write of it freely. Back at your own library in Udaipur, Your Highness, are many accounts of this same story."

The child kept his attention on Sanga. "So you think he's the greatest of our heroes, teacher?"

"Only one of them. But can you imagine a man who by the time he died carried 80 wounds in his body? How brave can one man be?"

Young Maharana Bhim Singh had no desire to be that badly mangled. "How many Ranas are there between Sanga and me? I know I am the 67th."

"Quite right. And he was the 50th. He died in 1528. His son Ratna ruled for only four years. He was killed by the Rao of Bundi but he likewise killed the Rao. And then came another of Sanga's brothers, Vikramaditya."

"He preferred the rougher people like prize fighters and wrestlers; he liked the people of low castes," his mother interjected.

"But you like Nina and she is of a low caste," he argued, reddening as he caught sight of Nina sitting nearby, listening.

"Nina is quite different, Bhim Singh. She may be born of a lower caste but she is a very fine person. I believe heaven must have made some sort of mistake and placed her with the wrong parents," she answered, nodding to the girl with a beaming smile.

Hari Lal returned to his lesson. "Our next Maharana was Udai Singh II. Our Udaipur was founded in 1559 and eight years later came the last siege and sacking of Chittor. Emperor Akbar was responsible for that."

"Why wasn't Udai also killed? You keep telling me of the thousands who die on the battleground, but there is always another Maharana to take over."

"Yes, Highness. In this case he abandoned the fort early in the siege, taking himself to safety down south into Gujrat's Rajpipla Hills. And we must never forget that wonderful woman who saved his life and the other woman who raised him from infancy. They are all real heroes of our land. Everyone who helped is a hero.

"Very next is our special Maharana Pratap Singh. You asked before if Sanga was my favorite. I revere him for all that he did for our kingdom. I sympathize with him and applaud him for boldly carrying on for so many years while inflicted with those eighty wounds. Still it must be Pratap who was the very greatest of all our dynasty. He had solemnly vowed to take back Chittor from Akbar and for twenty-five years he worked so hard to attain this goal. Often his family had told how he would feed them fruits from the hills." Hari Lal was thoroughly enjoying this day. His student had become seriously attentive as the tales wore on, completely impressed by his predecessors and probably trying desperately to decide which of them to emulate.

Maharana Pratap Singh, 65th ruler, from 1572 to 1597.. (Photo of a painting by Raja Ravi Verma located in the Maharana Arvind Singh's dining room, the Main Palace, Udaipur.)

"Hari Lalji, why does that suit of armor that Rana Pratap's horse Chetak wore look so funny?"

"The mail turns up to look like a great elephant tusk, doesn't it?" he replied. "This they hoped would startle the other horses on the battlefields, thinking Chetak to be an elephant rather than a horse, because for one thing Pratap's opponent rode an elephant. The battle of Haldi Ghat is the most special battle of our twelve centuries of reign, beyond any doubt. And now that you can read better, if you will walk up the steps into Jagdish Temple outside your palace gates you can read two verses which describe this battle. Verses 41 and 42. It's about how with his dagger in his hand he got into a fight and how he shattered the enemy and they fled away.

"But our poor Rana was wounded in this battle, as was his horse Chetak. Although it carried him further after being wounded, he was tiring rapidly. He came to a stream and those who chased the Rana had to swim as they could not take their elephants across the waters. This allowed more time for the Rana. In this couple of minutes grace period he heard another rider. He turned to see it was his brother Sakat Singh and thought this now was sure death. Pratap, his horse too near death to go further, could only stand and wait. When the Mughals crossed the river Sakat killed them. How stupendous. This was the same Sakat who had wanted his brother dead for so long and now he was coming to his aid. The younger brother asked forgiveness for the past."

"And what of the horse Chetak?" wondered the boy. He had always known it was a special hero of the kingdom.

"He fell dead at their feet and Sakat gave his brother his own horse to ride."

"But those were just battles like any other battles, weren't they? He doesn't sound that special to me, compared to some," Bhim Singh argued.

"What you do not realize," answered Hari Lal, extremely patient with the boy, "is that he was a true patriot. Not only would he not yield to Akbar but in fighting for his rights there were times when he had to retreat to the hills. I told you he sometimes had to feed his family only berries from the bushes. When in the hills the Bhils once more came to the rescue of the Rana as they had done off and on for centuries. They fed and took care of their other needs. Much of our lands he got back. He would not give in to Akbar, even retreating when it was necessary, returning another day to win. His name is revered most."

Narendra interrupted a reverent silence which followed Hari Lal's magical tales, fearful of treading on sanctified grounds. Hari Lal had become a peerless teacher, yet from the dark long-forgotten recesses of Narendra's mind the old man tugged and pulled to the forefront of his thoughts those unexpurgated legends he too had learned from father and grandfather. Narendra began, "There is another tale which tells of the Raja of Bikaner who once heard of a silly rumor that Pratap was going to submit to Akbar. He was so distressed by this news that he wrote something to the effect 'Pratap calling Akbar as his Emperor is as unbelievable as the rising of the sun in the west.' Some such thing he said, indicating there could be no truth to the rumor."

Hari Lal nodded for him to go ahead with the story.

"Pratap sent a message back swearing that 'By the grace of God Eklingji, Pratap would always call the Emperor a Turk, that the sun would always continue to rise in the east.'"

"That's a dumb story, Narendra Singhji," the lad replied, unaffected by it.

"Not really, Your Highness," Hari Lal took over the conversation. "It was the way of both men to stress the fact Rana Pratap could never in any way consider allegiance to the Mughal. He would remain ever stalwart, never giving in. It makes us extremely proud to be who we are."

There came at this point another lengthy silence. Even Hari Lal sat with a lump in his throat. The quiet continued until finally he chose to wind down his discourse in this manner: "It was Amar Singh who ruled next and he vowed the Maharanas themselves would never attend the Mughal courts.

"Some years later Rana Raj Singh took the gaddi and it was at that time Emperor Aurangzeb wanted to destroy the idols and you remember how Shri Nathji was carried about the countryside, no other kingdom wanting to harbor the lovely image because they feared war with the Mughals. Raj Singh not only allowed it to come within our boundaries, but you sat before it at Nathdwara with your mother but a few evenings past. The Rana also hated the Jazia tax levied on the poor people, already heavily taxed. But we shall get into those details at a later time.

"And now, Your Highness, I think you should take rest. I would beg your leave and will see you tomorrow." He arose without awaiting permission, throat parched, body and mind weary, old eyes heavy in the heat of the day.

Chapter 9

Loyalty is a trait worth preserving and none deserve its crown more fittingly than Panna. Queen Mother would not be able to pull off with equal magnitude her feat or that of Padmini. And perhaps escaping sati at her husband's death in favor of raising Hamir and Bhim to reign would hold no real merit.

Long ago the servant Panna worried about the progression of the kingdom, unaware she was fated to help. Always alert to danger, she knew of Banbir who ambitiously wished to gain the throne of Mewar and tried various methods of diabolically disposing of the boy. On one particular night Banbir stole into the innermost portion of the palace in which Panna had been wet nursing the child. Palace spies were many but among them were those loyal to the little heir, Udai Singh. It was thus that Panna came to hear of Banbir's stealthy climb into the zenana. She was able with the help of another loyal woman, Bari, to place Udai in a basket such as seen throughout the palace and village kitchens. Bari and Panna were of a low caste and had the same innate desire to protect the young babe. Walking innocently, basket covered with a tie and dye cloth on swaying hip, bunches of grapes draping from its side, Bari spirited the royal infant away from its home.

If Banbir had even noticed Bari he would have thought nothing of her, the basket, or leaving the zenana, a common sight. He reached the room in which Panna sat, asking gruffly, "Where is the child Udai Singh?" Panna hesitated as if in great fear, playing her part well, careful not to overact, and then pointed as if reluctantly to the swinging cradle near her. In it was her own little child, dressed in the Rana's lovely clothes and sleeping peacefully. Banbir hideously stabbed him, thinking him indeed to be little Udai.

It took time for the two courageous women to meet. Panna was careful not be followed, and at long last she came upon Bari, some distance from Chittorgarh, in the westerly direction which Bari had said she would travel. For a long time they moved about together over treacherous countryside, trudging afoot through tiger and leopard country, over ragged rocks, through tangles of underbrush, crossing streams. They were extremely careful not to leave any tracks for many days beyond the fort.

Queen Mother knew they must have been frightened many times, not knowing if and when they'd have to cope with cobras or jackals, afraid to sleep at night in the wilds. Nor was it hard for the Rani to guess at the grievous heaviness of Panna's heart, having sacrificed her only child and just as suddenly becoming a surrogate mother. Cold and dreary chambers of her heavy heart must have been unbearable, yet she continued on the unknown path with her companion Bari.

Avoiding the main traffic patterns it was a long time before they found refuge. Even the feudal lords of such places as Dungarpur and others of Mewar refused them admission, knowing that to harbor little Rana Udai Singh would mean disaster from a vengeful Banbir. The pair finally came upon a Jain lady in one of the fortresses who joyfully gave sanctuary to the child. Deep faith told the Jain that Udai Singh would live to rule, as indeed he did.

Queen Mother knew she too must retain such faith in herself to keep the kingdom whole and sound, and continued to ponder on it. In a few days her stalwarts would be leaving her at the Udaipur palace. Narendra would soon return to his beautiful though less intimate Kala. As for Nina, she was disposed to a lengthy, hot summer of dreary days and tearful nights. but not until she and Narendra would once more meet.

Narendra had asked Nina to go to Mira Bai's temple in the fort when the sun is getting ready to set. Her repressed heart quickened in impassioned longing for the nearness of this man. Lord, so many hours yet until dusk. Her day was dominated by anxiety and the sad burden of doubt. Doubt about whether she would advance her love and whether, in his terms it would be helpful or hurtful. From the day she realized her love for him until she would eventually lay upon her own pyre she felt certain there would never again be a man with whom she would make love. Kala was not justifiably worthy of the hurt that would come to her if ever she were to learn of any affair. Nina's moral standards knew it was not right, yet she did not know how weak would be her flesh next time she stood against the warmth of Narendra's rugged body. There was an eleventh hour compunction to remain in the servant's tent. If they ever did make love, tonight or any time in their lives, would she be forever stricken with remorse or uncontrollable guilt?

Hours were spent walking through wooded portions of the fortification. The more Nina pondered the possible calamitous consequences of this or future evenings and the role she would play in Narendra's life the more fretfully disgruntled she became.

Returning to the campsite, she stopped to play with toddlers sprawled on the warm ground, bare bottoms turned up to the sun. In the tender manner of all Indians she picked up one into her cuddling arms. There was always within Nina a motherly pang of regret that she would surely never have a baby of her own. Who was there who would marry her? Who to find her a husband? Her, now known as a "widow."

Nina too had known of Panna: how could a mother give up her child and to such a viciously murderous act? What courage to stand by and watch it happen! It was despicable of Banbir. To set the stage for the infant Rana's safety was amazing. Still, Panna successfully accomplished it. It obviously took a special person to revere the seat of the kingdom so much she would arrange that her own child be substituted in murder to save the ruler. "Oh, Panna," she said, almost aloud, "give me your strength that I might know what to do with my Narendra. He may not be a ruler but I love him as you didst your young king, your kingdom and your son."

Nina went to a well, drawing fresh water, washing face and hands. She tidied her hair as best she could, twisted her gagra around and set off for Mira Bai's little temple. Before entering she stopped momentarily in a small chhatri in which, she had been told, were the footprints of Mira Bai's guru. The swami had been a Harijan, an "untouchable." Standing beside his hardened prints she felt a new and keener sense of herself. If such an unquestionably saintly woman as Mira Bai could follow the acclaimed teachings of one theoretically low caste person, an untouchable shunned by so many, now she could understand Queen Mother accepting Nina not only as a faithful servant but as a friend. Rare as it was, it was not without precedent in this royal family.

Surprisingly, Narendra was already there in the shadows of the deity, painfully anxious for her anticipated arrival.

Through the long ordeal of the trip from Udaipur he had carefully avoided being alone with Nina. Each day brought a greater degree of longing for her private presence, though not quite in the same sense he had longed to rush home to his Kala in their first year of marriage. The raptures of his honeymoon were still in the forefront of his mind. With Kala he was the master of his home, her lord whom early on she pleased with kindness and affection. There had been much laughter; each day brought excitement. They had giggled together at the simple sight of a father dog playing coyly with his new litter, slapping his pups on their behinds, drawing them closer under his protective body. Everything had been genuinely fresh and new, beautiful and bright. Every day the sun had dazzlingly shone on their lives as if before their marriage the sun had not ever existed.

Now to Narendra there was a puzzling unfathomable stirring. Nina had cautiously rebuked him to be patient with his wife after her miscarriage. How long could he allow Kala to put him off in their private chambers? He dreadfully needed a solace which Nina could bestow. Ever-knowing Nina allowed him the freedom to be himself. They were friends in the true sense, certainly. Could Nina fill the foggy void? She came closer than anyone he knew. She entered the little temple and stood quietly at first barely noticing him in the somber shadow of the deity.

"Follow me, Nina. I have found a hollow where we can watch the moon pass cross the heavens." They reached a gnarled stump of a tree. In ribboned moonlight they could see it clearly for a minute, twists of knotholes changing shape as grey velvet clouds passed over the moon. Spellbound they watched the formations change from minute to minute, wandering shadows dancing ingeniously up and down the trunk. "I think the tree is talking to us, Nina," he chuckled.

"Is it asking us to sit? I think the old tree will protect us tonight, will it not?"

"I wonder what all this tree could tell us, Narendra Singhji, if it could but talk. It is so old and has seen so much. We can listen to the stories of Hari Lal and wise men, but who better to relate the tales than one who has really seen them. Perhaps in a future time the trees can come back and find a way to speak aloud to us so we can hear and understand and learn."

"Little one, you are a romantic at heart. What would you want the tree to tell us if it could? That Padmini sat beneath it with Ratan Singh and made love?"

"No. I think they would only have made love in his big palace. I cannot imagine anything else for them. No. If someone made love here it was a servant and one of the feudal lords who spirited her away from the confines of her quarters. Oh, no. Even that does not intrigue me. I would like to think of perhaps a chaprasi passing by, catching sight of another of a low caste, their body chemistry taking hold from afar, longing for a way to get to know each other. Or perhaps Panna rested her back against this tree when she was pregnant and dreamed of a happy future for her unborn child, never knowing she would place him in a position to be knifed to death. Narendra Singhji, I still cannot get over the kind of love that possessed that woman. I do not believe I would have been strong enough to give my beloved child to the knife of a villain, regardless of how much I loved my king or queen."

"It is a touching story, at the very least," Narendra said seriously. Then, in a lighter tone, "Right now I'd like a touching experience with you." Dancing shadows of the moon cast themselves demurely on the maiden, Nina, as he turned full front, clasping her curving shoulders tremulous with life. Warm gold of her early summer skin shone upward to delight his shining eyes. Inches from each other they remained and she came to anticipate pessimistically what might follow. The slightest touch of his hands and she knew she would be his if he'd but ask or take. Her uncultivated beauty did not elude Narendra and as with the first time he kissed her he again trembled inwardly though less perceptibly. Still, it did not escape her palpable senses.

She stood motionless. He saw a new loveliness in her face, charming angles distinctively different. Her composure confounded him. Nina neither pulled from him nor initiated another kiss. What was it she wanted? What did he want?

Her presence held him like a magnet, yet he could not get Kala completely from his mind. Impassively he seated himself against the gnarled tree, pulling her down beside him. Gently his arm reached around her, and gently his hand pressed her head against his shoulder. Compellingly winsome, it was becoming increasingly difficult to keep from making love. Her disarming simplicity became enchantment to Narendra.

Nina asked, "You must be anxious to return home? I hope you will find everything in better condition, Narendra Singhji."

He had not cared to be openly reminded of his wife, yet it was impossible to resent anything Nina ever did or said. "I am a little weary of this long trip, Nina. Unless Queen Mother wills it differently I shall see her safely to the palace and immediately leave for Jagatpur."

This time Nina knew it would be excruciatingly difficult without him near. Even on the days she did not catch a meagre glimpse of him, the knowledge of his closeness brought a spirit-piercing joy.

For Narendra there was also torment, still loving Kala, thinking of her daily, praying for the baby they both wanted, and lastly for the wisdom to successfully track and trace down the treacherous dacoits which had now become an obsession with him. And somewhere between the all-important matters of his life he found time to pray for the happiness of his friend Nina. She was very special in a hundred varied aspects. Suddenly he was aware of something he dreaded with a passion. He was in love with both women. He would try to keep it from Nina, but could he? She was so much more clever than he.

The night wind stirred in the mango trees and the poinciana. He could wait no longer, yearning for her kiss of youth which he would slowly train.

It was not until he was back in his tent that he realized how Nina must be hurting inside. Darling Nina. Always thinking of others. Always helpful. Certainly she had to know for her there was no real tomorrow. Yet Nina never complained. Earlier he had called her very special. She was every bit of that. How could one little commoner be so overflowing with the grace and goodness of a goddess? He had heard of mythical guardian angels of the Christians. Perhaps he had his own guardian goddess. Bless her for that.

Chapter 10

The Rani's intensified interest in Mewar's monumental background was even more heightened on her return from Chittorgarh. On entering the palace grounds she went immediately to the celebrated idol in the zenana which had once been in the possession of Mira Bai. News had come to her of more skirmishes between neighboring factions and it was to her pecuniary advantage to keep things peaceful. Neither her purse nor her temperament could countenance any major conflict now. Nor was she entirely sure every lord would remain loyal should real trouble break out, cleverly aware those who bowed the lowest could harbor devious dreams.

Although she did not frivolously seek the help of medicants as did Mira Bai, she did seek the help of the gods in prayer. She required the precious safety of her last son. Would he become one of those more illustrious heirs to the coveted throne? She prayed also for her own health. If Bhim Singh could not take control of the government at a reasonable age, she'd be compelled to steer Mewar's ship. Other queens before her had done their vicarious share. Was she pre-ordained to do likewise? With great effort she succeeded in placing a few trusted friends in strategic places in other forts within and outside her kingdom. No amount of care was too great.

Narendra had left for Jagatpur as he had said he would, immediately after reaching the palace, assuring himself first that all was well within the confines of the building itself. He and Nina avoided each other on the return trip, avoiding gossip. It was impossible to know how long it would be before they'd meet again. Now late April, the rain clouds entered more than just the heavens.

Queen Mother had grown sullenly moody and on a whim called for several artists, wanting to discuss part of their history which was to be put onto canvas. There are in the Mewari schools of painting those marvelous craftsmen able to depict the times, battles and picturesque countrysides. With remarkable skill each whisker on a man's face could be counted. Yet these are all miniatures, some pictures small, yet others immense.

Historians had written of the valorous acts of past generations. Mira Bai had her hymns to her lord. Architects left imperishable monuments dedicating all manner of glory. The Jain community entered into the arts with their magnificent temples and the Kirti Stambh in Chittorgarh with hundreds of figures on the tower.

So enamored of this heritage was the regent that she demanded a more comprehensive pictorial display for people of all generations to come visit, enjoy and study.

When the several artists arrived she summoned them to an open courtyard atop the palace where the breezes were more comforting. They had brought recent samplings of their work which she carefully viewed.

"I must insist that some of the most impressive stories of our land be put onto paper. I have here at court several persons prodigiously knowledgeable of our heritage. You are to listen carefully to each detail of the events they will be depicting so that your rendition can be as true to the story as we know it. Sumje?"

Queen Mother continued, "One of you must choose to do the battlefield at Gogunda. You will please to take notes. Now when his father died Jagmal took the throne. However the nobles were summoned and it was agreed that they were not satisfied with him. They therefore pulled him off the throne and seated Maharana Pratap. It is therefore considered that even in this kingdom of Mewar we have seen democracy in action. This was an unusual circumstance, and one that I personally find of lofty significance.

"For another painting I wish you to portray Maharana Pratap in the jungle without supplies for their meals. The Bhils and others got together bringing them figs and dates. The kindness and generosity was much appreciated by the Maharana and he asked that they sit and share the meal with him, although it is most unusual and improper to mingle with royalty.

"Your Highness, if I may speak?" one of the artists interrupted. She nodded approval. "I have had an idea for a very long time for a picture. With your permission I would desire to tell it to you."

"As you wish."

"It would depict the story of the long fight with many wounded men when the great Maharana Pratap told his nobles there was no reason why they should shed their blood for him. Did he not say to them that they might go? But what Rajput would abandon Maharana Pratap? So they told him no, they could definitely not leave him. I should like to paint them with their swords which they had laid down before themselves, symbolic of laying down their lives for him."

"It's indeed an excellent episode," the regent agreed.

Although Hari Lal was to have left for a well deserved rest after their safe arrival from Chittor, it was decided he would remain until fully rested, travel at his age being quite a strain. He joined the meeting late, bringing up a point he felt worthy of discussion. "The battles against the Mughals were lengthy and costly. When things looked particularly awful for Pratap the faithful treasurer of Mewar came through. He brought to the field the balance of their money and with it they were again able to secure the necessary arms, army and food. The treasurer was also a great man," Hari Lal added wistfully.

"You revere Pratap most of all our rulers?" an artist asked.

"Better than all the others," Hari Lal smiled.

Queen Mother interrupted, on her mind the distant future and preservation of the past. "Rajputs are chivalrous men. To illustrate this in one manner I wish a picture which shows the peasant girl after her capture. You know that she was presented to Maharana Amar Singh but he said that it is not our way to fight with the ladies, the war is with men. He subsequently ordered that she be sent back to her home with all the courtesies and respect accorded to her as it would be for any great lady. Do not therefore give her a look of sadness, for though this young peasant was in effect a prisoner, the Maharana was treating her like a princess. I'm sure that not even her wildest dreams would have conjured up such a noble gesture as my husband's predecessor accorded her. Let me see the face you have painted when it is completed. She must be surprized and thrilled."

Also in attendance at this meeting was Ramnathji, a noble extremely well versed in the history of the Mewaris — in fact, perhaps the most knowledgeable. Queen Mother asked that he give any other suggestions. He asked that they depict Pratap fighting the Mughal commander-in-chief who thrust his sword at the Maharana. So angry was Pratap that with one mighty overhead stroke of his sword he cut through his enemy's helmet, down through his body, through the body of the horse and right to the ground. "Such was the physical and spiritual strength of the Maharana. This is not a myth but written into our annals."

There were several minutes of discomfited silence in the aftermath of this amazing tale. Then Ramnathji continued, "Unfortunately Maharana Pratap's beloved horse Chetak was also mortally wounded in this battle. His younger brother quickly came to his rescue with another horse taken from a wounded enemy. Before mounting, Rana Pratap had the horse's armor removed from Chetak and replaced on his new mount. It is safely set aside in the palace when you are ready to paint it. We look upon it with reverence for as we touch this chain mail we are touching not only the spirit of our beloved Maharana Pratap but also the spirit of his brave horse who served him so well. There is not another horse in any history which was so beloved as Rana's Chetak."

The craftsmen took their leave with a quickened vigor. The work would be of superior quality, for their own sense of pride and to please their regent. They would be donating their time and talents while living here under her wing.

It was about this same time that Nina came to know more about Ramnathji. Hari Lal would be given safe escort to his home some seventy kilometers away. Ramnathji would remain close at hand to assist in details for the artists whenever necessary.

"Are you of Mewar?" Ramnath inquired one day of Nina with a slight smile.

"No." She dreaded the fact he might ask from where she had come. Although Narendra and she had contrived that old story, still it was not her nature to lie and whenever she could get by without replying to personal inquiries she did so with tremendous relief.

"There is a deep and abiding love in your heart for this kingdom, isn't there, Ramnathji? I can see it in your eyes when you speak eloquently of it and even in the way you walk. I saw you tie your turban one day and even that simple gesture was done with almost a prayerful attitude. In fact, Ramnathji, I do not think I have seen — not even in any of the nobles have I seen — the wondrous look that surrounds you. There is an aura about you. I do not know the words. I am not learned. But there is something most special as if you were a priest, a muni, a pious man who had just dropped from the sky, sent down by the gods to be among us," she said in awed wonder.

"You do me too great credit," he smiled. "I am merely a servant of the queen, one of the lesser feudal lords, though it is true I dearly love this heritage. Its legends are hard to believe. I would imagine that an outsider, someone far from our world, would find it difficult to believe all that has passed. We were and are unique."

"I would love to hear more epics, Ramnathji," she baited him.

"Perhaps some day." He wore his erudition gracefully.

Nina was grateful for having found another circumspect friend. The women of the zenana were still annoyed, unclear why she was favored. Resentment and exaggerated fear filled them all. Except for the Rani and Narendra's mother, whom she rarely saw, it appeared to Nina she was destined to have only male friends. She could be a true friend to Kala, but there was little chance Kala would stoop in that direction.

Open stretches of desert beyond the palace recorded 55 degrees Celcius in the overworked afternoon sun. Immensely thick walls of the palace kept the rooms from overheating but it also took alternating servants waving all manner of fans to keep the Rani and her Rana son reasonably comfortable. Queen Mother's favorite was the kus-kus mat lowered from a roof covering a select window. Topside, servants poured buckets of water across the kus-kus mat, its perfumed scent refreshingly cool. Soon they would be taking off for the monsoon palace, far less imposing but standing on the tallest peak of the Aravallis, certain to triumphantly capture whatever blessed breezes the gods should decide to send down. True, it was the marble palace in the lake which had the finest of creature comforts but the Rani would move into it only after her yearly visit to the hilltop residence where she could watch the sprawling countryside take on its new green growth.

Nina meanwhile, kept a close watch on the lesser important servants, impatient for a change of routine. She protectively covered her head from the direct sun, slowly walking to the fringe of Lake Pichola. There in the scrubby brush and small branching trees she followed the shade. Around to the western bank she strolled, dreaming of things which might have been, yet not allowing herself any pleasure of self pity. She had a good life here, far more than she deserved. What would happen to her after Queen Mother's death? She dared not think about it.

Nina sat on a short stump of a brittle tree, hacked away for kindling by the people of Udaipur. Although they sent their children faithfully scurrying about the streets and lanes of the city and beyond for each and every cow dung chip they could find. Carefully dried, it was a far better source of fuel than the spindly live limbs of the trees they were fast mutilating. Mother Nature was going to have to work mercurially rapid to replace what the people stole from her. Women sitting on their haunches within their tiny courtyards or doorways patted carefully the chips they were able to possess, flattening them against walls to dry in the frying sun, handprints deeply inset into the dark brown.

Three water buffalo wallowed in the edge of the fast sinking lake. Without good monsoons it appeared that by fall the queen and her court would be able to walk from her zenana on the mainland across a dry lake bed to Lake Palace. Long legged birds glided to landings on the backs of the water buffalo, turning their heads in all directions as if to see if more marauders would follow. The primitive buffalo were undistressed, black shiny horns dipping melancholically into the landlocked water. The birds found their evening meal in lice or pesky parasites on the buffalo's back. Large spoonbills came swooping in to rest nearby.

Farther beyond, toward the center of the lake, moved two well-defined objects which appeared as sticks with straight spines standing upright out of the water. Nina recalled the day she rode with the regent to the lake palace and seeing the same "sticks," reached innocently into the languid waters. The queen shrieked. So startled was Nina that she sat awkwardly trembling, hands in her lap. On rare occasions the queen had fits of temper and Nina wondered what it was she had done.

"What do you think you are doing, Nina?"

"Your Highness. I have distressed you. I'm sorry, but I don't know what I've done wrong." She stared into the eyes of the Rani.

"You stupid girl. Do you not know that those are poisonous snakes?" A shudder of horror and painful revolt ran through Nina's body, drawing herself into the smallest package she could make.

Then she heard the last remnants of the dhobis at their daily chores. Beyond Jagdish temple in the oldest part of the city which rolls down to Pichola Lake these people brought their clothing, beating it rhythmically against huge rocks placed at the water's edge. "How is it children never get bitten when they play in the water?"

"They are not spared, Nina, nor can I forbid them to swim. It would seem that the loud pounding of the dhobis in the early morning hours scares the snakes to the other ends of the lake. There are of course those children who have been bitten."

"Do they die, Your Highness?"

"No. While the venom is poison there have been those who by the grace of the lords have only been made ill and some temporarily paralyzed. It would be safe to say, therefore, that you should not court danger by trying to grab one of those 'sticks.'"

Nina knew also that nearby lived several alligators, though she had never been able to learn how they first got to this man made lake, not being indigenous to the territory.

She now waited until the sun sank behind Monsoon Palace high atop the overpowering hill before starting her long walk back.

When she could see nothing but scary shadows she thought of Narendra and the terror she first felt in Mandore. Cold shivers traversed her frame and then his booming voice strangled her breath.

She vividly recalled her torn gagra whipping fiercely around bare legs, dancing gruesomely back and forth to the shaking of her body, created less by fear than by activated anger of this man towering above her, the dagger held in his hand forced lengthwise against her fragile skin.

Counteracting stark fear was an unexplained sense of gentleness. Her fear had vanished almost faster than it arrived. Even from those very first voluptuous moments Narendra could not hide his true self from this astute reader of men. She vaguely recalled a story she heard as a child. It was of Sita and Ram. The details were somewhat fuzzy but she knew Ram wanted to show his love for the woman, Sita. He ripped open his chest with his hands, bearing his heart, so pure and unadulterated with love for her, so that she could see it and never doubt. Nina apparently had one similarity to Sita: she could see into Narendra's very being. Little escaped her.

Today her vision could not carry her to Jagatpur.

Had Kala outgrown the sadness of her miscarriage? Was she again able to become pregnant? Would she even try? For Narendra to be without the wife he loved in his bed was too harsh and cruel a punishment. She would pray that Kala would return to her old self. Good lord, Nina did not want him to start frequenting the places where he could lay with girls.

She thought he had been as close to making love to her as any man could come. Nina could have instigated a few moves and made it difficult for him to refuse, yet she could not resort to such a tactic. She wanted to. Oh god how she wanted to. But she could not.For him to sleep with Kala, yes, of course ... but none other. Several years had gone by since they first met, almost four in fact. What a strange life for a little girl born on a tiny farm, in love with a man who would be the feudal lord of a magnificent fort after the death of his father.

The monsoons were to come up any day now and Queen Mother, her son and a small party prepared to ride up to the top of that imposing hill beyond the west end of the lake. Nina rode on an unimposing wooden houda tied to the back of one of the work elephants. She was to hold a few of the regent's little treasures. It was a fun ride, at least near the palace, Nina enjoying the boisterous laughter of wholesome children in the streets, following the pachyderms. Nina's was the last in a small line, the Rani and Rana having each a gorgeously clothed beast in the lead positions. Atop the queen's was a mirrored boxlike houda covered with a gently shaped dome of gathered silk, the elephants' ankles jangling with the ever-present silver bells.

They paraded through the triple arch, down the cobblestone street past Jagdish temple., through narrowing roads to the outskirts of the city, swinging around in the direction of a neighboring lake, crossing a narrow bridge one elephant at a time, to the shuddering relief of Nina.

Little children ceased to follow, shouts of glee still echoing, as much for the sights and sounds of the tinkling elephants as for a glimpse of the regent and her son. They rode blithely over semi-desert until reaching the severely rising hill. Nina felt the houda shift its weight across the boney back, sure that now she would fall mercilessly down the brown hillside to remain forever a speck of dust, non-glorious, insignificant. She glanced up ahead at Queen Mother. Her houda wasn't shifting. It wouldn't dare.

In the first courtyard she disembarked, remembering all too vividly the story Ranmathji told but a night or two ago.

An order had been sent by one of the Maharanas to the sardars and jagirs of his kingdom to arrive at court. One man came but immediately began begging to be excused for something he claimed to be of prime importance back at his home. Whether the Rana was angry or merely playful at the time was not known but the sardar was excused with the whimsical comment that perhaps he could give an elephant and rider as a condition to his temporary release. Unquestioningly the feudal lord had taken literally the words of his Rana. When he reached home he ordered a mahut to ride his elephant to the top of an extremely precipitous hill in the Aravalli mountains, a chore even for a sure-footed elephant. The mahut also had taken the order of his master as gospel and unquestioningly obeyed, urging it upward. At the peak the mahut issued command to jump.. They did, rolled over and over countless times, picking up momentum until coming to a stop far below, each severely mangled and heroically dead.

Nina identified with the mahut, recalling how she too feared falling from her elephant. It widely opened Nina's eyes to the pre-eminence and respect of the people for the whims, orders and jests of the family and their subservient sardars.

On arrival at Monsoon Palace, Queen Mother went immediately to the westerly rooms watching the sun just starting to set beyond the Aravallis. A delicate pink reflected onto the marble surrounding her, so slowly giving way to soft rose shades. There was not a stirring of her body on this little balcony until the sun had turned the marble deep crimson-purple. How many years would be left for her to enjoy this scene she was so comfortable with?

It was still several days before the rains came. The fields below so vehemently brown spread like a giant canvas. For Nina it was a great part of what she had come to revere. The lake had been mercilessly swallowed by the sun until the Palace no longer seemed to swim, leaving the marble home sitting high and dry astride its massive rock. Jag Mandir, the other little island which once harbored Shah Jehan, the builder of the beautiful Taj Mahal, also was stranded. Water buffalo now had to walk further for a drink and the dhobis slid lower each morning to the bottom of their sloped rocks to pound their clothes. Children could no longer swim. Fishermen were having great difficulty and there was much speculation the entire stock of the lake would die.

From this distance Nina could see at dusk thousands of green parrots returning to Jag Mandir, having spent the day no one knows where. Swooping over the northern end of the lake they seemingly disappeared just over the top of the water, to rise again but briefly before reaching their nightly perches on the island's few trees. Their sounds became raucous, but noisy or not they were always entertaining.

Beyond the lake residence stood the immense main palace of Bhim Singh and the zenana of his mother, one of the largest private residences in the world. How had Nina ever been accorded the phenomenal privilege of residing here?

The rain finally came in great crescendoes, dashing into hardened ground in spreading fields. Three quarters of the people of Mewar were supported by agriculture. Wheat and millet could soon be raised after these rains, residents praying it would refill the lakes. "Thanks to the gods that Pichola didn't completely dry," Nina overheard Queen Mother speak to her son. Restocking fish would not be easy. Not only the palace but the people of the city heavily relied on the abundance and numerous kinds to help keep food in their mouths. Only the Jains and vegetarians avoided it.

The browns and sallow shades had now completely disappeared and before Nina now were the fresh feathery greens of a new world. Overnight.

A few weeks later the Rani longed to again settle into her lake palace, once again floating in water, looking more lovely than ever. She was hungry for the beauty of Kuuch Mahal, her room of happiness. "You see," she once said to Nina, "man can make things to look as beautiful as your most impelling dreams. If you wish sunlight in the midst of dark clouds why not have soft blue windows? Staring through them the sky is heavenly blue no matter what the reality. One should have everything for which he wishes." Nina wondered if that applied to servants.

It has always been said that little girls love to dream of being a fairy princess. Here in this land of ancient India there are thousands of princesses of varying degree, many of whom live exotic lives. But the boy Rana also had his dreams and knew well his lot in life, at times longing for the unencumbered childhood pleasures of other boys his age. There were the wistful moments when he would pretend to be fully grown, as he had done since Nina first met him, clearly discontent with those who did not jump at his voice or accede to his demands.

As Nina leisurely strolled to the room containing the golden sun-window she caught sight of Bhim Singh approaching the slight step which raised him to the window.

"So you, my subjects, will not go to work until the sun shines?" he spoke in an exaggerated deep gruff voice, no one about to hear him other than Nina. "I am a descendent of the sun, and so I mercifully shine my face down upon you," he spoke after unlatching the round golden window, pulling it inward and pressing his head into the opening. Seeing his auroral face, had anyone been lingering in the courtyard, they would have been free to attend their chores, for it had been said that in the early days of this capitol many did not go to work until they could see the sun.

The mile long **City Palace of Udaipur**, founded in 1559 by Maharana Udai Singh II, 53rd ruler (1537-1572). The large gateway in the left of the picture leads to the ladies' palace. To its right, above, is the famous round, **golden sun window**.

Nina suppressed a chuckle. She began to wonder what kind of a ruler he would really make. His mother was doing all she could in these early formative years. Later he would surely go to the college in Ajmer where many of the royal families sent their young people.

The kingdom had seen its golden years and was now fast slipping. There was the suffocating emergence of the two rival factions twisting and turning the regent with a vise-like grip. Her counsellors were less than reassuring, often fighting among themselves. How long could her strength of purpose endure? It was sometimes incontrovertibly good to be of a lowly estate, Nina could see, for the dramatic perils and vexing problems of the Queen Mother were enough to tear out the heart of the strongest of men.

The next three withering months led to a tempestuous autumn. A bright spot for Nina was the fact she would again be seeing Narendra's father, Arjun Singh, and she could catch up on Jagatpur news. Mewar had a martial system resembling the European feudal system of medieval ages. Escheat is of prime importance, a method whereby the land reverts to the crown in lieu of an heir. Arjun Singh had his heir, Narendra. One day it would be vital that Narendra also have an heir, or adopt one, to retain the family's lands. "Oh please, Kala, you must have a son," Nina prayed.

The duties of the lords and his vassals under feudal laws were corresponding. Each had to adhere to his duties properly. Nina had seen the lords attend court. Never could a vassal take leave of his lord without permission. He would have to ride with him when hunting, go to war for him and even give himself as a hostage if necessary.

Interestingly, the vassals had sub-vassals who also held land. Their deeds of grant showed they had to serve at home and abroad. Some of them lived many months at a time in the capitol of Udaipur. When given permission to return to their homes they could not depart until other vassals had arrived.

Most subjects of the royal family were extremely loyal and in Mewar's shining hours as many as 15,000 horses and men would go into the field from one jagir alone, so closely bound were they in their ties of fidelity. Smaller regions who might be able to send only 500 vassals with their chief, and on a very rare occasion, perhaps just a very, very few.

When Arjun Singh arrived for this next tour of duty Nina excitedly sat beside him on the cobblestones. "Tell me all. How is everyone at Jagatpur? Let's start with your wife."

"She is keeping well and has sent her regards, Nina."

"Please, sire, what of Narendra and Kala?" Nina inquired.

His voice became audibly different, like a leaking bellows, and he cast his deep-set eyes to the ground. "Narendra grows more quiet and I worry about that. Kala is with child again and we fear for her. Again the priests and the doctor had come to our home and we had the ceremonies performed which helped her get pregnant the first time, but she does not look well. Kala's once lovely skin is now sallow and she keeps to her room most of the time. My wife attends her each day, bringing nourishing food and making certain that she eats at least a little, but it's a real chore. She doesn't seem to care about anything, acting lethargic and preferring to be alone. She is not at all the happy young thing Narendra married."

"How dreadful for all of you," was Nina's earnest reply.

"I should not burden you with this except that I know the closeness you feel for my son, and him for you..." Nina turned scarlet. "Oh, not to worry. I know it is only a sister and brother friendship. My wife and I are happy he has you for a friend."

"How very perceptive," Nina thought. Aloud she said, "I wish there was something I could do. I shall pray for a healthy son, an heir apparent. Do you think if I pray it will help."

"It can't hurt," Arjun said, patting his hand atop her head paternally.

"Let us hope the nine months pass quickly and all will go well," said Nina. "When is the baby due?"

"January." There was a catch in his throat.

"I think, my friend, that you should go alone to some quiet place and cry."

"A Rajput warrior cry?" He was totally astounded with her suggestion.

"Yes, a Rajput warrior can cry as well as any other person. It does not make you less a man. Tell me tomorrow if I am correct."

The following day they passed each other in a narrow corridor on his way to an audience with the Rani. "It is no wonder my son tells me you are wise beyond your years. I finally fell into the soundest sleep I have had for many months. I shall never again say to my wife, 'stop your crying,' for I see now it is great medicine. Just as Narendra and my wife have told me, you are an uncut gem!"

Chapter 11

An unripened decade slid by, Kala unable to avert two more bereaving miscarriages. The doctor warned her life would be in serious danger if she again attempted to have a child. Strongly swayed by his remarks and her lessening desire to share the bed of her husband with no immunity to its remorseful apprehensions she had become even more of a churlish recluse.

Narendra seldom returned to Udaipur palace, always finding excuses to track down dacoits in each of the far corners of Mewar, an obsession which he fully allowed to overtake his being. Rulers from beyond Rajputana now sought his assistance, which he gladly gave. The few times he and Nina met were brief, always under the umbrellas of the tree where first he kissed her so passionately. Each fought valiantly to retain their quasi-platonic relationship though each time he held her tighter, sighs unrestrained, eyes of each sadder and searching.

The demon worry cast its pall continuously over Arjun Singh for the health of his son, once standing tall, strapping. He once resembled the straightest of the noble ashok trees but now his massive shoulders slumped in coordination with his disintegrating mood. Nina's heart yearned for the aging Arjun. He knew it was dangerous for Narendra to be any less than completely alert when hunting dacoits. Nina longed to return to Jagatpur to pay her undying respects to Bhadra Singh, but this she would not do unless both Kala and Narendra were out of station.

News traveled laboriously from forts to villages, to palace, Nina waiting impatiently for a day in which to surprisingly rejoice ... whatever the reason. Resignation to a kind of non-happiness as opposed to complete unhappiness filled her never-ending days and harshly lonesome nights.

As for Narendra at Jagatpur, his old friend Ashok found time to visit him after a marriage and several children. There was, in spite of his family, a crying need to assist Narendra in his endeavors against dacoits. He had managed long ago to make the acquaintance of Ali, the dacoit leader. Ali was both imaginatively elusive and difficult to know, cleverly regarding all outsiders as possible enemies. His men had to be at his side for long periods of time before he tested them. He insisted they bring young boys for his sexual pleasures. It was after Ashok had known Ali for five or six months that this demand was put to him. Foreign to Ashok's thinking, his moral standard would not allow him to do such a horrendous thing to an innocent young lad. Ali could see he was hesitant and said, "You have never had a boy? Come, you must join me."

Ashok could no longer hide his feelings. "I couldn't do that, Ali. If it is your wish, so be it. I personally desire my wife." He could not be sure of Ali's reaction, he told Narendra, and whether he would be banished from the confines of Ali's ever changing home. Ali, astonishingly, acknowledged the difference in their physiological makeups. He would continue to nurture Ashok's sporadic presence and doubtless he would be able to use him in another manner at another time and place. He would test his loyalty later.

This information and similar grievances by others rankled Narendra through the years ... but always Ali remained phantasmally elusive.

"Will you continue to work for Ali, my friend, or are the rigors too much for a family man? How is it you have managed to be away for lengths of time from your wife and children?" Narendra questioned. There was a definite limit to which he could expect his friends to stretch, and he had no desire to overtax their lives.

"It is not always easy, but there are times when I get the lust to move about, to race on my horse as we used to do together, remember, Narendra Singhji? I long to beat the wind and sit upon a rock waiting for it to catch up to me and laugh into its face. Life at home is dull. We are not at war now. Things may be verbally in turmoil for the Maharana but in my village there is not much to do. The elders sit around their counsel fires and look for things over which to argue. The wives stoop and converse around a steaming pot of hot water, forgetting to brew the tea, all day yelling 'chup, chup, chup' to their dirty-nosed little kids."

Narendra laughed. "You sound as if you don't enjoy being a father, Ashok."

"Oh sure I do. You know, Narendra Singhji, when a little toddler has weeping eyes and a runny nose, if he is yours you sweep him up into your loving arms and coo softly into his ear. But if that little kid belongs to the people down the road, then his dirty face is dirtier, his cries louder and his tears a blot on your own patience."

"Are you the same Ashok I've known all my life? It would seem you found it necessary to come visit me, not because of Ali, but just to get away. Is it?" Narendra asked.

"I guess so. I shall stay with you a few days. By then I'll be anxious to see my wife and children. When I again get bored, very bored, I shall take off once more and try to find the current whereabouts of that bastard. God, how I hate his guts. I think I want the personal pleasure of sticking a knife into him myself. He is far from entirely trusting me yet, and even so he will still have others all about him. I pray that Ali is killed, not captured. He'd only escape, laugh at us, and cause yet more harm."

"Remember Ashok, we are not murderers. Nor should we stand in judgement. It is when capturing them in dacoities that we are justified in killing, if they attempt escape."

"Sure, sure, I know," answered Ashok, a black cloud of depression obviously flung over his head. But Narendra knew from his reaction, given the chance Ali would not come out of any fracas alive.

"Stay on for a time and we'll ride again. I don't think we can beat the wind, but we can always try," Narendra suggested.

It was a week later, after Ashok returned to his village, Narendra received the inevitable news that Sultana's gang had been seen, or so they thought, in upper Rajasthan, close to the border. They too had been elusive. He felt the information was reliable. Arjun Singh was in agreement with his son that he should shortly set out to find the illusory mob.

Kala was indifferent to his leaving and it seemed to Narendra a good idea to stop at the palace and visit with Nina. He now had longed to hold her again, to truly make love. Enough of the put-off by Kala. There was just so much a man could tolerate and Nina at least did love him. This he knew.

Arjun Singh rode with his son for the first half day's journey, stopping to clasp his arms around his first-born, favored of all his children, intrepidly fearful he would not come back. What a disastrous blow that would be. He wanted Narendra to live to rule this fort after his own death. Arjun considered him wiser and more just than his brothers. The chance that Kala still would have a child not only dimmed but blackened. Failing that, Narendra could adopt a son of his brother. He then could inherit from Narendra. Arjun's number two son would surely agree to that proposal for it was an honored custom and would be to the advantage of his child to one day head this vast fort and all their domain.

With the departure of his father Narendra continued to indulge in the fancy of traveling via the palace on the pretense of telling Queen Mother his plans. They had become closer in recent years in spite of seeing little of each other. This would enable him to ask for Nina on the pretext he had a message from his parents. Psychoanalytically he arrived at a negative decision, bypassed Udaipur and hurried northeast to a village from which someone had been snatched, a reprehensible crime.

Padma was weary as a run-down timepiece. Her singing and dancing engagements had been many of late, dizzying tedium catching up with her. It was only ten in the morning but the sultry air already hung heavily over the desert state of Rajasthan. She heaved a gusty sigh. Beyond an open hole in the wall serving as a window she reached wistfully for a crumpled cotton tie and dye gagra, stepping clumsily into its brilliant colors. Awkward movements were abnormal to this young girl, her lithe body bending normally in sensuous gracefulness. Padma's odhni still caressed her soft swollen bosom as it had throughout the restless night.

Half stumbling into the tiny courtyard of her parent's home she spied Anil, a cousin-brother. "When did you come?" she asked in welcome. Anil had been a particular favorite of her seldom seen friends and relatives from afar.

"Last night. You were gone. Are you keeping well, Padma? You are looking weary ... but beautiful as always," he added after a second thought.

"I am alright. Just too damned tired only. It is hard work, dancing. I would rather dance than anything I know, but it is hard work. Anil, sometimes I think I must work harder than the men who plow the fields and till the soil. I know I certainly work harder than the women who follow their husbands into the fields, bending over to drop one seed at a time behind the plows."

"Dancing is the second best relaxation I know," he said with an unbrotherly wink and a silly smirk.

"Ah, you tease me, and you think that I am naughty, too, don't you Anil? A dancer and naughty both. Is that not true? Be honest."

He was caught. "I had not thought of it one way or the other, Padma. I do not know. It is not my affair."

"Perhaps not, but if I were your sister you would not want me dancing. All men think dancers will sleep with any man. I do not do that."

"I have never taken a tally, Padma. It is no concern of mine."

"In this vague reflective way you have already committed yourself. You believe that because most nautch girls and dancers prostitute their bodies, I too most likely do. And if I were your sister you would most probably hate me for it; because I am not your sister it is alright with you. Is that not what you think?"

"Padma, you are putting words into my mouth. I love you like a sister. I have not thought of it. I do not have a real blood sister, but it is true, I would not want her sleeping with all sorts of men."

"Damn it. You still don't see what I'm getting at, do you? All sisters and daughters should be faithful to their husbands! They should live for one man alone! It is a terrible thing for her to crawl into the bed of another man! Yet if a man wishes to be unfaithful to his wife, from where come these women with whom he lays? Are they not also someone's sister and daughter? You men..." She turned and walked briskly from him.

"Now wait a minute, Padma, I did not come here for an argument. I came here to see your family and my other friends. I want to be your friend, but not when you start a fight with me." He was completely puzzled. He had never known her to be perturbative.

Padma realized she had made him the innocent victim of her weary mind and body. She rushed back, grasping his tanned arm firmly and saying, "I'm so sorry, Anil. So very sorry. Please forgive me. You are my friend, I know, my favorite cousin-brother and I treat you like a pariah dog."

"Not to worry, Padma. After a day's rest you will be your sweet, beautiful self once more."

"You have come for Narain's wedding?" She remembered now. "That's to be in two days."

"Umm," he muttered, swishing around the last yard of cloth in his hands. All this while he had been tying a white turban around his asymmetrical head. "There; how does this look?"

Anil had not worn turbans often enough to become adept at tying them and she wondered why he even bothered on this non-festive day. "You look like the ancient mummies I have seen pictures of in books," she loudly giggled, for all his lack of good looks and grooming.

"You are most unkind," he replied, not the least angry, for he had thought even this outburst of laughter might change the outlook of Padma's day.

"Well it's good, very good, to see you again," she uttered earnestly, reaching for a wooden bucket of water for her morning bath, dropping it into the courtyard well. Her parents were one of the few villagers who were fortunate enough to have been able to drill for water on their premises, thanks mainly to the earnings of their dancing daughter.

She walked into the tiny shed-like device without a roof, constructed roughly at the backside of their pitifully small piece of property. It was on a slight rise above surrounding ground, making it difficult for voyeurs to get a peek of anyone bathing, though many had tried in the hope of catching luscious Padma in the nude.

Lazily cleansing herself she thought of Anil and her last visit to his village. She had voluptuously enjoyed that trip, walking down their side streets half way between Jaipur and Alwar on the way to Sariska.

Melodiously clinking chisels created long oblong slabs of stone by unremitting laborers. These grey slabs were everywhere to be seen in the neighboring villages and cities designating property boundaries and as floors and walls in the homes of all but the poorest. Begrimed faces were set in smiling molds, rough-hewn bodies somehow filled with an inexplicable masculine allure.

Near to the finished product stood a short row of gloomy-eyed camels, equally dusty, turning to spit at their owners laying upon the carts on which would eventually be carried the weighty market-headed product. Vividly Padma recalled sitting on a low stone wall listening to the rhythmic throbbing of the tools and how she wanted to set the sounds into song. The men's skills shone through their labors with camels adding only questionable charm.

Remembering all this Padma bathed as long as she could stretch out the single pail of water. Water in the desert is an immeasurably precious commodity and she dared use no more than this. The song of the stone cutters she had made up on that day two or three years ago eluded her. She knew it to be none too good. Padma was a raving dark-haired beauty with an exhilarating platinum voice. In unabated demand, her talents did not extend to the harmonious creation of new music, too discordant were her trials. Her thoughts went back once again to the ugly camels with their strange jaws mimicking the conceited sway of her body, jealous of her gracefulness, chewing their straw from one side of their drooling mouths to the other.

Padma donned the same wrinkled gagra and odhni, walking into the small kitchen. Everyone else had completed their morning meal hours ago but her mother had kept the dung fire simmering, a metal pot of left-over rice resting just above the dying red embers. A small ledge held a few chapatis. Padma sat on the dirt floor, knees in the air, gagra tucked heavily between her legs showing bangled ankles and bare feet. It was not until after this poor excuse of a meal that she really started to waken.

Rising slowly from the floor, covering head with her scarf she walked out of the house, down a bowered dirt road, past budding poppy fields, hoping to see a few of the young women her age at the well. She had to pass the Persian water wheel where friends worked slowly, moving the oxen backward and forward, dragging up from the much larger well than her parents' the skin buckets of water which were carried to the neatly planted rows of poppies used for opium.

For the first time she wondered what it would be like to smoke opium. After all, if it was good enough for the maharajas it should be good enough for her. She lived in a society which did not in any manner believe in equal rights or opportunities, yet in her imagination she could see herself as an equal to anyone she deemed worthy of emulating. White poppies fringed in vivid pink were lovely when in full bloom but it would be a few more weeks before they reached that stage. Irrigation was a rare thing but it certainly proved itself a boon.

And now the marriage season had come with several weddings besides Narain's to take place in her village alone. As anticipated, she saw some of her old chums and they gossiped at length, for the well was to all of them the local newspaper. Each girl was in her own way the gossip columnist-cum-society editor. There was nothing malicious about their talk, but they did live for their daily chit-chat. Padma joined them occasionally.

With nothing really new to be learned she rapidly wearied and strolled on once more through the budded poppy field into the open countryside. She had within her a strange longing for fevered excitement. When dancing she could see in the gawking eyes of the men impassioned longing, exasperating uncouthness; there were the hungry bestial types; blundering awkwardness; wholesome boyishness; demoralized perversity. Long for her as they did, she was immune to their voracious pursuit of her body. Yet she dreamed for someone to come set free her craving spirit.

The memorable night of neighbor Narain's wedding came. She had taken off the night from her duties to attend. All the ladies would be wearing their finest. All had unlocked their jewel cases carrying family wealth around necks, arms and ankles. There was nothing manifestly unusual about this. It had gone on for myriad centuries all over the Asian sub-continent. Family tiffs were forgotten during the days of festivities.

The hastily written, hand delivered wedding invitations had read nine thirty as the auspicious hour. The sun had sunk and formless darkness lunged into the village. From the wedding shamiana a drowning din of merry voices echoed in the desert. Padma sat restlessly with a few of her friends, her parents seated with others nearer their own ages.

Padma glowed in her natural beauty, appearing some sort of Hindu Madonna, if ever there was one, for who was there among mortals who knew each and every god and goddess and all their incarnations and attributes. She stared blankly as the priest placed a coin in the joined hands of the bride and groom and tied a new white cloth around their hands, ceremoniously binding the two together in holy wedlock. Another hour went by and the boisterous guests slowly stood up to shower the sober-faced couple with rice or flower petals.

Padma turned from the mandapam which sheltered the bridal party and walked from beneath the many colored canvas tent into an empty lot. The sound of blaring musicians filtered through the unjaded air even as she walked further into the pervading darkness. Suddenly she had the uncanny feeling someone called to her; her sense of curiosity kept her walking toward the unuttered sound. Her pace quickened. She looked around and even as her eyes became more accustomed to the darkness, she could see nothing in any direction. Still it sounded like her name being whispered, sent to her on a breeze. She stood quietly for a few moments hearing only the beating of her heart, no longer hearing her name, if in fact it ever was spoken. Nothing or no one could be seen, yet she sensed something, not necessarily danger. Or was it just a nebulous maze of abstract thought, that inner yearning for some form of diversified excitement.

A rough hand suddenly caught her over the mouth and a left arm grabbed her around her tiny waist. She grappled vigorously with this creature of overpowering strength, kicking her two feet into his shins as he lifted her from the ground. He flung her to another person who by now she could dimly see held a camel by a rope. How they slithered up to her without her seeing their advance remained a mystery to Padma. The first attacker flung a leg over the camel's back and beckoned for the still writhing form of Padma. The man spoke not a word but instinctively obeyed unspoken commands.

The crouching camel stood up with his usual clumsy jolt and wavered out over the desert sands, its driver kicking vindictively into the beast's sides as they galloped into the night.

Padma thought she should be experiencing an agitation of perplexity and alarm, yet was this experience not giving vent to her desires for a release from a hum-drum existence? To her friends she lived a life of excitement and glamor, wearing colorful sexy costumes, learning to apply her makeup elegantly over an already flawless face, being adored by all the men, young and old. But this was merely all in a hard day's work to Padma. Superficial. Without true reward. Another woman's wishful dream, Padma's monotony.

Tightly she clung to the young man's waist to avoid sliding down the racing camel's side. The moon remained in hiding, thus the night could shed no light on the features or form of the kidnapper. Her only clues were those which she could feel with her hands and body. He must be 15 centimeters taller than she, athletically muscular. Padma dug her arm into his ribs and clasped her hands at his middle. Her forearms felt the tumultuous irregularity of his pounding heart, though instinct told her this man knew no fear. Thunderous throbs of their proximity transmitted themselves from his body to hers.

Was this abduction a lark, a spur of the moment thing by wedding guests who started their festivities early with too much bhang? She smelled no liquor on the breath of either man, nor did they appear stuporous. The kidnapping could not have been pre-planned. They could not know she would be walking alone beyond the shamiana and crowd. Even she had not planned that. Possibly they decided upon kidnapping anyone who might meander alone. She was vain enough to know that she would be the best catch of the village females but the coincidence of her emerging alone from the tent was too great. It could not have been she whom they sought. All her fundamental rationalizing brought her no clinching answer.

Eventually the ride became more tolerable. Her illogical whims changed to the rhythm of desultory breezes. She whisked out the several pins which held her silky hair in a neat, matronly bun, whipping her head vigorously from side to side, the tresses now flowing behind her. Minute by incredible minute her mercurial mood and spirit lightened. Whoever and whatever this man was she was contented with the escape from dull routine, a condition which she deemed unnecessary for him to learn.

It was hours before they came to a halt, their pace becoming more leisurely. The camel knelt on his forearms, lowering his head, Padma almost tumbling headlong over the body of the driver. Instead, he reached his arm to her, lifting her gently to the parched ground, never loosening his hold. In the now accustomed dark she could vaguely see the features of his disdainful face, his black eyes shining. She spoke not a word, staring boldly into his eyes with no suggestion of fear.

Padma's quiet attitude befuddled her captor. She was determined not to speak until he had done so. His disappointment in her lack of fear both puzzled and annoyed him. "Aren't you the dancing girl?" he finally questioned.

So he hadn't known who he was kidnapping. "I dance and sometimes sing," she agreed, no trace of any quiver in her voice.

"Your name is what?"

Unflattered, she replied haughtily, "If you have seen me dance then you must know my name, because you would not have forgotten either me or my name."

"You will not speak to me in that manner," he bellowed, lifting his hand as if to strike her, finally holding back. She did not reply. Nor did she as much as blink an eye or move a muscle. "So ... you are a tough one, eh?" Taking a step back to better survey what he had acquired, he said, "Hmmm. Not too bad, I suppose."

"Not too bad?" she uttered, placing her hands on her hips, spreading her feet wide apart. "Too bad you'll never get to find out for yourself."

"Indeed. Well, I suppose you'll have to do until something better comes along." He attempted to antagonize her.

"You'll find none better," she again boasted, referring to her figure and beauty. Not until after she said the words did she realize he might be referring to sex. As many offers for bed partners and physical struggles as Padma had encountered she had never been a promiscuous girl. "How is it you grabbed me out of the desert? Why were you there?" the curiosity continued.

"We were bored," he admitted. "Thought we'd take a little ride, and then suddenly you were there. We couldn't leave you to the mercy of the jackal, could we?"

"Your concern for my safety overwhelms me," she taunted.

Padma's captor once more grabbed her arm, forcing her into a small hut with a lone oil lamp burning near one wall. There were other men inside who seemed to cower back against their walls in apparent unsolicited deference to the young man. In the center of the room stood a rickety wooden table, the only piece of furniture. Blankets of scratchy camel hair were heaped against another wall opposite the lone flickering lamp beneath the only window. All the men remained squatting somnolently on the dirt floor.

Finally getting a fair look at her kidnapper, Padma found him anything but repulsive although sober faced. Now the reality of the event took hold. What would he do with her? Thirsting eyes gave her an answer, but she would not give in to him easily, she decided. She had learned to ward off many a man. If he was to win her body, and the odds were in his favor, he would somehow have to merit it. Her real fear was with respect to the others. She dreaded the thought he might allow them all to share in his catch.

"Get out," he gestured to them. That was a reasonably good sign.

"Yes, Sultana," they replied.

"Sultana?" she gulped as the room quickly emptied of all but the two of them. "Not the infamous dacoit Sultana?"

"I prefer the word famous, not infamous."

"As you wish." For the first time her throat tightened with the sense of what was happening. She had not suspected it was dacoits who had captured her, just a bunch of fellows out for a good time.

"It appears you are not frightened of me. Let us see if I am capable of arousing in you any emotion, or are you made of cold snows of the Himalaya's? Even that snow melts, I'm told." He drew her to him.

"I didn't know I was supposed to be frightened," she smirked, cleverly wrestling herself from his grasp.

"You will submit to me. You do know that, don't you?" he was firm in his flat statement.

"You don't frighten me, Sultana. You are no different from any other man. If there is anyone who will submit, it will be you submitting to me ... if I wish it, that is."

"Why you..." He lunged for her, caught and held her so tight around the waist, his entire body welded with passion against hers. His mouth half opened and he tried hard to kiss her but found her more clever than he. Then in a moment of shame — not for what he was doing, but because he could not easily get the better of her — he disdainfully flung her backwards.

She walked around the barren room sensuously, touching the table, hips swaying more than usual. Her lovely bosom rose and fell like a tidal wave. Every movement of her pretty head was cocky and bold. She wanted him to want her with every sweating pore of his body.

"Damn it," he screeched, grappled for her and blew out the light. "This is the way you like it best?" he questioned, teeth clenched. "Your men must always fight like this to take you?"

"I have never been taken," she whispered.

His love making was to begin voraciously. After a short while he laughed from deep inside and said, "So, you are right. You have never been taken," and suddenly he became more gently caressing, and again ferocious.

After this Padma knew she would belong to Sultana. What she would do about her dancing or returning to her family she did not care to think about. Horrible as a dacoit was in her past imaginings, and the reputation of this one in particular, she knew she would end up his woman. Indeed, she was already his woman.

Intoxicating weeks had passed with Padma relapsing into a state of euphoric abstraction. Sultana would leave her behind as he and the gang engaged in raids. Often the areas were a day or two ride and the better part of a week would be spent waiting for him to return. Padma heard the men laughing over their sexual conquests and rapings. She warned Sultana if ever she heard of him raping one of the girls on his raids she'd cut his heart from his body and feed it to the camels. But in the feverish hours of loneliness Padma would sit dejectedly whittling twigs or picking at fingernails, daydreaming of home. She suffered touches of guilt for the inexplicable pain she knew she was causing her mother and father. In spite of her joyous nights with Sultana and her new way of life, nothing more than a doting mistress, she was painfully conscious of her wrongdoing. There were even moments of blinding shame.

Her parents were at least entitled to know she was alive and happy. This she talked over with Sultana, who was at first definitely against doing anything about it. As days wore on and with his growing fondness for the girl he agreed to let her go briefly to her family. Two of his men would accompany her to within a two camel-hour ride of her home. She would have to walk the balance. He did not want his camels recognized, for all they possessed had been stolen from one village or another, each bearing its original markings.

Sultana had the mutable custom of changing his "residence" frequently. Padma feared she would never find him again. It was agreed she'd be met exactly one week later at the drop-off point. They were not to be discovered. Padma's life depended on it.

Sultana cared enough to allow her this wish against the advice of the other gang members. Yet he knew she would not betray him. There was the oneness between them which only lovers can share. He felt completely safe in her keeping and sorely missed her after her departure.

The rising reputation of Narendra and his successes with dacoits justified Padma's parents in sending for him. In frantic desperation for days after her unexplained disappearance they paced their floor and courtyard. No one had seen her slip out of the shamiana and it was as if the earth had swallowed her. Nothing constructive was accomplished until one of the wise elders of the community thought of Narendra and the legend he was fast becoming. After all, a dacoit could have captured her.

"You would do well to send for him," the elder suggested to Padma's parents. A scribe was hired and a letter sent to Jagatpur by horseback. It would take a week to reach him, at the very least.

"And if he is not in station?" Padma's distraught mother asked.

"He will be found. Word will be sent to him. It is the best we can do."

It was well into the morning hours after the wedding that she was first missed and the revelry had died down to a quiet whisper. The young men were filled with bhang, the old men crazed with opium. By the time anyone was able to look for her, each had covered the other's tracks with their horses, camels or their own bare feet.

Narendra had been away hunting another band when he was finally found. Already a two day journey in the direction of Padma's village, it was ridiculous to return to Jagatpur. Thus he wrote a note to his father, sending it with the messenger. It was lengthy and detailed about both his good and bad fortune in finding those he sought. A few had been captured and already sent to Udaipur, for it held the closest jail. From there Narendra's men were to return home for a well deserved rest. Narendra in his restlessness determined to remain longer away from the fort and his husbandly duties. The slightest excuse seemed to keep him from Kala. How could he love her still, and yet shrink away from her uncaring coolness.

He headed to the northeast with a vague knowledge of where Padma's parents lived. How could people allow themselves to disappear? After prayers he spent the balance of the day riding Chetak, sorting out the limitless possibilities of Padma's distressing predicament. By now he knew of so many motives and habits of dacoits he could only surmise what happened. As for it being anything other than a dacoit, no. Young women, even a nautch girl, were too sheltered in Rajasthan to wander off on their own. Villages and hamlets are exceedingly small.

Men from miles around know each other from their occasional get-togethers, from weddings, from religious holidays. She would have been seen. She would have to have a place to live. Someone would have taken her in. This is not what happened, he was certain. She had to have been kidnapped. The message stated that no one else was missing and he was keenly anxious to question everyone in and around the village.

At last he came upon the place where Padma had been born and raised. News of his arrival spread quickly. Immediately he sought Padma's parents and started his interrogation. For the sake of unneeded confusion he ordered others to stay beyond the dilapidated fence encircling their small piece of property. Rigorously precise questions astounded the parents and beguiled the elders of the town when he much later sat with each, individually and then as small groups.

When Narendra completed his interrogation he told them that if they knew anything of the whereabouts of dacoits, he was the one to be told and the informers would be given whatever protection required.

After a day and a half of going over and over the same little things it was explicitly clear that no one, young or old, knew anything about Padma's disappearance.

Narendra had by now felt he knew the girl intimately. He sat resting his back against a ragged tree, staring into space, eyes growing heavy in the late afternoon sunshine, trying to decide his next move. Young girls were taking their water jugs in the direction of the village well. A few men worked slowly in their nearby ripening fields and wives had long disappeared into the shade of their homes for afternoon naps.

In the distance a lone figure moved, at first just a speck against the far-off horizon. It came closer, now grown into the shape of a human. And when it came near enough he saw it bore a swagger which many of the girls of India possess. Accustomed to carrying water pots upon their heads, the back of the Indian maiden is straight, her posture perfect, her swaying comely.

Somehow this female in Rajasthani clothing had a very special bearing. He rose to his feet, not taking his eyes from her.

She was wearying as if having walked a long while, yet the grace did not disappear. He looked around at the others in the vicinity, not saying a word. And finally one of Padma's friends let out a shriek, running toward Padma, arms outstretched. The girls embraced.

By this time Narendra himself walked toward her but she was already converged upon by friends who seemed to come quickly out of nothingness. All shouted questions to the tired traveler. "Are you alright?" "Where were you?" "What happened?"

Narendra broke into the conversation, wriggling his way past reaching arms, taking the girl into his custody. His overpowering bulk and firmness of voice left no doubt he was in charge. They accompanied her home, all remaining respectfully outside its broken front gate.

Narendra, too, remained outside the door of the parents' little cottage while the three united, but only briefly. He wished to be in on the beginning of her conversation and not receive her news second-hand, or oft-repeated.

Padma had plenty of time to think about her arrival and what she would convey to her family. Her conclusion was to say as little as possible and she would play it by ear. When the first tears of joy and excitement were drying the four settled down to an uncomfortable quiet.

"Where have you been, Padma?" her mother broke the silence. They intermingled their questions. They had searched neighborhood ravines, nullahs and broken buildings.

Padma was evasive and tight-lipped, Narendra finally resorting to interrogating her in private. She remained steadfast in her assertions that she did not know who the two people were who kidnapped her.

"Were they dacoits?" Narendra asked.

"I don't know. I don't think so."

"Were they farmers?"

"Yes, perhaps they were farmers."

"Perhaps? Then if they were farmers you will be able to relocate their farm and you can take us there. They must be made to pay for their crime." He hurried all his questions and statements to keep her in a state of confusion, entrapping her.

"No. I would not know how to find my way back to them."

"I will help you. I am a good guide. Do not be afraid of me, Padma. I am here to help you only. What did they raise?"

"I do not know. I am not a farmer."

"You did not work in the fields with them?"

"No. Never."

"But you walked around the fields with them, certainly."

"No."

"You stayed in the house all the time? They would not allow you to go outside?"

"I could go out. I was not a prisoner."

"Then when you walked outside what did you see? What kinds of trees were there? Was it sandy desert? Was it jungle and underbrush? Was it open fields? What was outside your door? What kind of fence was around the place? How many days it did it take you to walk back home?"

"I don't know. You're confusing me."

"You were not a prisoner but they did not let you walk into their fields? I do not understand, Padma. Let me help you. I cannot help unless you help me." Narendra tried to be gentle while the urge to strangle the answers from her was overpowering.

"I don't recognize different crops."

"But that is easy, Padma. You can tell the difference between wheat and rice, can you not? Were they wet rice paddies? Or was the crop taller? Perhaps wheat? It should be tall now for it will soon be harvest season."

"It was not either, I think."

"Mustard! What is lovelier than the swaying golden crops of mustard?"

"I have never seen mustard growing."

"Good. Then I know one district not to look."

Narendra's shrewdness nettled the girl, realizing she should never have returned. Getting back out of town would be more of a problem than she had dreamed, if not entirely impossible; she'd be closely watched by this calculating man. What would she do if she could never again find Sultana? What if he would tire of waiting for her, pull up stakes and leave. She longed to be with him at this very moment. Lord, she thought, if he came back to whisk her away there would be mass bloodshed. Sultana could easily become enraged and set torches to her whole village. It was too brutal a sight for her to picture. She would not allow herself to do so.

"Maybe they weren't farmers," she hoped he would give up the questioning.

"Did you help with the meals?"

"Yes, and I cleaned the house."

"That kept you busy all day? It must have been a very, very big house. If it was there must have been more servants besides yourself," Narendra's planned confusion kept its fast pace.

"There were no other servants. It was a small house. I cooked and cleaned and the rest of the time I rested."

"You didn't have to help till the soil or reap any harvests?"

"No. I told you. They weren't even farmers. They would go away and I do not know where. They did not tell me."

"When they went away why didn't you escape? You liked living there?"

"I didn't know where I was."

"Did you escape or did they let you go? How long did it take you to walk here, Padma? Two days, three days, a week? How long?" He lifted her foot from which she had kicked off her chappals. Though they were extremely dusty they were no harder than usual callouses or new sores. She could not have walked for too long. Certainly not for more than a day, but this he kept to himself. He had been told that the villagers had searched in all directions, well beyond this remote spot in which he now stood.

It was evident she was withholding all of the story of her disappearance. But he couldn't help wonder why she returned. "There is no wheat or rice in a day's journey. Much more than that, I too am sure they are not farmers. You have told me you understand their dialect but you do not know exactly what it is. Padma," he took her chin into his huge hand and turned her face to his, "they were dacoits, weren't they? If so, they would not let you escape. I have known too many. That they would not do. Don't you even want to help us catch them?"

"Oh leave me alone. Just leave me alone," she cried, elephant tears streaming down her face.

He would not relent. She was coming near a breaking point. "What about the nights you slept in the ditches, Padma? Were you cold sleeping out in nullahs and ravines? Did you have plenty of blankets?"

"I didn't sleep in ravines. Always I slept in a house."

"What kind of house? Kutcha? Pucca? Stone? Mud? Cement? Thatched roof? Tin roof? Tile roof? Stones on the roof?"

"I don't know."

"You cleaned their house for them every day, yet you do not know what kind of house?"

"I can't remember."

"And the morcha. Did you have to dig your own, or did the big strong men dig one for you to hide in?"

"I never said there was a morcha. I never dug a morcha in my life." The interrogation sped up, visibly confusing the girl.

"You said they went out. Did they leave someone behind to guard you while they busied themselves committing their dacoities?"

"No. The first time they left someone, but aft..." There it was. She had fallen into his carefully laid trap.

"Aha. Then they were dacoits."

Padma sank her tousled head down into her hands and cried. Harder and harder came the convulsive sobs. Desperado though Sultana was, she had intended not to betray him. Narendra talked to her longer before leaving her in the consoling custody of her bereft parents. Padma was now more confused than ever.

On the next day Narendra returned, and the next. Little by little he wheedled away at her, teaching her to see what she was doing was wrong, very wrong. When she finally confided Sultana's name to Narendra there was no doubt in his mind that he would search until Sultana was captured. Sultana and Ali, from reputation, were the two highest on Narendra's list of those he most wanted. He pleaded deprecatingly for knowledge of Sultana's whereabouts. It had been difficult for Padma to turn informer, yet she agreed that she return to his hideout and spy for Narendra, and secure information on a future job.

Narendra had also made every effort to have some of his cohorts quickly come to his aid. His legion was growing rapidly with his reputation and the excitement it brought. He told Padma he would arrange to have aid close to her, keeping her safe as humanly possible.

It was decided she would walk alone to the spot where she was to be met by Sultana's two men, avoiding suspicion.

That she had even seen Sultana, much less lived with him, was kept a secret from all but her parents. Her week was up and she returned to Sultana completely exhausted, Narendra's grilling and the worries of right and wrong tormented her night and day. Why she again left was never mentioned and the villagers soon tired of asking. All they were sure of was that Padma's parents lost their luster, ever after sullen, rarely even speaking to others.

She had agreed to spy for Narendra. What she would do once in the lascivious embrace of the man she made love with was another story.

The inevitable happened. In his arms, Padma instantaneously gave up the idea of being Narendra's informer. "I'd rather be a dacoit with you than an informer for a man who talks of right and wrong," she sighed, resting her head on his strong chest. "Take me with you on your next job."

"If you stay with me now, Padma, you can never return to your home again, but you cannot go on jobs with me. You would get yourself killed. What use is a dead lover?" he tried to joke.

"You can teach me to shoot and to use a knife."

"If you do join us you must learn a lot more than shooting guns and using knives. You must learn to be a lookout and how to defend yourself. You cannot run around in swishing gagra. You'll have to wear trousers like us and a turban. I do not want others to know we have a woman in our midst."

"All these things I can do, Sultana," she asserted willfully, "and some day I'll get that famous dacoit fighter Narendra because now I know him."

And so it was that Padma took to the arduous task of learning all the facets of becoming an outlaw practicing grueling hours. Eventually she learned how to handle a gun, to load it, and to wield a dagger. Finally good enough to join the commissions of dacoity, she helped in the kidnapping of several people. Held for ransom they were returned unharmed after receiving specified amounts of money. They had successfully eluded Narendra. But Sultana, knowing Narendra was on his heels, had taken to far off places. The band grew braver and luckier, moving frequently to avoid association with any given area.

Meantime Kala was quite ill. On a message to this effect Narendra rushed to her side, putting Sultana and Ali temporarily to the back of his mind. It was a long time before Kala physically snapped back but the coldness she showed her husband remained unchanged.

When Narendra had been gone from the region of Padma's parents for well over a year the expected happened. While in the midst of committing another dacoity Sultana was shot and killed. When the encounter was over, Padma and most of the others slipped away, leaving behind the man with whom she had intimately lived and through whom she had learned to herself be a desperado.

That much news eventually reached Narendra, and he could only wonder the outcome of the gang and of Padma.

The next most powerful person in the gang was a man by the name of Sinha. He immediately took over the gang and within a few days was planning the next offence. He also took over the woman who had belonged to Sultana. Nothing else changed. She fought at the side of Sinha, still wearing her male uniform, until the villainous group lamentably submitted to their tragic fate.

In another gun battle Padma was injured in the left hand by bullets from a villager. She had tried to treat her own wound but it was futile. An infection soon started and she acquired a fever. Sinha knew something must be done now. In traditional dacoit fashion he and a few gang members barged into the home of a small city doctor in the middle of the night, forcing him to treat Padma. By this time the wound had become gangrenous and the hand had to be amputated. The doctor who loved both his life and money was handsomely paid off in rupees and never spoke to the authorities of this ugly event.

It took well over a month for her injury to heal but when fully recuperated Padma was good as new. She compensated by teaching herself to handle the gun with her right hand only and remained very accurate. Once more she fought side by side with Sinha.

News of a beautiful one-handed female dacoit spread through Rajputana over the months and Narendra had a premonition she was Padma. There never had been word from her about the goings on of Sultana and most certainly he had either killed her if he learned she was to spy against him, or she chose to be loyal to him. Now there was this person running around two countrysides, Rajputana and Madhya Pradesh, bold and cunning. He must find and capture her, defiant of any pressing affairs of state in either Udaipur or Jagatpur, and Kala's health remained on the mend.

Narendra pieced together bits of stories from many villagers over endless kilometers. It had appeared that Sinha too was shot and killed. Although Padma had tried to disguise herself as a man she was far too beautiful, her skin too silken. With Sinha's death it was believed the woman had taken over the gang. At last Narendra was hot on her heels.

Then a further stroke of luck; one of the gang had defected. Laying ill and dying he told a group of men of some of the dacoits' deeds. Since the death of Sultana and Sinha he said Padma chose at random anyone she wanted to be her sex partner. One of these men fathered her only child, a daughter. Padma had taken her to a lovely home and left her at the door.

It was not unexpected when Narendra finally encountered Padma and her gang in the district of Morena in Madhya Pradesh; in fact she wondered why it had taken him this long. The police came to the aid and the fighting that ensued was horrendous.

Padma's taste for jewelry was insatiable. Once inside a relatively secured village she would immediately head for the homes which appeared to be owned by the most affluent of the villagers, little matter how plain. Nothing but the finest available bangles or gems would assuage this hunger. As she entered one house it took no time to discover the hiding place of the strongbox. Easily prying it open, she voraciously grabbed its contents, shoving them into a bag securely tied around her waist, her gun on the table beside the box. Looking up at the huge form just arrived at the door she immediately recognized the man she knew as dacoit fighter Narendra.

Instinctively she reached for her gun. Padma was not about to be taken alive, neither wanting a life in jail nor the prospect of facing her parents who would be dreadfully ashamed of her. Nor did the fighting last long, all quite haphazard and slipshod on the part of the disjointed dacoits. Grasping the gun firmly in her right hand she aimed for Narendra's heart. He would have much preferred capture but in this decisive flashing moment he had to fire.

Padma had come to live by the gun and knife and now she died by the gun with nine of her male companions.

Chapter 12

Aging Shrimati Bhadra Singh had been ailing for quite some time when news of her illness reached the palace by way of her husband. Arjun had again been required to serve his tour of paramount duty for the Rana and Queen Mother, disconcerting as it was at this particular time. All the way from Jagatpur he rehearsed his little speeches for the Rana, yet knowing all the pre-planning in the world would not help if the young king was not in the mood to let him go. Arjun Singh sought an audience immediately upon his arrival.

"What is this? Your wife is ill?" spoke the Rana, who had long since slid past his teens.

"She has been ailing for a rather long time but lately has grown considerably worse. I honestly do feel that I should be there with her at this time." Queen Mother was seated at the side of her fully grown son, silently listening and watching as he handled routine matters.

"Is your son Narendra off on some of those wild dacoit-catching expeditions? If not, he can surely see to his mother's needs. I'm certain your doctors are as good as ours and that she is accorded all the care and attention available," spoke Bhim Singh, rather irked with the lord.

"Narendra comes and goes, dependent on the needs to catch various gangs. Then too, he must assist me as our first son in the settlement of our many feudal problems. He is very busy, always. As for doctors, they are doing their best but whatever it is that is wrong, she just seems to whither away. I cannot bear to be long gone from her. I could not tolerate it if something happened and I was not there," Arjun continued to plead.

"But you have many sons and all their wives to aid and comfort her," Queen Mother broke in.

"True, all our children are now married and the wives should be capable of amply attending her, but you know how it is with daughters-in-law. They squabble among themselves and it causes more agitation for my wife who is always aware of the undercurrent. It is unrestful and I try to have only one of them at a time come sit with her for an hour or two each. It is doing my wife absolutely no good and she grows weaker and weaker."

"And your daughter? How is she keeping? Where is it she lives?" asked the Queen.

"Mughal Serai. She is quite well, and she has recently paid us a very lengthy visit," Arjun answered. "But at last she had to return to her own home and little ones. She could not bear to be away from them too long. She had two babies now in the almost four years she has been married, and of course she cannot shun their care." He was becoming quite ill at ease at this little meeting, disturbed for the health of his beloved wife and annoyed that they were giving him this third degree when he had so faithfully served them all these years. Others among the lords had become extremely lax, some not coming to court for several years at a time and getting away with it. He was performing his duty honestly and faithfully and the one being censured. There seemed no justice. About to argue these points, Queen Mother again spoke.

"What of the servants?"

"Ah, I'm glad you brought that up, Your Highness. There is none in this world like your Nina, is there? We should never have let her out of our home for early on we could see the extreme merits of that child and knew that she was indeed of palace quality. This being so, we said to each other we must sacrifice and give her up to Queen Mother for her very own, even though doing so would deeply grieve and deprive us." He was laying it on quite heavily. "Our servants are of long standing and undeviatingly faithful. They have spent their lives doing as told but lacking that extra-special quality which sets them apart as your Nina. I much prefer to return home immediately. Out of respect for Your Highnesses I came myself. But perhaps we can work out a compromise. If you will not immediately release me from this session at court, would you kindly release Nina?"

"And of what good would she be at the bedside of your wife?"

"You know her capabilities better than I. She is made up partly of some sort of heavenly being and a portion of common sense. To it has been added a calculating knowledge of what is proper to be said and to be done in any given situation. I have never known her not to come up with just the right antidote at the exact right time. You ask me what she can do. I do not know specifically what she will do for my wife, but Narendra and I are in full agreement we must have her caring for my beloved wife. That magic which only Nina possesses will work for us. I am sure she will make my wife well."

That was a pretty powerful statement. The royal family sat back looking at each other and thinking of this. The decision would have to be Queen Mother's for Nina was still her number one servant. Nina had patched for her many a heartache and cured her during fevers. The queen had to agree there seemed to be some magic, but could she dare part with her? She didn't think she'd feel quite safe without her. She didn't when she went off to visit her sister long ago and left Nina behind. But now ... perhaps for just a little while. Perhaps.

Arjun was quiet now too for the words he had just uttered really struck home. Until now he had not truly realized the extent to which he had become fond of her in a fatherly fashion. He would think of Nina often when Narendra was extremely low and morose and wish to send for her, but never was he entirely sure of the relationship between the two. If it was extremely intimate he would not blame Narendra, for Kala had not been hiding her black countenance from anyone. As for Nina, poor Nina. She too needed solace for her womanly woes. Still, he could never interfere. It was not Arjun's way to teach infidelity to his son, even though he was fast reaching the point of condoning it.

"I shall talk with her and give you my decision later today," Queen Mother promised.

As soon as Nina heard of Arjun's presence she wanted to rush to him for all the Jagatpur news, but Queen Mother demanded she sit at her feet for a chat. Explaining the problems and the suggestion of Nina's departure, she immediately interrupted, "Oh, Your Highness, it is several years since I've had leave ..."

"Stupid girl," the Rani bellowed. "You get your leave every year." But Nina explained to her when last it was she departed from the palace and the circumstances under which she left. The Rani was astounded to think that such time had elapsed, grimly aware the girl was right. "Why did you not remind me?" she asked sheepishly.

"I was required here by you and I thought only of serving your needs. Now it is that I'm required elsewhere by someone else I dearly love, and if you can see it in your power to release me for this cause, I would be extremely grateful."

"Very well. Stay a month or two; whatever it takes to make the woman well. They are good people. I'll return her husband to her side as soon as we have met on some very vital issues of state, along with some of the other sardars now in our midst." She was obviously the one calling the shots while at the same time forcing her son to take more active hold.

There was no tedium in this trip, over-anxious though she was to be with the woman she had not seen in some years, that sweet woman who taught her well. One whom she adored. She hoped to discover a way to assist and comfort her. As for Narendra, they had been unable to see each other except a few times each year and for very brief visits while he stayed at the palace. Nina's love never wavered but she was not entirely sure of his deepest feelings. To a small degree she had relaxed her worry over him and his dacoit fighting, believing their combined daily prayers held him in the safety he deserved. When meeting in their usual spot they would embrace warmly but each held back reservedly that last little touch which would take them from the range of best friends to lovers.

Kaushik and Nina passed Zawar where the fateful hooks still clung to the trees, the hooks from which the Bhils had hung the baskets of the royal babies. The Bhils had always seemed to come through when things were rough for the Ranas and their families, protecting women and children. Now if she could only come through for Narendra's mother.

Odd they'd request her help. But she welcomed the opportunity to repay this bedridden woman who had asked nothing of the low caste Nina, who took her in, feeding and clothing her. Perhaps best of all, she was taught a trade which made it possible to be accepted into the palace as a well-placed servant. Nina never thought to take credit for her own assertive personality. To her it was always Narendra's mother to thank for influencing her footsteps.

The fort loomed larger somehow when Nina caught her first glimpse of it in three years. With a sudden subdued gait she walked her horse through the fort, down the cobbled streets toward the main entrance of the compound of the Arjun Singh family. Here she'd be compelled to conform to the realism of everyone's station.

Kala was at her door, looking tired and frail, a lack of proper exercise and too many miscarriages, Nina surmised. She alighted from her borrowed horse, handed Kaushik the reins, for a brief moment acknowledged Kala's presence, then raced toward the doorway where she hoped to find Kala's mother-in-law.

Numb with heartache at the pitiable sight of her elderly friend, Nina drew back in unhidden surprise, cruelly aggrieved, uttering a quick silent prayer that she could banish the ill which had overtaken this grandest of women. Sensing someone's presence Bhadra opened her sunken eyes which lit as they had not for days at the sight of Nina. Sadness and ill health had worn deep channels into Bhadra Singh's cheeks. Tears swelled in the eyes of the girl as the old woman reached out her emaciated hand. "Do not cry, Nina. I shall again be well if God wishes; otherwise it will even be alright," she accepted her misfortune with gentle resignation. "What brings you to my side? This is the best thing which could happen to me."

"Your husband has arranged it with Queen Mother and Rana Bhim Singh and for me to stay as long as I am needed here. But then neither did I have a leave in several years."

"What a relief," tears hovering behind her smile, still holding Nina's hand. With such a wonderful family Nina was at a total loss to understand this depth of pleasure, making her responsibility a fearful awakening. "Come sit beside me on the charpoy and tell me all the news of the palace."

"It is sad you could not make it to the wedding of the Rana," Nina attempted to be somewhat lighthearted in conversation. "I was accompanying Queen Mother on that journey and it was very different and exciting. I wish you could have seen it. The shamianas for the meals were exquisite, trimmed with a million jasmine and rose blossoms. The mandap for the bride and groom I got to see before the wedding started and the poles at the four corners were entirely covered with these dazzling flowers. Oh, it all smelled so sweet. And His Highness, my did he look handsome. He stood so proud. Imagine my good fortune to be there."

"And his wife? What of her?"

"I have not come to really know her yet. She brought back to the palace all her own servants and they do not have anything to do with the rest of us under the wing of Queen Mother."

"I hear the Rani still runs the kingdom, Nina. Is she as busy as ever?"

"Yes, besides the durbars she meets with all the representatives of the other kingdoms who come to pay respects, and to all the jagirs and lords of our own land." Nina had years ago come to think of Mewar as "her" kingdom too. "She grows noticeably tired but when she relaxes and allows the Maharana to take over she becomes disturbed that he has not handled something properly. At least that is what it appears to me from the little I see of the business end of the palace. I am not a politician, as you know, and it is difficult for me to understand much of what goes on. Still, it is evident to me the queen is stronger than His Highness and she in fact continues so far to be regent."

"Have you seen Narendra yet?" the mother changed the topic.

Nina's face reddened noticeably and she said no. "I am here to care for you, so you had better make up your mind that from this moment on you are starting to get better," she ordered, raising a pointed finger at the sickly woman with a crinkled smile.

Even that bit of jesting perked up the old lady and she ordered that Nina bring a cup of tea. When it had properly brewed she held the cup while the weakened Shrimati Singh slowly sipped.

Kala had quietly stepped into the doorway. "It is good that you are here. It's the first nourishment she has had in the last two days," and turned to leave as quietly as she had entered.

Nina waited until well after dark to saunter to the ramshackle little temple in the far corner of the grounds. Perhaps Kala would have told Narendra of her arrival. If so, she hoped he'd come to her here. The wait was not too long, Narendra trilling the little bird call as he had on occasions past, Nina's heart dancing. Neither spoke and they once more kissed as they had on that very first episode. The night was to be a very long one in the temple.

"We must not meet too often," he cautioned hours later as they were about to part. "Let us make it every eighth night so that no one notices a pattern of every Wednesday night we are both gone, for instance."

"What would you say to every fifth night?" she suggested. "Oh God, but I'm glad you're here in Jagatpur. I didn't dare hope you'd be. I can stand these long separations no longer."

"When possible I try to stay here if father is serving his time at court, and now that mother is ill there is all the more reason. I am glad too, Nina. I've waited years for such a time as this. I think we both always knew we would come to this."

"I would wait another eternity if I had to, but I pray it will not come to that. See you next Monday night," she said, reaching up for the last kiss of the night and walking into the direction of her little room.

Narendra would circle around in another path he had created, climb a broken part of fence and re-enter his courtyard from the opposite side appearing he had been out in the city. He would sleep well tonight for it was the first time in several years he had enjoyed the presence of a woman, though he had forced Kala to submit to him a few months previously. He knew he would never do that again!

Patterned intricacies of Nina's current life in Jagatpur made her more happy than she had ever been. To nurse her ailing friend was of prime importance. Virtue was not the main ingredient of her days. Her meritorious services rendered before the gods meant nothing to her other than the sublime opportunity to assist in curing, by whatever powers and patience she might possess, the woman she revered. Nina took it upon herself to talk with the doctor about Shrimati Bhadra Singh's condition and how best she could help. It was pleasing to the ears to hear that Nina's presence alone had brought a sparkle to the eyes and a hint of color to the cheeks of the patient.

"How can I please you today, Mataji?" Nina requested earnestly.

"Sit with me again and talk of life at the palace."

"First let me give you a little exercise. You have lain in bed for too long. You will grow weaker. I'll call for help." One of the daughters-in-law rushed to Nina's aid, holding the woman firmly under the arms on either side, allowing her only a few steps of movement to a sturdy chair, a few minutes to rest in it, and then back to bed. This Nina would do several times a day, each time increasing the distance slightly until one day soon she was able to sit up for a half hour duration.

Bhadra Singh took more food with the urging of Nina who by this time had totally taken over all the chores of caring for the woman and along with the doctor issued all instructions. Bathing her twice a day, keeping her hair combed back and tidy, freshening her with frequent clean clothes made a terrific difference in attitude. If and when others would have suggested such treatment Bhadra Singh would send them from the room. Strangely, not only Bhadra and Kala but everyone else acquiesced to Nina's subtle demands. Perhaps it was because she served Queen Mother. Everything about the household including the kitchen ran more smoothly, Nina tolerating absolutely no bickering.

Nor was the problem of caring for the matriarch due to anyone shunning duties. Each of the daughters-in-law felt an abiding respect; none could help but love the woman for her gentleness and incarnate beauty of spirit. She managed to treat them all equally, hushing them with subdued tones in the budding stages of inevitable family arguments. Nina had become aware of this trait on several earlier occasions and learned from it that the quiet mannerism, the softened tones of speech did more to hush a room than the ranting uproars of others. This lesson she had learned well from earlier life at their home. It was now her turn to practice this method. And many other little things she was still learning from her "Mataji," her "respected mother."

Determined strength of purpose was prodigiously admired by the two ladies, each for the other. Both Nina and her patient wished they had the character of the other while in fact possessing it. Born in two vastly different strata, the women were much alike. Born of another mother and place, Nina could have been the finest of all Ranis; of this there was no doubt in the mind of Narendra's mother.

Nina had loved her natural parents yet she could not resist thinking at times how lovely it would have been had she been born the daughter of this tremendous person. Except, of course, she would have been Narendra's sister. She could not fathom him even as a rhaki brother, much less a blood brother.

"You look more radiant these days, Nina," the slowly recuperating woman started. "Could there be a reason?"

"It must be because I can see you gaining strength."

"There is no other reason, Nina? Sometimes I think you look more the blushing bride than any of my daughters-in-law ever did. I think you must be hiding something from me." Arjun Singh had just entered the room. With his wife's remark he suddenly became aware his son also had some spring of youth, much as he did when returning from his Laxmi Vilas honeymoon. Was there really something going on between these two? If it was Nina who restored life in his son's veins, could he be angry with her for this?

"I must bring up another point, Nina," the old woman again spoke. "Why is it you did not marry?"

"I have no dowry, Mataji. My parents and relatives are all dead and I am now long past the marrying age. As you know too, I was widowed," she had in fact almost forgotten that fabrication, "and I shall never remarry."

The darkness that fell suddenly across Nina's face brought secret tears and a mask of misery. Bhadra and Arjun each woefully regretted the pain this subject obviously caused, reaching out weary arms to the younger woman, holding her loosely. A weeping cloud crossed Nina's heart. They spoke no more of the prophetic sorrow inflicted and tensely remained long within each other's weak hold. If Bhadra Singh learned of this intimate relationship would she be banished forever from Jagatpur? But the old woman drew Nina ever closer. How strangely fate wove its web.

Secretly vowing to make up to the girl for the unkind question Bhadra Singh later called her son to her side. While Bhadra was the sickest Nina had remained in the room with her, sleeping on the floor beside the bed. Now that she showed signs of returning health, Nina slept more soundly in her own room.

When Narendra arrived at his mother's side she told of what had transpired; her inadvertent unkind remark. The distress was apparent, Narendra sick at heart to see such brooding. "It is but one of those things which happen in life, Mataji. You must not permit yourself to become so sad."

"I do not want Nina to be angry with me. She has been my mainstay. Without her I would surely have died." Her comments were sincere and heartfelt. "I had really forgotten she was widowed. Too bad she had no children. She would be the perfect mother."

"Nina would never be angry with you for anything, least of all something so simple as an innocent remark. You must give her more credit that that, my mother." He was dynamically forceful in his speech.

"But she had been so radiantly happy. She should not be serving others but caring for her own children and husband. She is so loving and adoring."

There was no need to remind Narendra of those attributes. He had come to realize this more than anyone else. When he had fallen in love with his bride he could not imagine loving another. Never would he know if his love affair with Nina would have progressed this far if Kala would have continued as a loving wife. Perhaps if she had no child-bearing problems there would have been no strain in their husband-wife relationship. Never had he forgotten their first few years of rapturous bliss nor the agony of the loss of their first child. Each successive miscarriage drove them further apart instead of closer as Narendra desperately tried. He wept for Kala, not so much for the loss of his child, but he tried fervently, diligently to soften her pains and to accede to all her wishes. She could have, should have been so happy. Now everything was beyond hope between Kala and Narendra. All doors were shut and bolted. Their happy years were too few and rocked with comfortless memories. He never spoke against her to anyone. He cared too much to do that.

Narendra's feelings for Kala had become an agape love rather than passionate. And now the woman of such lower status had won heart and soul. But Nina understood him. She never judged. She had pressured at one point for him to try harder to mend the cracks in his married life and when convinced the cracks had broken irreparably she submitted joyously, every bone in her body aching to cleave unto this man. He sensed all she felt. He was grateful. And he returned her love, no longer with any qualms.

At his mother's bidding he spoke to Nina that night, in the midst of the courtyard when all other ears were at a safe distance. "Mother is greatly distressed, Nina, that she has offended you. She broods gloomily about what took place."

"She told you of our conversation?"

"Yes. I too am sorry, my little one. I would not have you hurt for all the rupees in the kingdom. I know what it is you feel. You have said you wished to be mine in name, too. I know you feel this, as do I."

"Chup," she said loudly and firmly. His last remark was all she needed to know. It was what she longed to hear. Never had he said, "I love you." She felt in his love making it had to be, yet why did he not say it. His silence was the deepest hurt of all. She needed that verbal verification of what she felt was true.

"Love is a word I cannot use often," he explained.

"Can we meet tonight, later?" Nina asked.

"It is not our night," he started to reply but she urged him to break their five day span. With her eyes she touched him and he felt her need. Readily he capitulated, ever mindful of her feelings.

Very late that night before she arose she asked but one question. "Narendra, to whom did you make love just now — Kala or me?"

"I do not substitute, Nina. I made love to you."

That was the last nail required to pound securely into her mind the fact she was now loved, in spite of anything he might still feel for Kala. There was no jealousy harbored for the position Kala would retain in the family for the rest of her life; only a sense of pity Kala had been unable to give enough of herself to keep her man forever happy.

When Nina rejoined Bhadra the following morning they immediately embraced, neither discussing the trying moments of the previous day. All was as before.

A favorite broth of Queen Mother was occasionally prepared by Nina, the recipe learned when a friendly palace cook permitted Nina to watch as he worked. Palace food was superb, anointed with the best of everything. In Udaipur fish were caught in Pichola but Jagatpur had a fairly well stocked pond nearby and Narendra was able to send a villager for several fresh fish of a similar variety which Nina required. They were carefully cleaned for her. To cut open a fish or look at those staring, accusing eyes made her mortifyingly nauseous, but once completed she took over the role of happy cook, somewhat to the disgust of Bhadra's.

"Mataji," she said delightedly, "this is very good for you. Please try it. I am sure it will give you more strength." The flavor was all she claimed.

Nina also called for Narendra to assist her when he could spare a few minutes from his office desk and pressing matters. His strong arms were needed, although other members of the family were clamoring to be of help. The devotion felt for his parents was no hidden secret, but Arjun Singh and his wife continued to adore and favor their first-born and it came as no great surprise that Nina should summon him for assistance.

"The day is sunny and not too hot. I think we should walk your mother to the veranda and let her enjoy the freshness of today's air, shouldn't we?"

The son started to lift and carry his mother but that was not Nina's aim. "She needs to walk to strengthen her muscles, Narendra Singhji. Put her down. If she is too tired to walk back, it is then you can carry her. Place her where she can watch the swaying of the neem tree leaves and listen to the happy chirping of the little song birds."

Why she had developed more of a will to live after Nina's arrival remained a mystery to all, including Bhadra Singh.

Earlier in her career at Udaipur, Nina had painstakingly and with great effort learned to read and write. Determined to do at least as well as the young Maharana she practiced incessantly in her long lonely hours. When completely stumped she often scribbled words or phrases from books she labored over, catching Hari Lal as he entered or left the palace grounds seeking personal help. So pleased was he that this little peasant underwent such fierce struggles merely for her own sake that he gave undivided attention whenever possible. Thus she subsequently learned to read well enough to entertain even Queen Mother. Now she could do so for the revered Bhadra Singh, her uncrowned "queen."

A little at a time she would read this woman's favorite, *The Meghaduta*, by one of the most wonderful of all writers, Kalidasa. Both women were charmed by the story of the cloud messenger who sought the grieving wife, crossing the world's lovely plains and up over the mighty Himalayas. Reading was a little slow because the immensely difficult Sanskrit was hard for Nina to translate into Mewari. Much less poetic and dramatic though her rendition was, nonetheless it entertained the ailing woman. Nina would blush through it, not for the words she was speaking aloud to this motherly person but for her own love affair, clandestine as it was.

The lovers in the story had been geographically torn apart and Nina could never have Narendra totally to herself. Still, in this particular life on earth she had been born into a family which conceivably could offer her little, she had wound up living glamorously in Udaipur. Far, far more than that she was exalting in the privilege of loving and being loved. Certainly this depth of feeling could not be taken by everyone placed in this same world. Her good fortune was beyond belief. Could it possibly continue?

The lengthy morning ritual of Narendra's prayers never varied before breakfasting and taking to his father's desk. But on one morning he remembered some papers he had taken to his room to read the night before. Returning, he found Kala seized with nausea. Not again, he thought, with mixed emotions. Then he remembered the night not two months ago when raging anger had taken hold and he had grabbed his wife, tossing her heavily onto his bed. Rape is what he committed. Not passionate or tender love. It was rape of the wife who had turned him out. He was twice as angry when the act was over for it was demeaning to himself to lose his temper in this manner, and demeaning to a woman he once loved beyond all reason and still cared about. He knew after that episode he would never touch her again.

Now Kala was grievously nauseous.

"You are pregnant again, Kala?" he presumed. She merely nodded with an expressionless face. "The doctor has said you should not try to have a baby again," he replied remorsefully. "Oh, Kala, what have we done?"

"We? It is you who has done it. I wouldn't have."

All he could say was, "I'm so sorry. So sorry." Conscientiously he tried to hold her, to tell her he still cared. Sorely upset she jerked away, implacable disgust on her face, impossible to wash from his mind. Feelings of heinous guilt overwhelmed Narendra and he would work no more that day.

As for Kala, she had at great length considered suicide but if she would do so she could not have a Hindu's sacred rite of cremation. She and her child would be damned through eternity to a fate worse than hell. This she could not abide. Her personal pain and suffering would be over well before this time next year, whether or not she lived through the ordeal. And whether she lived or not was of little or no concern to her. She neither loved nor hated the man to whom she was married. It was to her as if he never existed. He had always been kind but it remained difficult for him to forgive her the coldness she had shown, just as she could not account for or justify her actions.

Narendra told his mother this latest news in the presence of Nina, the two women staring up at Narendra in open-mouthed awe. There were now eight grandchildren running around the family compound so grandchildren were nothing new to the elder Shrimati Singh. For Kala to again suffer the torture of another probable miscarriage and the clouded threat to her own life deeply grieved both the women.

"Why would you allow this to happen?" the mother reprimanded her son.

"It must have been that time, the only time, I have ever been angry with Kala. Something just came over me. It had to be that time. There were no others." All remained silent until, as an afterthought, he said, "I am, after all, her husband."

"I shall go to her if you like, Narendra Singhji," Nina suggested, looking toward the mother for her approval, too.

"You brought your healing magic to me, Nina. Perhaps you have some left over for her. Go."

"I have no magic, Mataji. There is nothing mystic about me. But I shall try to help if there is any way." She left immediately.

There was no way of being sure of the reception Nina would receive. On the other hand, Kala could not know of Nina's relationship with her husband. It had been brought about by her rejection and while this did not justify what Nina had allowed to happen, they were exceedingly careful that no one should know of the affair, mainly to avert the tremendous hurt it would cause Kala. Kala should be seeing Nina only as a servant waiting upon her mother-in-law. Nothing more.

Stopping first at her own quarters she picked up a bowl from which she daily washed and the ever present little shiny brass pot into which she poured fresh cool water. At Kala's doorway she called her name, both hands full. "I have come to help you if you need me," she said as sweetly as possible. Kala remained hunched in a corner of the room, one hand on her swelling stomach, the other on an aching head. She did not even acknowledge Nina's presence.

Slowly Nina walked to the miserable woman, once more convulsed in violent nausea. The servant knelt beside her, holding once proud shoulders firmly, the retching so terrible it made Nina's insides ache in reflected pain. Swabbing gently the face of this once lovely lady, Nina could only eye her with benevolent pity. She ran the cool cloth up into her scraggly black hair. At last Kala sat back on her bottom, earlier rounded breasts prematurely sagging were at this moment shaken as a tempest, on her face a mask of misery. Nina's grave pity amounted almost to horror.

Treating her as one would a child, Nina had slipped away for a few minutes, again returning with more water, taking over as she would with Queen Mother, undressing and bathing her. Kala voiced no objection; who knew, there might even be some ray of hope for herself. Oh hell, she thought, what does it matter one way or the other. Nina therefore had the questionable pleasure of doing with her whatever she willed. Nina even took the time to bathe the once lovely tresses in fine oils.

"How is Kala? Will she be alright?" Bhadra Singh later questioned Nina.

There was a mixture of annoyance and humor which struck this servant-cum-nurse, even in her extreme weariness. Laughingly she replied, "Since I am not a doctor I cannot know, but I would like to think that this time everything will work out right. We shall see that she retains some food and water for her sake as well as the baby's. I washed her hair in oils. I believe, don't you, that when your hair is pretty then you believe you are pretty all over. I think it will do her good. And now, if I may have your leave, I would like to rest a while. I shall come to you again later, also."

Nina's rest period was not to be for no sooner had she placed her weary body in needed repose when a messenger came. The doctor had visited Kala and wished to speak with the "nurse." "Will she carry this baby full term?" Nina immediately questioned him.

"That of course is impossible to say with any degree of certainty, but I would like to think so. Perhaps if you can stay attending her through this whole ordeal, watch over her closely, you may be able to make sure she does not make any sudden move to injure herself and the baby. We will want her extremely quiet and well nourished."

"But she must have some exercise, mustn't she?" Nina was puzzled.

"Definitely. It is quite important, but nothing strenuous. I'm sure you understand. This is one reason I wish you could remain to constantly attend her. For some reason this household must be afraid of you. They seem to do your every bidding. And be sure she gets plenty of liquids. You have been so successful with Shrimati Singhji. So my young friend, if God wishes it, and with your help, perhaps Narendra will yet be a father," said the doctor hopefully.

"But you must know I cannot remain here much longer. I am first and foremost in the service of the Rana and the Queen Mother. I must soon return to the palace where I belong. I've been here too long already. She'll have my head."

"Can you not impress upon them that you are needed here more urgently?" His voice was angry and demanding and Nina resented being placed in this absurd position.

"That's easier said than done. You see, I feel I have two allegiances, and that is terribly difficult for me to cope with. In different ways I owe my life and services to each of these families. It is not easy to be torn in half this way. You are pulling me physically apart as if you took my limbs from my body, giving half to the palace and half to the Arjun Singh family."

"I'm sorry you feel that way. But you must admit that none of us could do anything about Arjun's wife until after your arrival. We hope it will be the same with Kala."

"But I have never been trained in such things. I clean up Kala's vomit and bathe her. I do not see what more help I can be. And if I wanted to I could not stay. The Rani would really have my head. As for Shrimati Singh getting better, it is just coincidence that it happened after I arrived. I've done nothing except pray for good health and care for her and that's something all her family has also done."

"Nonsense," growled the doctor. "I shall talk about it with Arjun Singh. Perhaps something can be arranged," and with those words the doctor was gone.

Nina had been glad to see Arjun Singh return from court and surely Queen Mother must have told him to send her back as quickly as possible. Father and son had been spending many hours behind closed office doors trying to catch up on things which had transpired here in Jagatpur while Arjun stayed at the palace. Nina also wondered if Narendra might once more be baring his soul to his father as he had the first time he brought her to Jagatpur.

It was several hours before Kala awakened from a well-needed nap. Nina washed the oils from her well soaked hair, combing it back over her shoulders. She'd wait for it to dry a little before twisting it into the pretty bun at the nape of her neck. She brought fresh clothing and took jewelry from a large box. The pregnant woman finally spoke, gently thanking Nina for her generous time and caring but dismissed her to the first command of duty, her need to attend Narendra's mother.

"But it was both she and Narendra who sent me to you" she bowed her head and pressed her hands together for in the singular presence of Kala she felt more subservient than she did with anyone, including Queen Mother.

"If it is their wish," Kala replied, too weak and nauseous to argue.

"I know we are all going to pray very hard. If our prayers are to be answered you shall have the finest child in all of Jagatpur. Then the rose will return to your cheeks and a briskness to your step. I am sure you will be well soon," Nina lied, overcome by an overwhelming wave of compassion.

With a curse of unhappiness she answered, "I shall never be well. Nor do I believe that anyone would want it, least of all my husband."

"That is not so," Nina argued very loud. "It is because you are now so sick that everything appears bleak. The weeks and months will pass. Have they not in every other year? Time does not stand still, and you shall soon be free of this nausea."

"I do not believe. I'm sorry, Nina," she said plaintively, lips turning downward as did her eyes. Kala had become inundated with a desperate homesickness. "If only I could be with my mother and father at our home, like it used to be."

"You are in your home," Nina argued. "I can understand your wishing to be with your parents. I longed desperately for mine when I was in terrible trouble, but they were both dead and I had no one. I think every woman must want her mother nearby when she is to have a baby, but Shrimati Singhji, it would not be safe for you to travel now. It simply cannot be."

As always, Nina and Arjun Singh were genuinely pleased to see each other. He met with her briefly. He was so delighted at seeing the bloom returning to Bhadra's cheeks, amazed that she was now taking some steps on her own, and shaky though she was, the condition was almost beyond belief. When he had left for Udaipur the last time he felt such pangs of guilt for he was sure he'd return to find only the ashes of his beloved. Now his prayers had paid off. She would definitely return to fair health.

"I don't know how I can ever thank you, Nina," he spoke from the depths of his heart.

"But I have never known how to thank you and your family for all you have done for me, sire." She was equally honest.

"Then let us leave it that we understand and appreciate each other. I have asked Queen Mother to permit you still more time here."

"What did she say?" Nina was now very anxious to depart and quite fearful of Arjun's reply.

"She has released you for a while longer. Let us see what happens in the next few weeks, shall we?" With that he arose and walked to the rooms of Kala and his son.

A couple months longer Nina remained at Jagatpur, assisting both ladies in their daily ablutions. It was unyieldingly and psychologically more difficult for Nina than the physical suffering of the two women, each of whom was feeling remarkably better. Caring for Narendra's beloved mother was still a considerable privilege; caring for his wife offered overpowering emotions. Nina and Narendra still met regularly in the temple grounds. By this time neither could bring himself to break the enchanting spell and its respite from an existing grim world. What Narendra or no one else knew was that now Nina was also pregnant. She would have to leave Jagatpur before her condition was discovered. She must supplant responsible reasoning into her pedantic thoughts. She would return to Udaipur, sit beneath that tree where she and Narendra had often kissed and held hands. Perhaps there an answer would come to her about her baby and future.

Probably she would have to run away from the palace and lose herself in a remote place, have her baby, beg for food to sustain it until grown. She knew only one thing for certain. Narendra could never be told he was its father and preferably he would never come to know she had delivered a child. Her greatest fear was that Narendra would stumble upon her at some future point in time in his extensive travels through this and surrounding kingdoms in his quest for dacoits. Where could she hide from this man?

After a while Narendra's mother was considered to have made a miraculous recovery, gaining close to full strength. While Kala's vomiting had adequately dissipated she continued to look pale and wan, moving listlessly only within the confines of the home grounds, never venturing into the bustling streets of the bazaars which once she enjoyed.

"I have done as much as I can here at Jagatpur," Nina spoke to the elder Bhadra Singh. "It is time I move on to Udaipur. Queen Mother has been most generous with my time and I must not take further advantage of it."

"It seems you only came yesterday," the old woman lamented, knowing things would never be quite the same, so heavily had she and others of the household relied on this servant-friend.

"I have been here almost five months." Time had moved breathlessly. Nina knew she could not much longer hide the abdomen which was swelling, although the garments of Rajasthan did a superb job of concealment for a lengthy period.

"With your leave I shall start tomorrow," she addressed her remark to Arjun Singh.

There was nothing left but say goodbye to Narendra and she desired a quick one. Seeing him in the courtyard, hearing of the abrupt decision, he was caught off guard. He asked that they again meet in the usual place but Nina adamantly refused. "God grant you safety in all your quests," she simply stated.

"And will you not wish for me that healthy baby boy for which I am longing?"

Nina's heart caught, throat tightening. Which, if either of the two women, Kala or she herself, would have a healthy baby boy? Waiting until she was sure he was at morning puja she left Jagatpur expecting never again to see this fort nor this man.

Chapter 13

Held at bay by Queen Mother for five long days after a tedious return to Udaipur, Nina was certain she lost all favor with the regent and, perhaps through her dominance, also the favor of the married Rana. Being refused an audience she could do nothing more than wait silently in her quarters, each crawling dawn more fearful of her secret becoming known. Was her job also at stake; had she already lost it? The isolation of her life became terrifying. Growing violence of loneliness could not be assuaged.

Desolately forsaken, she too gave thought to suicide. Even in heaven she would not have her Narendra beside her; he was not hers to live with here on earth, and what was there to this place some called hell? Could it be more dismal than her present existence?

What of her baby? Narendra's baby? Perhaps she should wait to see what it was she was able to produce with the combined help of her body, her love for Narendra, her amorous act, and the grace of God. "I'll wait and have a look," she'd tell herself. That's surely better than suicide. Why kill the child. It might be the only one Narendra will ever have, and though he would never come to know of it, somewhere off in a vague and misty afterlife the two might somehow meet." It would be too late for her to share in any joint family happiness, but perhaps not for Narendra and his child. Could such a mystical thing be? Her beliefs of any future life, any reincarnation were perplexingly vague.

Nina thought too of Kala. With masterful strength she forbid Narendra's wife to labor over well-founded fears. Could she not be sufficiently strong to resist brooding over her own human complications? Unlocking old resources of will, she would bring herself to fight not only for the child she carried but for herself as well. There would have to come a way. God surely must have meant that she bear this babe. It must have been pre-planned somewhere up in the heavens far beyond mortal sight. How could she question God's actions.

Nina's spirit forcefully rejuvenated and neither Queen Mother nor the Rana could any longer intimidate her by their apparent anger with her lengthy leave. Some day she would again be received by them, of this she became strangely certain. When the time came she would hold her head erect and look into their eyes. She would not be cowed. She had listened to far too many stories of pride, bravery in face of defeat, super-human strength of purpose. She too was now a Rajput, to her way of thinking, and would admirably act as one.

If the lengthy silence on the part of the royal family was intended to intimidate Nina it had the reverse effect. She had finally gained all the strength she needed. The last thing remaining unresolved was where she'd have her baby, and that too would work itself out if only she would give it time.

At last Queen Mother summoned her. "You've been away a very long time girl. It would seem you've taken enough leave for ten years. Is all to your satisfaction at Jagatpur?" Nina replied with a brief rundown.

With his mother still acting as part time regent, the young Maharana showed no remarkable aptitude toward the exigencies of State affairs. Lessons, per se, by Hari Lal had ceased years ago, the political good it did the young Rana somewhat questionable. It seemed Queen Mother still inflicted her will upon her son.

Nina felt it a form of penance when told she'd accompany the family on the arduous trip to Sardargarh. "Will the young Maharani be attending also?" Nina inquired.

"Of course, child. It will be a holiday. I want you there also to look after their needs if required, and to be certain Her Highness's servants are held in check." This would obviously be no easy task for it was clear to everyone concerned there was no love lost between the servants who had arrived with the young wife of Bhim Singh after their marriage and the original servants of Queen mother and the Maharana.

"Will you be joining us, Your Highness?" Nina inquired.

"I do not know. There is an ever present rising and ebbing of political tides. I cannot say at this time." Nina had the feeling Queen Mother no longer felt as free to talk with her and it certainly was unwise to press any issue, at least not before she could regain her old comfortable status.

But if this trip was indeed to be a mark of penance or a form of punishment for the servant it would have the reverse effect. While Nina dreaded the chore of having to keep an eye on other servants she nonetheless welcomed the opportunity to get away from those who thought little of her in her own quarters of the palace. This stroke of luck was more than hoped for, but the glee it brought was short lived.

Maharana Bhim Singh's wife instructed Nina to come to her rooms, insistent upon a new wardrobe for the trip to Sardargarh. "I shall have to request permission of Her Highness, Queen Mother," Nina replied as courteously as possible.

"I am the Maharani, wife of the Maharana. I am the senior woman here," she fumed.

"And I am the servant of the…" Nina almost said "regent" and caught herself, "…Queen Mother," she replied, bowing respectfully. "I beg your leave," and without awaiting a reply sped from the room.

"Do as she bids, Nina, for I have no stitching needs of you at this time. If she thus acknowledges that you are superior to her handmaidens in this regard, you should be flattered."

Dispensing with the flattery came easily to Nina who wished as well to quickly complete the chores. Stitching for Bhadra Singh and Queen Mother was a rewarding pleasure. To do so for the Young Highness would be a despicable bore. "I shall have little time for a wardrobe if we are to leave shortly," she pleaded.

"I have reconsidered the matter, Nina. You shall not be departing as soon as I anticipated," said Queen Mother. "I have already sent word to Sardargarh and I mean to keep my son here with me longer. There are pressing matters on which I need his assistance and the trip will be postponed."

Changing plans at the drop of a turban was as common as a sneeze in a dust storm. And it was definite in Nina's young mind that Queen Mother needed no assistance from her son when she made up her mind that something was to be accomplished. Probably she wanted him to witness how she was about to manipulate an important issue. She was still not above teaching him a "lesson." But remaining at the palace any longer would reveal Nina's not too well hidden secret. She was already tying her gagra higher around her middle and it appeared even her breasts were swelling enough to be noticeable in the tiny bodices of the region. If only she would again be free as once she was with Queen Mother, telling her the situation before it came to her as salacious innuendo from gawking eyes near her tiny room. Putting off a bad situation made it no better.

"Your Highness, I'm going to have a baby," she blurted.

"Oh lord. Narendra," she bellowed back.

The response was so astonishing and quick, it caused Nina to laugh even as it stung her heart. "No. Not Narendra. Of course not. He loves Kala. It was someone in the fort."

"How could you come to know anyone in the fort if as you said you were constantly busy with Bhadra Singh and Kala. I do not believe you, Nina."

Implicating any specific person in the Arjun Singh household was unthinkable. Nor could anyone be allowed to try tracing down the imaginary person on whom Nina had carefully placed the blame. The three or four dozen servants of the Singh family must emphatically not be implicated. "I would walk in the bazaars when I had free time. We met. That is all." Lord, how Nina hoped her story would sound believable.

"Does he know?" the regent questioned, paying little mind to the fabrication.

"The baby's father? No."

"I mean Narendra."

"Narendra? He does not know either, nor shall he," Nina was insistent. "In fact, Your Highness, you are the first person to learn of it. I beg of you, please do not turn me away. I shall work for you all the harder. Day and night if you like. I will take no money and share my food with my child. Please. I was lonely. I have no one in this world. No family. I know I was wrong but I must have this baby. At first I did not want it because I can never remarry. But now I know I must have it. It will be something of my very own. Everybody should have someone, isn't it? I do not care what others day, but I ask your blessing, Your Highness. It is very important that I have your blessing. This I cannot live without."

The ardent plea was temporarily cast aside. "No one at Jagatpur knows of your condition?"

"No one."

"You do not keep babies a secret, Nina. How do you expect to do that?"

"I only know I must have my baby and keep it. If you will not allow me to remain at the palace, so be it. I shall then have to move about the villages until I come upon a place where I can stay with my child, begging for its food and mine. I would be repeating some of your history, is it not?"

"You do not have to beg, Nina. You have been a good and faithful servant to me, and ofttimes even my dearest friend and confidante. I shall not turn you to the outside world. And your child can remain with you, but I will not decrease the amount of your duties because of it."

It was four months before the regent and her son settled the affairs of state with neighboring kingdoms. negotiations had been tedious and tiring, bringing ire into everyday conversations. Nina stayed as distant from the royal family as possible, stitching dispassionately the younger Maharani's wardrobe, now far more extensive then originally anticipated. There were those evenings, however, when Queen Mother requested Nina's strong hands rubbing her shoulders in humanizing relaxation. She'd look at Nina growing slowly larger, sending her to an early bed. To the older woman it was almost akin to having her own first grandchild, as yet having none.

Feeling the need of a holiday at the last moment she decided to accompany her son and his entourage. She'd mention it to the Maharana whenever she got around to it. Excessive gear was added to the already huge mounds of tents, furnishings, food and water. Nina's few clothes she had carefully washed, sun dried and folded into a neat small package. Little would she miss the jeers of other servants. The more pleasant ones who were in the traveling party accepted Nina's condition as a way of life, uncaring about the male relationship. It was not the first time this happened to a servant, nor would it be the end of an age old curse.

Eighty kilometers to the northeast they would travel, until reaching the right bank of the Chandrabhaga River. Only about twenty kilometers a day were covered in their semi-leisure, and after several days the imposing fort of Sardargarh raised its glorious head on its semi-wooded knoll. Nina stood in long silence. Though not as grandiose and uniquely different from foreign Jaiselmer or Jodhpur, it was nonetheless the most lovely of all the Mewar forts Nina had seen. Far more imposing than Jagatpur. All that surrounded it from below remained unspoiled by nature and man. The thakurs of this fort had never allowed anyone to build near it with a resultant view so magnificent as to make one's soul cower before it. Already intimately acquainted with the grandeur the entourage remained stationery at length, impelled by its natural beauty.

The thakur came to ostentatiously stand below the entrance of his fort, awaiting in prideful silence his liege lord and the Maharana's mother he had for so many years loyally served. Opulent were the rooms prepared for the royal family, the thakur and his wife having thought of every possible means of comfort. Fresh fruits had been brought by camels from various directions: bananas and coconuts from the south, apples from the far-off Kulu-Manali valley farther northeast. There were papayas which it was said were brought at great cost due to the lord of the fort sending villagers scurrying the countryside, buying any they could find which were edible, paying a high price for each, their season being just past. There were mangoes from which would be prepared the soft mushy mango-phool, so delicate in flavor and which the thakur knew to be a particular favorite of Queen Mother.

Bolsters had been recovered in silks of all the pulsating peacock shades. Mats on which to sleep were freshly covered. Servants of the fort wore new uniforms for this auspicious occasion. It was a rare thing for the Ranas to accept the hospitality of a family of lower standing, normally visiting only other kings and queens, or meeting their vassals in tented fields for tiger shikars, or in times of war and stress. Willful as she was, Queen Mother determined her son would see first hand the manner in which all riches were brought to him and the abstruse problems of the nobles, though the latter was of far less concern to her. It was at intermittent times enough for her that she had their own nobles and personal problems with which to deal.

Swallowed up in the tiring journey and exquisite comfort of their new quarters the royal family remained at rest until time to dress for the nine o'clock dinner hour, a meal certain to be sumptuous and drawn out. Nina had naught to do but rest in quarters beyond that of Queen Mother, thankful for the leisure, the trip harder on her than anticipated. Though gratefully she was never afflicted with Kala's nausea, as months wore slowly on she wearied easily and it was beginning to appear the baby could be of very large size, especially for one as petite as Nina.

Even Queen Mother feared she'd rue the day she issued the executive order for Nina to join the crew, the travel an unjust ordeal for a girl whose only crime was that of loving a man. Queen Mother was certain the father of the babe must be Narendra. She could not believe Nina would bed down with another man while being so in love with the dacoit fighter. Never had she appeared flirtatious with others in the years of palace service as did the normal servant. The Rani could not envision her as promiscuous, sleeping with anyone from the fort, not even in her lonesomeness. But Queen Mother would not press the issue. There were sufficient problems of greater importance, although she had in fact retained that motherly instinct toward the girl, perhaps even more protective now than any time in the past.

Detached impersonality overtook the fort after a week of flattering meetings, colorful musicians, dancing girls of Rajputana, and semi-ribaldry. Nina quickly wearied of the sounds from party rooms echoing through the fort and came to know reasonably well the major servants and aides of the thakur. They were as justly proud of their thakurs' forebears as were the Maharanas of theirs, for this was the oldest noble family connected with Their Highnesses, the rulers of Mewar. The present thakur is a descendant of Dhawal who came to Mewar from Gujrat to the south in 1387, they would proudly tell Nina. Dawal and his ten successors all died in the battle, fighting valiantly for the Ranas of Mewar. The proud moustached man who last week stood at his massive gate commanded twenty-six villages, yielding a fair income and paying tribute to the durbar of one hundred seventy five rupees. Save for resurrecting the dead this lord was as close to the Maharana as anyone could be, the first family of the first-class nobles or umraos of which there are sixteen.

He has the hereditary privilege of guarding the Maharana's person in time of war, his servants would explain to Nina, although it was hardly a thing she would have forgotten. As at Jagatpur they had their own judicial powers, jail, police and revenue officer, first-class magistrate and their own court.

From across a courtyard one day Nina stared at the thakur. His brows and moustache hairs of salt and pepper grey had grown more wiry in ripening years. Nina had readjusted her original opinion of him, once so fiercesome. Underlying stories of his ability to be extremely harsh and cruel if and when circumstances warranted no longer affected her. She knew him to be extremely proud and haughty but the years which mellowed her gave her also a sense of more than pride which was due a family steeped in tradition. It was this man's forefather who surveyed the deteriorating position of his liege lord on the battlefield and contrived an outlandish scheme.

Akbar was one of the mightiest of the Emperors who invaded Chittor. At that time the grandfather of the man at whom she stared went surprisingly one day to Akbar. Sandu was his name.

The Emperor wanted to know what boldly brought him onto this battlefield to stand before the Emperor. Sandu had arrived alone and while this would in itself indicate no immediate danger to the Emperor's person, he was nonetheless searched and carefully watched.

Sandu devotedly loved his ruler and the fort of Chittor and all who resided within. He could not bear to think of its capture and explained to Akbar that he had come to beg him to make peace at the fort and in all surrounding areas. Akbar certainly must have been amazed at the strange request. He had asked how he could do this without Maharana Udai Singh's presence, even if he should want to. "If he comes and asks me, then I shall consider to accept," spoke the bewildered Emperor Akbar, feeling certain that our beloved Udai Singh would not countenance doing such a thing.

Being the immediate closest person to the Maharana, Sandu also knew only too well that his Maharana would not do this, appear before Akbar, begging him to leave this place. But Sandu had hoped his own plea would suffice and was willing to take the sporting chance to ask this boon, whatever the risk to his own life.

Nina walked to the Sardargarh lord and asked, "When your grandfather spoke to Akbar that strange request, what was it the Emperor said?"

"The Emperor stared uncomprehendingly at my forefather. Just imagine, if you will, what he must be thinking. A man so brave as this who would risk his own life in an absurdly impossible request for peace. That such a great man as Akbar, about to be unconditionally victorious would, because of an inopportune request of one lone enemy accede to his demand and walk away — well — it was cause for laughter. But Akbar held back his emotions. He could use many men such as Sandu in his own army. What general could not? Yet this strange man must be the loyalest of the loyal. No way he could win him to their side. Nonetheless he tried. The attempt naturally was fruitless.

"Also, grandfather knew, even before coming to Akbar, that his request would not be honored, but in his heart he had to do this thing, not knowing where the event would lead and rather expecting an axe across the neck. And even if his Maharana would come to Akbar, there would be no earthly reason why Akbar would listen. Certainly he would not grant the wish for peace after already fighting so hard, so long. The coveted spoils of war were about to become his.

"'Your noble bravery stands you in good stead with me, sir. Instead of sending your lifeless body back to your king dustily draped over your horse, I shall munificently reward you. What is it that I can give you?' asked Akbar.

"Worldly riches were on no importance to grandfather and he told the Emperor, 'I want for nothing, Your Excellency. I can have no needs, for surely tomorrow we will die, but I could never rest in peace in any hereafter if you were to bury my body as is the custom of you of the Muslim faith. I would, of course, wish to be cremated and my sacred thread first removed from my dead body and preserved.'

"Akbar was a bookishly well educated man and knew that all faithful Hindus wore their sacred thread around their necks, these threads having been given us at a ritual in the forefront of our lives. He knew there was a special prayer or scriptural passage told to the boy children which is kept lifelong to themselves. Akbar thought long and hard about this request. He had to respect this. In hammering silence he tried to envision his own forces completely annihilated, his foe cremating all left laying on the battlefield. For himself he could not bear the thought of cremation. He would therefore honor this brave man's simple request. It would hardly be a cumbersome task to cremate one lone defeated Hindu soldier. But there was one little detail which would create annoyance.

"Turning to my forefather he spoke, 'There are thousands of warriors. You will all be killed. How would I recognize your body amongst all the others?'

"'Under my dress my trousers will be one side red and one side yellow,' was his diabolically clever reply.

"This did not sound a difficult task, for he'd stand out superbly in the midst of all others and surely his bravery warranted this special attention. It was the least a mighty man like Akbar could do. He told Sandu the wish would be granted.

"Sandu returned to the fort of Chittor and called for a gathering of all the people around him. He had something most amazing to tell and much work to do."

"Everyone listened avidly to Sandu's strange tale. All were in agreement that they could hold out no longer. Akbar's marshalled forces were just too strong. Brave as the Rajputs were, fighting to the death, about one last encounter would end their attempt to retain their precious fort of Chittor. Food, ammunition, soldiers were diminishing in comparison to Akbar's army.

"'What is there left for us to do?' many asked.

"'It is simple, very simple,' my grandfather spoke slowly and deliberately of his well thought-out plan. 'If it is true that we shall all die on tomorrow's battlefield, let us leave for the Mughal invaders a wearisome task and one which will suit us admirably. None of us could tolerate the thought of burial in a mass grave such as they would dig for our dead. Or they might leave us to the buzzards or jackals if they choose just to ride off. But no. Let us all be cremated with the honor to which we are due.'

"'You must be mad if you think Akbar would waste his energies on behalf of his fallen foe,' one of Sandu's old friends asserted.

"'I have carefully set a stage,' Sandu answered. 'Let us each play our part well. We shall in the best tradition of Mewar fight our best fight, killing as many of our malicious enemy as possible. From there it is up to Akbar himself. I have always heard he is an honest and just man. Let us hope those stories are true. This is our kismet: we will all wear the same dress exactly. Now everyone get busy and see that each of you has made for himself the pair of half red and half yellow trousers I told him I'd be wearing when he promised to honor my wish and cremate me instead of bury me. He can have no choice other than to cremate all of us. And our sacred threads shall stand tall, as a monument to our greatness.'

"Sad as they were to again face losing our beloved fort, but happy for the iconographic scheme they would, in a manner of speaking, be saved.

"On the second day all of the Mewaris on the battlefield died valiantly. Akbar had not forgotten his promise, honor being a profoundly important part of the emperor's lifestyle. He gave peremptory orders to all his men to search for the body which wore a pair of trousers of half red and half yellow.

"'Here it is,' one of the soldiers called almost instantly. Another in the field hollered back, 'I have him here.' 'Here.' 'Here.' 'Here' echoed buoyantly from all across the vast fields.

"'What nonsense is this?' the emperor must have raged. This could not be. Legend says Akbar himself walked across the battle-scarred, blood-drenched fields and everywhere he looked were upturned dresses revealing half red, half yellow trousers. All were the same and there was nothing for Akbar to do but order a mass cremation for the men who had so cleverly outwitted him in life. He would thus honor them, and most especially Sandu, in death. Now he owed him even more a tribute. Sandu had been exceedingly clever. Never once had Sandu hinted at an ulterior motive. More than ever Akbar wished that Sandu had fought at his side.

"Before the funeral pyres were lit and the bodies thrown upon them, Akbar's men were first ordered to remove the sacred threads, remembering well this was an important part of the agreement. They were stripped from the necks and thrown upon a scale, weighing 74 1/2 maunds, almost three tons. So you see now why we write the figure '74 1/2' next to the address on our letters. Have you not always done so? None would dare to open such a letter for everyone fears the curse that comes with it."

The royal family remained at Sardargarh longer than planned, enjoying their well-earned holiday. Nina worried about Kala and her fate, knowing the time for delivery had come and gone but there was no Jagatpur news. She was also anxious for herself, secretly afraid of the wearisome trip home in her productive condition. While she had remained healthy throughout the pregnancy she was not eager to face a difficult birth, or worse, a miscarriage. Already huge she feared being torn badly by the child, especially if it should happen between Sardargarh and Udaipur. As a servant she could not hold up the procession, nor should she be entitled to ride in a palanquin. She would ride a horse yet feared a misstep and the animal's natural jostling. Being her first child she was not entirely sure what all the physical movements within her body meant, the baby exceedingly active. She'd speak to Queen Mother about remaining at Sardargarh until after the birth.

"I would guess the baby will soon arrive and you would be of no use to me at the palace the way you are if it's delayed a week or two. And for your sake I hope that doesn't happen. I'll make the necessary arrangements with the thakur," Queen Mother spoke gently. "Perhaps you can remain for a week or so after delivery. Some arrangement will be made for you to find your way back, but how you will carry your baby if you come on horseback I do not know."

"You are most kind, Your Highness. I shall hurry back, and do not fear. I'll find the way."

The thakur and his wife treated Nina with kindness until the departure of the royal family. Once out of sight the woman brought hordes of cloth requesting sumptuous embroideries on her finest silks and georgettes in return for room and board. And the look in the eye of Ganesh Lal, the thakur's aide de camp, Nina feared was anything but fatherly in spite of her huge proportions.

Each evening, weary from tedious stitching, she would walk laboriously across the courtyards to a hillock where she could see over the fort's reinforced walls down into the surrounding lush valley. Disconsolate and uncomfortable with the weight of the baby pushing on her small ribs and breathing more difficult, to Nina pleasure came only in fond remembrances of walks and rides with Narendra and their love nest in the corner of the old temple.

Was he now a father? Hoping desperately that all was well with Kala and the infant, Nina nonetheless resented the awkward situation. If anything happened to Kala's child and Nina's was born well, how tragic for Narendra not to know of the existence of his heir. It was unfair to both Narendra and the child. But how could she speak of it if Kala again lost hers? Nina would find it impossible to further hurt Kala, admitting to an affair with her husband while at the same time caring for the ailing pregnant Kala. In other parts of the kingdom women such as Nina would gladly give up their child if its future could be ensured. The baby's bloodline did not have to be perfect. Narendra was not the heir to the throne of the kingdom. Her baby's inheritance was not so grandiose. Narendra's inheritance, although terrific, was only a small part of the kingdom. And so it was that the brightness of delivering her own child, a child of the man she loved, offered only mournful resignation of the secret she must keep all her life.

With silent endurance Nina bore the early pains of labor. Relentless throes of agony kept beady sweat upon her body until at last she could stand it no longer and cried aloud in frenzied torment. Watching the suffering, another servant at last called upon a dhai to attend Nina and shortly thereafter a sturdy baby boy cried loudly as he was placed within the arms of a much relieved and thoroughly exhausted mother.

"My little Arjun," she kept whispering to him over and over, named after his grandfather. If anyone were to mention the name she intended to claim it was in exalted respect to the man who befriended her at Jagatpur. It would seem only natural. The baby was the most beautiful she had ever seen and she longed for Narendra more now than in any time past. He too was entitled to the raptures known only to new parents of a healthy child. There had been the pain of childbirth which was quickly forgotten. Could she tolerate the excruciating pain of keeping her secret from Narendra?

The child was but one day old when the thakur's aide de camp came to Nina suggesting she return alone to Udaipur within a few day's time, that he would arrange to have the baby cared for at his fort. There was another who could wet nurse him.

"Why would I want to do that?" she asked Ganesh Lal in complete astonishment.

"You could spy for me at the palace and bring back any news of important events and developments within the various factions of our government. For this I shall pay you handsomely, and keeping your newborn will be an excellent excuse for you to return here for it. You can say you just couldn't any longer bear being away from your child."

"You must be mad," she roared. "I would never leave my baby for any reason, let alone for something so disgusting as your proposal. I'd rather die with my baby on the road to Udaipur than dishonor myself in such a way. I've always been the most loyal person to Their Highnesses. Never would I do such a thing — not for any reason."

"It is precisely because of your past loyalties that no one would suspect you, Nina." He never lost the smirk on his face and it was fast becoming nauseous to the new mother.

"And what of you if I should tell the thakur or the Maharana or Queen Mother of your suggestion?" Nina countered.

"You will not, Nina, for if I thought for even one moment you harbored such an idea, neither you nor your baby would ever be seen again. Don't test me because I am quite capable of arranging it. They would think the tigers or jackals got you both."

There was not the slightest doubt that he was capable of such an act. As for the thakur, he must have been oblivious of the haughty request. Taken with her true Rajput loyalty, and knowing her to be his regent's favored staff member the lord of Sardar offered Nina an escort all the way back to Udaipur. She thanked the thakur kindly but declined, not wanting any further connection with Sardargarh, terribly afraid of his assistant, Ganesh Lal.

Nina left the fort a few days later when the sun had barely risen, not knowing how she would make it back those 100 kilometers. To ride a horse would be impossible for her while holding the infant. Something else would come to her, or she would walk. That she did not mind except for the terrible length of time she'd be gone. She owed it to Queen Mother to return as promptly as possible. God had once more been so great to place in her keeping the good looking little son of her lover. He would surely continue His goodness and reward her with safety and some form of accelerated transportation.

Sitting beneath a leafing dal tree nursing her infant she could envision Narendra. The babe was going to be very large, just as his father was tall. He was already handsome, having lost the reddish wrinkles and fat cheeks of the jubilant strain of birth. She played with his little coral-tipped toes and smiled at his round face, his yet unseeing eyes like a blind angel's. Softly she sang to him and he nursed and the warmth it brought caused Nina to close her eyes, to see and feel Narendra in all those moments of pure love and happiness which she'd most likely never again recapture except in memories. How dreadful that she would not share this child with him; but how much worse for Kala if she was to learn of little Arjun's existence and father, especially is she again lost hers. Hour after hour, day after day these thoughts pounded at her.

Persistently nagging at her were the questions of whether Kala delivered a healthy baby, hopefully a boy heir to Jagatpur. Surely she went full term. She would tell herself if only it's healthy, then I can keep my little Arjun's father a secret after all. No one but I shall know. Kala's baby will be Narendra's first born, the rightful heir to the seat of Jagatpur. Why was this the most difficult thing with which she ever had to deal?

A creaking oxcart interrupted her dreams and prayers, stopping a few paces from Nina. "Are you going toward Udaipur?" she called hopefully to the whithered old man seated with his children and grandchildren in the lopsided wooden cart.

"We go to Kotah," he answered. "If this will help there is room for yet one more. We can take you at least that far."

"There are two of us," Nina smiled broadly. God that made her feel good. What an accomplishment. For the first time she felt fulfilled.

"Of course. I meant we have room for the two of you. Come along. Hop onto the back."

She sat upon straw which worked its way through her cotton garments, tickling. Looking up into the heavens she said to herself, thankfully, "Somewhere there is someone watching and He had sent this regal chariot for the two of us." To Nina not all the gold or glitter of the finest palanquins or elephant houdas and trappings could have compared with the majesty of this her bumping noisy oxcart. From Kotah she'd get another ride, or she'd walk. It did not matter. She was on her way. She was going home with her child. Her child and Narendra's.

"We go to Tigon," he showed sad. "It is well, I say time is now to go at one mage. We can have a few of Bass that (I)

"There are two of this Mita, smiled broadly," God thee thanks his carnage. What an accomplishment. For the first time ever. On her.

"Of course Ismaru? we have room for the two of you. Come safely and rest," the book.

... which explains us every day? A few ...

... performance us of Dawn appear of hope...
by public no — — from You it she's not another side of
Each side her mastered. She awaits in her servants. Veneine
— — — — furnished to — the —

Chapter 14

Passively Nina went directly to Queen Mother on her return to the palace, waiting outside the zenana door until permitted entry.

"In honor of your past exemplary service to me and my son," the woman's voice was authoritative, "I shall allow you and your child to remain here, Nina, as promised, with the understanding that the boy will also be in our service when sufficiently old. However, if the father of this child had not come forth to claim his heir, assuming you still do not acknowledge Narendra as his father, no other man is to be accepted here with you under any conditions. Is that understood?"

Nina was not prepared for this condescension, but in a manner totally Nina, she looked into the eyes of the matron, "Sumje. I understand, Your Highness. There will be no one here to claim his son. I shall be Arjun's mother and father."

"So be it. Then let us once again be about our business. The silk walla will be here within the hour with new fabrics ands I shall want you to help me choose. I have been long enough without something fresh and pretty. There is to be much embroidering and stitching and you shall take time out only to suckle your child. Is that also understood?" It appeared Queen Mother still had not forgiven her for the lengthy stay at Jagatpur.

"Yes, Your Highness. Your Highness has always been very generous and kind. I shall do all in my power to demonstrate my thanks." Nina was doing everything imaginable to return to those inestimable good graces of her benefactor. Once lost could they be regained?

Conflict came in the form of duplicate demands from the wife of the Maharana, the Maharani, who long was aware of the superiority of Nina's talents, and while the girl prepared many pieces for her before the Sardargarh trip, the woman wanted more and more. Though she had brought from her home at the time of her marriage all the servants she required, she often tried to spirit Nina away from her other tasks. Nina's first loyalty would ever remain the Queen Mother, the wife of the Maharana could only be second in her way of thinking. This pot would brew as long as the three women resided at the same palace.

Since baby Arjun's somewhat odd arrival Nina was called on far less often to idly sit and chat with Queen Mother, the elder woman disinterested in the presence of the little child, especially while Nina was still nursing him. And so it was that the return to Udaipur became a more lonely stint that the servant had ever experienced.

Then came something which Nina might have expected one day. Queen Mother sent for her on a very bleak morning. Entering the room where male visitors were received Nina's heart was instantly touched with aching pity. Seated in the middle of the room, Arjun Singh told of the Jagatpur tragedy, his face mottled and swollen with weeping. Was Narendra killed by dacoits? Was Bhadra Singh crucially ill again? Or...

"The Rawal of Jagatpur has requested to speak with you and seek your help." Queen Mother's voice was gravely sober, eyes reddened.

Instantly atremble, Nina sank to shaky knees before this old man she nobly admired and after whom she had named her baby. "Tell me quickly. Who is it?" she begged.

"It is Narendra," he started slowly. Nina swayed visibly, certain he was dead from the knife or bullet of a dacoit. Desperately she fought a fainting spell just as he continued. "I have asked Queen Mother that you come home with me at once. I have ridden straight through with little sleep. My wife insists you are the only one who can ever help. You are better than any doctor. Oh Nina, you must come. Her Highness must let you come."

He turned to the woman still seemingly part time regent and once again begged. "I will do anything for you, Your Highness, if only you'll allow Nina to come to his aid. All my money you can have. Anything."

"His aid," Nina swallowed hard to spill out the joyful words. "Then he is not dead?"

"Dead? No. What ever gave you that idea?" the man frowned at her. "It is Kala and her child who are dead. Did none of you know?"

"My God," Nina wailed. "When did it happen? How did it happen?"

"It is going on three months now. She was in labor and it was so difficult. We called the dhai and then sent for another midwife. The doctors came too. My wife went in to assist also but no one could seem to do any good. My wife thinks she did not push hard enough, did not want to have it, but I don't believe that is true. What woman does not want to have a baby? Everyone was so helpless. Each of the people there would take turns at what they thought was best. They all tried and everyone prayed but it was not enough. The incessant, mournful wailing around the house you cannot imagine.

"When the baby finally came out it was strangled and dead. Kala heard one of the dhais say her baby was dead and Kala moaned over and over, 'I am cursed. I am doomed. I can never have a baby, an heir for this fort.' She would not be stilled, though miserably weak.

"The doctor said to me later that he had told her and Narendra she could not try any more to be pregnant but somehow she was again. You know how sick she was, Nina, but then little by little she gained strength and some color returned to her cheeks. When her pregnancy lasted more than eight months we were all sure that she would be well and the baby would be born safely. No one thought otherwise. It was such a shock."

"And Kala?" Nina wanted him to continue.

"From the instant she heard the baby was born strangled she just moaned and laid her head back on the pillows Narendra had gently placed for her. She kept her eyes closed as if she could not bear to look at her husband or any of us. She was weak, you know, and after the long ordeal of the birth she just succumbed to the inevitable. We believe she did not want to live. Narendra begged and begged her, 'Speak to me. Tell me you forgive me,' but that she definitely would not do. Steadfastly she refused to answer or to look at him. She wanted to hold her baby. For a few minutes they let her do so, but after they took it away to prepare it for its sacred rites she lay motionless. For the rest of the day and the next she refused even water and would speak to no one. Then as my wife was still sitting with her she simply stopped breathing."

This fine strong lord was rocked by his own convulsive sobs. When he could again speak he said, "We tell Narendra that Kala and the child are both happy in heaven but it is as if my son has gone deaf. Now it is he who will not eat anything at all, nor drink. Is he trying to kill himself as his wife did? He had to be held back from throwing himself on her funeral pyre. It took the strength of Ranjit, Pandu, Ramesh and others who had come. This hunger strike will kill him soon if it continues, and killing himself will do no one any good. Not Kala, nor his child born dead, nor anyone else.

"My wife and I believe that if there is a chance for him to live, if there is anyone he will listen to it is you, Nina. His men friends, even those he likes best, Ram and Pandu, none of them will he see, and if they barge into his room we think he cannot hear them. He does not listen and looks even more furious, like a wild tiger. He's dying, Nina. Without your help he will surely die very soon."

The terrifying bind in which she had been placed brought total frenzy. She longed to rush to his side regardless of the outcome. But what of her baby? How could she thrust little Arjun at his grandparents and natural father, — a total disregard to the sacred dignity due Kala and her memory. Flaunting infant Arjun now was too callous a thought to countenance even for a moment. What to do?

"But I cannot just up and go. I have only just returned to the palace after an absence and I spent nearly seven months at Jagatpur. More than that, what can I do? I'm no doctor. He loved Kala and he is tormented. Is that not natural? Who would not be tormented? Surely he'll outgrow it. Force him to eat and drink. You are stronger than he." She could not believe a person as strong-willed as Narendra could allow himself to be as his father described him. Surely he must be exaggerating, a ploy to get Queen Mother to sanction another return to Jagatpur for Nina. That must be it. Exaggeration as his weapon against the Rani. Yet Arjun Singh was not a devious man.

The regent too was visibly shaken by the rendition. "Narendra is a fine young man, Nina, and I am agreeable under the strange circumstances to let you return to Jagatpur if there is a chance that you can save his life. I do not know what powers they think you possess but it appears the Arjun Singh family believe themselves helpless without you. Are you capable of miracles?" Only a little smile crossed her lips. "If it is true, as they say, that it was you alone who healed his wife and helped his daughter-in-law early in her pregnancy, then perhaps it is true you can also help Narendra. And your affection for him has never been hidden from me. I would agree that it is worth a try."

Turning to the feudal lord she inquired, "When will you depart?"

"I have already requested a fresh horse readied for Nina and one for me. We shall leave the instant I can get Nina onto the back of hers. I am ready this very minute."

"What of Arjun?" Nina asked her queen in dismay, not prepared to discuss the baby in its grandfather's presence.

"Arjun?" The elder Singh was perplexed.

"I have a baby born just several weeks ago and I have named him Arjun after you."

Stunned, he turned to the regent. "I did not know. When did she marry?" His mouth remained open wide.

"There is time for all that later," Nina suggested. "If Narendra is as bad as you say, then we must rush to him, but I cannot take my baby with me on such a flying trip." Although Nina had prayed ceaselessly Narendra would never learn of the baby's birth, she was smart enough to know he could not be kept a total secret. "What to do?" she beseeched the Rani.

"Go. Bring the little one to me and I shall find a wet nurse. There's always one around the palace grounds. He shall be well looked after in your absence."

"But I fear for him, Your Highness. The staff here does not like me much."

"Not to worry. He cannot be safer than here in the palace under my watchful eye. I will guarantee that."

"This is fantastic news in the midst of darkness, Nina. Everyone will be so happy for you. Soon you will have to bring him to our fort. Oh what a blessing. My wife and Narendra will be so pleased for you." He asked to see his namesake. He'd wait here in this same spot to offer his blessings before their departure.

Nina prayed he'd find no strong family resemblance, a deadly strain of anguish overpowering her. Taking the babe into her tender arms, refreshing him with cool damp cloths, she carried him not draped across her left hip, as the typical Rajasthani mother, but serenely snuggled against her breast. She stood before its grandparent ashamed not to acknowledge that relationship. Concealing heartache she reached it out toward Arjun who took it gently into his strong arms.

"He looks just like..." His words frightened Nina and he remained quiet a moment. Reconsidering what he almost said, he began again. "He looks like a very healthy baby, Nina, and I bless you for naming him after me."

Queen Mother took him next, calling for Karnawati, one of the wet nurses. In another five minutes Nina was on the horse, prepared to leave.

The ride to Jagatpur was formidably arduous for her body, still weary from the difficult birth of such a large baby, the uncomfortable oxcart ride to Kotah, a second rickety slow ride on tonga, and finally a day and a half walk to the palace carrying her infant. Work beginning in earnest on her return did not allow for the physical rest she required. Now this new emotional strain was almost more than she could bear. She was astride a horse on the way to the man she loved, who desperately needed help far greater than any she felt she could offer. The unfathomable story Arjun Singh related in the palace was just now settling in. Futility of searching for words for Narendra's ears and heart brought despair. The whole idea of the Jagatpur scene was as unreal as any mist she ever beheld. Sore at heart to think of his lethal brooding obliterated all other thoughts. Her drooping head ached, heart busting from the depths of despair.

When the two stopped it was only for a couple hours sleep, again to continue riding at a rapid pace, the father's eyes like those of a stalking tiger. From where would the strength come when first she would face Narendra. What, if anything, did he feel for her now in the midst of all this horror. In his life-deserting misery would he banish her from his sight as he did his parents and friends? The two riders spoke very little and when she ventured to break the silence it was to ask if Narendra still continued his morning ritual of lengthy three hours pujas.

"On the contrary. I think he never prays now. I believe he has banished all the gods from his mind, just as he has us mortals. He believes himself forsaken. He will not light any lamp in his room. From dark to dawn he remains in the gloom. He screamed at any servants who ventured to take water or food to him and now all fear him deeply. And he is the one who had been loved most of all my children by everyone who knew him, nobles and chaprasis alike."

"But what can I say or do?"

"I only know you are the one we have faith in when it comes to healing, Nina. And you are our last resort. We should have sent for you long ago."

"And if I fail?"

"Then I will have lost a son and you will have lost a ..., a ...," he turned to look at Nina. "I know you are more than just ordinary friends. I make no judgements or accusations, Nina, but rather there is a special quality about you. Narendra saw it when first you met, apparently, for otherwise why would he have brought you home for 'salvage,' as he once put it to me? And from that moment on there was something incomprehensible, a strange something binding you to each other which neither my wife nor I have ever witnessed on earth. We are grateful for it, whatever it is, for all the caring and loving affection you showered upon my son, my wife and Kala when she was so ill. In my mind there is no doubt you will find a way to help."

Slowly creeping into his thoughts was the timing of the baby's birth. He would have to place her in Jagatpur at the time of conception. Could his son and this woman indeed have been lovers? Who was the baby's father? Now he recalled how Narendra's unhappy life suddenly took a radiant newness. And hadn't Bhadra remarked to him more than once how Nina sparkled and glowed like a bride? But Arjun senior would not bring up the subject at this moment lest she become so defensive she'd turn running back to the safety of Queen Mother and the zenana. At this particular moment it was more important to see if Nina could bring his special son to his senses and back to life. And if they were lovers, if the baby was his, might this not make her task at Jagatpur consummately easier. That news should return him instantly to his old sanity.

As for Nina, she resented their placing so much confidence in her so-called abilities. What abilities had she? There were no powers of magic as some of the family alluded. She could only sew. Oh yes, she was a good listener too, with a great many years of palace practice, but if Narendra was not speaking, to what could she listen? Yet how could she have refused to try? And how astonishing her queen so readily let her depart from her chores when she so adamantly opposed the last release from duties.

The travelers exchanged weary horses for fresh ones at one of their customary stopovers. Nina took these few minutes to rest her back against a tree stump and remember the day before Narendra's wedding when they stood in his tent. She recalled her last words. Perhaps he would remember also. She had said to him, "Always rain falls from the skies and if you should ever need to be made dry, come to me. I shall always await you." Fondly remembered was his soft reply, "I shall come to you if ever the rains fall on my life." Now she was on her way to him and perhaps this would be her entree.

A sickening mist covered the fort of Jagatpur the next morning and everything before it and to both sides. Nina knew from this spot in which she halted her horse that the crenellated walls should be before her but blighting gloom stood in the path. She and Arjun had slept but a few hours the night before, rising in the dark to rush onward to his emotionally exhausted son. Concentrated essence of sorrow permeated the heavy air. There were no sounds from any direction. The jackals would have scoured the jungle and now been at rest. Too early for the dhobis to arise, there was nothing to break the still of the air for the washerpeople must have the light of the morning sky to aid in their rigorous pounding of soiled clothes against wet stones. Birds did not chirp. Slowly now they angled their horses toward Narendra. The ascetic despondency which hovered over Arjun Singh and Nina was as shapeless as the dreadful night.

Arjun watched the girl, face drenched in tragedy, as they moved onward. Her obvious misery touched him almost as much as his son's. Gently he took her reins, leading her slowly toward the sloping entrance to his home fort. Shaking the nervous, feverish yoke of misfortune he would not again allow her to stop, so fearful was he of finding Narendra truly at death's door — or worse, already having passed through it.

The gatekeeper was startled by their arrival, never allowing anyone inside at this early hour, but then Arjun was his headmaster. He held the massive gate wide for the two on horseback, closing and bolting it noisily behind them. Cobbled lanes resounded in the clickety-clap of the two animals' hooves and not until riding through the entire fort and coming to the oldest of the bazaar stalls did they find any walla awakening, bowing deeply as they recognized their master. By the time Arjun reached his private entrance to his joint family home the gatekeeper had opened wide the entryway, ready to grasp the horses and reins, but Arjun rode through the courtyard right up to the closed door of the main room in his son's quarters, Nina on his heels, both dashing into the darkened room.

In a far corner, with just the slightest suggestion of light from a single window sat an emaciated Narendra. He looked half his normal size, shoulders slouched and drooped, bare feet crossed in front of him, hands paralyzed laying one over the other, palms and thumbs pointing upward. He made no move when they came in, no indication that anyone was there.

"My son, it is I, your father." The silence continued. "Can you not speak to me? Can you not say something?"

Nina had come closer, sickened at the sight, watching for any suggestion of change of expression. Accustomed to the dark her eyes could focus on the brooding shadows of his face, but not a single muscle moved. She longed to clasp him in her arms. It was true what Arjun had said. If anyone could bring a response to him most probably it would be she, though certainly no one else could grasp the closeness which they had enjoyed, the fervent intimacy in which they had lived. Not even Arjun Singh. She dared not give this secret away, choosing not to touch Narendra for the time being, at least not in the presence of his father. Poignant heartache conquered Nina far beyond anything she had yet felt. How could he be saved from himself? There had been no exaggeration in the old man's rendition of Narendra's physical and emotional state. Nina could not imagine her lover living through another day like this.

She continued neither to speak nor touch him as his father relentlessly begged and pleaded for an acknowledgement of their presence.

At last Nina touched the sleeve of Arjun Singh. It was as if he had forgotten his mission to bring Nina to Narendra. He looked at her half in wonder, and then at his son. "I have brought you a wonderful surprise, Narendra. Do you not see her here in this darkness? It is our dearest Nina." The two stood warily constrained before the dying man, awaiting his response. There was none. For several more minutes the three were maddeningly silent. Arjun repeated himself. "I have brought you a special surprise. Nina. Myself I rode to the palace and back with her, trusting the chore to no one."

Had they not been glued to his facial expression they would not have noticed the subtle twinge of a cheek muscle.

"Narendra Singhji, I came as soon as I heard the news from your father's lips."

Narendra raised his head painfully slow, looking first at Nina and then at his father. Silently he wished they had not entered his circle of doom. Too weak and heartsick, he still did not speak.

"Could I talk to him alone now," Nina requested, no longer able to resist the overpowering urge to cling to him. Perhaps a physical gesture would bring more response. Arjun nodded consent backing toward the door. Believing him gone, Nina knelt in front of Narendra, reaching her clammy hands around his waist.

"Oh my beloved, I am so sorry about Kala and your child. How can I ever tell you? But I am here now and you must let me help you get better. We all need you so desperately. It will kill your father, too, if you do not get well, as it will kill me." Still there was no response.

Many minutes droned by and when she repeated herself he announced in a barely audible voice, "Oh, my little one, it is too late for me. I have killed Kala and now I too wish to die."

"That is utterly absurd and you know it," she replied in semi-harsh tones, but he sank back into his new life of silence.

Arjun had listened though he was not entirely certain of his son's verbal response, so low were the words. But the fact that he did reply justified the faith he had placed in Nina's special attributes. Nina's loving words also brought a greater curiosity of their previous relationship. Was her child Narendra's? She **must** have been living at Jagatpur when she conceived and in the present dark of room and mood she didn't hide her love. Again he counted backward the number of months. It had to be while at Jagatpur. For many hours he waited for Nina to leave the room, finally asking to speak with her well beyond the hearing of his son.

"Who is the father of your baby, Nina? I insist on knowing."

"He was someone who just happened into Jagatpur, sir. He has long ago left and even I shall never see that man again, the one who fathered my child." She felt her words were not far from the truth but even Arjun considered them a metaphor. Indeed, thought Nina, that man I once knew so well might never again exist. How badly is he damaged?

"If it is Narendra's baby the very knowledge of its birth would change his whole outlook and bring Narendra from the bowels of hell in which he now wallows," Arjun tried to trick her. "If only it is my son's child. Lord, how I pray it is."

"Perhaps he shall one day take another wife and have your grandson. I hope so. There must be many lovely kumaris to marry. Certainly there is one to make him happy."

That perplexed Arjun. If she could speak thus to him perhaps the baby Arjun was not Narendra's. She obviously cared deeply for him as well as the rest of the family. She would attempt to woo Narendra for herself if they were lovers. That way she and the little baby could live in ease and comfort in this fort rather than subserviently at the palace. Perhaps he is not the father the elder man halfway conceded to himself.

"Would you say Narendra's condition is about the same as when you left him to fetch me?" Desperately she needed to change the conversation and anxious to get to the urgent business at hand.

"Definitely weaker," he said.

"There is the very slightest chance I can help," she said. "Please, may I again be alone with him? Do not raise your hopes too high, but I have seen a glimmer." Arjun left for his private quarters, eager to convey to his beloved wife even the mere suggestion of a change. He'd keep Bhadra from the room, permitting the privacy Nina demanded. This attitude he could respect. They'd look in on the pair some time later.

Nina was beside herself, not only with the grief brought by the very look of this once strong body, now so haggard, a grotesquely impure form of tragedy. But first ... what was right and just for her to do about their child? Arjun was correct in stating that the knowledge of his having a child could bring life back in his body. Surely he would be so proud, even if it was a servant girl who delivered it. What Nina knew and Arjun senior did not was the deep love the pair felt for each other. Had she a right to deny Narendra this pleasure? Was it her duty to inform him? Kala was gone and baby Arjun's arrival could no longer hurt her.

But what would happen to her and the baby? If the family insisted that Arjun gain possession of the man child as the rightful successor to the lordship of Jagatpur, probably they would not allow Nina to marry Narendra and sit as his wife, she a lowly servant and mother of an illegitimate heir, and all of them believing her to be a widow. It would be bad enough for any Hindu to marry a widow, but an heir to a feudatory? From what she had learned in all the lessons to which she had listened with His Highness it would appear they would most probably keep the child in their home, raise it as a member of the family. They would try to marry off Narendra again, hopefully the next time to come up with a legitimate heir, Arjun then becoming something of a cast-off.

Nina would be an outcast and to be torn from her baby she could not bear. If she had carried it those nine months she would want to raise him and watch carefully over him. He would have nourishing food and some sort of work at the palace later on. Was that not far better than the trials of many of the farmers in seasons of drought or the countless problems of poorly experienced laborers. His lot in life could be far, far worse. She knew she could fend for him until he could care for himself, and in him she would always see the man she loved when she conceived and adored more fervently each passing day.

If little Arjun could not be heir to the fort, she would in no way give him up. To be the illegitimate son in a home where one day a younger legitimate son would hold the hearts of parents and relatives would make for a miserable life for little Arjun. To know she wrought such suffering to her own innocent flesh and blood was intolerable. The secret would remain hers. There was no real choice. Besides, was she not entitled to something in life?

Walking back into the room, the sun had risen a trifle higher issuing softest shadows in the melancholy gloom. She found an oil lamp and lit it, placing it carefully on a table out of his immediate reach, lest he once more become angry or wild and hurl it across the room.

"Will you speak to me now?" she asked in a sweet low voice. Again that horrible quiet. "You called me 'little one' before. I believe it to be a name reserved only for me, is it not?" Still there was silence and no physical movement. "You are too gentle and kind to hurt me like this, Narendra love. You would not hurt me willfully. Your father has gone to much trouble to bring me here. He felt that I could help you regain your strength. Won't you let me try?"

He continued to be morose and she decided to try to adhere to a routine pattern. For a half hour she would sit with him and say nothing, then she would try to force some tea into him, if only one swallow, then becoming quiet. If she could keep this up long enough to get his kidneys working then she'd start to introduce slowly a more solid food. She'd build up his strength perhaps without his knowledge of what she was really up to. She'd be diabolically clever and persistent these next days.

Bhadra Singh finally came to the room, warmly embraced Nina, shortly to be escorted out by her husband. It had been agreed before Nina ever returned to the fort that she would be allowed to work her wiles in whatever manner she chose, for who could understand the strange ways and mystical wonders of this outstanding woman — a servant, yet one of the wisest and most helpful persons they knew.

By evening of the first day Nina had been able to get Narendra to sip a tiny amount of tea and retain it; before bedtime, two small spoons of a thin soup. Prior to that were those prophetic words, "I told you if it rained in your life I would come to you, but I didn't expect a monsoon." A barely audible laugh sounded in the room followed by just the glimmer of light in Narendra's eyes. He had reached out to Nina, touching her hand. She knew she had won the battle. The crisis had just passed.

She had chosen to sleep on a mat outside Narendra's door in case he awakened and called to her, but before laying down she walked to the entrance of Arjun and Bhadra Singh's rooms. "I think it will be alright now, one day soon. He has passed the crisis," was all she would explain, departing. Tearful rejoicing of the elder Singhs echoed through the courtyard.

In the days that followed Narendra spoke at length about his guilt. If he had not thrown Kala on the bed when she wanted no part of him she would not have become pregnant. But he did and she was dead, as well as his boy child.

"You cannot blame yourself for everything, Narendra. You are a man and she was your wife. She knew that too. I'm sure she loved you deeply in her way. She was just frightened of what might happen. She wanted babies too. What woman doesn't? But it was not to be."

Then Nina turned philosophical. "Narendra, remember that big rock that the whole fort of Jodhpur was built on? Remember when we first met?" He nodded, squeezing her hand. "Narendra, you are like that rock, and also the wind, the heart and soul of India. You are the fire we all worship. And if you are all this as I say, then you are strong. When you are fully well you will be stronger than ever before. I truly believe through deprivation we grow. I have seen it happen to Queen Mother. You <u>will</u> be strong again. I will see to it."

"You make me sound like some kind of god, Nina. I am not a god. I am only a miserable man who makes the cruel mistakes of a man, only mine are worse. Nor can I bear to face anyone, not even my own mother and father, and you know how much I care about them."

"Have you heard what you just said? You made a mistake of a man. All men make mistakes, do they not, or else they would be a god, and you are correct, you are not a god. Therefore it is only through a mistake of a man that this whole thing has happened. God forgives mistakes and so you are already forgiven. Of that I am quite sure. So you have but to cry when you will, regain your strength, accept the sorrows everyone endures. Remember Kala kindly. Remember her as when you first met.

Of those first months and years when you both were so much in love and happy. Forget all else, Narendra. I beseech you.

"Once, when we first met, you had killed a man and thought you could not live through the ordeal and pain. Now you believe you've killed your wife. It took a long time to live with yourself before. This sadness is immeasurably worse because the dead woman is your love. But time will pass and the burden become lighter. Before this can happen, however, you must come to realize it was not your fault. Please concentrate on that and on remembering Kala as the loveliest thing in your life, that you were so lucky to have her even for a while. After all, my darling, what is there among us mortals which is permanent?"

"You, Nina, who have made love to me ask that I remember her that special way? You do not ask that I forget her and think now only of you? You do not ask for anything for yourself in all the time you've been here and now you want me to remember the best of Kala. You really are special, aren't you?"

"Just mortal; like you. I'm not being noble. It was a wonderful love for however long it lasted. I have lost count of the years. It seems like only yesterday you found me in Mandore. I was but your second love and perhaps it is never as great as the first. Perhaps one day you can love someone very beautiful again, even have ..." her throat tightened and she could say no more. Somehow she was able to share Narendra with Kala but another woman would be far, far more difficult, too cruel.

"You are wrong about the second love not being as great as the first, Nina. There is a difference to be sure. The first love is all magic and wonder and starry skies. But the second I think settles down to a greater reality or acceptance of what life is all about. Never say my second love is not great, for it was and it is. I still love you, Nina, though strangely I cannot say those words very often."

Hearing this again brought a lightness to her heart beyond description, yet it also brought a wretchedness of mind with her decision to keep her baby's parental background a secret. At the time of her capture by Motilal and his sinful months of lust which followed, her heart smarted with wrong. Now was she again creating another deplorable wrong? Could such wrongs ever be righted? Would they be irreconcilable? A writhing torment clouded her path and somehow a final decision would have to be made. From whom could she seek advice? No mortal soul could she confide in. The temple would be the place to go. It would be quiet and she would be alone. No longer a consecrated place of worship, it was a temple only to her heart and the love they had shared within its crumbling walls. Long ago all gods and goddesses in their carved imagery had been removed. But Nina could still pray there.

She found the hidden paths grown higher with scrub brush, catching her gagra on bristles. Once at the door's lintel she dared not step through it for to Nina the love which created little Arjun was the most sacred love and minute of her life. To step upon that hallowed spot where she and Narendra had lain was for this moment blasphemous sacrilege. She would pray to whatever powers that be for a clinching answer to her dilemma. She had no favorites in the Hindu religious pantheon, yet somehow called on Ganesh to supply her with intelligence to handle her vexing problem through his powers of prudence and wisdom.

The air carried a gentle breeze and sounds seemed to whisper to her alone. She sat at length repeating over and over in silent prayer that she must be just both to Narendra and to their son whom she loved all-discerningly and equally. Certain she would receive the answer at this very spot she stayed on and on, at last shouting aloud in anger at Ganesh, "Can't you hear me, or don't you care. I ask you for help and you do nothing. What kind of god are you?" Angrily she stalked back to her tiny room, distraught and dismayed. If Ganesh was so filled with wisdom and would not share it, to whom next could she turn?

The week that followed showed increasing signs of ultimately restored health to Narendra, although he was still significantly weak. Now agreeable to taking small amounts of solid food and liquids and having a greatly improved mental attitude, Nina announced unceremoniously it was time she must return to the palace. Narendra did not press her to remain; at a future time he would possibly want to take up their relationship where it had left off. As for Nina, she was very unsure whether that could ever be possible. Neither spoke of it.

Telling Arjun of her decision to leave, the older man brought up the inevitable. "You've told Narendra of your baby?"

"No. I could not bring myself to do so after such a tragedy. How could I?"

"You remain too close to him not to. He would be delighted with your happiness and it is not right to keep such a deep secret. Go to him. Tell him. He will want to know."

"How can I tell him I am a new mother when he has lost both wife and son? It's too unfair."

"It is right you kept silence when his death was imminent. Now I can see your wisdom at that point. In that you were far more clever than I, but now he is stronger. Please go to him."

"And your wife?" Nina inquired. "Does she know?"

"I have kept your secret until now but she must be informed too. First go to Narendra, child. You must. I insist." There was no longer any doubt in his mind that this baby was his grandson. What he could not believe was that Nina would hide its identity and not come here to live with him. He was sure his wife would gladly welcome Nina into their household just as he would, and how they'd love that grandson. Nina had been closer than all their daughters-in-law at gravest family situations. That she was not of high birth the elders could overlook. It would be hard on Nina, Arjun knew, to share the same spotlight of the other women for they'd resent her suddenly being raised to exalted status. It was an unprecedented occurrence, yet in time he felt it would work itself out.

How they would come to a decision of the rightful heir to the feudal ownership of this fort and Arjun and Narendra's passing would have to be decided conscientiously and discreetly. There was still plenty of time for that. Lord, how he wished for the truth to be out in the open.

Nina could not tolerate the thought of news of the infant reaching Narendra through anybody else. She moved uncertainly back towards his rooms. Choking back a frenzied paroxysm Nina spoke in subdued tones. "I have a baby, Narendra Singhji."

He could only stare at the woman. In his agony he never thought to realize that Nina too might be conversant with tragedy, or happiness. She had a life of her own. He had never asked about her. Kala's misfortune could conceivably happened to her. But this was good news! His life so long lost to the world, he had forgotten all but himself and the ill-fated Kala and her child. "A baby? How can this be? Why wasn't I informed? What tremendous news! Is it a boy?"

"A son. He is now a month and a half old and I must hurry back to the palace and care for him."

"It's mine, isn't it. It must be. Why didn't you tell me?" He rushed to her, grabbing tightly her small shoulders.

"No. You don't know the father. He's long gone from here."

"I am the father. I know it. You could not make love to me as you did and sleep with yet another. I know you too well for that. It is mine. I know it is and I want to see him. What is he called?"

"I named him Arjun after your father. It was the finest name I could think of in all of Rajasthan. I hope you do not mind."

"Yes. I would have chosen that name too. You named him Arjun after his grandfather, isn't it?"

"I named him Arjun for the deep respect I have for your father. He is not your son. I have told you. Why won't you believe me?"

"Nina, I don't know why you are lying. I suppose you have a reason which you think is right. But if I have a son I must know it for sure and it is not your place to lie on such a grave matter. You realize, Nina, that my first son is the heir to this fort just as I will be sardar after the passing of my father. Can you honestly deny such a heritage to your own flesh and blood? <u>That</u> is not in the Rajput tradition."

"But he's not even legitimate, Narendra." She had stumbled badly in her reply just as he had cleverly tricked her. For years he interrogated people deftly, bringing them to submission. Even in his weakened state, he remained the master of that trade.

"So he is mine. If you will not admit it before me then perhaps my father can get you to realize the gravity of this situation. This kind of thing has happened before in the history of Mewar. Father will know what is to be done."

"You have no right to try to trick me into saying something which is not so. I have not said he is your son, nor will I."

"If he is a month and a half old then you conceived him while living here at Jagatpur." Narendra's arithmetic worked the same as his father's. "There is no way you slept with any other. I can never believe that. If he is my son by heaven he will be my heir."

"If he were your son he could not be your heir. You will again marry and have legitimate heirs who will not be mothered by a servant but by someone high-born. And then what of Arjun's life? He would be treated cruelly by his step brothers and sisters and this I could not have. But he is not yours and so there is no problem. Why do we even argue about it?"

Narendra could understand her reasoning and delayed further dialog until he could discuss it with his father, a matter Nina refused to let him do at this moment in her presence. She was too vulnerable to the passionate love she still felt for Narendra. A renewed strength would have to be built up before letting herself in for further arguments. The future of her son must be at the forefront of her decision. She was sure she had already made the right one.

Nina left early the following morning, determined she could now travel this route alone, unafraid of wayside bandits, fully familiar with the terrain she had crossed a sufficient number of times. Narendra, though on the upswing, would be far too weak to make such a journey for some little while and it would allow her sufficient time to bolster her courage to stick to her decision.

By the following January Narendra's strength had fully returned, his conscience sufficiently eased to make life bearable and both he and his father arrived at the palace, happy on two counts. He would at least get to see the child he felt was his, trusting that in these months Nina would have come to her senses and admit his fatherhood. Arjun senior, meantime, had disallowed any thought to an earlier trip, knowing Nina to be a willful woman who would not easily be swayed in her thought of right and wrong with regard to her son's future. And of course there was the minute chance that perhaps little Arjun was not Narendra's.

The second reason for arriving at this time was the tiger shikar on which they had been invited. Neither man had been on an organized hunt for a couple of years and to join His Highness, Maharana Bhim Singh, was first a distinguished honor and second a fashionable pleasure, not to mention a chance for father and son to be together for something they keenly enjoyed since early boyhood.

Immediately on arrival at the palace they asked for Nina and her little one. Nina placed the baby into the arms of the grandfather. He was a happy babe with a broad smile for all those who cooed or talked to him. Black eyes as round as puri and curly silk hair made him the most precious little thing on the royal premises, although His Highness and the Rani also had started to raise a family.

"He looks just like my son when he was a baby," Arjun spoke hopefully. After Nina's departure from Jagatpur Narendra admitted their love affair. Narendra instinctively believed the child to be his but loving Nina so deeply and already hurting badly from his first love he wished to tread slowly and lightly until the matter could be settled amicably. He could not tolerate the thought of another disaster with the second of his two loves.

"Many Indian babies look alike, sir," Nina had replied. "I wish with all my heart I could give him to your son to replace the one he lost but you know I cannot do so."

"I know you will not do so unless you have a change of heart..I am authorized by my wife to tell you," Arjun senior spoke, "that we would all welcome you to the house of Arjun Singh and adopt the child even if you will not openly admit that this is our grandchild. You can live at Jagatpur for the rest of your days, and not as a servant, watching your son grow up in an atmosphere grander than that of living with the sons and daughters of the servants of Udaipur."

"Your offer is most generous and I thank you," Nina interrupted. "I shall think further on it, but I do not believe I can accept. I have vowed to care for Queen Mother as long as she lives and it seems she needs me now more than ever. There is much trouble brewing between dissenting factions in the government. She is growing older and the problems exhaust her." Then in the lowest whisper she added, "It would seem she is not content with the way her son handles all the affairs of state and she presses so hard to do all she can in the span of a day. I try to interrupt and get her to rest more but sometimes this is not possible. I must continue here, sir, but I cannot express my gratitude to you and your family for the generous offer."

Narendra had taken the child into his arms, playing with its tiny fingers. When Nina looked at him there were tears starting to roll down his tanned face. In that instant she wanted to blurt out, "Yes, he's yours," but she had steeled herself against this urge ever since leaving the fort. She knew these moments would come. But Narendra was sure to remarry and have more sons and she would place her baby in primary importance in her life, caring first for his future. She must not let Narendra's tears sway her. God how she loved that man; how she longed to be with him, live with him, make love with him again. How could she hurt him this way? How could she not?

Several days passed, the two men gleefully playing with the baby at frequent intervals. Then the group was ready for the shikar departure. Two days earlier elephants laden with tents, water and food were sent ahead to locate a good spot in which to camp. There were still plenty of tigers around the palace but

Bhim Singh had wanted a camping trip well beyond the confines of Udaipur where he could loll each night with his nobles, tell stories, eat in excess, drink, and those who used opium could have their fill. By the time the Maharana and his nobles would arrive along with the many hunters and another retinue of palace servants, the first wave of help would have found a fortuitous spot near a well with sufficient water for bathing, cooking and a large flat stretch of land in which to circle their tents, the dining room tent placed strategically in the center.

Elephants and horses departed Udaipur ceremoniously, children squealing happily as they ran alongside, not stopping until completely out of breath.

Narendra was looking forward to this stimulating trip with his father. Corroding time partially separated the two, the younger with dacoit hunting, Kala's illnesses and death and those dreadful months of remorseful grieving. With loosened shackles he would try recapturing the bounteously carefree days of a vanished past. In the easy casualness surrounding shikars, flippant moods of the hunters could tangibly return this saddened giant to his majestic old self. He had come to count on it. Nina was right to force him back to life and he'd not betray her faith in his Rajput manliness. He had listened to her as life ebbed; heeding her words he grew stronger, for she spoke to him with an all-persuasive authority within herself.

And Nina. What of Nina? Could he dare ask her after a reasonable length of time to marry him? Would his father and the elders of the fort sanction such a marriage — whether or not little Arjun was his? Would Nina ever accept? He loved her more than ever since the harvest of their joint naked suffering. She had been alone with her unborn child. God knows how Queen Mother reacted to her news. There had been no one to care for her other than the nourishing food of the palace. The staff would have scoffed and spurned her. Lord, why did she keep such a secret from him? Why indeed! Nina was not one to upstage another.

A free man again, he was able to think of no other woman. Kala was a beautiful wife whom he adored and respected. But Nina was brought up minus all the luxuries of the wealthy, yet she possessed all that he could love and honor in a woman, servant and low-caste be damned. If the elders would refuse to accept her as the next head woman of the fort, what then? He would not dishonor her by making her a concubine and marrying yet another. That would break her heart. And still, could he remain forever unwed, never to rear a rightful heir to the fort of his revered father and forefathers? Arjun had judiciously warned Narendra to make no hasty decisions with regard to his altered future, aware he might come to think along undulating lines.

Poor Nina, would sense the turmoil wrought by bringing her illegitimate child to Jagatpur, whether or not she'd live with Narendra. Had he ruined Nina's life by making her pregnant? Or had he in fact given her the chance to be a mother, a chance she otherwise would never have? That too was a curious possibility, albeit never considered at the time of conception. He owed it to the hapless girl to make her uncertain worldly future as secure as possible, her immortal future a worthy seat. Who in the Arjun Singh household could deny a spirit of God dwelled within her. He had seen God living within her as she painstakingly nursed him, transferring His power through her.

Charitably beneficent was Nina in her dealings with others, seeking nothing in return, her sole reward the friendship and admiration of those she served. He must handle her with a sensitive grace worthy of the most compassionate and heroic of all women. Narendra resumed his lengthy daily prayers, asking where his first duties lie: his father and their feudal lands some day to be under his care; the strange little low-caste who nobly helped mold him into the man he had become; a method to learn beyond all doubt whether little Arjun was his son and all its monumental ramifications. He prayed too that the answers would come soon, perhaps in this change of scenery. Perhaps in the familiar surroundings of home he had not heard a voice. Would it speak louder in the beauteous stretches of vibrant jungle and illimitable desert?

A symphony of ruddy browns and sparse greens spread every direction from the man standing at the curve in the dusty road. Old with ageless dignity his sole duty was directing the traffic of the shikar entourage in the paths of their home for the duration of the hunt. They had passed no one in the past six hours, so remote was the ostentatious campsite. The second bend brought into view assembled tents of beige, subtly blending with the terrain.

Narendra and his father chose a tent close to the Maharana. Sardar, because of protocol, was immediately next to His Highness. Some quickly took to opium, relaxing after the long journey, preparing for an early sleep. Narendra chose a less stimulating thirst-quenching nimbupanni of sweet lime and water. Removing top clothes he sat in full rays of the undying sun. This early in the calendar year it was still pleasantly bearable, even in the desert afternoons. Night brought a noticeable chill circumvented with wool blankets and many hours of unstirring sleep. Warm morning baths scintillated their bodies.

By morning Narendra was thirsty for the kill, spirits high, and he anxiously awaited the Maharana's distribution of hunters across the fields.

"Tiger, tiger," Pushpender called, rushing into the midst of the tents on his stallion. He too was one of the umraos, an avid hunter, and always anxious to be at the side of his Maharana. A lightning fast tiger had been spotted at a new kill, having eaten its fill, settling down for what was sure to be a lengthy sleep. Pushpender had been scouting the night before, remaining in a hopefully safe spot until morning when he could report his beautiful find to his Rana. From the description of the animal the hunters were eager to get moving, already completing their sumptuous breakfast.

Horses were to be ridden this day, although on others they might be taking the elephants. Bhim Singh was glad his mother had decided to remain at the palace. She too loved tiger and leopard hunts but opted to continue trying to assuage angry desenters of a few major problems. Had she been in camp she would have taken longer to prepare for the hunt, a point which never failed to derisively antagonize young Highness.

It was a good hour and a quarter before the hunting party had reached the circumscribed area, quickly leaving parched desert and swallowed by lush green jungle. His Highness viewed the kill, a baby water buffalo, neatly covered with nearby brush by the sly and wily tiger. He had not allowed anyone other than Pushpender to accompany him to this exact spot, doing so on foot and without even a whisper. The two men backtracked the kilometer to the others in the party, as stealthily as the wild animals themselves moved. The tiger was thought to have gone in the opposite direction for a lengthy rest.

It was the privilege of His Highness to make the decisions on the small pairings of hunters, certain that in each little group there was at least one superb crack shot. He had no desire for a frenzied animal stalking a village, taking out his revenge on innocent people. Man-eating tigers, once having tasted the blood of a human, look for another. Quietly and stealthily they were known to pounce upon unsuspecting persons who might for any reason leave the safety of their huts or perimeter of their village. When critically wounded they are doubly fierce.

His Highness set himself up with Sardargarh's thakur and a servant. Beyond them at least another several hundred meters, hidden from view, was to be another threesome, and so on down a straight line. They were spaced far enough apart that they could not wound each other and the beat would begin to the right of the Maharana, about two kilometers away. This beat would not start until it could be decided that the hunters all had sufficient time to settle down in a good spot. They would all be hushed for an hour or two so that any other lurking tigers or leopards would be unaware of their presence, hoping any slight breeze would not change direction and carry the foreign scent of the humans. With each duo of hunters there sat a servant with a baggy pocket of oranges.. Should the day become too dry and throats scratchy, and that was sure to happen, sucking a piece of juicy fruit would greatly lessen the chance of anyone coughing or clearing his throat, which was to say the very least a severe offense. Should the tiger be scared away by such non-jungle sounds His Highness would in all probability go into a foaming rage.

Narendra and Arjun were seated next in the sequence of hunters to the left of His Highness, their job to kill the animal if by chance His Highness or Sardar Singh were to miss or only wound it. And so it would be for the others to follow suit in the unlikely chance they would also miss. Too, should a female be scared into running in their direction they would all have the great pleasure of viewing her. Greatly honored is the female for her cub-bearing properties and none of the hunters would stoop to shoot one, save in a life-threatening emergency.

The tranquility of the jungle and ceaseless subtle changes ever enthralled Narendra. Langurs intrigued him. With their long tails they would zoom from tree to tree screeching the coming of the tiger, a sentinel of first order. Bushy eyebrows seemed to make them scowl, comical looking with funny little tufts at their chins. Yet the hunter respected them for their awareness of imminent danger and their personal private telegraph system left nothing to be desired.

There was another theory of Narendra's, too, that also told of the coming either of tiger or leopard. In evening hunts of olden days it was his hypothesis porcupines clustered about, moving nervously, quills standing upright. At such times Narendra usually found the larger animals stalking their prey.

Two hundred beaters had been sent into the fields, well behind the area where this tiger was resting. They had gathered from numerous villages to faithfully serve His Highness. A sort of honor guard, they were unpaid for their chores, often taking their life in their hands flushing out a tiger or spotted leopard, driving them into a rage. This chore they were to consider an honored privilege. But their leaders were uncannily skilled at flushing out the beast, forcing him to run in one specific direction by assiduously placing the front runners in strategic spots. Behind them the others would follow, all on foot. Many had metal pieces which they'd bang together. Others had long poles to which were attached small stones dangling on a rope. When struck against the pole it made a sound like a large bore gun. Such noises would violently flush the creature from his daytime lair, for normally he is a nocturnal beast.

When two hours of quiet had passed Narendra and the others could hear the shot-like sounds and the loud wailing of the beaters in the distance. There would be no let-up until at last, after a long spell, the hunted tiger would pass in front of the place in which the Maharana has taken cover. On this specific day they had chosen an area along the edge of a narrow stream just barely trickling with water over its large rocks. On its westerly banks, beyond tall shrubby bushes, each party was well hidden, and finally the tiger made his way past the royal party.

Because of his station in life the Maharana had the first crack at killing the gorgeous tiger but he was not a particularly good shot. When his gun rang out it was quickly followed by that of Sardar Singh. He too, for some strange reason, had taken bad aim on this inauspicious day, one of the two of them only wounding the cat near its rear, doing no apparent appreciable damage.

Momentum would carry him a great distance before he would fall if he had been wounded mortally. There was on this occasion only a short time between the first attempt at a kill until he reached Narendra and Arjun, so swift was he. It had been pre-planned that Arjun would be given the next shot, and it was never likely that he would ever miss a prey, especially when it crossed through open area. He had positioned himself at an angle where he could get him in the heart as he ran, rather than broadside, ruining his pelt. Nor did these two men ever like to shoot at the head. Incongruous as it seemed, they were softies about the looks of the beast even after death, to be seen as something flawless. It was, after all, one of God's most glorious creatures.

So accurate was Arjun's aim the tiger jerked upward with impact, spun automatically into a twirl, falling dead without an instant of suffering. It would be taken home after skinning and a lengthy tanning process, preserving its beauty for all time.

In the solitude of their tent later that night Narendra asked his father whether he would do anything special with the tiger. "I'll present it to Nina for having cared for my family," he simply stated. He intended its tanning to be done at Jagatpur, keeping it there until Nina herself would decide where she wanted it kept.

Nothing was killed on the second day. The wildest game around was the partridge and quail killed first thing in the morning for their breakfasts. And then there were the donkeys which ambled near the campsite, strayed from heaven knows where to a few scraps of food the cooks tossed them. Eight adults and two little ones who brought infectious laughter, scratching behind their own ears with wobbly hind legs, comically entertaining lazy hunters.

Then came the intervening respite, several hours of sleep in the shade of their tents, flaps at the front and back left open to capture hoped-for breezes. After that would come a quick pick-me-up wash, their finest clothes, a few jewels, and a sumptuous evening meal. Nothing of grandeur was spared in these shikars.

There were intermittent hunts, His Highness permitting others to have the place of honor on alternating days. On the seventh Bhim Singh bagged two lovely male tigers and as a third crossed his path he ignored it. A noble from Durgarpur managed to get that one. On this day the men had placed themselves on machans built into the trees, placed at safe distances from each other.

While many were of the mind tigers were God's most beautiful four-footed creature, the leopard stood close behind. Its disruptive camouflage made viewing extremely difficult and Arjun promised his wife a skin if possible. With a couple dozen species it's remarkable, he would tell her, how unique each is, every one so different from the other. Their heads are strangely smaller than tigers, the males weighing about 70 kilos, the spots something like a name tag. No two alike. Although they look upon villagers as their only enemy they do not prey on them as do the tigers. Still, the leopard is a dangerous wild animal and all due respect must be given when anywhere near their possible presence. Before they broke camp Arjun made his kill.

Many of the hunters went separate directions to their own private homes, this fun-duty to their king temporarily paid. While they would, of course, create their own hunts, in no way would they compare in voluptuous elegance. Narendra and Arjun would stop briefly at the palace, seeing the Rana home safely. It would be one more opportunity to see little baby Arjun who radiated so much winsomeness. Besides, who knows, maybe Nina would have had a change of heart and was ready to return with them to Jagatpur — permanently.

Chapter 15

Udaipur had found its portentous level as a city of vast charm. Narendra never tired of returning to it. His few weeks of hunting with others contentedly relaxed him, melting his problems from a vast reservoir of doom to a straddling pond and as he entered the old part of the white desert city of Nina's fairy-tale dreams he thought once again of her and her child. No decision had been found out in the open campsite as he had prayed, yet he would not loose faith that in the greatest moment of need an adaptive solution would manifest itself.

He sent for Nina and the child intending to impress upon her the need to have her close by in Jagatpur. But any discussion had to be sheltered. Waiting within the confines of the palace was his trusted friend Ashok. Exchanging hurried greetings Ashok was nervously anxious to speak privately with Narendra. Nina quickly returned with her child to her working quarters.

Ashok, Narendra and Arjun found a spot well outside the palace walls under spreading shade trees to talk of his venture, far from listening ears of servants and others. He'd not jeopardize his mission with even the slightest chance of being overheard by a prying spy.

"Beyond Kotah I learned you were on tiger shikar," Ashok started, the three seated facing each other on hard ground. "I felt you'd have to come back to the palace as the Maharana's escort before returning home. I sought an audience with Queen Mother, telling her I must discuss with you the capture of still more dacoits. She was sufficiently busy or disinterested and didn't press me for details, for which I rejoiced. I don't know how much of your work she knows about or sanctions. I did not wish to jeopardize your standing with her, yet I wanted to remain here until your return and not miss you. She graciously offered me a room for visiting servants. I was more than grateful. And I must add that the kitchen here is remarkable, isn't it?" Ashok was so wound up he just kept rambling on with the pace of a winning race horse.

"You have news of Ali, Ashok?" Both men were anxious for him to get to the point. "I had received your message long ago that he had settled in Afghanistan, well beyond my jurisdiction. He is back now?"

"He has crossed the border into India again, has traveled through Jaiselmer district and now again settled in Marwar. Does your work take you out of Mewar, or do you restrict your hunting these criminals to our own kingdom?" Ashok had seldom fought alongside Narendra, at times tied up with infiltrating Ali's hangouts or lengthy visits with his wife and family, a place he much preferred.

"As you yourself have demonstrated, dacoits know no boundaries. Yes, we sometimes go abroad with the request and sanction of other rulers. In the past I've discussed Ali with His Highness Marwar and I've been asked to assist them when and if he ever entered their domain. Can you give me an accurate run-down on what he's been up to lately?" Narendra requested soberly.

"It is the same as always before. As you know he is greatly worshipped by the Muslims and in the Jaiselmer district there are even some Hindus who revere his very presence. Everywhere he has gone people go crazy. And I don't mean from fright. They become blind to everything else which is decent. They prostrate themselves before him in mind and body. I tell you, you cannot believe. Many offer him all their jewelry and cash. Still more even give him their wives."

"It is difficult for me to understand how normally good, law-abiding citizens can become so rabid. Are you sure this is not just hearsay," Arjun suggested hopefully.

"No, my friend. I have seen first-hand."

"But you have said he is a homosexual, Ashok," Arjun Singh reminded him.

"Since I have lived in his camp I have come to definitely know that his preference is for young boys but he sometimes also has women. They think he is all powerful and great. He has as disciples the Gazi and the Fakir. The Murid, the ordinary people are his favorites. Narendra Singhji, people really do worship him. I make no joke of this. They think him a god or an incarnation of a god. Even I have been forced to carry him ceremoniously in a palki on my shoulders with others helping. From place to place he would have us do this, not settling down too long in any one spot."

"They literally did bow down before him?" Narendra questioned.

"They have even cut down trees and made roads for him when he chose to move on to a place where no roads stood before him. And gladly they would do it. They made slaves of themselves, joyously. It makes me sick to pretend I am a part of this. Sometimes I cannot sleep. As you know I have been watching his activities from time to time these many years, yet spending as much time with my family as possible. When I would again learn of his whereabouts and could spare the time from home I would again join him. I hate it, and I hate him, but it has become my crusade.

"At first he would question my leaving him, fearing I was a spy, but in the more recent past he has come to trust me, I suppose because of the number of years, and because I do return. What I really cannot stomach is the things he does against human nature. Now-a-days he puts boys in a cage and at night he takes them out for his use. He has had for himself a very fine palace and three forts but apparently was not content to live in even that extravagant luxury.

"Then came the time that others have told of his imminent capture and it has scared him back into the largest of his forts," Ashok continued. "Now that he is closer to our land we should get him once and for all."

"What capture? By whom?" Narendra demanded.

"I have checked and checked and can find no one who knows anything for certain. Sometimes I think it is all a myth, yet he feels sufficiently threatened to bury himself in the fort, sending others out for all the supplies necessary to feed his ever increasing number of followers.

"Oh god, Ashok, to do to young boys ugly sex acts is not being worthy of living," Narendra fumed. This old disgust welled up ever more strongly and he vowed he would not again put off Ali's capture. He'd return to Jagatpur as quickly as possible, round up as many of his faithful fighters as he could, preferably a couple dozen, and plan his strategy after reaching a safe hiding spot near Ali's fort. From there he would personally evaluate the bizarre situation.

The men paid their respects to Queen Mother before departing the following morning for Jagatpur, Nina being advised briefly on Ali and his following. When he could get back to her they would have to have a very long and serious talk about the child. Ashok meantime swung around to the east, making a very quick trip back to his wife and children before wanting to depart with Narendra, leading him to the fort and Ali.

With each passing day Nina grew less sure that she was doing right. While she held tight to her decision she felt less justified in doing so.

By the time the men reached Jagatpur, rounded up the others and took off for Marwar another week had passed. Narendra had become diabolically clever about learning the movements and ways of his foes. It was no different this time. After swift travel another ten days were spent camped well beyond the fort, artfully dispensing pertinent questions less cleverly answered. They soon knew all that was required to mastermind an ingenious scheme to entice Ali from his den.

Narendra used the good office of his friend the Maharaja of Marwar to arrange a quasi-tiger shikar. If he was suspicious of all others in planning his capture, surely Ali would trust the Maharaja. But the procession would have to look real and none of the servants must know the truth. No one was to be trusted. Only His Highness, Narendra and his closest assistants could discuss the master plan.

Several days later scores of beaters left the Maharaja's palace, passing near the fort. Earlier an invitation had been sent to Ali by the Maharaja personally inviting the outlaw to join the hunting party. In exaggerated importance of himself Ali felt the request to be authentic and well warranted. Of course he would accept.

When he felt the proper moment had come Ali left his palace and fort, swaggering pompously to the regaled elephants thought sent here for himself by the raja. Instantly he was arrested by Narendra and his crew. Placed in the jails of the Maharaja under heavy guard it appeared the trouble had only begun. So upset were Ali's disciples they became inscrutably hostile to everyone near.

"I do wish you could stay on with me at the palace as my personal guest, Narendra Singhji," the Maharaja soberly requested. "It would be helpful if some of your friends would do likewise. While I feel relatively confident Ali cannot escape from my jail, I am inclined to feel things on the outside are definitely going to grow much worse. Such a following that beast has."

The two men took little time in agreeing to further aid this ruler. And so it was that Narendra again sat with the Maharaja, devising a systematic plan, along with the ruler's personal police force and most loyal members of his army to quell the wild followers of Ali.

Each of Narendra's men drew from his own personal experiences with their fearless leader and each had his own special little talents. However, in the aftermath of Ali's capture the damage was becoming so terribly widespread and instantaneous it took the whole army to spread out well beyond the Maharaja's capitol city, to the outlying villages and every place in between. Martial law had to be declared, and as Narendra and his men joined the official police, they were finally able to put an end to the vengeful terror that was wreaked, but it had taken another two and a half weeks.

Instead of being gone from Jagatpur a month as anticipated, several had lapsed. They were now in the midst of the monsoons, cooling rains a blessed boon to the sweltering days preceding the downpours. Narendra would return to Jagatpur once more stopping at the palace to fondle the baby which would possibly by now be attempting to walk. Resentment would set in whenever he realized he was missing out on important parts of the child's growth, by now accepting beyond doubt the assumption he had fathered the boy.

The two disconsolate lovers were to meet once more in the tree-shaded fields beyond the palace where they could sit at leisure. The child was left in the custody of one of the older women who since the birth of Arjun decided it was time she befriended the young mother.

In nervous preparation for this soul-trying meeting, Nina attempted desperately to convince herself never again to enter his tender arms. To do so would be never to leave them.

Most of all her heart screamed for a final decision regarding her son and his father, a decision with which she could live in peace; there had been none thus far. Thinking mainly of little Arjun, putting him before his father brought no solace to her soul.

They accidently met near a grove, a distance from their favorite tree. It was difficult walking beside him, not holding his long-fingered hands; not allowing her swaying side to swipe past him. Conversation was casual: weather, people of the town. For once she did not even want to get into the subject of dacoits he had just rounded up and the reasons it took so long to handle the situation. That would take up too much precious time. She was content only to know he and his men had returned to safety.

Still fully leafed although more stooped was their private tree. Standing against it, afraid to look up into the fierce glitter of his eyes, his unblighted masculine charms once more captivated her. To be desperately in love with a man and not hold him close was something Nina could not easily reckon with. Quickly discarded were all the things she earnestly told herself she must shield against. In his nearness she could hear his heart beating fast — or was it hers — feel the air his lungs expelled. Grabbing him ferociously the two were lovers as before.

Health fully restored, his body was once again perfection, flawless, and he clung adhesively as if she were a goddess. Rhythmic undulations held them in sway until she insisted on returning to the palace.

"Not until we talk about Arjun," he said firmly.

"What about Arjun?" Nina asked in unjustifiable fear.

"You know that I want to marry you, Nina, but to do so at this moment would not be kind to the memory of Kala. I would want to at least first celebrate the one-year anniversary of her death before we could take such steps."

"I have never said that I would marry you," she argued.

Ignoring the remark he continued, "It would be best for the boy to be brought up in Jagatpur. As with any grandparents, my mother and father would look after him well. They have eight others now so he would have many playmates. My parents will love little Arjun equally with the others. There he would have a life of freedom, a playful boyhood to which he is entitled and the important thing is he would not have to live in servitude."

"I do. I manage," she almost whispered. And there was a long silence.

"As for Arjun's paternity, I do not know why you try to shield it from me. I cannot condone what it is you are doing," Narendra spoke fiercely.

Interrupting, she argued in her defense. "More than once you have settled for my decisions. How then is it that you do not accept the fact someone else could have fathered the boy?"

"Because you are too much in love with me to submit, under any conditions, to anyone else. I know that what you do you believe to be just and fair. I wish you could come to see it my way and send the child back with me. On the other hand I cannot be too harsh for I can see what he means to you and it would indeed be cruel to take him from his mother. That is why I think you should leave the palace and come with him to stay in Jagatpur."

"I cannot leave now. I keep telling you that. I owe something to Queen Mother and I must remain, at least a while longer."

"I think you owe something more to the boy, as well as to me, Nina," but these words he spoke softly and respectfully.

No amount of arguing would change her absurd position even while knowing deep in her heart it was wrong to implacably deny his fatherhood. Totally confused over the fundamental issue she often wished it was but a wild dream, that everything would right itself in the morning. Life was never that magnanimous.

"I know this whole thing is a complete mess, Narendra, but some day it will work itself out. You know you always used to say to me: slow and easy wins the race. Let us take this slowly," Nina begged.

"Slowly?" Narendra asked dejectedly. "He won't even be a baby much longer. Nina, there are many things to be considered. My father is starting to show his age to me and I wish to lighten his load when I am not out fighting dacoits. Soon I must sit only with him and go over the books and his records and learn still more what it is like to operate our fort and all the villages within our personal realm. I must remain up to date on problems and governing. It will ease father's burden and it is something I must do at any cost. I therefore do not know when I shall again be able to take the time to come to Udaipur, but rest assured it will be as soon as possible. I hope you will have come to your senses and return then with me to live forever at Jagatpur.

"Keep well and take good care of the child. If you change your mind before I get back send word. I'll come immediately. That you must promise me. Besides, there are always rumblings of troubles within and beyond the kingdom. If anything should ever happen to Queen Mother, you must not stay here. Understand? As long as I live you will have a place at my humble dwelling. I want you as my wife, but if you continue to refuse I at least want you safe within our walls. Promise me you will not forget this." It was completely beyond his comprehension how she could say for years that she wanted to be his wife and now given the opportunity, after a polite period, she would not take it.

"We will be fine and you can be sure I will always do what I think best for my son."

Narendra left the next day for Jagatpur, Nina once more settling down to a busy life of sewing, running errands, talking with Queen Mother about inconsequential trivia, sitting with her when she wanted to relax, and always lending an ear when she felt the need to speak aloud of plans for a newly arising problem. Nina's working hours were long and the tasks harder as she grew older, or so they seemed. Sinking into a morose spell she'd drift between the desire to grow old watching her child develop into a fine young man, and wishing the years would dissolve quickly, leaving her soon to join Narendra on his funeral pyre. She didn't know how she'd manage that, but it was her last intense desire to join him in heaven, consumed in the same sacrificial flames, those flames once faintheartedly feared, and now which held the possibility of making them one in death, if not in life.

As for her son, she worried excessively about his future, what trade he might learn and with whom he could work. She wanted more for him than to merely carry trays of food or pipes of opium to the Maharana, or shine the brass and wash the crystal furniture. She would teach him at a very young age all the lessons she had learned while listening to Hari Lal's classes, or talking with assorted nobles as they came to court. Each had fascinating stories of their family's past encounters, some repetitious, others lending charm by intrigues, for intrigue was a word synonymous with court life, whether at the head seat of their Maharana here in Udaipur, or in any of the forts of Mewar.

Narendra was right. There was no doubt that little Arjun's living in Jagatpur would have a more satisfying childhood and manhood. His future would be secure. But would he be happy? There was no end to Nina's torment.

Meanwhile at the palace, there was always that underlying current of faction against faction. To quiet the controversies Queen Mother and Bhim Singh had to continuously find ways to appease either side. This was never easy for sometimes they had to betray their own moral standards or integrity. Awakening to his responsibilities Bhim Singh joined his mother more and more for penetrating discussions. They not always produced an accord but at least he was taking the helm more swiftly since his marriage had settled down to a routine and he became a family man. The Mahrattas remained a constant threat to their kingdom.

To the northeast there was ever recurrent destruction. Countless wars and battles brought great wealth to the Mughals who sat in Delhi. Unfortunately for themselves their barbarously despotic rule created tumultuous chaos. For several centuries the Mughal emperors sedulously collected all manner of prized possessions of their foes, gems and jewelry, works of art, monies and even the finest of their women, except of course for the unbending Mewaris.

The Persian despot issued an order to his soldiers to burn their own city of Delhi. They were to kill all the inhabitants and thus leave the emperor free to abscond with the entire wealth. Insidiously cruel and wantonly unjustified as the order was, he imperiously demanded that his orders be carried out in half a day, burning the city after the swift and unprecedented annihilation of the people. To further add insult he had most of his subordinates blinded, murdered or despicably maimed.

So it was that the British took a strong hold within India, attempting to straighten out the chaos, creating another geographical place on which the sun would shine for the British Empire. It was because of the kingdoms of Rajputana, and mainly that of Mewar not submitting to the rule of the Mughals, that the princely states came to fight each other.

Queen Mother thought Mewar was writing its own death warrant in many of their acts with the Mahrattas and others. She grew older and less able to suffer the extreme mental tortures of the task of regent, giving in often unwillingly to the forces of her son, now planted firmly on the throne. She found him one of the significantly weakest of all the Mewar rulers and often powerless to rectify his inane deeds. Often Queen Mother thought of her grandson Amar and whether he might amount to something greater than his father Bhim. Whatever hopes, whatever dreams, or desires the Rani had for his future greatness, they were wasted. Amar was still a youngster when he died, leaving his second brother, Jawan, with the probability of gaining the gaddi. Bhim had fathered besides these two boys another named Ummad, also destined to die in childhood, and the sweetest of all little girls, Krishna, a winsome child who became his pride and joy.

Years slipped by, Narendra never having broken Nina of her fear of having Arjun move to Jagatpur. Saddened by her decision, he eventually learned to accept his baffling fate, yet never completely giving up hope that one day she would relent. Nor would he listen to mother or father with regard to remarriage to any other. He remained cautiously occupied with the business of their portion of the feudal kingdom, returning to Nina whenever it was possible, but always for short durations.

A temporary peace settled over Mewar with regard to ravishing dacoits. Ran, Pandu and all the others were at last free to remain indefinitely home with their families, each of whom were raising fine youngsters. Narendra envied their lifestyles, more carefree than his.

Beautifully virile as he was, the eldest Singh would argue, "Son, it goes against a man's nature not to remarry. You must have a woman to warm your bed."

"The only woman I will have is Nina but none of my arguments help," he confessed.

Systematically the elder Arjun demanded that Nina and the boy be forced to live at Jagatpur where they rightly belonged. Never had he condemned his son or Nina for their relationship. It happened all the time with concubines. What was sinful to Arjun was that Nina would consider anything less than life within their compound. "We have been everlastingly good to her," both he and his wife would argue, for Bhadra too had been told the secret of their intimate relationship. "Her cruelty in keeping the child from you is intolerable."

But Narendra would argue back in Nina's defense in spite of the fact every sinew ached for the child and Nina to live within his arms. "I shall bring her to it one day, and then we can have more babies."

"You'll both be too old," they'd reply in duet.

There were other things on Arjun's mind. For one, thirty years were up and the land tax would have to be refigured. As the men from the capitol were making the rounds of various feudal estates Arjun instructed Narendra to join all of them in the fields so that he could watch how his unique tax was figured.

In no manner of speaking was Narendra an agriculturalist but when the time came for the men to appear he and Arjun rode their horses to the site of the soil testing. The ground would fall into one of three classifications. On their return to Udaipur the facts and figures would be compiled and presented at durbar. In all probability this prescribed payment would apply for the next thirty years.

More time was now spent in Arjun's private halls where all forms of work were accomplished, insisting Narendra be at his side, viewing what was done, helping in new decisions, in effect taking over many of the duties. He had become magistrate, judge and jury.

A servant had stolen a painting from the walls of Arjun's sitting room and was later caught. What was to be the justice? Long ago he'd have lost his right hand for the theft. Today Arjun and Narendra considered this too severe, yet all too clearly came to Narendra's mind the night he severed both hands of Motilal for the plundering, burning of the village and the rape of that poor young woman who had then thrown herself into the fire. Years had mellowed the Rajput and it was ultimately agreed the thief would serve a lengthy time in the Jagatpur jail under heavy guard. The Singhs felt it undeniably necessary to make the punishment a deterrent to others. A lord who would deliberately allow any culprit an easy penalty would be forfeiting his rights as lord and master and setting the stage for more serious crimes. The punishment would have to fit the crime and they would have to retrograde or increase as did the offense.

Another problem within the fort was the ever hounding Mahrattas who often enticed the best of an army to their side with promises of greater pay or other forms of remuneration. The Singhs knew they must more carefully rebuild their personal army and set about to think out good schemes. They must be attractive for their men to remain loyal to the causes of Jagatpur and Mewar; they must be paid an adequate salary to maintain their homes and families; always in the forefront of Arjun Singh's mind was a sense of loyalty for their ancient hallowed kingdom. A good soldier, he always argued, is a soldier who knows well the values of being a Rajput warrior, dying for a cause if need be, and ever aware of the pride of having been born in this time and place. To Arjun and Narendra Singh, where could there be a spot on the globe which more richly deserved obesiance than Mewar and any of its feudal estates.

Arjun had also started a school system for the youngsters of the fort, urging parents to make arrangements to send them. There were many lessons to be learned, sufficient persons within the fort to act as responsible teachers and certainly an illiterate society would profit no one. He himself had studied at the college at Ajmer as did his son but most young men would not be able to attain such formal education, but he did feel the most possible should be done for the youngsters. As for his own grandchildren, they would have private tutors until college age, as did his sons.

Classrooms were inexpensively constructed and a uniform system drawn up for their classes. It was Narendra's suggestion that they add to it some form of exercise and given periods of time were allowed for games and fun. It soon became a great thing for the young fold of Jagatpur fort to attend, as well as a privilege not endowed everyone within Mewar. Outlying villagers still relied only on parents for the teaching of what little the farmers or others had learned through the years by helping in the fields when soil was laboriously tilled, seeds were sown, or crops harvested; beyond this there was no education.

Life for the most part was good for the Mewaris when the Mahrattas were not bothering them too greatly, though their numbers were rapidly diminishing. And then as quickly as it had fallen asleep, there was an awakening of dacoity in the districts not too far distant from Jagatpur and once more Narendra's friends were forced to band together to wipe out the scourge. The big difference this time was that he'd depute Ran as head man and himself remain behind.

Nina had been correct in her original renditions of the working and thinking of dacoits. It was true that various bands of dacoits made up their own set of codes, many bands not touching ladies while in the commission of their crimes. But those of low castes or clans such as barbers and dhobis who had turned to dacoity usually had no moral standards, frequently choosing to rape the helpless young girls. Oh, to be rid of dacoits once and for all. Narendra and his friends were so sick of this. Arjun Singh and the local governments had set up heavy rewards to be paid those who helped capture these gangs and if a leader knew himself to be thus hunted he would not even trust his relatives, so fearful were they of being turned in for this money.

On Narendra's head was the grave responsibility of dozens and dozens of men, all good friends and effective fighters. Overburdened with this charge his years wore heavily upon him. They were early in the nineteenth century, still fighting the bandits. Would there never be an end? How naive to think at the onset of his endeavors he'd rid Mewar of this evil permanently. Still, the dacoit menace did keep growing smaller.

As Nina put it to Arjun Singh one day a year or two ago, "As long as there is a Narendra Singh, his rising tide will continue to inundate the scourge of dacoity in Mewar and Rajputana."

Chapter 16

Years indolently passed since the death of Kala and her child. Nina's little Arjun was growing tall and straight with the same buoyant spirit as his father. More and more Nina was coming to realize she was irrevocably wrong in not joining her lover in Jagatpur, whether or not they would have married. Little Arjun played at the palace with the children of other servants as well as the Maharajkumars Jawan and Ummed when they wearied of being alone. Ummed, the third son of Bhim Singh, was a sickly child, devoured by listless idleness and grateful for Arjun's company.

Ummed grew weaker and more pale until finally he was no longer allowed beyond his bedchamber. The little prince. like Bhim Singh's firstborn, died in early childhood. Now only the middle of the brothers remained, which in itself caused the Maharana a restless ghost of worry, difficult to steer successfully through already murky times.

Conversant with tragic misfortunes, Queen Mother looked to Nina a catastrophic human mask of suffering. No longer did she laugh at Nina's little jokes, a morbid sentiment resting upon her being. Seated together in the zenana one day a servant announced the arrival of an emissary from the court of Arjun Singh. Nina's quickened pulse was evident to the Rani, graciously suggesting Nina accompany her to the hall of private audience in which she would receive the ambassador. Neither woman spoke, Queen Mother old and tired with the cares of kingdom and family. Nina was convulsed with pangs of worry.

Formalities brushed quickly aside, the Queen demanded the travel-weary man quickly make his point.

"I have come, your Highness, with an urgent request of both the lord of Jagatpur and his wife for the servant Nina to again attend the lady Singhji who is dying." An audible gasp erupted from Nina's throat, but he continued. "It is their earnest desire that you will kindly agree to temporarily dispense with your maid until the inevitable parting from this world by a woman who looks only to Nina for care and comfort in her few remaining days or hours. This she most humbly and personally requests of you as a dying wish, Your Highness."

"And by what right can she again request the services of my Nina? This would be the third time I have allowed her to leave for such a request. I am very much afraid that I cannot agree to it. She is too sorely needed here. I am not so sure but what I too am dying, and who would be here to care for me? No, I cannot agree."

"Oh, Your Highness," Nina begged, "may I not do her bidding? She has been as a mother to me. I owe this to her, and if it is her final request in life should it not be answered?"

"To whom do you owe your allegiance?" was the sarcastic reply.

"Oh you, of course, Your Highness. You too have always been kind and fair to me and my son. You too have been even more than a mother to me and you know I always feel indebted. Yet without the help of both Narendra's mother and father I would not have found my place here with you, isn't it? Besides, in over twenty years I have been to Jagatpur only about four or five times. I have taken very little leave so I could be with you ... and that was as I wished," she hastily added.

"Some of what you say is true, girl. I had almost forgotten. Narendra brought you here when you were widowed. I suppose I have always taken you for granted. But no, if your allegiance is to me then let it be so. You will remain here at the palace and care for me. I once more sense doom, and you know how such past prophesies have been correct. I also fear I shall not long be in this world but it does not matter too much. That is not the doom of which I speak. I am old now and the young are ruling the States. I must have you here beside me to care for me, and to watch over my other handmaidens and bring me what solace and comfort you can."

Nina's sense of loyalty was again being challenged, in her heart believing she owed an equal debt to each woman, and on the surface it appeared Arjun's wife nearer death's gates than the lady seated before her who was merely wearing out. Somehow she would have to sway the Rani's judgement. "With your permission, Your Highness, may I please remind you that again I have not had a leave in almost five years. I have asked nothing of you for my own sake. I think you can bear me out on that score."

"Not five years?" she bellowed. "You cannot mean this is so."

"Yes, Your Highness, and I promise not to remain a day longer than actually necessary. To know she is dying and not be there ... my heart would not be in anything I do here. And if she does die, would I also have permission to remain through the one-month ceremony? That would not be too long, would it? You and I both should grant her dying wish. Please let me go."

The silence which followed was lengthy. Finally the Queen Mother replied, "You will forgive an old lady. You are a big part of me, a good servant and faithful friend. You may take leave. Offer Shrimati Singhji my warmest regards. Now be gone. Both of you."

The prospect of young Arjun going on a trip with his mother was an exciting one. He was not a rider, having neither horse nor opportunity. Nina being of small build could possibly hold him on hers. Yet, he was growing so very big. Soon he would be full grown, as large in frame as her Narendra. The ambassador, however, had brought extra horses and instructions to be certain the boy accompanied his mother.

Bhadra's condition was critical and the traveling party was to start at the earliest moment. From the kitchen Nina took whatever foods could conveniently be placed into a knapsack. The emissary and his escort would accompany them back, six horses in all. In a mood of abstraction they left the fort with the terrible inevitability of what she would find. Nina could not easily resign herself to renewed sadness which was sure to lie ahead.

All the way to the estate and into the room of Shrimati Singh she called repeatedly on heavenly powers to stay the hand of death, but it was not to be this time. A brighter look and tiny suggestion of a smile crossed the face of Narendra's mother on Nina's arrival, but Nina could see the stories of her approaching demise were not false. All the family was either gathered around the bed or seated outside her door, moaning dolefully. Nina ignored everyone for the time being, even oblivious of Narendra and his father's presence, taking the old lady's hand in hers, stroking its palsied but silken flesh tenderly, tears rushing down Nina's imploring face.

"Do not cry for me, my friend. I am old and it is time I die, but I must talk with you before I leave this place." With that she requested everyone, even Narendra and her husband, to leave them alone.

"I have come to know the story of you and my son being lovers, Nina, and that you are not a widow, although that in no way matters to us." The younger woman's blush was as red as the most scarlet of sunsets. "You need not be ashamed. We here have all loved you and never forgotten how beautifully you not only nursed me back to health but also Kala when she was ill with her last baby. I know too how you made Narendra always place Kala first in his thoughts and not you. Yours is a deep and true love, Nina. And we shall eternally be thankful for you bringing my son back to life when he was out of his mind over her horrible death. Such a madman he was and you alone could handle him. But for you he would have died." Her speech was agonizingly slow, each successive word more difficult to utter. Nina tried to silence her but she would not be stilled.

"You and I have not always seen eye to eye on important matters. For years we have fought you for the sake of your son and mine ... and now I once more implore you, mother to mother. I know the boy must be my grandchild and I would like to see him before I close my eyes for the last time, but the reason I requested your presence is that I cannot die without asking that you allow Narendra to help raise the boy, acknowledging him as any father has a right. You saved his life once, Nina, but you are now killing Narendra slowly and painfully. You cannot seem to see that your denial of the truth is killing him emotionally and psychologically. Is that not the worst of all deaths? Your little Arjun, our Arjun, would be the next keeper of this estate after my son's death and this high nobleman's position in life is one you have no right to deny, especially when it is rightfully his." At this time she became quite forceful, Nina fearing each breath would be her last. She choked and coughed hard on her words and efforts, laying back on her bed unstirring and quiet for a long while after the coughing ceased. "He has always refused to marry anyone but you and so he could have no other sons."

At last Nina replied, "We have gone over and over that, your son and I, but now you must rest. We will speak of it again tomorrow."

"For me there is no tomorrow, and it is for this very reason that I have brought you here, child. Not to nurse me. I know that it is too late. When I told my family I'd go to Udaipur in a palanquin to beseech you to do this for Narendra, they had to agree to send for you ... although, make no mistake, I would have gone if there was no other way."

Nina knew she meant every word she spoke, but what could she do now?

"This is my death wish, Nina, that you admit to Narendra in no uncertain words little Arjun is indeed his son. There must be absolutely no room for doubt. Then marry him and live here where you belong. Would you deny a dying woman her last wish?"

"I couldn't deny you anything, Mataji. I would rot in hell if I did not accommodate your wish. But I had reasons..."

"I know your reasons. I have heard all the arguments and we are all of one mind, that Narendra's son belongs here with him. You believe you are doing what is best for your son, ignoring your own chance of happiness. Oh, but you have been so wrong, Nina. So wrong. I too am a mother doing what I believe is right for all three of you.

"Now, Nina, if you are as wise as I have always given you credit for being, then marry my son before he starts taking his nights in ugly brothels. I am amazed he has not done so long ago. Narendra must have this son. It will probably be the only one he will ever have. And he has told his father and me that since the arrival of young Arjun he will not consider adopting the son of his brother."

With this she was completely exhausted, laying her head back flat, the last words barely audible. Nina was totally silent, useless to further argue. With great effort the old woman finally begged, "Promise me. Promise me..."

"I promise," Nina answered and watched as the woman drew her last gasping, rattled breath, a blessed contentment crossing her furrowed face as she heard Nina's reply. She could take to her heaven the knowledge her son would have his child and the woman he loved. Pity she herself never got to see the lad.

The other sons and daughter of the elder Singhs and their spouses and children strenuously objected to the indifference shown them while heaping concentrated attention on a solitary servant. They chided Nina for the attention received when it was they who should have been at the side of the dying woman. She'd atone for this visible affront, said some of the women, no matter how long it would take.

Stronger than they, Nina had already suffered far more emotional stress in her lifetime than Narendra's brothers or their wives. She learned to wear an armor about her feelings and heart and while she would not have chosen to be the sole person with the dying friend, neither could she part her bedside. There was absolutely no doubt the woman forced herself to live until after the fearless confrontation with regard to the young boy and the affirmative answer for which she fought. For the moment their personal feelings were inconsequential, nor would Nina let herself brood over it later. It was done. The matter was closed. A new way of life was to manifest itself. Perhaps Bhadra Singh was right. Regardless, the long rusting die was finally cast.

Narendra reigned at his mother's funeral, certain she was properly bathed and dressed. The cremation took place promptly, Nina bringing her son to the pyre before the fire was lit so that he could have his proper look at his natural grandmother. Not until her ashes had been placed into the nearest river the following day did Narendra and Nina speak of her dying wish.

The bedside conversation was finally discussed with Narendra and his father. Arjun was almost in his teens and at last he had a father. Through past years when he'd ask an explanation he'd be told only that when he was older he'd learn the whole story. The wait displeased him but he was powerless against his mother.

It was tacitly agreed Nina would leave him here at his new home with his father and grandfather. She would remain only until the day after the all-important one-month ceremony, returning to the palace to explain why it was she must leave forever the employ of the Queen Mother. This she could do only in person. After a very short goodbye she planned to hasten back to Jagatpur and make arrangements for an intimately small but proper wedding.

Still going through Nina's mind were the psychological problems of running the estate after the eventual demise of the elder Arjun. If Narendra's brothers or other officials of the feudal estate would bring undue pressure to bear on him at that future time she could not tolerate the knowledge she had created this accumulated unpleasantness. It would reflect on her son. If his uncles and cousins chose to be churlish, as she fully expected they would, then perhaps the three of them would be driven from this home. Her feelings of guilt never left her, always allocating the blame for everything negative in their joint life entirely on herself.

She took the time to discuss these aspects with the elder Singh. He took both her trembling hands into his, looked into her saddened eyes and said, "I too an growing older and know not how many years I have left. All I regret is that it took so many years to convince you."

"I did what I thought right for the boy and his father. Now I am more worried than ever for their future happiness."

"If you love each other and stick close together you can lick any problems. It was you yourself, my son has told me, who said that always the rain must fall. Can you not tolerate that same rain on your own head? Look to the future with joy, not sadness, and all will right itself. You have summarily punished yourself too hard and too long. Now go seek my son and settle whatever remains burdensome in your minds so that you can very soon come to the date of your wedding and get about the business of running the lives of you three as should be." With that he patted her firmly on the shoulder and left.

That night she told Narendra of her conversation with his father, or rather his lecture. And now it was time for a clearer picture of what they should do, what they should say to others, and how they should act. This she wanted made incontestably clear before taking off for that last visit to Udaipur and rendering her resignation. Queen Mother, of course, would be furious.

Overstrained moods were not conducive to love-making and the two sat outside their abandoned private temple, Nina trembling in the rumpled breeze. When Narendra spoke uncompromisingly he repeated his mother's conversation to Nina as she had told him. "What is there left to say or do? She made a death wish. You promised. Both of us will abide by it. We will be married when you return from Udaipur."

"Narendra, you sound as if your mother is putting a sword to your heart."

"Not at all, Nina. Have I not asked you repeatedly all these many years to bring the boy to me, for us to marry? Now it is done. My mother has made my dreams come true and we have but to wait for an auspicious day, after you come back, which I pray will be very soon."

"If only we had not made up that story about me being a widow. Even your mother died believing I was one. I am not a widow. But because of that crazy thing you will now be shamed if you take me as a wife. I cannot believe that your family or the people of this estate will allow you to sit in your father's place with me at your side when the time comes. And it is all because of our monkey-faced lie." Her voice drifted into nothingness.

"That part is all my fault. But how could I have known that we would love like this and want to marry? I was a fool. I do not see any way to retract that tale, do you? I have, of course, told my father the truth. We are discussing whether to tell mt brothers and I believe the truth should be told, but I have asked father to say nothing until I have a chance to talk it over with you. It is your life that matters most. To retract my story of your being a widow would mean that we must tell of how you lived with Motilal and the reason for our lie. I don't know what in all this mess would be the least painful to you, Nina. What would you wish us to do?"

"Somehow I cannot imagine that your brothers would believe the truth; at least their wives would not and would probably spread ugly gossip. That would only hurt you and the boy. As for me, I do not care. I am past being hurt more. I sometime think I am perpetually numb."

"It seems that since we can't marry before you leave Jagatpur, then we should think longer on it and make a final decision on your return. I do believe, however, that that decision should still be solely yours. But as long as you are my wife, I promise you I shall always love and care for you, as well as our son. I owe you so much, my little one." He moved to where she rested on a broken plinth which once held a solid pillar, placing his loving strong arm around her shoulders. "I wish I could go to Udaipur with you and bring you quickly back."

"You must stay at your father's side. He's never needed you more that at this moment. The days and months will be very bleak for him. I only hope his namesake will be able to shed some joy."

Each time Nina had been forced to leave Narendra it had grown more difficult. This was by far the hardest in spite of knowing she was to come back to live within his massive shadow, under his protective wing. Protection of this sort was something she had not enjoyed since he brought her safely home from the Mandore cenotaphs. The regent had bestowed her especial favor, keeping Nina free from famines and beneath one of the most far-spreading roofs of an imperfect world. Queen Mother's patronage was a fabulous boon but Narendra's protection was of a personal nature, a rendering independent from palace life.

Nor had she been separated from her precious son since his infancy when he was wet-nursed at Udaipur while she sped to the side of the dying Narendra. And in her heart of hearts she knew she could not make a brief, cold announcement of permanently leaving the palace and then depart. Queen Mother had to be persuaded to free Nina from her obligations forever.

The remainder of the month was spent playing and walking with young Arjun, Narendra at their side whenever he could manage time away from the rigors of official business. He had pressured the old man to remain in his living quarters regaining physical and emotional strength after the numbing ordeal of watching his beloved wife die. Old Arjun Singh thought of battles he had fought and how merciful it was to be killed outright rather than suffer the pangs of drawn out hammering pain. One day he walked with Nina and his grandson round and round the private quarters of their home, desiring no disturbing interruptions from well-wishers in this old fort city beyond his private gate.

Young Arjun looked up at this old man and his broken visions and even in his youth could see he held tight memories of a radiant past. "Grandfather, now that I am going to live here can you tell me stories of when you were my age?"

Wizened with the intelligence which resides in old men of his calibre, Arjun senior delighted in the awareness he would have a captive audience. "But not today or tomorrow, little grandson. Another time for certain." There had never been doubt that his first-born son was his favorite, and now, bastard or not, Narendra's son appeared on the threshold of claiming that same desirable position in the growing chain of grandchildren. Whether this would help or irreparably hinder little Arjun and his father within the larger family circle would remain to be seen. Nina could only worry it would have horrendous effects in their already awkward position.

On the morning Nina was to leave she arose early, the sun not yet too far into the partly darkened sky. It was the peacocks squawking which awakened her and she strode one last time to the door of the room in which she and her son slept. There in the little courtyard to the rooms she had been issued — she no longer shared the servants' quarters — were three magnificent peacocks.

"They've come to say goodbye to you," a voice startled her. Narendra too had arisen early, as was his custom, preparing to say goodbye before entering his puja room for morning prayers. "Aren't they the biggest showoffs you've ever seen?" The gorgeous birds commenced a spectacular show, the two males indeed the cocky ones, spreading their turquoise and green iridescent feathers into immense fans, dipping them softly and low to the ground, again standing them up in the air. As they did this they danced and screeched, Nina and Narendra standing across from each other for a quarter hour. He clapped his hands loudly, the three birds flying into the neem tree in the center of the main courtyard.

"Oh, you've scared them off," Nina pouted.

"They've stolen the show from me. It is I you should have eyes for this morning," he teased. "I expect I shall not be seeing you for another month. Can you wish me a proper goodbye?"

Nina walked to where he stood, straight as an arrow, stretching her neck and standing on tip-toes to gently kiss his mouth, pulling his head down to hers in order to do so. "Take care of my — our — son," she said. "I'll be back as soon as I can set things properly with Queen Mother."

Narendra was certain she had every intention of doing just that.

Well-nigh exhausted from the long years of wholeheartedly serving at the helm of her country Queen Mother moved slowly, seeing Nina only after a lengthy nap on the afternoon following her return to the palace. "I hope you conveyed my regards to the dying woman?" she asked of Nina.

"Arjun Singhji insisted his wife waited until I came before she would die, Your Highness, and I do believe this is so.

She was so pathetically weak and frail," tears again coming into Nina's eyes. "I did not have time for idle chatter. She died very soon after I got there. It was she who did all the talking, weak as she was."

"What was there to talk about with you, Nina?" she demanded.

"My son."

"Then he truly is Narendra's?" The Rani sounded like a village chaprasi eager for idle gossip. "What did she say?"

"Yes, he's Narendra's son as you always expected. I would never openly admit it before because I did not want him brought up there as a bastard, nor did I want ever to be separated from him. But my son's grandmother, on her deathbed, made me promise to let Narendra raise him as his eventual heir, bastard or not." Nina choked on those words.

"And you have left him there?"

"Yes."

"Well, I guess that's alright. They're fine people and will look after him well. Do not be dismayed about it. You can visit him on your yearly leaves. I have said he was to remain here and be a servant of the palace, but since it is your son and Narendra's heir I shall make an exception."

"It's not that simple, Your Highness. I was made to promise just before she stopped breathing that I would marry Narendra."

"But you are a widow!" she roared.

"For the first time since Nina came to know the Rani she was furious. "I am not a widow!" she yelled back, an act for which she was repaid with a hard blow across the face. "Narendra and I had agreed we would say I was a widow for a very special reason. A reason which I do not care to discuss with anyone."

"And who would believe that story?"

"I would have hoped that if anyone would believe me it would be you, Highness. Whether you believe it or not, it is true. Nor do I expect his family to believe it. This is what makes marriage with Narendra so difficult. It is why I kept the arrival of my son a secret from him as long as I could. It is why I kept refusing to marry him before this. But one cannot hide a child. And it is difficult to take back a lie."

"Well, I suppose if you must honor the dying wish of an old woman you can marry him, leave young Arjun there and return here to the palace to live out your remaining days in our service."

"But that is the whole point, Your Highness, if I marry I will and must live with Narendra and little Arjun. I could not do otherwise."

"Strange. I remember you saying before you left for Jagatpur that you owed your allegiance to me. I too am not well, and while I expect I may not be dead by tomorrow I know I do not have many years left. I expect you here to care for me. In fact I demand it. I've groomed you for it."

"Are you saying you will not let me return to Jagatpur?"

"If I demand that you remain with me then it would seem you have no choice."

Nina was completely befuddled, the Queen's reaction provokingly unexpected. She had anticipated something of an argument and disappointment but Nina hoped she could appease the woman by remaining a short time, achieving an acceptable compromise. Narendra expected her back in a month. What to do?

Bigotedly adamant Queen Mother would not reverse her position and Nina could not just simply walk away from either the palace or the problem. She set about spending her idle private time praying for a suitable answer to a seemingly invincible problem. Painstakingly she wrote a note to Narendra. Searching the old part of the city with much difficulty until she found a rider who would be going beyond Jagatpur whom, for a price, would agree to deliver the note. Thanks to the goddesses that Narendra had insisted she take money with her. It was still a commodity which seldom reached her private hiding place.

In her note she described most carefully the outcome of her discussion with her benefactor-cum-employer. She was sure the Singhs' interlocking minds would in due course arrive at a suitable solution; after all, she was not imprisoned here. Or was she? Come to think of it, that's what she wondered when she arrived way back in 1778.

The Mahrattas were becoming strong again and what would happen if they should once more take over Udaipur and perhaps even occupy the palace? It could conceivably mean Nina would be free to leave the royal family. Or would Queen Mother and Bhim Singh demand she accompany them to some obscure place, one of the smaller palaces where her work could double or triple with a smaller staff, each living virtually as prisoners. She had to clear her head. She took a long walk and sat in silence to think.

She ambled through the old part of Udaipur, past a place they called Chetak Square in honor of Pratap's noble horse. Fondly she thought of the first Chetak she knew, the beloved horse of Narendra when they first met. Grown old, he was kept in pasture, well fed and cared for until he could live no more. Narendra had mourned him even as he would his best friend. It was not until quite a few horses later that he found a young stallion he could buy which he felt worthy of the same name. When Nina recently left Jagatpur, Narendra spoke of teaching their son to ride and after mastering the skill the newest Chetak would be his.

With his father as an excellent teacher he should do well. Nina had realized, however, that unwittingly he had been coddled. Bhim Singh had not allowed his sons to enter into rough sports because of the frail health of his first and third. Subdued games like chess took the place of more robust fun and such leisure had to apply likewise to Arjun. Narendra would surely see to it that their boy who was far more precocious would at last develop into an independent person, expanding both physical and mental growth. Each day now she realized the child's grandmother had been wiser than she. Nina should have been strong enough to give him up to Jagatpur early on.

Dhao trees spread leafy arms into a welcoming shade as Nina walked beneath them close to the cenotaphs of the Maharanas. She hoped ardently that there would not be another need for a local cremation for a long time. What would Queen Mother do? Bhim Singh's middle son stood in line to take the gaddi but Nina was sure Bhim's wife would not be brilliantly prepared to act as regent as had Queen Mother twice consecutively during her lifetime. Nina had had sufficient court life in her decades at the palace to feel a furtive closeness to the multitudes of problems. "Oh, dear God, don't let anything happen to Bhim Singh," she prayed ardently. Long ago she knew he was not the greatest of the Maharanas but at least he had some feel for existing conditions and how to handle them. As fellow students Nina and Maharana Bhim Singh grew up with a winking closeness; a very special sort of friendship, but it was difficult for her to determine how clever Bhim's son would be on the gaddi.

Nina's mind glazed over ten centuries from Bappa. Not much that went on was commonplace. Chonda who had given up his birthright. Kumbha who ruled for thirty-five years to be murdered by his own son. The glory of Mewar due to Sanga. The modernization from the use of battering rams and catapults to various guns and cannons. How one Queen Mother, not even a Mewari but a Rathor, had gone into the battlefield to lead a fight and was killed instead of remaining safe in her palace. The honor accorded Nina by Queen Mother as they danced together on Holi one year.

Nor would Nina ever forget that sweet and gentle Hari Lal, now long dead, who would say after lengthy lessons, "Now you must take food for the body; you've had sufficient for your brain for one day." It had been a thrill learning under his tutelage.

In his youth Bhim Singh had come slowly to know the artistic nature of his people, the sterling character of some of his predecessors ... or their ruthless guile. Always he had listened in silence to the stories of his guru, nightly pondering situations, placing himself in the role of the hero. The more stories to which he listened the more he knew he would have to become quite a ruler to overshadow the drama of yesteryear. Once in a great while he would speak of it to Nina, the great listener. Perhaps his awareness of his potential problem had even stifled him.

A rumbling had been softly whispered about one of the aides d'camp. A certain Mohan it was said was a plant in the palace for the last several years, having been born in another kingdom. He had been a loner in the quarters of the palace reserved for such help, either having no family or not having brought them with him. He spoke little to anyone but on two separate occasions in the recent past a couple of the free-spirited had laced his drinks with opium and before he fell into too deep a sleep they pumped him with questions. In something of an incoherent tone he uttered a suggestion that perhaps one day soon there would be no young Jawan awaiting the throne of his father.

When the Maharana had been confronted with the news he shrugged it off as meaning his other two sons had been ill, perhaps Jawan too would die in childhood. The Maharana would allow no other credence to the drugged rambling and told everyone to forget it, forbidding mention of it to Mohan.

Nina, on the other hand, could not forget it, word by this time having spread to all the servants. Retaining a deep inner fear that Mohan meant to do bodily harm to Jawan, if the Maharana would do nothing about it then she would. But what?

She reached Ahar, determined to work out a plan and for the moment at least to forget about her own personal problems, for as Narendra always said to her, "Man proposes, God disposes." She had to believe that Narendra and Arjun senior would work out an idea to release her from her palace duties once and for all and that God, through Narendra's fervent prayer, would quickly dispose of the problem.

Nina relaxed for a while on a flat rock across the road from the cenotaphs. Ahar's excavations revealed a civilization existed here 4000 years B.C., the men working the dig so proud of the shards of pottery, exposed lanes and remains of houses. Today all was quiet for the workers on their Sabbath. There were, in fact, only a few participants from Europe and America camped nearby.

With an agitated mind, Nina returned to the cenotaphs of Bhim Singh's ancestors. Perhaps here a spirit would invade her thoughts.

If indeed Mohan intended doing away with the youngster Jawan then she should definitely do something about it. It was unwise of Bhim not to worry about his son's life, even if it was a false alarm. She did not want to disturb Queen Mother about it, already overburdened with other major predicaments. Women of Mewar had been so artfully cunning in handling major premeditated crimes Nina would permit herself no less crafty privilege. She must concentrate. Resting her back against one of the cool marble pillars, eyes closed in deep meditation, she reflected on the numerous deeds of the past. Somehow something of the past would give her a clue if she thought hard enough. And what of women other than Mewaris. There was always Alexander's wife. Aha. That was it. How had she manipulated the safety of her husband, "the Great?"

Especially in the days of old there was sometimes a great need for a woman to have a brother who would aid and protect her. If she did not have a natural brother it would be arranged that an "artificial" or adopted brother would serve the same purpose. Tying of rhaki could be of great importance. It was in the times of the first Hindu rulers of India that the lovely wife of Alexander the Great worried for her husband's safety. When he invaded India she knew that the Hindu king Porus from across the Indus Valley was sure to have a fight with him. Alexander had been valiantly successful many times in wars and battles but she had an unfaltering compulsion to protect him from the fateful harm she feared was surely coming. She skillfully planned her maneuvers sending a note to the king that she wished an audience with him.

Certainly he must have believed this to be some sort of trick but with her exalted station in life, the wife of the man who deemed himself ruler of the world, would preclude any dismissal of seeing her. She announced on her arrival that she wished to tie rhaki on the Hindu king thus making him her brother. Not knowing the motive he was hesitant but a Hindu king could not ignore a request such as this from another of high rank. Tradition was tenaciously strong.

The young woman tied the rhaki bracelet around the wrist of Porus and whether or not he would want to have her for a sister he had been caught. The ceremony completed, he asked his new sister what it was he could do for her. What could he give her? Customarily it would have been his place to present her with fabulous gifts: silks, brocades, jewels in great chests borne by many elephants. Away at war with such frivolous items safely left at home he could not honor such a thought, but obviously there must be something he could give her in its place.

"I want nothing for myself, my brother," she confessed, "but if you should meet my husband on the battlefield tomorrow or in days to come, my request of you is that you spare his life." There was nothing Porus could do but agree to her command, to this degree did the honor of a rhaki brother extend.

Her suppositions were correct and it was but a few days later when Porus and Alexander the great came face to face on the battlefield. In their struggles Alexander dropped his lance, laying defenselessly at the feet of the Hindu king. Porus drawing his sword was about to thrust it into the handsome body of his arch-enemy when the raised wrist bound with his new bracelet came into clear view. Porus looked down at the invader who had conquered so much of the world, but his solemn promise to his new rhaki sister spared the life of the Emperor.

Nina had long regarded this as one of the most poignant stories she had heard and vowed that such an act would also work its wiles on a potential menace to the throne of Mewar. Mohan and Nina were the most casual of acquaintances. It was not the custom in a Hindu palace to become very close with members of the opposite sex. But having already known Mohan she would make herself a little more evident and when she could manipulate the best moment she would present him with the idea of becoming rhaki-bund, explaining she had no family. It would be at a later time that she would issue her request of a promise to do no harm to the throne or its next Rana. She could only hope he too would be honorable enough to accede to her request, if indeed he did plan on killing Jawan. The brother/sister relationship is so extremely rare and wonderful in that part of the world, Narendra often told Nina that brothers would ignore all others, wives, parents, in preference to the sister if she was in any form of trouble and needed his help. If so, if Mohan would honor this code, then she could keep him from treacherous villainy.

An opportune time did not present itself immediately, which became increasingly troublesome. How would Nina know if and when any such horrible betrayal would take place. She finally forced the point one day when many of the servants sat about in the shade of the triple arches capturing whatever breeze made itself available. In the presence of all these others he dared not decline her request to tie rhaki.

Stunned with the suggestion but figuring no evil motive Mohan said they couldn't do it until their horoscopes had been checked. An auspicious hour would have to be set. On that point Nina was in complete agreement for it was most important that the plan be successful and she'd not tempt the fates by having it done other than through the workings of the stars and a worthy reader. Together they went to a priest who agreed to perform the ceremony, suggesting in turn a particular astrologer who would forecast the best possible time for it to take place.

When the strange day arrived the priest came to the palace. He had made known the fact that the ceremony, simply done, must happen between one and three in the afternoon. If it could not for any reason be performed within that time slot they would have to recheck the two horoscopes and set another date and time, presumably not any too soon. Nina was sure to be there by the stroke of one, praying that Mohan would not be detained by the Maharana. Luckily this was the luncheon hour and nothing kept the brother-to-be from the arrangement. A thread bracelet ornamented with a gaudy paper flower was tied around Mohan's right wrist while the priest recited strange passages in Sanskrit. She placed a tika on his forehead mixed not only with the red tilak powders but rice grains and a smattering of exotic spices.

"I have a present for you," he smiled halfheartedly as he extended a tiny parcel in her direction. "I hope you like it."

The present was a beautiful Rajasthani solid silver bangle with a strange oval bead at the end over which was laced a rounded firmly braided thread loop holding it on her tiny arm. Nina was truly delighted for she still had never been able to afford any of the pretty jewelry of the country, nor had anyone offered her such gifts in the past. Still holding it in the palm of her hand she looked at Mohan and said, "But brother, I was going to ask a favor of you instead of having you give me a personal gift."

"You don't like the bangle?"

"I have never owned anything as pretty as this," was her honest reply. "I love it very much and I would like much to keep it, but I must ask a favor of you."

"Then ask."

"I cannot in the presence of anyone else. It is a secret."

Walking to the other end of the courtyard he asked, "And what is the secret, my sister."

"You know I have many, many years been in the employ of the palace and I love the family more than life itself. You are an important aide d'camp and have the Maharana's respect and his ear. I have heard there is someone who would kill Jawan and I would ask that you watch over him very carefully and see that nothing comes of this terrible tale." Nina could not accuse him of the plan outright. In the first place she had no proof, and secondly she was desperately afraid of him, but she did want him to know that the scheme had somehow been detected.

"Where did you hear such a thing?" he asked in anger.

"That is not important, but I fear it is true."

"Do you accuse me of such a thing?"

"I wouldn't have a brother who would perpetrate such a horrible deed. Of course not. What I am asking is that you make sure it doesn't happen." Nina had chosen her words carefully. "But for the sake of argument, if you had been the one to do this, now it would be your sacred duty to lay aside your plan, for your sister has asked that this not happen. Will you abide by my wish as an honorable Rajput?"

"It would seem I'd have no choice — if, that is, I was the one who would have done this thing you speak of."

Nina slept easier that night for she had the innermost feeling Mohan would be a man of his word in at least this one instance. There was enough loyal Rajput blood in his veins, that strange concoction outsiders cannot fathom. Nina was now certain young Jawan would be safe, at least from Mohan.

Chapter 17

A comprehensive working plan to retrieve Nina from the midst of the royal family had been unavoidably delayed due to extremely pressing matters with the estate of Jagatpur. It was not too bothersome to Nina who felt the longer she stayed here the easier it would be to talk Queen Mother into her final dismissal. Besides that, she knew she would be humbled and subjugated by all of her sisters-in-law after she married Narendra. They'd be hard put to accept her as an equal and certainly more so as the superior she would one day be if the elders of the estate were to accept her as Narendra's legal wife. She would be alone and lonely in the midst of a very large joint family. It would not only present terrible difficulties for herself but her husband and son as well. This was exactly what she had fought against all these years. Now each day she clung more tenaciously to her sheltered environs at the palace. Most of the other servants had envied her the supreme position with Queen Mother, some jealously attacking her, but she had learned to ride with those waves and through the years that misery had subsided.

There were heard no further rumors about harming Jawan, that ubiquitous situation apparently coming full stop. But there were the invincible problems of Queen Mother. She had on several occasions of late failed to keep her rendezvous with death, three times becoming very ill. Nina had successfully nursed her back to a somewhat healthier state with childish willfulness. The friendship of the two women so far removed in class had grown again into a rich hue with the assertive faithfulness of one for the other. Now Narendra's plans, if any were soon forthcoming, would have to be set aside. Once more Nina would have to attend her Rani. If a fourth illness should occur Nina was sure she was too badly weakened to successfully combat it. It was now three and a half months since leaving Jagatpur and she missed her son dreadfully.

At the fort Narendra had taken him for daily rides within the compound on the young Chetak. There was no doubt that he would become a skilled rider in the true spirit of all Rajputs. Soon he would take him out of the fort and into emerald fields where he could more freely learn to gallop. Young Arjun was naturally anxious for this promise to take place but father was often busy resolving more pressing matters. "Why can't someone else do the work?" the boy would ask.

"Some day you too will have to understand this job and handle it yourself for it is not always expedient to delegate chores to others. There are such times as you must tend to business yourself. Grandfather is growing old and more and more of my time is demanded. Do not fret, my son. You have many years before you of riding with your friends as I have often done with mine. It will not be much longer before we go into the fields."

His prediction came true. With further news from Nina that she was once again tied up with the nursing of the Rani Narendra grew restless. He had successfully completed the problems of the fort and their villages, fully expecting a wedding to take place soon and perhaps the three of them riding off into some distant sunset for a lengthy holiday. Apparently it was not to be ... at least not quite yet. He'd occupy the future weeks and months with further training of his son, one of the greatest pleasures of his saddened life.

Back in Udaipur Nina wondered what would be the limit of the fixed span of life of Queen Mother. Inevitably she would have to yield to the gods and lay her head down in death; if Nina could make it painless she would want to do so. When she was not sitting fanning the Rani or wiping her head and hands with cool cloths she took time to play with Bhim Singh's youngsters, Jawan and his darling daughter Krishna. How she missed her own son!

The festival of Gangaur, the ceremonial worship of god Shiva and his wife Parvati, came and Nina vowed on this year she would be down at the base of the lake to watch the festivities.

All the unmarried girls of Udaipur were anxious to participate in the gaiety. It's believed that in the old days Parvati herself used to do this puja with the object of long life of her husband, Lord Shiva. Now in these modern days the married women perform the same worship service for the prolonged life of their partners. By the same token young girls hope to shortly capture a choice mate.

Nina recalled an old Hindu proverb which says, "Even the gods know not in advance a woman's mind or a man's fortune, then how can we?" Nina wondered about Narendra's fortune.

Just recently a collection of firewood piled high brightly lit the March sky, the beginning of the seven day festival of Holi. When cold, the ashes were collected by the ladies, made into balls. At the end of the seventh day they'd be immersed at the Gangaur Ghat.

Images of Lord Shiva and Parvati are made, decorated garishly and taken in procession. All the Maharajas of Rajasthan rejoice in this, one of the most colorful ceremonies of the year, some cities being more elaborate than others, but Nina knew only of the festival right here in Udaipur. Maharana Bhim Singh made his way down to the Gangaur Ghat, stepping onto his royal barge to ride to Parvati Niwas opposite Jag Mandir. For four days these processions would go on, each day the colors of costumes different, the same color costume to be worn by the Maharana. Even the ferry was painted the same color.

Nina returned again later one evening to watch the women dancing with the Gangaur on their heads. From the courtyard of the zenana the women of the palace paraded out the palace gates, past the elephant corridor, through the main entrance gates. From here they turned into the narrow cobbled path leading down to the Gangaur Ghat built for the specific purpose of immersing the clay images of this God and Goddess into the blue waters of Pichola. Others had already arrived, singing and immersing, and doubtless wondering how it would affect their destinies. Nina merely watched silently.

Nina had grown tired of sickness and grappling death, eager for the questionable life of harmony. Then came the day a servant called quickly to her. Queen Mother had taken a turn for the worse. Doctors at her side tried vainly to console her with blundering words. It pathetically angered the old woman, body shorn of strength, and waved them from her room. Only Nina was desired at her side, holding her time calloused hand. For four days and nights this lasted, rarely taking time out for tea and a few bites of food, but never out of her Rani's room. Only after Queen Mother would sip a rare drop of water would Nina allow herself a few moments of sleep.

"Look after my grandchildren," the weakened woman would repeat over and over.

Nina wanted to scream at the old woman. The grandchildren meant nothing to Nina. Why must she now look after them? She had her own son to look after. "I can only promise to do my best," she told the Rani, careful not to state she would soon be leaving forever. Besides, their mother, the Maharani would have something to say about this. Nor had Nina in any way forgotten her promise to Bhadra Singh.

Bhim Singh and his wife had been called to the Queen's chamber. There they remained until the gauntly weathered old woman was taken from their lives. Bhim Singh was now completely on his own. No longer could he call on her for judgements often superior to his.

"You will stay on and attend me?" the Maharani asked Nina to her astonishment. Though in the early years of this marriage the Maharani would have little to do with the original servants of the palace, it had become quite clear that Nina was a jewel in the crown not easily replaced.

"I am honored that you ask, Your Highness, but I must return to Jagatpur to my son. I have stayed this long only at the special request of our dying Queen Mother. I am long overdue and must leave as soon as possible."

"If you change your mind, do let me know," she said, turning to depart and make preparations with her husband for the funeral service of her mother-in-law. The venerable Queen

Mother had served the palace and the kingdom for a great many years, first as the wife of a Maharana, then as regent for two of her sons. Now the dowager Queen Mother was dead and the State of Mewar must be told.

As soon as it was feasible Nina left Udaipur for what she expected would be the last time, choking a goodbye to her rhaki brother Mohan. Before reaching the fort on this wearisome, journey sounds of distant laughter pleasantly greeted her, recognizable as Narendra and Arjun.

Presently she caught sight of Narendra playfully pulling their son from his horse and looking for all the world as if in mortal combat. Nina rushed headlong into their midst yelling, "Mar, mar; war, war." Momentarily the boy's young arms circled his mother's waist, his father standing back, allowing them a respectful few moments alone.

"Little one, I was thinking I could take it no more, this life without you. Now you are back and we can marry one day soon."

"I shall certainly honor my promise to your mother, and I so much want to be yours, but for the time being let's just be carefree. I'm so weary."

They sat on the calloused ground, Narendra opening a little packet he had the servants wrap for him, expecting to picnic in the shade of the forest with his son. They ate and chatted of many things which had happened in the previous months. Narendra's problems with the estate and how he settled some of them through continued good judgement of his revered father. Nina had questioned him on the old man's health, intensely relieved to learn he was in splendid condition for his advanced age. They spoke of Queen Mother and her dying and the surprise request to remain at the palace and aid in the upbringing of Jawan and Krishna Kumari.

The sun was starting to slide down its final path of the day before the trio took off for the fort. Arjun would be highly pleased to see his future daughter-in-law.

For several days both Narendra and Nina avoided conversation about their expected marriage. Finally he suggested they talk in their usual spot, the old temple grounds. The puzzle might sort itself out far better there.

Bhadra's request and Nina's promise were the opening part of the discussion, Nina following with the expected remarks that Arjun would always be called the bastard of the family and even if the estate "fathers" gave their sanction to this marriage it would be dreadfully hard on both Narendra and little Arjun.

"It'll be hard on you too, won't it, little one."

"Of course, but then I'm much accustomed to problems.

"If you can tolerate whatever is handed out to you, then certainly so can Arjun and I," Narendra argued. "Do not impugn us by suggesting that you are stronger in character. Our son is also a Rajput and as such he can stand up to any test. If my brothers or their wives insult us, as I fully expect they will, we can always do something about it.

"Nina, my little one, you cannot solve all the problems of tomorrow's world before you even know what those problems will be. Let us worry about each day as it comes and let the rest wait until we reach it. There is time enough for trouble. While the days are good let us enjoy them that way. Let us not borrow trouble for it may come all too easily. But I have full faith that when and if it does come we will find a way to handle it. I am of Rajput blood. The Rajputs have always found a way to handle their problems. It will be no different for us now."

"And what if they make it so difficult for you that we cannot live here in this home of yours, Narendra? What if they refuse to accept me as your wife because I am a 'widow' or because I've been a servant? I have thought and thought about it and I do not believe we owe anyone an explanation about why I am not really a widow and how we came to make up that ugly story, one that now we have both lived to regret. What I cannot bear is for them to ridicule you, my love." Nina placed her soft head on his chest.

"Nina. You are not to worry on my part. I can be like Chonda, you know, and give up my birthright. I have been thinking for some time perhaps we should follow in his steps. He pulled up roots. We too can go off by ourselves. Just the three of us."

"I've long forgotten the lesson of Chonda, Narendra. Refresh me," asked Nina.

"Who could forget Chonda? I too may become a Chonda and the three of us may go off by ourselves, but though I have thought and thought of a place we could possibly live, we should take each day at a time and try to work things out, not borrowing any trouble. Chonda is really father's favorite story though, Nina. Come. Let him tell it to us. It will please him."

When they reached the quarters of the elder Singh, being a warm night he had pulled a charpoy out onto the verandah of his large bungalow. Sitting there wistfully smoking an old pipe, Narendra told why they had come. The old man pulled both his feet together, boney knees pointed outward, resting in the very middle of the charpoy. "One of you on each side of me," he ordered, "while I speak of that strange and wonderful man once again. He was one of Mewar's best."

Many times traveling back and forth between Jagatpur and Udaipur they had all passed the tin and silver mines, sometimes stopping nearby for a rest. "In the fourteenth century," the elder Arjun said, "there was not a great deal of work done in the mines but there was some production. Lakha was the Rana at that time and he had two sons, the older of which was Chonda. But it was his younger brother who was exceedingly handsome and everyone around from village to village had come to love him.

"Well, one day the Rana was just sitting around and an emissary brought a coconut and the announcement that it was intended for the eldest son Chonda. He could have as his bride the princess Hansa from Marwar.

"I can see it all so clearly," Arjun Singh started to rock with laughter. "'I certainly didn't think the bride was being presented to me.' The Rana laughed, bringing the whole room into a gleeful uproar. By the time the news reached Prince Chonda he became terribly indignant, refusing the coconut, sending word to his father that this was a terrible personal affront. The Rana tried to explain to his son that this was just a chance remark and that to offend the throne of Marwar was to invoke war and they could ill afford it. True, the mines were doing a bit of work and there was a little other income, but nothing great enough to support a full-scale all-out war.

"But Chonda remained livid; his father had no right to make light of his proposal of marriage, especially in front of the foreign delegation. In private he met with his father stating that he could not marry Hansa, fearing he would be the laughing stock of all Rajputana. 'I refuse the Princess,' he adamantly replied. 'Send the coconut back in the morning.'

"'For the sake of honor and decency you must marry her, Chonda,' the father begged.

"'It is honor and decency that I am thinking of, father. It was you who taught me that honor is synonymous with the word "Rajput," with the very name of Mewar. I shall not have Hansa and let there be an end to it.'

"The Rana definitely had to come up with a satisfactory answer. He knew. He'd wed her himself. Besides that, if they had a son it would be that son who would inherit the gaddi. Chonda would have to accept the fact that _he_ would not inherit the throne.

"Now you must remember, children, that Chonda was thrilled with this solution. There would be no war and he would not have to sit on the gaddi when his father died, assuming Hansa would have a son. It pleased him greatly. And, as you know, in due course a child was born, the boy they called Mokul. The Rana loved him just as I love your Arjun.

"But the Rana was a strange one. While he had said they could not afford war with Marwar, in the years that followed he became bored with life and decided upon a war with the barbarians of Delhi. Yet he feared he would not return alive and also feared for Mokul. But Chonda had pledged years ago to go along with his father's demands of Hansa's son becoming ruler.

Chonda would see it was carried out and in fact would assist little Mokul in any way he could until he would be old enough to handle things on his own — provided, of course, the Rana was killed on the battlefield.

"Chonda was definitely a man of his word and with a lighter heart the Rana went to war. Alas, even with all the thousands and thousands the Rana and nobles could muster, the Rana's forces were too weak. He not only lost the war but his life. Chonda started to immediately govern in the name of his little half brother.

"For a reason I guess none of us will ever know, the Rani Hansa wasn't happy with the setup. Perhaps she didn't trust Chonda, which was foolish on her part. Saddened by her attitude, Chonda and 200 of his best friends left the fort, leaving the Rani to fend for herself and solve problems as best she could.

"She was completely beside herself as worries multiplied and she sent for her father and brothers from Marwar to assist her in her need. My, how they must have loved that. Coming to the aid of the woman now running their rival kingdom — their daughter and sister. 'It's nice to be once again in Chittor,' they must have gloated. It really was lovely in Chittor, you know, Narendra and Nina. Of an evening high above the surrounding countryside the air might be still and warm, the sun an intoxicating blood red at eventide. All could be beatifically peaceful.

"The men remained to permeate in the life of Chittor, interceding in Hansa's affairs. Little by little they wheedled away at her until eventually the dissipated Mewar nobles were ousted from their positions. Not too much longer the father and brothers were running the kingdom of Mewar. Hansa's self respect had been destroyed by her kin. She'd have to do something soon. But what?

"Then the strangest thing happened. A faithful maid came to the Rani explaining that while the grandfather was playing with his grandson, all of a sudden there sat the grandfather on the royal throne sacredly reserved only for the ruler. It was an innocent gesture to be sure, nonetheless it did appear he was the Rana and it completely rankled the maid. She begged and begged Her Highness to do something at once. Her father's affront was the last straw to Hansa. She had seen the error she had made. Now it seemed the only person to save her and the kingdom was Chonda, the man she had driven from the fort with her foolishness.

"Chonda's younger brother had stayed on at the palace with nothing to do after the others had left, so long ago. She considered sending him after his brother but her family must have considered him a threat, even in his quiet, unassuming manner, and she found him viciously slain.

"Now Hansa was more troubled than ever. If her family had killed the prince they could just as easily kill her son. It would not surprise her after seeing how her father gloated as he sat on the throne. Nothing could now allay her fears for her son's health and well-being. The false god of revenge tormented her constantly. But to whom could she turn for help? There seemed no one to come to her self-denying aid.

"In the dark recesses of her shadowy room she nervously sat at night, and in the same dark a spiritual light shone upon her. Suddenly she intuitively knew what she must do. It was Chonda alone who could save Mewar. That she had known. She remembered a trusted servant and asked that he sneak from the fort, seek out Chonda from wherever he hid, and bring him back to the palace. She explained very carefully all the stories the servant should repeat to the rightful heir to the throne. Now she prayed these cabalistic words would not fall thunderingly on deaf ears. And now she would have the protracted vigil of waiting to learn if her impassioned plea would be answered. 'Prayer is the only thing left to me now,' she'd say to herself, hoping this would bring not only Chonda but the metamorphic sleep she so desperately needed.

"It took many days before the servant found Chonda and he laboriously told the many pathetic stories. After that he was given a hearty meal and sent for a well needed sleep while Chonda and his men devised their strategy. Very soon after the arrival of Hansa's 'ambassador' the first few of Chonda's men returned to Chittor. Reaching the gates of the fort they explained they returned because they wearied of being with Chonda. Hansa's father and brothers were unsuspecting of any foul play, so few would saunter in on any given day. They were allowed to move freely within the palace grounds of Chittor, careful to bring no suspicion to themselves."

Nina interrupted the old man. "Narendra, if we were ever exiled from Jagatpur, where would we go? Could we ever return? What of our young Arjun and his eventual seat?"

"Let's hope we don't decide to go that route," he replied.

Old Arjun chose to ignore the remark and took up his story. "Chonda remained behind, the Rani Hansa not knowing he had a scheme. Meantime in a dramatic act of atonement Hansa one day ordered a great feast be prepared. When the enormous amounts of food were ready she ordered the nurse to dress the Rana and join her. Down into one of the villages they traveled, along with the entourage bearing the prepared foods. In devotion she had the feast spread before the villagers. All were exceedingly pleased, for not only could they use the excessive amounts of food, but the presence of the little Rana and his mother was a true joy. They were greatly heartened with the act of fidelity.

"After this the Rani felt a new sense of jubilation when she returned from such trips, now making it a custom to conspicuously visit a different village on each occasion. Her brothers thought nothing of this strange event, as long as their bellies were full. As for her father, he was always so drunk with opium and with fulfilling his bodily desires with his new mistress that he had no time to watch the meanderings of his rebellious daughter.

"Diwali, the Feast of Lights, was to be celebrated as it had been for endless centuries, in honor of Laksmi the goddess of good luck and plenty. Everyone for hundreds of miles in each direction would be gay and festive. On this occasion the Rani decided on a particular village five kilometers from the entrance of the fort of Chittor. She sent word to them that they were to be the village honored on the night of Diwali.

"What a thrill they all felt for not only would they have their stomachs filled but it would be a beautiful night. Each year hundreds of clay lamps were molded, but this year with the intended visit of the Rani and her son, Rana Mokul, they determined to have an unusually large number of lamps to outline their flat roofed homes and fences, their barns, the perimeters of individual pieces of property and the entire village.

"For many warm days the lamp makers sat around their various yards fashioning little mud pots in which they would burn their oil. Laboriously they would set them into the hot sun to bake. When the night of Diwali finally came the lamps blazed from every home from the tiniest little hovel to the largest of the village. It was the village of Gossonda where the merriest of these feasts took place and it was to be especially joyous for the Rani. One of the followers of Chonda who filtered in to Chittor much later than the first arrivals brought word to her that Chonda had a plan and would make an appearance at the feast of Diwali at Gossonda. But she did not see Chonda and as the night grew late she felt betrayed.

"With weary heart she turned to make her agitated departure from the village and reenter the fort. She must have wondered why Chonda would send a message if he did not intend to come. Had he met with foul play? Could no one save Mewar?

"As they neared the gates of Chittor the noise of thundering hooves reached out to Hansa and the group. Turning, they saw the feathery dust and counted forty horsemen encrusted in dirty and ragged clothes. Riding past the Rana and Hansa and giving a gesture appropriate for their station, the riders went on. Moments later they reached the gates.

"'Who goes there?' they were asked.

"'We were at Gossonda at the feast and were honored and privileged to escort your Rani and the Rana back to the palace,' the leader lied.

"There was certainly nothing suspicious of this. For many weeks the Rani had been delivering feasts to the villages and always horsemen accompanied them on their return to Chittorgarh. At each of the successive gates they were asked the same question and gave the same reply until the seventh gate, the Gate of Rama. On a higher rise the gatesman could see in the distance more armed forces and became suspicious. 'Who are you, Chieftain?' he wanted to know.

"The reply was a drawn sword by the leader and at this instant the war cry went out. Huntsmen from all around had been expecting something to happen on this day and were prepared for any eventuality. All came to instant aid. The gatesmen were taken by complete surprise, overpowered or killed. All gates were quickly opened to the men of Prince Chonda. Some of the followers of Hansa's brothers rushed out of homes, swords drawn, but were not too successful in their attempts. Hansa's father, deep in opium sleep, was stabbed to death.

"Chittorgarh was now rid of the horrible men from Marwar who had undeservedly taken over the important position in Mewar kingdom. Once gone, Rana Mokul again came to full power, but only with thanks and help of his elder half-brother Chonda who rightfully should have been sitting on the throne, but who because of a promise to his father had allowed his little brother to occupy the seat. And remember too, Nina, he could have been Hansa's husband, had he not considered his father's joke as a brazen affront. But thanks to his forgiving nature he came to the aid of the woman who banished him with humiliation from his kingdom, then sought his help when none other could." Arjun senior concluded his historic tale.

"How exactly does this apply to our problem?" Nina questioned.

Narendra replied, "Chonda was willing to give up his throne if his father chose to have another take it. By the same token, should my family or the elders of Jagatpur find it impossible to allow me to serve as ruler of this jagir's estate on the demise of my father, then I like Chonda can go elsewhere and live. We three would move to a place where we could live in quiet solitude. While I love my country dearly, still I must be my own man. You will become my wife and we'll go somewhere to bring up our son where we can still live honestly and simply."

"It would be a far cry from the life young Arjun would have as the lord of a feudal land," she argued. "On the other hand I cannot rid from my mind the fact he would be so totally unhappy if all his cousins and others were to condemn him for being my son. I no longer know what is best to do. I have caused great trouble by ever coming to Jagatpur with you when you found me in Mandore. If my running away alone would solve anything I would have done it long ago."

Resting his withering hands upon hers, Arjun senior stated, "I'm attempting everything possible to make the whole family see that there's nothing wrong with my son marrying a widow. I know the real truth. If you will allow me I shall explain to them that in fact you are not a widow. As for myself, I would want you for my daughter in any case."

"I do not think any story will satisfy them, father," Nina spoke. "But I am ashamed of nothing. Whatever I've done, I've done in the name of love, true love."

"And without that love my son would not have a son," the old man smiled. You know, Nina, of all my sons' wives I favor you the most. It was you who brought the greatest joy to Narendra and brought comfort to my wife. The others are undoubtedly higher born, but you have been the wisest and kindest. My wife could never forget it, nor shall I. And now we must talk of plans for the wedding."

Elated with this long awaited settlement it was agreed the wedding would take place within these grounds on the first auspicious day. Tomorrow the priests would be consulted, as would the two horoscopes. Meantime Nina would try to make friends with the other women. Tomorrow should be easier to live with.

Chapter 18

Marriage plans for the bride and groom would not crystallize for almost another two months when the first auspicious date appeared on their horoscope. It was frustrating to each to be patient after such a tense wait of so many years. They had been in love for into the third decade, their son now into his teens.

Haggard with apprehension, Nina feared something again might happen to keep the most wonderful day of her life from dawning. Arjun senior lectured his other sons and their wives to treat Nina with respect as the family's newest member. At least for the time being they were decently civil although not abundantly warm. Nina accepted it as a pre-wedding blessing and prayed it would continue while fully expecting it would not.

Narendra once more took to the trails with his son, teaching him not only to ride well but to jump and now he had graduated to the stage of learning to stick wild boar. His real "target" was one of Pandu's arms wrapped heavily in yards of thick cloth, dashing to the side of the horse as the youngster attempted to spear his arm with a blunted weapon. This taught Arjun not only to aim at the target, lean his body weight carefully to the side of the horse, Chetak, but to properly rein in, turning him swiftly without losing balance. With each passing month Arjun became more beloved to all of Narendra's friends.

There would be those times too when young Arjun would beg to be taught the art and wiles of capturing dacoits. Why could he not follow in his father's path? Furiously both parents forbid his ever thinking along such lines. Narendra had now for the most part given up these never ending searches and fights.

Time was undeniably on Nina's side insofar as growing accustomed to a permanent life here at Jagatpur. Since her final decision she could barely wait out the last weeks before the actual wedding ceremony. The pair had remained physically apart since her return from Udaipur as if a maidenly modesty had overcome her. They would wait until after the final ceremony before again being one, a matter which they had no need to discuss.

It was also at this time that the elder Arjun, Narendra and Nina discussed cool-headedly and at length the boy's need to know the true background from which he came. He was old enough to understand about Nina having been spirited away by the infamous Motilal and all its gross implications. In fact, thought the grandfather, this might even serve to clearly emblazon on his mind the viciousness of dacoity and his father's reasons for fighting these villains for so many years. But more than that the elder Arjun wanted his grandson to be absolutely sure he understood the type of life his mother was forced to live and her loyalties which were many and uncomprehendingly deep. Young Arjun was called to join the trio. By the end of the discourse the old man had practically beatified Nina.

But Arjun Singh took the discussion one step further and said, "Young Arjun, everything and everybody in life is not entirely just. There are times when we must accept things which we know to be less than right. If we can set them straight, well and good; but often it appears there is little we can do about situations. It is at those times that we must learn to live with them, just as many of our forefathers and friends have had to do. Understand?"

"I think so, grandfather."

"I hope so," he said, holding the teenager's strong hand.

"You have something on your mind. Why don't you tell me what it is?"

"I should not speak against others of my sons and grandchildren and I do not know quite how to say it well. Arjun, there will be those among us who will be jealous. It is often that we bear these ignominious traits. We should be above all that, but unfortunately it is not always so. I think what I'm trying to say is if your cousins or aunts or uncles should look at you differently than they do the others here, try to overlook it. Perhaps in time things will become equal. There are several things the more self-righteous among them feel. First, they still believe your mother to be a widow and to many this is an irreparable shame ... not that she was widowed but that your father would marry one. Some would not believe the true story because they do not wish to believe. No matter.

"Second, they will call you a bastard and as such they will not think you the appropriate one to take over the duties when your father will one day die. But only time will work that out.

"Third, things will be difficult for your mother because they will regard her still as a servant. Personally I think she has more royal blood than all of us put together. Now when things should be the brightest and easiest for her, it will suddenly, with her marriage, become the most difficult. Treat her always with the greatest reverence, for never can you understand the beauty and light she has brought into our lives. There is none more worthy of happiness."

It was several days later that it became visibly apparent to both Nina and Narendra that old Arjun must have been quite emphatic with the priests who were to perform the marriage ceremony that Nina had never before been married. The various rites were performed as if she were a first-time bride. If others about the household questioned this they were sharply criticized for interfering and each of the day's plans went forward flawlessly.

An entire retinue of Narendra's friends had arrived in Jagatpur, the most intimate of whom camped with their families within the private grounds of Arjun Singh, growing each day by the half-hundred. No one ceased to love and admire Narendra and knowing the wedding was his most cherished dream they all joyously came to offer sincere best wishes and help in the rejoicing.

If there were those in the immediate family who wished ill for Narendra and his second bride, outward signs were hidden and everything proceeded graciously. Seven days before the big event seven married ladies, Narendra's sister and his sisters-in-law, gathered together at the far end of the family quarters. They had purchased a bright substance, grinding it into a powder. Narendra was summoned. Bashfully he removed his kurta, as ordered, standing giggling as they childishly tickled his bronze skin, shiny from perspiration. They had mixed the powders with oil and now his lissome frame glistened more than ever as they doused him.

The room vibrated with open-hearted merriment. The wedding ceremony would take place on the ground floor of the elder Singh's. The courtyard outside was smoothed over with cow dung. From now until the marriage a barber would come each day, massaging and smoothing Narendra's palpitating body. He was now considered a bridegroom, no longer free to roam the lanes of the fort. Each night the relatives would take him to yet another home for meals. On the last three nights they performed the rite of Pithi. Oil and spices were put on his head, after which he knew the marriage must take place.

On the auspicious day of the wedding the barber once more returned. A cord was put around Narendra and then he adjourned to take a bath. In the absence of the groom's mother his sister handed to the barber the clothes which would be worn for the ceremony.

At the same time several of the sisters-in-law watched closely to make sure Nina had her luxurious and religious bath, relaxing in the spiced and scented water. The clothes which she had been wearing previous to this were given away in traditional custom. Nina could not help wonder what her groom was thinking. They had not spoken of love for several months now. Could her past behavior have changed him in even the slightest manner?

So resolutely besieged with activities, pujas performed by the ladies in the room next to him, Narendra had no time to do much thinking about anything. After bathing and his invigorating massage the barber handed him his trousers, then his shirt, brought by his maternal uncle as traditional gifts.

The appointed hour finally arrived, a magnificent Arabian steed waiting outside in the temporal courtyard. Adorned with long strands of white flowers it stood patiently for the equally adorned groom. By this time Narendra had placed upon himself a soft pink aachkan, buttoned all the way down the front. A lengthy red sash graced his swivel hips and on his sun-baked head a Mewari turban. At his side dangled the ornate tulwar, the curved sword resting in its embroidered blue velvet sheath.

A toran was placed in front of him and it was then that his married sister, acting on the part of his deceased mother, approached her "son." Now it was that he must take from his "mother's" breast a taste of her milk, then remount his horse. Ceremoniously his sister-in-law came to him and would not let go. Expected, he paid her something and presented her a gift, a new sari purchased for this specific occasion. With that she released the mount.

The band in all their finery had assembled and the festal procession started, self-taught musicians playing their droning instruments, marching in slow cadence in front of the man of honor. He reminisced how he had done this once before and that is should not be happening again in this manner. It should have been a simple, discreet wedding, but his mother and father had decided upon this detailed affair for the sake of Nina alone. Old Arjun was determined his dead wife would have her wish, whatever the payoff to the priests. Narendra thought also of the moment after his marriage to Kala when on leaving the room he pretended to trip and whispered into Nina's ear. Could it have been way back then that he was in love with her and would not admit it even to himself?

The procession had left the grounds of the Singh compound, walking slowly through the major roadway of the fort, circling back and returning to the compound where the mandapam had been placed for the official ceremony. Through the circuitous route they continued picking up friends and neighbors.

Normally at this point the father of the bride would have presented something to the bridegroom. Nina, with no living relatives, had chosen Ramesh to take her father's place. He took Narendra's arm and walked with him to a small room near the main entrance of the compound. Here he found his girl "sleeping" on a cot, or so it would appear. All the ladies around pressed him to sit on the bed while she presumably slept on. Nina lay very quiet, eyes closed in humility and her face covered.

Dutifully he refused to sit on her cot. And then the ladies proceeded to ask many questions. They were giddy and foolish, one asking, "Narendra, who is behind you?" His smile was sick and he wanted desperately to get the whole day over with. He half turned around. "Everyone is behind you," they told him he should have replied. The bride and groom were too old for this nonsense; couldn't anyone see it? What to do? Small portions of food were brought to be shared with the little children in the gathering; they too had a special spot in the day's events. If Nina had had any young brothers or sisters they would have been the very first to join him in this little feast.

Now the main priest arrived and once more Narendra entered the arena along with his esteemed father, the priest chanting to various gods and goddesses. Coins and colored powders were pressed into the hands of the bridal pair, tying them together. After a ten minute ceremony they were led to the holiest of the places, the Chamwari Mandap, where the actual rite would be preformed.

The appropriate mantrums were read with the help of six Brahmans, on conclusion the bridal pair walking four times around the sacred fire, Nina preceding Narendra. At the end of the third time she became his legal wife. On the fourth turn it was Narendra who walked in front. This then became the permanent marriage. The husband now sat on the right side of his wife; heretofore he had been on her left.

When one of the little ones asked for an explanation of this his mother had said, "They have promised each other to love through their life, to speak truth, not to steal, to look after their family with love and he would always be on her right hand side. If she does not obey this then he will only be on her left side. It is a symbol."

The parents of Nina should have presented many cows and horses or money. Had Nina still been the ward of Her Highness it is highly likely because of their great admiration for each other the Rani might have taken this chore upon herself. This Kanya-dan or daughter-gift was taken over by Ramesh who chose to offer a few symbolic gifts.

After this they went to the elder Arjun Singh's house, Nina entering and bowing very low before him. Finally they had won her, this woman they had all come to revere so many years ago, a perfect mate for his son.

The bridal pair slept separately this night, Nina feeling a sense of relief in this out of guilt and even a touch of hypocrisy. But in the early morning the two arose, bathed, dressed and went out to worship together in all the temples of the many gods and goddesses throughout the fort, commencing with their personal favorite in the far reaches of the family grounds.

Night brought more drum-beating and the high pitched voices of the local women in their customary Rajasthani songs. On the following day they revisited all the temples. When the religious part of the day was over they reentered their games of childish delight, searching for rings in slippery little tubs of gooey water.

Then came a sober moment. The sacred threads which had been tied around the hands and feet of the bride and groom were removed. A special place in the house was found for them to be kept and the last of the ceremonies to be observed. From that night on Narendra and Nina were truly husband and wife. After so many long years of suffering they were now together, thanks to the foresight of his mother and the added endeavors of his father. They felt destined to live a close family life, probably not to raise more children. So much time had lapsed since the birth of their son. But "God is great," to use the words of Narendra, and who could know what was to come? They would leave it all in the hands of their lord.

They took off with their son for an extended holiday riding through the forests and woodlands, stopping to watch deer and sambhar roam the wilds, listening to the stories of the whimpering monkeys; it seemed at times Narendra understood their language. Arjun caught sight of his first great tiger close up, standing still to watch, obviously down-wind of the gorgeous creature. A civet cat one day caused them more problems than the larger animals and through this extended outing Arjun learned better than ever to respect the craftiness and beauty of the animals of the wild.

Many friends were visited and the most important to Nina were the young men who had come to her assistance offering a dowry. Stopping to pay her undying respects she would accept no hospitality except for tea. They had already done so much.

Arjun had come to love his mother and father equally and was astounded to be included in their honeymoon. He had a separate tent and would lay in it in the night's quiet, happy to hear the muted laughter of his parents, for in their happiness lay his.

They stayed almost two months, each in his own way dreading the return to Jagatpur, pushing it into darkest recesses of their three minds. Some of Nina's fears were well-founded. The celebrations were over, several of the sister-in-law had dropped all pretense to niceties. Now things reverted to the days after the announcement of the wedding when with a special hatred they looked upon this woman who would sit with her husband, the next feudal lord of Jagatpur, ruling over the land and claiming its richest rewards. All this glory and tribute for a woman who had been a servant in the house of Mewar and bore an illegitimate son to Narendra even as Kala was carrying her last child. The majority of the family could not understand or forgive. Narendra's sister was the kindest of all, perhaps because she was a born romantic. She had gone from the fort to her own home in the city of her husband shortly after the marriage. Nina would miss her sweetness and the opportunities to sit idly chatting in the shade of the neem tree.

For the sake of Narendra and their son Nina would pretend to be unbothered by the injustices and innuendoes of the family, only and always expressed in the absence of the elder Arjun Singh. Perhaps Narendra would not notice and in time this too might go away. She would live for that moment in time.

Things did not get better, however, the little cousins picking on Arjun, taunting him with snide remarks. Arjun nonetheless was his father's son and learned rather quickly to turn a deaf ear, never speaking of it to either his mother or father, understanding quite well how it would hurt them. Instead he took such worries to his grandfather who kept reminding the young man of Nina's great caring and concern for all. Young Arjun was old enough to place his own values on these truths. He could only love his mother and father more for all they endured. He kissed his grandfather, an act seldom seen among the men of Rajasthan, telling the old man he had done right in uncovering for him all the uncertainties with which he had to live.

Young Arjun hoped fervently his grandfather would never die, but a little more than a year later he was taken very ill. The daughters-in-law said of Nina, "She has taken care of the others. If she is such a magician let us see if she can heal our father." When he didn't get better they'd taunt her with, "Where are your miracles now?"

Nina had sent for all the doctors they knew of in the fort and from nearby towns. If there was the tiniest suggestion of something new to help she did not want that chance to be missed. With the passing of Arjun she knew a great part of her heart would also die and she could not easily bear this thought. Difficult as it was to lose Bhadra Singh and the Queen Mother, it was tremendously more difficult to sit and watch Arjun Singh slipping through her fingers. She could do little to comfort the old man wading through the deep waters of his various afflictions.

An expression of great suffering crossed his face, not for his own excruciating pain but for the pain he knew Nina was enduring as she watched him die. One night he sent all from the room except Nina, Narendra and young Arjun. He asked that she hold his hand and said, "My child, there are infinite varieties of suffering and in your face I see the deepest of them all. You feel for me as I lay here dying, but do not fret. I have had such a superior life. I was fortunate to be born into a rich house. I've had a pleasure and success running this estate. My wife and I raised a fine family, although I realize they treat you badly and for them I apologize. I'm a crumbling old man and it would be futile for me to remain here longer, even if I could. I leave my estate in good hands, for you, Narendra, are very capable of running it flawlessly. Promise you will always be careful should you decide again to chase more dacoits. Our original thoughts and ventures were noble, but we could not know this form of life would take such strong hold and run rampant throughout so much of India. We know now that you cannot lick it single-handedly. Like prostitution, it will be here forever. Take care. You have a family now to care for.

"Young Arjun, I charge you to watch over your mother and father. Look after them in old age as they have looked after me. This I insist."

"I will, grandfather." Huge tears streaked down his reddened cheeks.

"Nina, be lovers always, you and your husband, just as my wife and I were. I hope you have already come to know that marrying my son was the finest thing you could do. Live here in peace with the rest of the family, and Nina, thank you for coming into our fold."

His words touched her deeply. She had always known he cared for and admired her but until this moment she never realized to what extent. Narendra was forced to take the wailing Nina and Arjun from the side of his father, returning alone to sit with the dying man through the balance of the night.

No longer did Arjun have control over his biological infirmities and all the nursing, caring and prayers could not save him. Arjun died three days after their lengthy talk. The bickering again stopped during the time of cremation and other religious ceremonies, each person enveloped in his own sadness and how to deal with it. To light the funeral pyre once more was dishearteningly difficult for Narendra. His father and best friend was dead, a good part of himself dying with this feudal lord, but it was the duty of the eldest son to oversee the chores and light the fire.

As for Nina, she knew nothing would ever be the same and feared not for their mortal lives in Jagatpur but for a sanity to prevail if Narendra's brothers and their wives should become as despicable as she suspected they could. Always Nina had a sixth sense about such things and she was not likely to be wrong this time. The month that followed was quiet but slowly thereafter there arose little twinges of malcontent in the compound. Nina tried to remember her father-in-law's words. She was strong enough to fluff off some of the contemptuous banter, turning to other things to brighten her days. She sought from Narendra conversations about the handling of the estate, local and village problems which were constantly being brought before him and the politics of the country which he would invariably get from the palace.

It would soon be time for another tour of duty to Udaipur and though he was conversantly familiar with the routine, he and the estate were running short of money and duty at court was a costly thing for all the rawals. He would most probably be gone for a number of months. In the past years there were wars. Thank heavens they were supposedly at peace at the moment. Duties would be longer and costlier. In the years when crops were bad the revenue brought to the rawals was limited; this year there was not an excessive amount coming to the Narendra Singh estate. Also, during festivals it was obligatory that the nobles come to the palace and spend a good deal of time in more or less entertainment for and with the ruler. Occasionally a rawal or rawat would try to excuse himself but this was for the most part quite difficult, the rulers not too anxious to have their numbers depleted, and besides, it was something of an affront.

The nobles had to bring with them their own staff when they served at court, in most instances living as high on the proverbial wild boar as the Rana. They were accustomed to a large retinue of personal servants, bodyguards, and so on. But it was from the pocket of the nobleman that the bills would be paid, and not by the Rana. Thus it was that often nobles hated attending too many large functions for too long a time. Payment for these jaunts dipped deeply into their tightening purses.

Still feeling the romantic bridegroom, Narendra insisted that Nina return to the palace with him, to live at his side. He also invited Ramesh, Pandu and Ran as well as other close friends. All the major servants would attend him, as they did his father, and by the time they counted their numbers they were 53. This would badly strip their coffers but it was a must, especially being his first time to serve in Udaipur as Rawal of Jagatpur.

Nina would be glad to see the Maharana again and his pretty daughter Krishna Bhai, the young Maharajkumari, and

Jawan and all the dozens of others Bhim Singh had sired through his numerous concubines. She wondered how he was making out ruling his land now that his strong-willed mother was dead. She had often said to Nina that it would be difficult in these times for the strongest of rulers and she knew Bhim Singh to be relatively weak.

The journey with its many people took a few days longer than usual, stopping more often to pitch their tents, prepare their food and rest. Rumblings were rampant over the countryside and he was certain the durbars would be anything but festive.

Everyone reaching court took their allotted places, settling down as comfortably as could be expected, servants jammed into small quarters with the vast numbers. Nina sought an audience with Their Highnesses, receiving one rather promptly. They were genuinely happy to see her, the Maharani asking if she reconsidered and would come back to remain in their custody. Nina explained that she had married, which raised a few eyebrows, no doubt in view of her supposed widowhood. She explained that she accompanied her husband, the Rawal of Jagatpur, just to be at his side, but that another joy in the trip was the opportunity to see Their Highnesses and their children.

Graciously Nina was offered the many courtyards in which to stroll and to sit with the children whenever she would happen upon them. Nina even surprised herself at how rapturously happy she was to be back in the home she had so long loved. If she could be of any assistance to the Maharani during her husband's stay she would be honored to do so, she told the queen. Besides, it would help speed the hours.

It was not long after their arrival that a durbar was called to discuss mounting problems with the Suktawuts and Chondawats, the ever-feuding rival clans. Their fights were normally nonsensical but nonetheless real and causing undue problems for many. Representatives of the two groups were called before the durbar to answer charges of their latest quarrel. Placed before the Rana they were superstitiously reluctant to discuss anything to do with it but under a penalty of a fate worse than death they were forced to openly admit their latest clash had to do with which of the two clans would be first in battle. While others of the world might fight for a place at the rear of the lines, these Rajputs, ridiculously strange as they might appear, held the brave contention the most worthy of all soldiers were entitled to the place of honor, the first in battle.

The Rana's counselors called him aside, taking the stand a medium ground had to be found, too detrimental would be the cause of finding the one more competent to handle the esteemed position. Nor would scorn or derision of either group help the Rana either in times of war or peace. While Queen Mother was still alive she sat openly in favor of the Chondawats. She gave them greater attention, helped them secure the best of arms, allowed them to sit in some of the durbars and thus they came to know most of what was going on or being craftily planned within the kingdom. All this information was used to the Chondawats' eventual gain, oblivious of the fact that without the Queen Mother's sanctions none of the good would have ever reached them. They appeared to owe her no special allegiance as their foothold within the kingdom and especially around Udaipur grew stronger. She, like Hansa, had done a foolish thing by taking one lone faction into her confidence, whether ill-planned or spontaneously happening. Under the Chondawats she felt less and less the regent. Her son was too languidly weak to help, and the entire mess was of her doing. Bhim Singh spent more and more time with his beautiful bevy of concubines and wives, siring numerous children. To Nina, her son seemed less and less a bastard as more and more babies were born in or near the palace.

Living close to Queen Mother's torment through many years Nina was quite aware of the inner struggle in her Rani's heart. She had permitted one faction in her kingdom to come close to complete rule. Like Hansa, she had to seek outside help, but where could she find it? Locking herself into the quiet of her favorite room she prayed and prayed for an answer to the confusing riddle. The only thing which kept popping into her mind was the opposition — the Suktawuts.

That incestuous change was worse than nothing for with her shifting of patronism, civil war was started. The futility of her move and worthlessness of this other side caused grievous harm, not only to the nation, but to the Rani as a person. Nina was sure it was this time in her life and the events surrounding it which led to the spiritual and physical downfall of the regent. Unveiled were her errors, by then too late to correct. With the decadence which followed there were many murders within Udaipur and in most of the feudal seats of the nobles. Jagatpur had not been too seriously affected because all were aware of the viciousness of Narendra should his anger be aroused and with his stout following of dacoit fighters it would be perplexedly difficult for murderers to seep into the fort or Jagatpur's villages and get away free and clear. It simply was far easier to plunder and instigate their misdeeds away from Narendra's watchful eye. As a Hindu god has a third eye, they thought Narendra to have one in the back of his head. Little escaped his notice with his network of crime-fighting friends.

During those frustrating years Queen Mother had frequently asked for and received Narendra's assistance in quieting problems, but he could not be everywhere and while he helped considerably, the troubles could not be entirely eradicated. Queen Mother could only hope to reasonably control the pervasive evils and trust in time a new solution would make itself known. Now she was dead and the problems rested on the shoulders of Bhim Singh, his counsellors, and the men meeting in his durbars.

Reflectively listening to the numerous predicaments laid openly before the durbar, Narendra wondered how the kingdom could stay together at all. Fearful that too many mistakes would be the complete ruination of Mewar he knew they must all band together with an intelligent approach to each problem, yet with a consistency conducive to good management. To lose Mewar was disturbingly problematical and Narendra came to resent the folly of the opium-filled evenings and drowsy headed thinking of the days following. To the extent that he could, Narendra repeated over and over to the Rana and all those seated in the great room that this was a crucial time in the life of the kingdom. Others argued there had been many crucial times throughout the long centuries and though things could have been better at times, they were none the worse for the occasional devastation which preceded them.

Narendra found this a curious argument. "Why settle for mediocre when it's possible to have the best?" he'd lament. Certainly he knew personal life or that of the kingdom, any kingdom, could never be completely upbeat, and while it was necessary for hundreds of thousands of Mewaris to accept sad fates in times of dire trouble, there was no need to let down all holds and wallow in the dregs of whatever your enemy wanted, and certainly the Suktawuts and Chondawats were the enemy in this regard.

Many men issued numerous commonplace solutions, some to attenuate the clans, but nothing seemed to resemble the cleverness of their august ancestors. None had the style of the sardar asking to be cremated and having all soldiers dressed alike. What a joke to play on the enemy; what a clever plan to arrange for cremation of himself and his friends instead of the dreaded burial. But no one, Narendra included, could parallel that brilliance.

After the durbar adjourned the Maharana called upon a man by the name of Sindhia for help. Narendra thought him too sly and cunning and was totally against using this man in any manner, but Narendra was quickly overruled by the Rana. It was just before the end of Narendra's tour of duty at the palace that word reached the Maharana their mighty fort of Chittor had been surrendered to the man Sindhia. "How could that possibly be? What has happened?" Narendra asked his king.

"There are those who will do anything for a bribe."

"I still don't understand. What exactly took place?"

"All the news I have so far received is that the Chondawats surrendered. What it has cost me in the way of a bribe I still do not know, but I am certain to know before long."

Narendra was terribly ill at ease with the lack of further knowledge of the events at Chittor. But he was not Rana and his functions were dreadfully limited.

There are many quirks of fate in the ways of politics. The disliked and untrusted Sindhia had an aide who fought in any way he could against Mewar for a great many years. Yet it was now this same man who began looking after the affairs of State and the best interests of the Maharana. By the time Narendra and Nina took off for their home in Jagatpur, several months of palace duty over, this odd man by the name of Umbaji was already acquiring some of the lands which had been lost to Mewar. Nonetheless Narendra worried about his real interest and warned the Maharana to keep close watch on him.

"How can he be planning anything against me when he is giving me back some lands earlier lost? You do not make sense, my friend," the Maharana shrugged off Narendra's warning.

"Perhaps not, but I still believe he bears close watching, Your Highness." And with that he took his leave and moved with Nina and entourage toward Jagatpur, happy they were many in number, for an uneasiness embraced him.

Chapter 19

It was business in tenacious earnestness immediately after reaching home. Narendra was quickly apprised of many local problems. There had been a forcible breakout in the jail and he was anxious to look over the structure making it more secure to avoid repetition. There were the ever present misdemeanors of villagers and fort residents. Court had not been held in Narendra's absence because he chose to sit as something of a superior judge. Arjun had ruled over such matters with an iron-clad fist and brute courage. Narendra would do nothing less while keeping ever mindful his decisions must be just. There were even such petty things brought before the court as husband and wife squabblings, Narendra's sense of justice normally leaning to the side of the man.

By the time Narendra made it through a solid week of such events he came home one night discursively running down the simplest and the worst of incidents to Nina. She whispered in his ear what he was in need of was a mental anesthesia and she knew just the cure and even the place. Waiting until long after dark he knew her intentions and the two walked together hand in hand over the path she had laid out so many years ago. More emotionally tired than those earlier days, their ardor never failed them. Since their marriage their intimate lives were as enthralling as if they were young in years and their special bond brought them as close together as humanly possible.

Narendra now came to think less and less often about Kala but when he did it was with a special reverence. He never spoke of her to Nina, nor did he mention Kala's name.

Things went along surprisingly well for Nina in running the household. Her servants adored her for Nina having been one herself so many years knew the tender traps into which one can easily fall and was careful of their feelings at all times, never overworking them, paying compliments when deserved, a huge thing in the somber life of one subservient.

It was really Arjun who took the brunt of apparent nastiness, his cousins resenting his being the heir apparent to the rule of the estate. When they tired of taunting him and his disarmingly clever way of turning a deaf ear they refused to let him play with them or ride in the fields. His only friends seemed to be the sons of his father's friends, Pandu, Ran and Ramesh. When he was permitted to take his horse Chetak into the villages and seek out these families he was at his happiest. They adored the lad and could not be more pleased that he would occupy Narendra's seat. In fact they preferred it to the so-called cousin-brothers of Arjun, too bullying and spoiled and untrained in the workings of business.

Narendra had always promoted the idea it was to their best personal interest as well as that of the joint family to have each of the males, as they reached their teens, take an active interest in the management of their estate. All were flauntingly lazy in this respect, content to sit back, allowing Narendra and his studious son to handle all matters, large and small. It was evident that in approaching manhood they would resemble their fathers who took only the barest interest, preferring to hunt and ride or sit in the shade in idle gossip.

The only exceptions were Narendra's eldest brother Akhil's first son. His name was Amar. Since the latest return from Udaipur's durbar it was obvious that Amar, aided and abetted by his father Akhil, had an obvious eye to the seat of power in his own right. Narendra welcomed them into the offices, discussing whatever details most interested them and the manner in which each would be handled. Nina, distressed by what she felt was in the offing, took a dim view of this sudden change in attitude.

Deciding to change the tempo of things within their joint household Nina determined to give a party at their home for the leaders in all the various fields of civil office, and for their wives. It would be large and festive, hopefully bringing a needed cohesiveness to the estate. She talked over the details with her husband and son for several weeks. Nina cleverly sought the aid and assistance of each of her sisters-in-law, drawing them into the activities, making them feel they held a place of great importance. She asked their suggestions, though in fact she desired none. Narendra and she had thought of everything. She had been well trained in planning parties of great magnitude with the Queen Mother; this would merely be on a smaller more subtle scale. She would wear her prettiest clothing and some of the new jewelry which Narendra had bought for her in Udaipur, the first lovely jewelry she had ever owned.

A comprehensive menu was decided upon, not much different than her wedding which was indeed one of the finest banquets anywhere. All the invitations were painstakingly written through quite a number of days, and hand-delivered by their son Arjun. That took the better part of a week, involving not only seeking out the right persons within the fort but riding into many of the towns as well. No one was to be slighted.

The day of festivities came and while it appeared on the outside everyone was in great spirits and happy moods, the sisters-in-law had banded together, the worst of them placing carefully into the minds of the others that Nina devised this day as a means of showing them up to all the others as menial; Nina alone could afford to give such a party; Nina had managed in her cleverness to win over the hearts of the elder Arjun and his wife and place herself comfortably into the heart and home of their oldest brother. For such a woman, a simple maid to Queen Mother, now lording it over them was a serious affront and they were not about to take it lightly.

Narendra had been busy moving about with the men, making certain everyone was exceedingly happy. They were delighted he had come up with a plan to be together under such happy circumstances and he forbid the talk of any form of business or civil matters.

All of those from outlying cities camped within the compound of Narendra's home or stayed with relatives in the fort, the party lasting well into the third day. Narendra and Nina thought they had surely done something extremely clever.

A discomfited silence followed the frivolities after everyone retreated to his own home, including the noticeable deafening silence of the women of the compound, none now willing to even speak to Nina. Lightly she passed it off the first day or two believing they would get over their petty jealousies. Her goal had been to draw them all closer to her. It didn't work that way. Each in her own way persuaded her husband that what was happening was unjust and should not be tolerated. The eldest brother Akhil soon lived such a miserable life with the rantings of his selfish wife he was forced to either leave her or speak to brother Narendra about how things should be changed for the better.

"What is it you would have me do?" Narendra asked bewilderingly. "We have tried all we know, including this expensive party we could scarcely afford."

"It is for you to decide," Akhil laid it back in his brother's lap. "You're the eldest and you must know that we cannot have such discord within our compound. You settle family disputes of the villagers and others. If you're so smart surely you can suggest a way that we can all live here more peacefully. My wife swears she will not talk to me again until the homestead is free of your wife. While it may not seem entirely fair to you, I think you should look at it from where we stand. We are many against you three. Your son is but a bastard and how can we let him one day take your place?"

"And if Nina and I were to have another son, what then? We are married and he would not be a bastard. Would you or your wife think it right for that son to sit on our father's seat in place of my first born son Arjun?" Once more Narendra thought of Chonda giving in to the will of his Rana-father so that his little half-brother would sit in the place of honor, and how the widowed Hansa had driven Chonda from Chittor with the same childish foolishness these women were displaying.

"I had not thought of that aspect," Akhil answered. "Is Nina again pregnant?"

"That is none of your damned business," the elder brother raved, "but I would like your answer. What if we had another son?"

"Then I suppose he would have to take the place of honor, but it would be under protest from all of us."

"Wrong!" Narendra screamed. "He would be our second son and only after Arjun would he rule."

There was little doubt in the mind of either man that the women did not intend for Narendra and Nina to live within the fort under any condition, Akhil's wife long eyeing the prestigious position as head lady of the estate. Not only would she be deferentially raised in esteem, the dispossession of Nina from her lofty perch would subdue the awful rancor which she herself started. If she could take over Nina's position in life all would return to peace and quiet and her favorite son Amar would thus be in line for the revered spot when Akhil was no more.

Narendra, however, was not to give up a fight easily and turned from his unworthy brother by saying he would think on the conditions, but could not believe any change was necessary other than having the women mature and act more wisely than they were now doing. That last remark was a definite slap in the face of all the family, acutely aware it would not sit well with any of the ladies when they would undoubtedly come to hear of it.

Life in fact got so much worse that Nina made it an unsavory point never to be in the larger courtyard when any of the others were present, something of a prisoner in her own home. Narendra was too busy with business to see this happening day after day, but it was forcefully brought to his attention when the unsettling condition raised the vengeful ire of their tender hearted son.

"What to do?" Narendra asked Nina when the subject was brought out into the open, the three sitting together in labored thought. "Would you be happier if you lived away from here?"

"A woman's place is with her husband, no matter the conditions. You are cleverly capable and well trained to handle the politics. You're fated to handle the task and perhaps should not turn your back on it. Yet, if it's too much to bear, then let us think of where to go." Nina continued, "Arjun, you are an integral part of the family. Any suggestions?"

Wise beyond his years he spoke of seeing the hatred building up. He felt to escape it one of two things must happen. They must move on, or the whole family must go — which, of course, was unthinkable. That left little more to be said. "Let Uncle Akhil and Amar worry about the work. We can hunt and ride, and of what use is money if we cannot enjoy it here? Can we not take just enough for food and shelter and be done with this?"

"I can see you have much of your mother in you," Narendra managed a half-smile. "But be aware that by leaving you probably would be forfeiting your rightful inheritance. This cannot be taken lightly and as you know, grandfather made this clear to all."

"What does station matter if one is always unhappy, father? Amar spits at my face as if he was some ugly desert camel and me a lowly chaprasi and the others stand back and giggle. For a long time I ignored him but he does not stop."

"Well, perhaps he has the mentality of a camel," his mother replied.

"If that were so, our estate would be relegated under his tutelage to the lowest of the low and then what would become of everyone else?" his father went along with the conversation. In all probability his predictions would not be too far afield, he was certain, if the place could not be maintained in its highest tradition and proper consistent thought given to each of the problems as they would arise. Perplexing social problems had a way of interweaving one with the other.

"The boy is right, you know," he said, turning to face Nina. "Perhaps we should leave. Let Akhil and the rest run the place. He did not want to sit in on any sessions of court and other matters when father taught me the ways of our government. If he cannot wish us to live in peace here together, all of us, then my son is right. Let us give thought to going, but first let us make sure that what we are doing is right and that we have exhausted every avenue which could prevent such a tragic move. Giving up my birthright is tragic, you know."

Nina tried to convince him that he could never be happy carelessly roaming the countryside, playing games with Arjun. For years Narendra had traveled in search of dacoits. None could know it better. Their son would soon be fully grown and have to enter a life of his own at some sort of thought-provoking work or a job with substance, keeping his mind active. For Narendra to think even for a moment that he could be happy roaming around was absurd. For him there was always a purpose in life. He would need to work, if only to put in charitable time. And where could this be done? "If we are to leave the home of your father and their fathers," she said to him, "think first on it long and hard. Think of a place you could settle down at something constructive or you would quickly come to hate me and the misery I have brought upon you by becoming your wife. This would never have happened if I had not become your wife and brought Arjun here to live. Now do you finally see why I fought all those years, denying he was your son. I knew this would happen. I knew it."

"You could never bring misery to me, Nina. How can you think such a thing? I would be miserable without you. You should know that."

"Nonetheless it would happen, and the day I would waken to find you looking at me as if I were some contemptuous enemy, someone whose sight you could not bear, that is the day I wish my life to end."

"I'll send out some feelers for things I can do," he said. "Meantime it will be work here at the fort as usual, as though nothing had happened and we shall discuss this with no one. Who knows, maybe things will change for the better for us after all. As for Akhil, he had known since the smallest boy that he was only first after me. Certainly he could not have spent years believing he would one day be completely in charge. It is the poison of the mouths of the women which has inflicted us with this tumultuous confusion. It is unjust and uncalled for.

"I have been brought up to do this job when my day would come. I have always known it is what I would do. But I cannot stand idly by watching them hurt you and the boy in this manner and will not tolerate it. Our son is right. Happiness is more important than any station in life. If it takes our departure to bring happiness that is what we will do." Narendra was firm in his convictions. "But I agree with you, Nina. It is too serious a step to jump into without due process of thought. The lives of the three of us are at stake, and for the youngest of us it is immensely crucial. Let us all earnestly pray for a change in conditions here at our ancestral home."

But the only change was for things to grow increasingly worse. The women continued to be the greatest of bullies. Nina stayed in her rooms or walked quickly out of the compound taking exercise in the narrow lanes of the fort, pretending to be shopping for one thing or another. At least at Udaipur she could sit and listen to the ramblings of the other servants, even in the days when they did not talk too much with her. It was conversation, and while much of it was idle gossip, nonetheless it was the sound of other human voices and something to think about, laugh over, or be saddened by. Here at her new home if the sounds of others ever reached her, the words were mainly slanderous and cruel. She'd sometimes walk to the little temple dusting the few stone remains of carvings with her fingertips, wishing desperately to find a way toward peace with the family. Years ago she screamed at Ganesh for not answering her plea and she no longer begged in prayer, but only hoped.

She had her most precious of private places, yet she feared going to it every day, too sacred to be discovered by others, most especially her in-laws. She took, therefore, to the much longer and round-about paths designed by her husband to hopefully avoid detection. The advantage of her hideaways in Udaipur had been the easy access through the postern of the palace, past those who sat selling short pieces of tree limbs for kindling, toward the sculptured trees spreading down to the southern shoreline of beautiful Lake Pichola. In just minutes she was away from all prying eyes and the only sounds were those of birds bedding down for the night or an occasional squabble between the soft gray langurs which roamed between the forests and edges of the palace from which they joyfully would swing.

Or there were the times when the wee little Indian squirrels would busy themselves about the tree stumps, hiding in root systems to emerge a few minutes later, cheeks bulging with newfound food. There was more of nature for Nina to watch while at her old home, unless of course she chose the lengthy walk through the whole of Jagatpur fort before reaching its massive outer doors, followed by a long stretch of open ground, the better for lookouts to discover approaching enemies. Not until after that point could she reach the wide stretches of luxuriant jungle.

Narendra refused her a horse if she would ride alone through this part of their country, ever fearful of straying leopards and tigers. But Nina did not always want an escort, even if it was only her son. How could she reminisce or think out new problems if there was another person hovering over her. And so it was she generally spent her time, if not in their assortment of rooms, then in the little temple grounds. Between times she would still frequent the bazaars.

Disintegrating misery forced Narendra into calling a meeting of all his brothers and their wives, as well as Nina and Arjun.

"Brothers, it is clear to my wife and myself that you are none too pleased with things as they now are. Nina, the boy and I shall be leaving for an unspecified length of time during which you are free to run this place as you see fit. Our father was always careful to be fair and just with all within our jurisdiction and it would behoove you to do likewise. Akhil, it is now up to you to see that our dues are paid at the court of Mewar on time. There is to be no exception in this, for if you wisely collect all monies owed us there will be more than sufficient to pay our debts on schedule. The soil classification has recently been done so there will be no changes in regulations. Be careful if any of the Chondawats or Suktawuts filter into our fort. Watch them very carefully. Things have not gone well for either clan in recent years and neither side is to be trusted. This was a major concern at the last durbar.

"We will be leaving in a few days and I wish you all well. You'll not be able to reach us. And we shall be back only when we feel the time is right; that is our option."

Akhil started to protest but Narendra added, "This is a situation brought on largely by your own wife, Akhil, and multiplied by all the others of the family. If you could not control her tongue do not expect to control me. I will say goodbye now. But I warn you, be very careful of all you do, for unwisely handling any situation can be your complete downfall and you would stand to lose Jagatpur, our homes and all else for all of us forever. Remember your history well."

For the first time Akhil felt maddening pangs of fear. He was apprehensive of this work to a degree of cowardice. As for his wife, she marveled that she had been clever enough to arrange their departure and now could sit in the place of honor. Regarding Amar, Akhil wasn't sure he'd ever grow up with sufficient intelligence to handle the fort's complex problems.

Saying goodbye to Ramesh and Pandu on their departure, the friends asked where Narendra could be located in the future if they were needed. "Who is there to need me?" Narendra asked sadly. "I would tell you if I knew, but I clearly do not. I have a few ideas but I shall have to work them out. Should we decide to permanently settle down somewhere specific I shall send word to you somehow. Take care, men. Watch over the place from your back seats. We'll each miss you." The parting was sad but without recourse.

Narendra had taken the time to send a message to the palace that he was taking an extended leave and may be gone for many years, that his younger brother Akhil was now in charge. Though he owed his allegiance to Mewar he may even leave the country if he could find no suitable employment within its boundaries, and there seemed little likelihood of that. There was, of course, no forwarding address thereby making either a reply or objection from the Maharana impossible.

Pandu questioned Narendra during their very brief departure-meeting about the continuing fights against dacoits. "What shall we do about them now?"

"They're on their own, Pandu, unless of course you and some of the others want to continue pursuing them. As for me, I simply no longer care."

Nina knew this attitude was one of deep depression and that the tides would change, bringing her husband back to the interested and caring person with whom she had fallen in love.

Her love must now be stronger than ever to assist him in carrying this aggravating burden.

They circuitously traveled for many weeks more or less in the direction totally unfamiliar to Nina. From that standpoint the trip was interesting. They had come upon Mina tribespeople, a group of adavasis heretofore unknown to her. She thought them colorful but strange, learning they had no cultural traits such as crafts, relying on someone else's manufacture for their cooking utensils, their clothing and the ornaments they wore. The Mina huts in the little village the three travelers came upon were very low, made of bamboo, grasses and mud, all held together loosely with cow dung. Nina stopped at a distance to watch a woman grinding her meal on a stone, silver ornaments in her hair, hanging from her head, heavily encrusting her chest, arms dripping with silver, yet the inside of her house Nina was told would have but one cot, if any, perhaps a couple of scratchy blankets against the desert cold nights, a few utensils in which to cook and certainly a plow for preparing their fields. Looking at the cattle and children, both tied up near the door of the hut, it was difficult for Nina to discern who was better off.

Nina suggested to Narendra inasmuch as they were in no hurry, why not rest here for a couple of days before going on, getting to know more about the Mina tribe, if he thought it safe. While their ancestral background had been one of stealing, they were slowly coming around to settle more permanently into little villages, divided into gots or clans. Narendra saw no reason why it would not be safe. He spoke with one of the elders of a particular got, asking the old man's permission to pitch their tents nearby for two or three days. The elder consented saying it would be good to have another person from afar stop and talk with them. The trio looked harmless to him.

"Which is your wife?" Nina asked. He pointed happily to quite a few women seated nearby. Everyone had lost first inhibitions by now, freer to sit and converse. Nina then pointed to one of the younger women at random, "Is she married?"

"Yes."

"And what will happen to her if, for example, her husband would die."

"Oh, she would be well taken care of," they smiled.

"By whom?" Nina inquired.

"Why, by her new husband, of course. She would then become the property of her husband's younger brother."

"I have heard," continued Nina, "that in some cultures and foreign countries there are people who even choose their own husbands and wives. Can you imagine?"

"Oh, that is not too strange," said the elder. "We, too, have a similar thing. If a woman should want very badly to marry a particular man and she is already married, they can arrange with the first mate to let this happen. Of course it is expensive, for then the second must pay the first husband twice as much as he originally paid for her. If she'd get passed around the village too much and has too many husbands this could get very expensive," he chortled toothlessly.

An uneasy feeling came over Nina and that night in the confines of their little tent she begged Narendra to pack early and leave this place. She could not put her finger on anything special and certainly the Mina tribesmen had been most courteous to the Singhs, but there was an underlying feeling of dreaded hero worship here, heroes who could be dacoits, or perhaps leftover strains of the Mina forefathers who secured any "wealth" through plundering.

Many more weeks went by in a lazy, slow moving fashion, the three settling down for a few days when they were weary or when they were particularly interested in the terrain, when there was a need to hunt for food, or simply wanted amicable quiet dialogue. By the time their third month ended they were relatively near the outskirts of the rambling fort of Amber, a kingdom northeast of Mewar.

Narendra had not necessarily planned to visit here but since he was so close there was no reason why not to pay his respects. The Amber royal family and Arjun Singh had been acquaintances for decades and Narendra knew the young Maharaja casually. The Singhs camped across from the sloping hillside for a couple of days of rest before bathing one bright morning, putting on their cleanest clothes and starting the ascent up the long excessively steep ramp. Three quarters of the way the slope turned an abrupt 180° angle and they continued to climb. Looking straight up they could see the small windows from which they knew they were being watched. And then came the massive wooden door at which Narendra knocked.

As they waited Nina stared up at the intricately carved windows so high above them, knowing this surely must have been one of the most romantic forts. Two days earlier they had stopped beneath lovely pink Hawa Mahal, the wind palace built at the time of her precious Lake Palace. From it the ladies of the court could watch the goings on on the main streets of the city of Jaipur. Could these also be zenana windows above her now at this beautiful fort?

One day she and Narendra would have to take their son to visit the astronomical observatories built by Maharaja Jai Singh near the city palace, although neither of them pretended to know anything about astrology or astronomy. Nina nonetheless had to admire Jai Singh II, known far and wide for his wisdom in arranging for this observatory to be built and it was done with such accuracy that through the sun's shadows cast by its fantastic arrays of concrete shapes, those knowing how to read the shadows can tell the exact time in all major parts of the world, and any place in between; a testimony to the brilliance of this designer. This is the largest in the land of India although he commissioned others to be built in Delhi, Mathura, Banaras and Ujjain. Aside from all this he was a lover of art and architecture, renowned scholar, soldier and scientist, and an ancestor of the present Maharaja. Much of this Nina learned years ago while studying under Hari Lal and now perhaps she could pay tribute to some of it. Perhaps the Maharaja would let them stay for a few days to view these things and refresh their weary bodies.

Still waiting for someone to answer their knock at the massive gate they turned to look at the sloping hills beyond the point where they started their ascent. The expansiveness of the great fort had been awesome and now at its front door they could view the hills and valleys with its breathtaking panoramic view. Through the pass far below one could easily imagine thundering hordes converging on the fortress in times of war, however unsuccessful they had been. The ridges of the surrounding hills were walled, the tops crenellated.

"How did they come by the name of Amber?" Nina inquired.

"Actually I believe it is for the Goddess Ambu, a title of Shiva. It had taken a hundred years to build this fort. I often wonder why they bothered to build Jaipur city."

At last the huge door opened. Armed with credentials which Narendra never failed to be without, the threesome was shown through the outer courtyard, up a steep ramp, through wooden doors laced with spikes and to the Diwan-i-Khas, spread open in the ambient air, save for its ceiling. Beyond that they walked beneath the black implanted image of Ganesh who smiled down on all who entered. That doorway took them into a lovely garden of roses and an exotic flower Nina failed to recognize. Farther in the shade of a porch they were asked to await His Highness who would be with them as soon as he could.

It was a little over an hour and the three, now restless, decided to stroll around the garden in the shadows of the overhang. They instantly felt a cooling breeze and to their amazement noticed a little trough in the tile flooring and through the trough slowly trickled cool scented water.

"You are enjoying my cooled air?" a voice spoke to them. It was His Highness, Maharaja of Amber, or Jaipur as it was sometimes referred to. In sheer filmy white kurta he wore only one string of pearls around his neck, four monstrous sized rings of precious stones adorning pudgy hands, and an earring dangling from one lobe. The trio was startled by the voice and the sight of the ruler who arrived unannounced, Nina instantly apologizing for strolling through his gardens without his permission.

"Not to worry," he smiled, lightly touching her arm, moving them in the direction of the larger porch. It was tremendously lovely, the walls covered with beveled mirrors cut in leaf shapes and flower petals. Imbedded into a special plaster they formed many versions of urns filled with bouquets. Even the ceiling of the porch was decorated in the same manner.

This must be the place, thought Nina, where His Highness also had a special room for wondrous nights. It was said that when its two doors and the window were closed tiny oil lamps were positioned in numerous niches in the walls. The sensuous room, its countless convex mirrors and flickering oil lamps lit the room magnificently as millions of stars could not in all their heavenly majesty. How many night of nights had there been here?

In the last several decades Nina had the unique pleasure of having visited many palaces in Rajasthan, mainly within the kingdom of Mewar. She never failed to marvel how each differed so greatly from the next in its dreamlike wonders, too perplexing to form a favorite.

His Highness had allotted substantial time to sit and leisurely chat with Narendra, his wife and child, outwardly content to renew an old acquaintance and trying, Narendra thought, to remain friendly with a possible enemy of the soil. But it seemed unlikely war was imminent. His Highness Amber had a need to be courteous, asking discreetly that they remain as his guests for as long as they wished. In getting to know more about this rival kingdom Nina learned the fort in which they were now seated had been the capitol of Amber for almost 600 years.

The Diwan-i-Am of grey marble to which they returned was quite lovely, 40 sandstone pillars supporting the luscious roof. They were shown to their guest quarters, Narendra deciding it politically as well as adaptably expedient to accept the generous offer of hospitality.

Narendra started the following morning on his lengthy puja in the exquisite Kali temple near the front entrance of the fort. This he found was the special place of worship for the rulers of this family but he was most welcome. The sanctuary itself was massive and extraordinarily clean in the midst of a grittily sandy country. Kept closed were the large double doors of pure silver, deeply chased and ornamented. Inside, a large silver drum boomed a deep-throated welcome, hearkening the call to attention of the goddess of destruction, Shiva's consort. Priests reciting their Sanskrit scriptures blessed the foreheads of the three foreigners with red tilak powders. They remained at great length praying for a way out of their personal and private dilemma.

The next week was spent in absolute luxury and relaxation, and just about the time Narendra thought he must make some sort of move, the Maharaja came up with a singular idea. "I know you are wise about horseflesh, my friend, and I have been wanting to breed some horses. If you have chosen of your own volition to remain away from your home for a period of time, perhaps you would do me the honor of assisting me in the purchase of some breeding stock. I shall want stallions and mares and I am told there will be Arabians for sale in a place to the northwest of us some several hundred kilometers, towards Afghanistan. If you could accompany and assist me I would be most grateful. Your wife and son will remain here, of course, and by the time of our return you would then be able to consider whether you would be retiring to your own place or staying on with me to breed my new prizes. Perhaps you will even wish to consider some cross-breeding. I do not know much about that."

"I'm flattered that you would ask me, Your Highness. I can certainly accompany you and it would be a privilege to assist in choosing and buying some of the Arabians. There are none finer. I would not mind having another myself. In fact, on further speculation, perhaps it is just the kind of thing I've been looking to do. Yes. Yes, I think I'll accept your offer, Highness. I would enjoy it very much. I do wish, however, that you would consider allowing my son to join us. He is an excellent rider and I'd very much like to teach him the ways of looking over a horse for purposes of either buying or selling. An auction or sale would be of tremendous value. Would this be asking too much of you?"

"Not at all, Narendra Singhji. As you wish. Be prepared to leave at any time although I would assume the departure will be three to four days hence. I shall let you know."

At last Narendra would have something to sink his teeth into, utilizing his qualifications. Nina was bathed in delight. He was effortlessly fast making friends and a creditable friend was always something to diligently cultivate. Once their kingdoms were mortal enemies but cementing a bond of friendship could come in handy at a later time. Nina's major concern, however, was for Narendra to retain an active, alert mind and body.

As for herself, there would be little to do other than the usual things the queens and princesses did during long warm days, sitting telling funny stories. One day Nina learned one of the Maharajkumaris was attempting some delicate embroidery on a very fine piece of silk, each stitch making more of a shambles. Nina quickly became a teacher, thankful for some little thing to do. So lovely did it develop that almost everyone in the zenana took up the craft, developing it almost into a cult.

Meanwhile the Maharaja's entourage found no problems in travel to and from the site of the animal sale. Following beneath the ridge of the ever beautiful Aravalli mountains they found hundreds of majestic horses corralled safely. Bargaining was laboriously slow and difficult, the leader much a novice leaving Narendra wide open with this capable skill of looking over the flesh and bodies, walking away from them as if demonstrably disinterested. At a short distance he would describe salient points to his son who would then take a close look, the teeth, the forelegs, stomach muscles, strong shoulders — whatever it was Narendra did or did not like about a given animal.

"You're going to let the best of them get away from us," His Highness was white with rage.

"You have done me the honor of seeking my assistance in choosing and buying. Now please do me the honor of allowing me to handle this in my own way?" he suggested solicitously, yet with firmness of voice. "If you look anxious to buy all the nobles who have rushed to this sale will want the same stallion. His price will go up and up..."

It was the Maharaja's turn to interrupt. "But I can afford the money. I do not care what it costs. From him we will raise many others. What does the money matter?"

"In life there are many sports, Highness. One of them is bargaining. I wish to buy him for less than is asked, not ten times what they are asking, for in but a matter of minutes it would jump that much if everyone else comes to notice him. If they see I want him, those who know me will also want. Trust me that I know what I am doing. I will buy him for three quarters of what they are asking and if you do not admire having saved that money, then perhaps you will give the other one-quarter to me and I shall buy myself another horse. I feel great need of another."

"It's a deal."

It was a long time since he had had this much fun. Narendra engaged in ever more vigorous arguments with the trader, first having pulled him aside beyond the earshot of all other interested parties, while at the same time pointing to some mares in a corral at the opposite side of them.

Not only did Narendra buy for the Amber stud farm the stallion which he wanted so desperately, but a dozen others almost as fine, several mares, and chose for himself another fine horse which the Maharaja threw in as a total gift. Amber's Prime Minister who had also joined the tour made his own deals and with two dozen horses of prime quality they left a day later for a slower journey back to Amber, intensively resting the horses in the manner a mother would coddle her newborn infant.

Once they returned to the fort Narendra spent considerable time roaming the terrain choosing the best grazing land and the place in which he would rear the horses. He then settled down to design a fine wall which was painstakingly built, creating an honorable shelter amidst virgin fields in which they were free to roam.

Nina once made a gentle hint to the court ladies it would be nice to go on a long impromptu outing. Subsequently it was arranged they would visit Sariska, an area abounding in wild life, a very long all day trip. They would stay in a guest bungalow for travelers and the groundwork was laid so that when the entourage arrived none other than the royal travelers would have access anywhere near the encampment. They roamed the wilds, well guarded by palace staff and an adequate number of hunters, the queens and princesses carried in palanquins, including Nina, stopping to watch the langurs, the most fun-loving of all monkeys. There were hares, ugly jackals, sand grouse, spotted deer in vast numbers, sambhar and blue bull and keeping out of sight were the feared tiger and leopard. The ladies camped here for a full week, accompanied within that time by a warden visiting some of the little lush valleys in this veiled sanctuary. There were so many animals. Vegetation was never greener and small limpid pools reflected date palms swaying ever so feebly. Hues varied greatly from the lighter green salar trees to those with reddish touches, the interesting dhok and several varieties of accacia trees. And oh those magnificent peacocks. Nina thought this must have been their original mating ground. Never had she dreamed there were as many in the entire world as the numerous peacocks and hens she had seen while visiting here. For that alone her trip was worthwhile.

Anxious as Nina had been to get away for a respite she was equally anxious to return to Amber. On the way they took the time to shop the stores in the city of Jaipur, looking for nothing in particular. Yet it was another languid way to wile away the pallid hours. Carefully planned before its construction the city of Jaipur stretched east and west from the center, laid out into a rectangle. At the traverse roads little open squares facilitated the flow of camel traffic, all roads terminating at the gateways in the city walls, there being eight in all.

While here the ladies of the court chose many jewels, some already set and others just gems which pleased their eyes, for Jaipur was one of the major gem cities in all of India. Nina herself longed for some of the lovely baubles she watched the others handling and while she and her husband were not poor, their chosen state of exile was not conducive to spending money on trinkets, nor for carrying excessive amounts of jewelry in their unplanned travels. Although Narendra was more accustomed to handling dacoits and better qualified than all others, there was no reason to tempt fate, and so it was that Nina remained merely a window shopper.

Returning home they passed again the white grazing cattle, tiny fields of old farms and the lustrous Rajasthani clothing. Here it was ever as beautiful as in Mewar, the main difference of dress only in the turbans of the men, and the language, although the dialect was close enough they could readily understand each other.

An inner peace and joy by now captured the three Singhs and every night after the labors of the hot days they could sit near the night blooming jasmine, drink in the sweet fragrance and keep locked in some deep dark corner of their minds the problems of the past. The Maharaja was exceedingly kind to the trio, treating Arjun as one of his own, permitting Nina access to the zenana along with his women. Perhaps they had never come to know she was once a mere servant in the house of Mewar for they accepted her as a near equal, a manner totally different from her latest home in Jagatpur. Slowly her mind came to rest, delighting in the pleasures of what she would have regarded as a fictitious world. Isolated as she was from her real environs she reveled in the pulseless existence newly created.

Arjun had so quickly grown, turning so much like his father. Years gnarled with unbeatable events interpreted by Nina now as a means to accumulate parabolical wisdom. Early fears by herself and Queen Mother of an untimely death of Bhim Singh were now allayed. Those apprehensions were replaced by grimly alarming threats to the life of Jawan. Her meritorious act in saving his life in at least one instance she considered divinely inspired. Heroically she had faced unfathomable deed and misdeeds of many and now the awesomeness of past years should have forever been silenced within herself. She was free; free from servitude and free from worry.

Even Narendra was no longer a worry to her, forsaking the contemplative frenzied and dangerous chases of vicious dacoits. Most probably none other would ever compare with his diligent and masterful art of tracking and capturing such desperadoes. Nina had successfully convinced him the time had come for a younger man to take over if there was to be a continued stand against this menace. He had valiantly taught many the necessary skills and thinking. Some were excellent pupils, others taking to it too lightly, a fact which they'd surely one day come to rue.

There was plenty of fresh air and exercise for Narendra and son who had joined him in his new labors, keeping their good health, but Nina who sometimes sat too long in the gorgeous shadows of intricately carved stone windows of the zenana grew pallid. She took to long walks up the hillside within the palace walls of "amber" colored stone, a second reason for the name of this magnificent place. With her she would take some of the children of the court, choosing different ones each time. They loved her company, quiescently sitting with them in the shade of a salar tree making up funny little stories, youthful variations of the jovial side of life as she knew it at the palace in Udaipur, or the innumerable true tales with which she had become intimately familiar. They knew her to be their friend, perhaps their best friend. They quickly learned she could be relied upon to pet and caress them for their tiniest little hurts, to listen to their tales of woe, to romp freely with them in needed exercise and to bring out the best of each one's character.

"Auntie," they would call her; "come play with us," or "tell us another story." Ofttimes she had to stretch the imagination indulgently and while all this served a manifest communal purpose for them as well as their ayahs who were temporarily relieved of their duties, it was observed by Narendra as serving a salubrious goodness for Nina. Never in her life had she been able to sit with idle time at her heels. Nor had she ever wanted it that way. To live a completely idle life was not only against her natural instincts, she believed God put people on earth with a purpose and it was her duty to discover what her role was to be. Certainly she had lived the greatest part of it already, she had amassed a certain tremendous knowledge for her caste. She came to believe God meant her to do something with whatever her brain now held, but what was that illusive purpose? It began to torment her.

Narendra would tell her she had already served her purpose on earth, she was a good wife and mother and what else could a woman expect? "Something much more than that," she'd reply. "If that is all I was to have done while in this life, why was it that He placed me in the illustrious position of one so close to Queen Mother? This surely did not happen to others. It was something special for me."

"Maybe He rewarded you for your good deeds while still in this life instead of waiting until the next," Narendra suggested.

"No. I had done nothing good before I met you. I was the most ordinary person and suddenly my life became grand. But it is more than that, my husband. It is the lessons I have learned.

I still believe it was intended that I should somehow use that knowledge."

Laughingly he answered, "Perhaps you should open a school here at Amber for the children of Their Highnesses."

"What? And teach them about their neighboring Mewar? Hardly."

"Well, Nina, I would not worry about it. I am sure that if as you believe the gods intended you to do something more in this life they will make it known to you when the time comes. Meantime, why don't you forget about it and just enjoy the children and your playtime with them. It appears to me that such as you do with them is in itself rewarding and should be so regarded. I know His Highness and all the members of his family are grateful for your inexhaustible concern."

Nina dropped the subject but it never completely left her mind. The year wore slowly on, things changing remarkably little.

Late one vapory morning Nina awakened to the gentle touch of a young maidservant. Turning her sweaty body on the bare floor, the meek girl announced the arrival of a visitor from Udaipur who requested an audience. Bewildered, Nina could think only that a Mewari spy had discovered their whereabouts.

She would take her time in bathing, dressing and receiving the messenger, fearful of his news. Desperately she wished the man had arrived while her husband was at her side. She would be in a quandary, cautiously replying to the expected queries. This slow gear into which she arbitrarily put herself would give her time to divergently think. Had Bhim Singh died with young Jawan now on the gaddi? Did the Maharani feel Nina's help was inescapably required? Her mind strayed from person to person but there was no way to come to a lucid answer. Without the news how could she form a reply? Whatever the mission she would give no definite statement until it was discussed with her husband; to that she earnestly set her mind.

She recognized the rider Sanjeeva instantly, exchanging pleasant greetings. He had been on the trail many days, arriving just outside the palace gates extremely late the night before, sleeping in the fields. He too had slept later than anticipated, weary from his ride, and took a lengthy bath in the nearby tank of a very insignificant temple. Refreshed, he was now ready to challenge Nina. She had ordered a substantial breakfast for him; meantime they could have their discussion.

"I am filled with wonder and confused, Sanjeeva," she started. "How did you know I was here and what happened at the palace that you have come?"

"We have known of your whereabouts for many months now due to some Mewaris being at the same Arabian horse sale as your husband and Highness Amber. Naturally we had known of your leaving Jagatpur through the correspondence sent His Highness Bhim Singh by your husband. Had it not been for the horse show I don't know when we'd have discovered your whereabouts. Everyone was sad to hear of your going and I am entrusted to say to you and your husband that the court of Mewar wishes you will soon return. The Maharana wishes you would be living in our own kingdom and not one of a potential enemy," he whispered these last words.

"Are things so bad that they sent you all this way?"

"Worse. Knowing the help you were to late Queen Mother and the close ties to the Maharani's husband, Bhim Singh, the Maharani asks me to advise that there is serious trouble brewing in Udaipur and urgently seeks your presence. I am asked not to return without you."

"I have finally come to have my own life," Nina was visibly perturbed. "Besides, I do not see how I could be of help."

"The point is, Nina, that you are well versed in the events of several decades, conversant with trouble, discerning in the wiles of court..."

Nina interrupted, "They have counsellors to aid them, That is what their job is. That is why they are paid. I know nothing of politics and it would not be my place to open my mouth if I was in the palace. I still do not see, Sanjeeva, what it is you want of me."

"If you would but let me explain, madam." She bowed consent, a little red-faced that she had been so defensive. She sat still, barely breathing. There was scant desire to return to Udaipur and definitely no wish to leave her husband and son. Poor Sanjeeva was but doing his job and she was making it perplexingly difficult. Although her days were tediously long she was more comfortable here than in Jagatpur and it was categorically certain she did not want to serve another tenure at the palace.

"As I've been trying to explain, there is much trouble in the land and within the family. Their Highnesses are attempting to arrange a suitable marriage for the Maharajkumari Krishna Bhai. The young princess would like for you to personally attend her, and in the words of the queen, 'you have a way of quieting disturbances.'"

"Does she not remember that I am happily married and intend to live the rest of my life in the home of my husband?" Nina questioned perturbatively.

"She has not forgotten but feels perhaps you could give a little bit more. Can you consider it a duty to your country? We know a great pride envelopes you. The royal family would make the effort worth your while," he argued on their behalf.

"I am sorry, Sanjeeva, but I truly do not believe this can be arranged. I will promise, however, to discuss this matter with my husband and shall give you a final answer tomorrow. Meanwhile I shall make arrangements with His Highness to have you sleep in the servants' quarters where you will be comfortable and well fed. Should you have need for anything, send word to me." She turned to walk away and with an afterthought added, "It is good to see a familiar face from home. I'm very glad it was you who came."

Waiting to talk this over with her husband developed a full-fraught strain. It was well after dark before the opportunity presented itself in the veiled sanctuary of their room. They had comfortable quarters down below the back wall of the Kali temple in a space just before the rooms of Amber palace's own private servants.

At last she could quote almost word for word Sanjeeva's plea, expecting a doggedly negative response. Instead, Narendra said, "While I would miss you dreadfully, Nina, perhaps you should consider going. The palace had been good to you. I am not sure but that you owe them this much fidelity. They must have full faith in you if they sent this far."

"I vowed my time there was fully served upon the death of Queen Mother, Narendra. I do not know why you want to send me back. Of what possible good could I be?"

"If it is said by the kumari that she would like you, there is probably a special reason, mother. I too think you should go." Young Arjun was always included in family decisions.

Shockingly abhorrent as was the thought of leaving son and husband for an indefinite period, Nina agreed to constructively think on the suggestion. It had taken a long time to trace her; no need to rush the decision. They did not say the request was a life and death matter.

Sleep did not come that night. Going off by herself the next day, refusing to speak further about the question with Sanjeeva or her family, she prayed for an answer to her dilemma. Allegiance. Lord how she came to hate that word. Didn't she owe herself some allegiance?

Little by little it came to her that perhaps it was after all a form of life and death, but just whose or why she could not figure. Why was it she was unaccountably chosen? Was this the something extra God wanted her to do while still on earth? That was the bothersome part. Motivated by curiosity Nina returned to announce she had reconsidered and would be leaving within a few days' time, accompanied by Sanjeeva and the handful of men who had ridden with him.

Chapter 20

Thirteen days after leaving Amber fort Nina entered the palace grounds with skeptical misgivings, met almost instantly by the Maharani. Most of their half hour together was spent in aggravating idle chatter. How is Narendra's health? What is the age now of her boy? With the old Queen Mother she could have cleverly handled the conversation to reach the point of her being there. This Rani was not to be dealt with in such a manner, their relationship only the barest kind. Sanjeeva had stated even the young kumari sought her assistance. Perhaps by asking of her health Nina could force the issue of why she was called back.

"Is the young Krishna Kumari keeping well these days?" Nina asked.

"Tolerably healthy but she grows nervous and repeatedly asks for you," the Rani stated.

"Why me, Your Highness? She never was in my care. I do not understand. I would have thought she would remember me casually, if at all."

"She has never forgotten your unassuming gentleness with her and with her brothers," the Rani said. "And it has been whispered all through the palace some years ago that it was you who saved the life of our Jawan. And I hadn't even known his life had been threatened! Krishna Bhai is not content with her servants nor does she trust them and she has begged me to send for you. The longer we waited the more restless she has grown. You are the only one who will quiet her spirits. Now that you are here I hope it will do some good."

"At the outset I must explain that I cannot remain long. I cannot come back to the employ of the palace, Your Highness. You must know that before we discuss anything further. I came because my husband felt I owe the royal family a debt of gratitude for past kindness. I am naturally eager to know of Krishna Kumari's plight, or any problems you have brought me here to discuss, if that was your intention. I shall stay but a few days and make my way back to Amber where my husband now works for the Maharaja. You can understand I cannot be gone from him and my son too long."

"We shall speak of that later," she dismissed Nina, "tomorrow when you are not so worn."

Excruciatingly annoyed with this behavior she could see herself being put off for perhaps weeks on end. These things happened many times before and certainly the ways of the royal family had not changed since her departure. If the dilemma should grow that bad she would simply state a definite date for withdrawal and that would have to be the end of it. More and more it looked to Nina just a cozy way to get her to return to their fold, trusting the good aspects of palace life and securely entrench her. But Nina would have none of that.

In the cumbersome days that followed she discussed with both palace guards and old servants she had long known about the problems of court, if they knew of any. Cleverly she asked for reviews on events past. They spoke of the rascal Sindhia and how the Maharana Bhim Singh asked him to get back Chittor fort and how he was in fact able to cleverly regain some of the lands which Mewar had lost throughout the years. He was also ingenious enough to decide he was entitled to hold this country of Mewar as a fief. His reasoning was sufficient to do so in the thinking of a great many. The ruler had asked that he do for him a specific service, namely get back some of the lands they had lost. Accomplishing it, he therefore was entitled to withhold these lands from the crown as a reward. It was a cut and dried fact and in almost anybody's set of rules he could do so.

Sindhia then sat as the overlord, demanding due payments for such land. What could the Rana do?

This question Nina asked of the wiser and older at the palace and it was said Bhim Singh had taken all the ready monies for these payments so cruelly demanded of him. Now it was time for more payment. "My lord," Nina grunted, "what will he do? What kind of justice is that?"

"It is said she has asked all the ladies of the palace, his wives and the princesses to give to him whatever they can that is of value," one of the women candidly explained.

"But he can't do that. Their jewels are precious to them. Some will need them for their dowries, and the older women ... well, they're entitled to them. How can he take such things from them? There must be another way."

"I'm sure they would all love to hear of it if there is," one spoke despondently.

When next Nina was sent for she found the lovely fifteen year old Maharajkumari Krishna in the stagnating windowless room of her mother. The door was left open to its private courtyard but there was little breeze, and a foreboding air to the place.

"You have grown even lovelier than when I last looked upon your pretty face," Nina was truthful in her opening statement. From a young girl she had suddenly changed into a lovely and gracious lady. "Many will be sending the coconut." The girl suddenly turned, dripping huge tears onto the shoulder of her mother. "What have I said?" Nina asked, terribly disturbed that she had created suddenly something tantamount to catastrophe. From a girl made of sunshine she was instantly deep shade.

"It's not your fault," answered the Rani. "You see, this is why we need you so badly. Krishna Bhai feels with you in our midst perhaps something can be done. She knows of your invaluable help to her grandmother."

"Something can be done about <u>what</u>?" Nina was still bewildered.

"Father wants me to marry Sindhia who had already asked for me. I simply cannot marry him. Do you know what he is like? What all he has done to Mewar? It is dreadful. How can father ask such a thing?"

"Sindhia who stole our land and robs the coffers? But you have counsellors who are wise. Surely they will be just and some arrangement can be made to avoid him as a husband if you are so set against it, as indeed you should be. As for me, what could I possibly do to help? I am nobody," Nina argued. "I have influence with no one."

"Grandmother always said she could not have managed without you when she was regent. So many times she would say so," Krishna sobbed.

"Your grandmother was a great lady and no one in the world knew her better than I, Your Highness. I miss her very much, but there was nothing I ever did about anything. I sat through the years with her and served her the best I could, but if anyone thinks I ever made a decision about anything they are very wrong," she spoke honestly and firmly. "I always listened and at times I believe she made big decisions just by talking them out, hearing in her own voice the flaws, polishing over and over the myriad details until her plan was workable. Always she gave great attention to detail. I was merely a small instrument. Not even a sounding board. I loaned her my ears, she always had my heart, but the wisdom was hers."

"That's not entirely true. You are too modest. We know there were many times she listened to you. Do not deny it, Nina, for we would not believe you. Even those who disliked you at the palace, those who were jealous of your closeness, told us so. I am sure you can help. Just stay here with me for a while and you shall see how bad things are. We know you can help. Please say you'll stay."

Maharajkumari Krishna's impassioned pleading tugged at Nina's heart, knowing she must remain at least another week or so. She thought about the problem long and hard, deciding to pay a courtesy call on His Highness, the ruler. Perhaps she could get a feel of his pulse. Something might coherently develop at that time.

Genuinely glad to see each other Nina hoped it would not incur too great a wrath if she brought up the ugly name of Sindhia. "Ah, we grow poorer all the time because of him," the Rana said. "Once again I must ask my ladies to give up more of their jewels and precious possessions just to pay him. There is no end. And now he has ventured forth with the insolent audacity of asking for my daughter as his wife."

"You will not let this happen will you?" Nina seized this chance. "None of your illustrious ancestors would, nor should you. That would be worse than giving her to a Mughal emperor."

"By all the gods in the heaven I could not do that, Nina. How could you even suggest it? Little Krishna Bhai is the dearest thing in the world to me. None can compare."

Intensely relieved Nina reflected on how beneficial it might have been for Sindhia to be his son-in-law. With Krishna as his wife perhaps he could turn the flow of these murky waters. Thank God Bhim Singh loved her enough to think of her first. Nina had never been sure he was quite that noble a person. Perhaps she had underestimated the man she had grown up with.

"What brings you back here?" he asked.

So he didn't know his wife and daughter had sent for her. She lied, "Just missed everybody."

Happily Nina reported to the Maharani, though she insisted she not be quoted, that the Rana had no desire to marry off Krishna to the dastardly Sindhia.

"What a relief," said the little princess who restlessly paced the floor. "I think I would do almost anything for father, but not that. I could not bear that. Not for the country and not for myself. And Nina, thank you. We knew you'd arrange it."

"I didn't arrange anything, little one," Nina half lied. "I just found out what he was thinking, that's all." She didn't want this family to think of her with magical powers too. "You can sleep easier now, little Kumari," she took the liberty of calling her familiarly. "In due time I am sure your father will settle only for someone very special and worthy of you. I think you no longer have anything to fear."

With that she turned to the Rani and suggested she stay on only another day or two.

"But you have come so far and have been gone from us so long," they both argued. "No need to rush. Stay on yet a while."

It could do no harm and she agreed to another week, meantime she would search for anyone traveling the direction of Amber, to deliver a message to her husband that she was well and would shortly be returning. Before the letter was ever written or a rider found there came from Amber an ambassador who also requested the hand of the lovely Krishna for the Maharaja. What an irony. He had a lovely wife and beautiful concubines, thought Nina. She had come to know them exceedingly well. Why must he have one more? True, Krishna Bhai was younger than the others and her beauty had become well known, thanks in part of course to Nina herself who now felt like a traitor. She definitely recalled speaking of the little girl's loveliness and her disposition sweeter than jellabies. Now she had grown and Nina had not especially thought of her as marriageable, but she certainly was. His Highness Amber must have listened well and been shrewdly calculating. Had he surmised the reason for Nina's return to Udaipur even when Nina herself had not?

Nina knew that at this age of fifteen a husband would have to be found before much time passed. Krishna Bhai was getting old, especially for a princess, and the older the more difficult for a suitable match. All the lovely princesses of Rajasthan and surrounding kingdoms were spoken for early and there as yet were no plans for her.

Her Highness, the Maharani, again called Nina to her side, distressfully telling of the proposal and that the House of Jaipur was considered in very low regard. Amber's esteem had fallen drastically when the very first of their daughters had been given in marriage long ago to the Mughal invaders. Of all the laws of Mewar, written and unwritten, the most stringent was the protection of their bloodline and the fact any of their women marrying a man of Islam was to commit a desecrating sacrilege. Whatever else Bhim Singh was, no matter how pathetically weak, he could not countenance his beloved Krishna married to the throne of Amber. It was bad enough in his estimation that Narendra, the rightful lord of one of his feudal estates, would go to work for the man and bad enough that Nina said they were quite content within his care. This Amber proposal, in another sense was as degrading as that of Sindhia.

"How can you even think to live within their palace?" Their Highnesses asked of Nina, who was currently up to date on Amber's affairs.

"His Highness Amber has been most kind to the three of us," she explained. "He has done nothing wrong as far as we are concerned. My husband and I, for personal reasons, needed to leave our place at Jagatpur — if not permanently at least for a lengthy while. We did not know exactly where we were going when we departed but the Maharaja has been exceedingly gracious to us, and now Narendra is happily content with his newest labor of love, raising horses."

"This is very strange," said Her Highness. "It is common knowledge that His Highness Amber is very cruel and evil."

"I have heard such comments too, but for us it has not been so. Perhaps he is pleasant with us because my husband is of good use to him. Without him there was apparently no one qualified enough to help with the raising of his new breed of horses. His stables had been in sad shape. At any rate we have no quarrel either with him or with his treatment. We are all well fed. Our son is more contented than he has ever been since growing up. Amber is the first place he has lived where he has not been ridiculed," Nina spoke truthfully. "Also, some people fear Narendra because of his work with dreaded dacoits. Perhaps that alone intimidates His Highness. I had not thought of it before, but I suppose it could be so."

"Is it that you don't believe the stories about the cruelty of His Highness Amber?"

"There is always gossip," Nina replied. "I sometimes have difficulty sorting out the truths and the falsehoods. What I do know is that if as you say Jagat Singh is a bad person then he must not be permitted to marry our Krishna Bhai, must he?" She started to blush. What right had she to say "our?" Their Highnesses could easily have taken this as a terrible affront for "our" placed Nina in the same category as the royal family. Before they would catch the ill-bred remark or reply sententiously she quickly apologized. "I beg your forgiveness, Your Highnesses. I meant only to say it would be sad to have the beloved child I watched grow from an infant to the lovely creature which she is today to be married to anyone unworthy of her charm. She comes from an illustrious family." Nina secretly referred to ancient forebears rather than current. "Only the best would be good enough. Certainly nothing less."

"No insult taken, Nina. But remember Krishna is already fifteen, soon to be sixteen. That is quite old for a good marriage. Soon we would have to settle for someone even worse than the two who have already requested her hand. The ambassador is housed here with us and I shall think on it further before sending a reply. But it appears I may have to settle for Jagat Singh. Even you would agree he's better than Sandhia. I shall see." With that the ex-servant was dismissed, forbidden to discuss the situation with anyone, save perhaps for the intended bride herself.

Thinking of all the famous royal houses and going over and over all horrid possibilities with his wife, the Rana was in due course required, he felt, to accept the request of Maharaja Jagat Singh, Amber. The ambassador left Udaipur jubilantly after receiving the good news, taking with him not only the message of the Rana but a short note Nina had written for her Narendra.

My dear husband,

It seems a year has passed since last we were together. As you read this you will also be learning of the acceptance of H. H. Amber by Udaipur for the hand of little Krishna Bhai. You will not believe how lovely and straight she has grown, but somehow I am deeply worried. I know when the bridal procession comes you will be among the riders. You had best bring Arjun with you, too, please.

Your loving wife,

Nina

By the time the note reached Narendra she had been gone a month. Between the lines Narendra could read the despair in her voice and he personally thought the union a particularly bad one. While it was true the two men got along famously he could not picture wee little Krishna Bhai in the arms of this man. He was at a loss to open his mouth and even utter one word. His position was too precarious, it was none of his business, he was not of this kingdom, and he wished badly to remain at this work, content with his labors and pleased with the kindness shown his wife and son. Yes, he would ask to accompany the procession on two counts. First that he could offer protection from any bandits who might come upon the heavily laden group. With his knowledge and skill at rounding up dacoits his help would be invaluable. Second, as a feudal lord — he had not formally given up his position in that regard on the outside chance he might not like the way the estate was being run and could conceivably want it back — he should for the sake of protocol be at the wedding ceremony. In fact, if he still acknowledged his rank it demanded that he be there. Jagat Singh could not dare refuse to let him attend and to bear his wedding gifts would perhaps be helpful to Jagat's questionable position.

The bridal paraphernalia took a long time to pack, precious presents of all manner boxed and readied for the elephants' backs. The entourage could take longer to reach the palace than it took Nina. Narendra was overly anxious for the sight of his adoring wife and the uneasy sound of her note made him want to race to her side. Nina was no alarmist and if she asked his arrival with the procession it must be for good reason. If there was trouble at the palace Nina was certain to know of it. Definitely her note would have been read before it reached him and she was astute enough to word it carefully. He was sure she sensed danger and either wanted her two men out of the grasp of Maharaja Jagat, or they were sorely needed at Udaipur.

While the gifts were being packed at Amber, the Udaipur scene again changed. Nina heard that a third suitor sent his ambassador. That hopeful bridegroom was a man by the name of Maun. This Raja had succeeded his brother and now sat upon the throne of Marwar, the capitol of which is Jodhpur. So it seemed that now Narendra's friend of that kingdom too was dead. Nina had not known that. She wondered about this younger brother Maun and if Narendra was likewise acquainted with him, and what sort of man he was. There was a great disturbance and Nina could not conceive of Krishna's problems getting any worse ... but they always did. In the presence of Nina Krishna Bhai questioned the Maharani about the conversation with her father.

"Well, it would seem, my daughter, that the present Raja of Marwar would also like you for a wife."

"I thought father already promised me to Amber. But what is this new man like?" she wanted to know, hoping this was a way out of the ugly fate in which she found herself. She did not care to be married either to Sindhia or to Jagat if the tales of their cruelty and selfishness were true.

"Neither of us have met him, little Krishna, but they say he is stronger and a better man than Jagat. However Jagat's gifts are already on their way here we would suspect and soon the marriage will take place, and so we have sent Raja Maun's ambassador back to Marwar, thanking him kindly for the proposal of marriage and stating you are very shortly to be married to his rival, Amber."

The distraught princess could only throw up her hands in dismay. It would seem things were completely beyond her control, as it usually is in Hindu marriages, and she would simply have to obey the dictates of her father. But this would not keep her from wishing her prince could be charming and as lovable as the old Persian fairy tales. She had become convinced, however, that fairy tales were nothing more than that, sadly not true to life.

The Marwar ambassador was travelling alone on horseback and would move much faster than Narendra and the elephants of Amber who would be ready to depart in a day's time. It would not be too long before the lone rider would arrive at the throne of Marwar, advising Raja Maun of Udaipur's statement: Krishna was soon to be married to Maharaja Jagat Singh of Amber.

Raja Maun sent the ambassador back the very same day, permitting no rest, stating Krishna had earlier been betrothed to his brother while he still sat on the throne of Marwar. The ambassador was to unequivocally state to the Maharana, "Inasmuch as Krishna and Raja Maun's brother were betrothed, she is now betrothed to Maun Singh, for it is not the man she was engaged to but the throne, and now Maun Singh sits upon it. Therefore she is legally and morally to wed him, as heretofore promised."

The ambassador rehearsed this over and over on the way to Udaipur, certain that his argument was valid and he would come out victorious, could return to Marwar and make all necessary arrangements of gifts and so forth.

"You cannot be serious," roared Bhim Singh on the man's return visit. "Our arrangements are with the man himself, not the gaddi. Besides, any day now we shall be receiving the bridal entourage of Amber. Enough of all this crazy story. I will see that you are fed and then you shall return henceforth to your Raja in Jodhpur and your throne that talks. Krishna will not be married to Marwar."

"I cannot do that, Your Highness. The deal was clearly put. The Maharajkumari Krishna was betrothed to the ruler of Marwar. Raja Maun Singh is now that ruler and you must honor this. There is no other way."

Once more their Highnesses spent a restless night going over and over this provocative puzzle and how to get out of this most precarious predicament. "I do see their point," said the

Rani. "Maun Singh is his brother's heir. If indeed the verbal contract stated she was betrothed to the throne, I cannot see what else we can do but have her marry Marwar."

Poor Krishna meantime was more upset and confused than ever and would hardly let Nina out of her sight. Walking the floor nervously day after day, wringing her sweaty hands, she'd say over and over, "What to do? What to do? I know my father loves me and would do his best but whichever man I marry there will always be anger for the difficulty he had to face in marrying me. And god alone knows what will befall my father and Udaipur when the other men are rejected. Would it not cause a war, Nina?"

Poor little Krishna Bhai was too innocent and unworldly to be so beset with earth shattering problems. Who ever would envy a princess her lot in life? Krishna Bhai deserved the happiness which should accompany thoughts and preparations of weddings, the girlhood dreams of seductive romance. "Let us not worry such a pretty head with awful thoughts, Krishna Bhaiji. Just be glad that your father is attempting to do the best for you. And you should be flattered that you have two men now fighting for you, let alone that awful Sindhia. Aren't you thrilled?" Nina attempted to appear light hearted.

But Krishna was not flattered. She was terrified. Though not a politician she was wise enough to know that no good could come of all this. It would be well into the middle of the night when Nina would finally console her enough to drop into sleep, cradling the child's head in her lap for hours.

How many years ago had she come here, Nina wondered. It was now 1808. She had lived through much of toil and trouble and now there was a battle going on militarily between Marwar and Amber. Raja Maun Singh neither had the military strength at this point in time nor the cleverness to win his fight. Terribly ashamed and dejected, and realizing winning Krishna was doubtful, he drew his tulwar to stab himself to death. Saved from this act by a friend, he returned to his capitol, his army continuing their battle. Problems continued to plague him.

His men fought haphazardly and he continued to remain hidden in his palace, yet he would not call an end to the battle with Amber.

At this same time, Jagat Singh sat in his luxurious tent in the battlefield while his wedding entourage neared Udaipur with his gifts. The two armies were camped near each other when Jagat received a message from his fort, the women fearful the enemy was about to capture it. If there had been confusion before, it in no way compared to what followed. Many changed allegiance on both sides and it was difficult to tell who fought with whom. Jagat made it back to his fort quickly, but only after bribing a good many people to allow him safe travel.

Narendra and his group backtracked a little when he learned of the fighting, remaining a safe distance from the actual battles, not wishing a conflict brought upon Mewar inasmuch as he was their feudal lord. But seeing the result of this unmanly series of episodes he could no longer have respect for Jagat. Narendra now knew he would never return to Amber, thankful he had sent Arjun on to Udaipur alone.

Jagat's foe had honored his request for safe return, accepting all his bribes, but he was doomed to live forever in disgrace of all who heard or spoke his name.

It was quite some time before Narendra assembled all the details of what had transpired and continued on behind the trail of his son, finally reaching Udaipur. Seeking out Nina first, relating the whole story, together they asked an audience of Their Highnesses and filled in all the blanks.

"Jagat should now be disposed of as a possible husband," Bhim Singh stated. "Such a coward. I shall not accept his wedding gifts. But there are still the others to deal with." They waited out the course of events, Bhim Singh taking the opportunity of Narendra's presence to attempt to talk him back into service at Jagatpur. Narendra was unrelenting. If ever he would consider it, this was not the time. He would wait longer and see.

Raja Maun Singh was the 1808 counterpart for the saying "all is fair in love and war" and now he finally felt he had won in both. He would again send word to the kingdom of Mewar and his Ambassador Ameer Khan was to deliver the message at the palace in Udaipur to Bhim Singh personally.

"Enough time has elapsed and a decision must be made immediately. Maun Singh has asked for the hand of Krishna and you, Maharana of Mewar, must now decide whether or not you will give your daughter in marriage to Marwar — promptly — or put her to death."

When the message was actually spoken to Bhim Singh he could not believe his ears. Sitting dumbly he asked the hateful Ameer Khan to repeat what he just said.

"You will either give your daughter henceforth to the Raja Maun Singh of Marwar or you will put the Maharajkumari Krishna Bhai to death."

"By such a statement you think I shall turn her over to you without further ado?" the Maharana wailed.

"The choice is yours." He bowed low, long, stepped slowly backwards until he reached the door across the lengthy Diwan-i-Am. He would await the decision in his majestic quarters.

In the room next to his were the huge piles of gifts sent by Jagat as wedding dowry. Narendra had dismissed the men he had accompanied, assuring safe conduct to Udaipur, and sent them back to Amber.

Once more the Rana called in his wife and his chief counsel. Bhim Singh found it exceedingly difficult to talk with the minister on this specific matter for he did not trust him. He knew his counsel and Ameer Khan to be friends and he could certainly guess what the counsel's reply would be. As for his Maharani, how could she condone putting to death her own and most precious child. It was bad enough she lost two sons in childhood, but Krishna was clearly her favorite, just as she was her father's.

Word of this terrible Marwari ultimatum came to Nina via the Rani who wept uncontrollably because she, more than anyone else, knew how weak her husband was. Could he indeed do such a terrible thing? And why should he? Nina offered to discuss it with Narendra. Perhaps they could jointly think of a plan which the Rani could present to her mate. So shocked was Nina that she could scarcely speak of it to Narendra. "It must be some ugly, villainous joke," she hoped.

"I think not, Nina. But let us pray the Rana will do nothing so dramatic as death. Let us sit and work out all the details, the options, go over all the requests and events which led up to this decisive moment. Surely he should quickly marry her to someone and either take the consequences, which are sure to be terrible, or perhaps something might yet come up which would appease everyone." That seemed too good to hope for, but hope and pray they would most vigorously.

Bhim Singh grew more distraught each hour. Humbling himself before Maun Singh was formidably difficult. The Rana's counsel was no help, undeniably biased in favor of his friend and Maun Singh. His wife would not speak to him unless he quickly came to a decision in unmistakable favor of Krishna. Bhim Singh could not even be at ease with his favorite concubines, spending his nights in an otherwise empty bed.

Krishna grew grimly silent as the invincible riddle wore on. Fearing the worst, even faithful Nina had no control over the Virgin Princess's feelings.

Circuitously tortuous days followed with no glimmer of a satisfactory solution when at length Bhim Singh determined his darling daughter must die for the sake of the kingdom. His word had been given to Marwar. That unpalatable fact remained in his mind as firmly and strong as the mighty Himalayan mountains. He had but one choice besides death — marriage to Raja Maun. If he honored that plight, Jagat was sure to round up another Amber army, for weak and dishonorable as he was, armed with his Rajput pride Jagat would stand up to the brazen affront. He'd fight Mewar and win.

The Maharana spent catechizing days implanting in his enslaved mind the tortures of another war. He had already lost so many parcels of land. That which he sought to regain through Sindhia he himself had to pay taxes on. To lose more land and nobles would precipitately weaken Mewar's position as a kingdom and Bhim's questionable place in history.

Then another option came to mind. He'd keep her in the harem in the zenana. But that dream quickly faded for Sindhia would amass his own armies. Treacherous as he was, he could easily make that happen. Sindhia and the Mahrattas would march into Udaipur and take this palace and all the women, leaving everything in ruin, just for spite. Krishna as well as himself, plus the heir to the throne, Jawan, would die by Sindhia's hands. Besides that the whole city would be laid to ruin. Udaipur was a lovely little city but completely unfortified, nor was the palace reinforced. It would be bad enough for himself and all his nobles to be killed, but the fate of the women, if taken by the Mahrattas, would be more than he could bear. It therefore boiled down to a mathematical question. How many would die? One girl? Or hundreds, maybe thousands, and worst of all a great many women dishonored. It seemed his decision had been made for him. Tradition was strong. At least that's what he told himself.

The next momentous issue was who was to slay the hapless girl and how was it to be carried out? There was no way this Rajput king would permit the killing other than by the hands of royalty. For countless centuries throughout the world it had been the unwritten rule that only royalty could kill other royalty. Narendra, as a noble, was one of the first to be called, the Rana considering him a loyal backer of the throne, but the notion was so appalling Narendra could only retreat the room in nauseous disgust.

Narendra went to Nina and told of the plan laid against the Virgin Princess. "Keep her safe from her father," Narendra ordered his wife. "I will do everything I can to help, but of course I do not have access to the zenana."

"That may be easier to order than carry out, Narendra. Should we flee the palace?"

"That too is undoubtedly easier to speak of than do, my wife, for she will be heavily watched from this moment on. We can't hide her in a basket of grapes like they did Udai. We must tell the Maharani of the ill-contrived intention and see if she can reason with her husband. Meantime, don't let the child out of your sight."

On hearing the news the Rani rushed straight to her husband begging, pleading, screaming, crying, pounding at him, trying to reason with him, using every cogent argument and even things less potent. How he could plan the death of his darling daughter when he loved her so much was completely unfathomable. The king barred his wife from the room after this outburst and she could only entreat Nina and Narendra for any manner of help. She could not be sure of trusting any others, not even those long in her employ.

In the meantime the Rana called in one of his trusted ministers, one he felt had a greater sense of loyalty than Narendra. "It is for the good of the entire nation of Mewar," he argued. "Certainly you cannot think I would do this if there was any way out of this dilemma. I have loved her as I've loved none other. Not to kill her would bring doom to all of Mewar and we must think of the thousands of other lives we are saving," Maharana Bhim Singh argued, attempting really to convince himself he was right.

"I'd rather die on this very spot this moment," said the noble. "There is no possible way I could do such a dishonorable thing."

"It is not a dishonor if you do it in the name of Mewar," the Rana reasoned.

"To willfully kill either a queen or a princess cannot be termed a credible thing. No. It matters not what you do to me now, nor what you think of me. I shall not kill the sweet little virgin princess."

It had not occurred to the Rana that this act would be so difficult to bring about. The decision had been made and he did not want it hanging over his head. Nothing about the verdict pleased him. He must rush to have done with it before too many others heard of the plan, causing more perplexing settlements. He called in yet another man, putting the statement in the form of an urgent command, wording it to sound as if the noble would be single-handedly saving the lives of all those within Mewar.

The man took his dagger from his sheath. Out of the Maharana's chambers he walked through several courtyards until coming to the entrance of the zenana. Even the guards at those portals stood back in amazement, doing nothing to stop the man. He walked past several doorways, glancing inside, until he came to the room in which sat the Maharani, the old servant Nina, and the doomed princess.

Sweetly the girl looked up at him, by this time desperately praying for an end to all this mess. Clenching his dagger so tight his knuckles became snow white, he stood above the child. Nina's muscles tightened, bracing for a quick lunge at the jagir, one of the lesser nobles, both women angry enough to tear him literally to pieces. They poised for his next move but he just stood there looking at the child in her pitiably forlornness. Her tender sweet smile which she somehow managed and the look in her huge round black eyes isolated him from his agreement with the Maharana. He dropped his dagger on the marble floor and turned to leave.

The Rani could do nothing more than sit beside her daughter, holding her firmly, shedding tears as large as her contempt for the man who fathered her child. Krishna, however, remained amazingly calm, still choosing not to move a muscle.

The noble turned in the doorway, bowed very low to Their Highnesses, and told of his entire discussion with the Maharana and how others before him refused to carry out the king's order. A black abyss of shame had overcome him, evident even to Krishna. She was the first to forgive his actions. He left the zenana and Udaipur, not to return for many years.

Considerable time had passed, Bhim Singh continuing to look elsewhere for someone to carry out his instructions. Maun Singh's ambassador was still waiting for an answer he was sure would come each day. Bhim Singh thought of the many baby girls who were killed at birth by daggers or excessive opium, sparing their fathers the need to find suitable husbands for them. Perhaps there would come a day when such infanticide would be abolished. There were those moments when he sincerely wished he had done the same with Krishna. The youngster had brought many pleasant days to his life, and now she was causing great pain.

Fate could only decry an executioner, for in what palace or fort from China or Japan to the Middle East would there not be someone who would carry out the ugliest of royal decrees. There is always someone who hates enough to do the puzzlingly unfathomable, or whose price can be met. The virgin princess was to be no exception. Even she had an enemy.

The day came when someone brought to the princess a drink. "Your father has sent this to you, Your Highness," were the coaxing words.

Krishna took the cup and drank the contents immediately, to the dismay of her distraught mother who walked into the room just a moment too late. "Krishna, Krishna, what have you done? Do you not know you are to beware of anything said to be sent from your father? If he sent a man with a dagger you can be sure this drink has been poisoned." The woman was beside herself with hysterical grief.

Nina had rushed into the room immediately behind the Rani. Overpowered with intense horror they were both certain the girl would be dead in just a minute. Taking no chances, Nina immediately mixed a brew which would make the princess vomit. After a short spell the youngster looked up at her mother and wondered at her mental agony. "I'm not afraid to die, my mother. Am I not a Rajput, and a Mewari at that? What of the thousands of others who have marched to the johar fires when they knew all else was lost? What of the queens who have donned armor and fought on their husbands' battlefields only to be killed? Am I not as noble as they? Am I to be different than they? Am I expected by you, my mother, to be _less_ noble than they? If I am your daughter how can this be? I would instead thank my father for letting me live instead of putting me to death when I was born."

It would seem that Nina's potion was stronger than the poison for Krishna lived through this ordeal. Later that night Nina left her to talk over the events of the day with her husband, the Rani glued to the side of her child. Nina thought perhaps the gods had not wished the young lady to die for her life had been once more spared. "Is this not a sign? I can think of no other reason, can you? Perhaps now His Highness will give up?"

Narendra reflected hard and though his religious attitude toward life should have made him agree, he instead suggested that perhaps the particular brew was not made strong enough. If that was the case he was sure they would try the same trick again and probably be successful the next time. On the other hand perhaps there was something about her very physical condition which would keep repelling the potion. In that case he felt certain they would think of still another solution. If the Rana had gone this far he would not back down at this point.

Narendra was correct. They had brought three times to the princess a cup of the same brew, each successive time a little stronger than previous. Each time she would take the cup from the shaking hands of the person handing it to her, and each time she would smile beautifully at the double-faced donor and drink it down. Each time it would be vomited until she finally wished to scream to them, "Be done with it ... one way or the other," but she said nothing and her smile did not betray her thoughts. Nina and the queen were helpless.

A fourth time a cup was brought and she silently prayed it would be stronger. It tasted different and smelled as sweet as their little flower garden. Krishna became very sleepy, laid down before her mother or Nina could find her, and the strong scent of opium within the cup told them on reaching the sleeping princess that this time the drink had not failed. She had fallen into her last final sleep. The virgin princess would never be anything more.

Ameer Khan was still within the palace walls when the Rana's dastardly counsel told him the demands of Raja Maun Singh had been carried out. "We have murdered the princess at your king's command." Now Bhim Singh could be certain war with either Marwar or Amber was averted and he should be safe from Sindhia.

"What?" Ameer Khan turbulently shouted. "You people of Mewar have always called yourself valorous, yet you would do such a thing to your sweet princess? This is valor?"

"But you yourself demanded death on behalf of the Raja."

"You fools. You damned fools. Yes, I said that, but certainly we did not expect you would carry out such a sentence. It was a figure of speech. You're a disgrace."

Throughout Udaipur, to the villages and cities and forts of Mewar the story swept, everyone hearing of it weeping in both sadness for the girl and disgust for the father.

Narendra was anxious to depart the palace with his wife and son but Nina coaxed to stay a bit longer while she sat out those first awful days with the distraught Rani. So overcome was the Rani in Krishna Bhai's untimely death and her inability to stop it that she refused to eat or drink. She was willing herself to death for she could no longer countenance the sight of her husband. Nina was defenseless to aid her as she had others in their troublesome times and came very shortly to know there was nothing else she could do at the palace. If she could not save the princess she could not help the mother. Narendra was right. They should leave very quickly, although they had as yet no time to decide what options were open to themselves.

The Rana meantime had his own misery, stunned into a mental paralysis of his own doing. He lived amidst a whirling vortex of political quicksands. Other nearby clans began condemning as dishonoring the race, having committed an act from which they could never clean themselves. Some of them considered it a destiny willed by the gods and that nothing would follow except doom.

Others came to argue with him that the enemy was not pounding at his door, ready to batter it down. How then could he justify his act by saying he was saving Mewar? Saving it from what? When he would argue that the enemy would have surely taken their women and done unspeakably awful things to them, they would taunt Bhim Singh with evidence that they were not near the palace gates. Would they not all have fought for the defense of the women as they had the past 1000 years?

One of the angriest of men said to the Rana, "I have come here to speak to a Rajput ruler. You are not a Rajput. A Rajput would not do such a villainous thing. A Rajput knows how to fight and how to die while their wives are busy also dying in the flames."

"But we all would have died in an inevitable fight," the Rana argued, armed with very little validity.

"You are wrong, Bhim Singh," he dared to speak to him familiarly rather than addressing him with respect. "Even if a war had followed not every one would have died. There have been many wars and hundreds of battles in the history of our kingdom and always some were saved or fled to rule another day and even in another place if need be. That is why we have an Udaipur. The gods would have seen to it that someone of our Suryavansa line would have been saved, but you have defamed us and now we <u>will</u> all desolately die. Now we <u>are</u> doomed, thanks to you."

Although not a prophet in the strictest sense, his words did come true; quite suddenly the wife of the Rana's counsel died as well as the counsel's two sons. The Rana had borne ninety-five children, and only three were going to live, and of those three only one was a son, Jawan. The Rana did indeed feel doomed but he still had twenty more years to sit on the throne. It was now only 1809.

Chapter 21

The Singh family plans were desperately in need of meritorious injections, an intense need to be physically and morally away from the palace. The three moved to the old trysting place where Nina and Narendra used to make love, toward the trees which would not carry their conversations further. Once more they asked their son to listen attentively and give thought to where they would settle, for he was infinitely vital to their future. "We must come to a decision soon," Narendra said. "Let's consider the past and see what we can come up with for the future."

To return to Jodhpur where he and Nina had met would now be unthinkable. His friend the Maharaja was dead and he did not really know the newest Raja Maun Singh. This man would surely be extremely angry over his loss of Krishna Bhai. He must have seen some political benefits in that union. Visiting him at a time like this was implausible.

He could not go to Jaiselmer for his old in-laws would never cease blaming Narendra for Kala's death.

Returning to Amber palace would be just as bad or worse. Jagat's wedding gifts had all been returned to Amber before they were ever officially accepted at Udaipur when Raja Jagat shamed himself by begging a disgraceful retreat to his fort. He would also be distressingly angry. Besides, Narendra had no desire to work for a man that weak. Why hadn't he seen these traits earlier? For that matter Narendra might not be welcomed into the sanctuary of his Amber fort. An unwelcome guest would not be permitted to attend the Arabian horses and maintain the stud farm he had created. Breeders and trainers could be replaced. Each of these kingdoms was definitely out.

Should they stay within the confines of Mewar? Should they return to their own fort and take back the seat he had temporarily given up? He had been wise enough to leave a return date completely open. Would they return to live in disharmony in their own home, but a home where they rightfully belonged?

"We need to reassess our own personal values, Narendra," Nina suggested. "Where do our loyalties and priorities now lie? Just as we could not instantaneously leave Jagatpur when we married and trouble started to brew, neither should we jump into any flapping flames now. Once more let us take it slow and easy. Can we not roam around and show Arjun more of our country? One day a candid answer will come to us."

Arjun, at this point, was completely without ideas.

Night came more sweetly to them, the three huddled together under the favorite of all the trees, Arjun unaware of the many satisfying kinds of love that were shared beneath its limbs. Nina had become a powerful reinforcement to Narendra, removing turmoil from conflicting decisions. Narendra had circled back to become the whole and marvelous person Nina had first known.

Before dropping off to sleep Narendra considered all the major things of his life which were influenced by his wife, his present happiness, thanks to Nina and everlasting credit to his mother who had forced this marriage. She had been infinitely wise. Regarding Arjun, he was a good boy and Narendra owed him the very best upbringing he could arrange. If this was so, then surely it was meant that they return to Jagatpur. How long can one run from problems? Their cortege of woes must be forced into the open before they could seek complete acceptance of Narendra's family if any real contentment could ever come to the three of them. Tomorrow he would talk Nina into returning to Jagatpur.

Tomorrow brought an even stronger Nina and a Narendra who finally gave in to her demand to roam the land a while longer. "You are just afraid of what awaits you," he said. "You never before were intimidated. That is not your way. That is weak and you are strong."

"You're doubtless correct," she replied. "We have been through so much, especially in these last months. The treachery has made me sick at heart and tired, too. I cannot rush back into yet more problems. They will wait for us. Let us just be free for the time."

"If you promise to one day return."

Nor was Arjun overjoyed at the prospect of seeing the loathsome Amar. Once back at the estate, if his father returned to the top desk young Arjun would be sitting with his father, learning the business. Probably his cousin-brothers would be of little or no help and life would be expectantly lonely.

On that subject Narendra had firmly stated, "Forgiveness is a divine power, Arjun. I hope you have been endowed with it and will forgive your cousins just as I shall forgive the women who have been mean to your mother and me. If your grandparents were alive today they would ask that we acquit the family and so it is that I am now asking you on their behalf to do this thing."

"I shall also try," spoke Nina. "There are things lately I cannot wipe from my thoughts. Bhim Singh was but a little boy when first I came to the palace. His lessons were my lessons. The kingdom's problems were his mother's problems and little by little they became his to solve. I saw his weaknesses and his strengths. I watched him make mistakes and do some things which were fine and noble. I was but a mere servant and then though providence might have created me someone equal in rank, still even then I could not have sat in judgement. Who is there who can live out our days without mistakes. If that were so we would be gods and we are but mortal flesh. Hari Lal would ofttimes tell him, "Your Highness, you will err and by erring you will become wiser and hopefully stronger. The point is not to err too often, nor on too big an issue.

"There was great sadness for me, my son," Arjun's mother was resolutely serious, "in having suffered with Queen Mother through all those years of strain and struggle, trying to keep Mewar from the Mahrattas or anybody else. She tried her best. She too had made mistakes but I think not too many. And presently all the worries became her son's and she was freed from her earthly cares.

"I am certain Bhim Singh loved his mother very much but he was too young when his father died to remember much about him. What Bhim Singh liked best was always hearing of the heroic deeds of his forefathers and I'm sure he wanted very much to emulate them. Somehow he just could not. Every man is not born as resolutely strong as he would like and it simply was not his kismet to be the most beloved of the Mewar rulers. And to be sure, the times in which he lived had much to do with this."

Nina continued, her son sitting silently beside her. "In a certain way I loved him too, Arjun, for without Hari Lal's marvelous teachings and without continued kindness by their Highnesses I would not have developed into whatever I am today. I am certainly a much better person than when your father found me. God has been great. What I have been allowed to share in the major part of my lifetime is tremendously unique. Can you yourself imagine any servant brought up almost as well as a princess?"

"But you did not have fine jewels and clothes like a princess, mataji."

"I had for my roof the most beautiful palace in the world. For my friends the Queen Mother and the Maharana, his teacher Hari Lal, and in the last years the rani and young Krishna Bhai. But realize the real importance lies in the give-and-take of life, the seeing and doing. Material things are of little consequence if you cannot appreciate what is around you — the earth, the sky, the people, what horrors they have suffered and lived through. Such things make a people great: their being together, suffering, laughing, learning."

"And that is why the three of us must stay close together, Nina," Narendra interrupted, reinforcing his firm statement that one day before long they should return to Jagatpur.

Nina smiled wryly, "Oh Narendra, I cannot get out of my mind the look in Krishna Bhai's eyes. That sweet innocent child with the meek and mild manners. I don't believe there ever was one so sweet as she. And her mother, oh lord how she suffered. There was hardly a time we would leave the girl alone, but always when we did that is when they would bring the poisoned cup to her. We would be with her almost every moment of the days and nights but they must have watched our every move. They always came in those few solitary moments and the guilt which comes from this I shall carry the rest of my life."

"I forbid you to talk of it, Nina. You will make yourself as sick as the Rani became. You had no way to save her. You did whatever you could, as did I. There was no possible way of dissuading the Rana. Let her soul rest wherever it is. She loved you, Nina. You served her as you did her grandmother and if they could speak to you now they would utter their thanks. You have done your job well, and now it is time for you to come home with me and let me shelter you from the world's cares just as you used to say you would care for me in the rainy times of my life. Remember? Now it is my turn to care for you. This is my sacred promise, just as I henceforth promise to prepare a place for Arjun in the seat of his father and grandfather and those before that when his time is come. We must leave this world one day and I too grow older. I must not waste much more of my time. Let us make of it what we can."

"Just a little longer," she begged. Narendra kissed her forehead.

"What will become of the Maharana now?" Arjun wanted to know.

"He must pull his wits together and see if he can arrange for stronger counsel. They have been deliberately torn apart more each passing year until now things are in great disarray. I hope he does nothing else which is foolish."

"What of the British, father? Will they one day come as far as Rajasthan, or will they stay over there in Calcutta and Delhi as we hear?" Arjun considered the possibility of having to deal with them in some distant year when he or Akhil and Amar would hold the position now officially covered by his father.

"There are many stories filtering down to us, son, some good and others very bad. I do not myself know what harm or good the British would muster should they reach Mewar, nor what we can do about them. There would have to be a durbar of great magnitude and perhaps all the Rajputana States would have to band together against them if ever they should threaten us, for individually we are very weak now, but joined together we could be incontestably strong if we all set our minds to it. I believe there is no immediate concern," Narendra informed his son, although he would one day come to know he was very wrong.

Changing the conversation, Nina said she wanted one last walk through the old city of Udaipur. A final farewell for she had no wish ever to return, not even as the wife of Jagatpur's lord while on durbar or any festive occasion. The scars were far too deep now in spite of the unique past. She wanted to be alone on this jaunt.

Walking through their bowered sanctuary Nina started in the direction of the great palace, through the tiny break in the wall covered with brush, used often by sentries. She nodded to a few of the guards as she passed, even stopping to pat a white oxen drinking from a trough in the largest of all the courtyards. At the spot where she had fallen on her buttocks on her original entrance with Narendra into the palace grounds she stood. The elephants were not lying here today, resting their backs on gentle concrete slopes, awaiting those fights she hated. For a long time she stood looking up at the windowed balcony where she first discovered Queen Mother staring down at her in delighted laughter, and where some years later she had danced with this same regent on Holi. Through her misty eyes she thought she could see her again, that kindly face, a woman of highest rank who stooped to make a friend of a low-caste servant. And then the image disappeared. Nina could see nothing more through burning tears.

Further down the palace front, just to the south of the long steep outer steps was that remarkable round golden sun window at which she'd catch the little Rana so many, many years ago as he played at being an adult, beaming his rotund face down upon anyone who might be looking, shining his ray of light upon them.

Passing through the middle of the triple arches, standing next in silent salute to the many sentries she had casually known in the thirty years valiantly served here, and to those servants attending court with their superiors. Downhill she'd go to Jagdish Temple, not only for praying for Krishna Bhai but for wisdom to be granted the Rana. She stopped now as she had on those other days, rumpling the hair of the youngsters, swatting their behinds in matronly fashion, joking about minor matters.

Removing her chappals to once more feel the cobblestone on bare feet as she had in most of her earlier days, she came to rest at the foot of the temple. Glancing up the 32 steps and beyond to the heavens she was afraid to wonder what was in store for the balance of her lifetime. Slowly she climbed to the top, handing a paise to the beggar who still sat here daily as he did on her first arrival in Udaipur. With three twisted limbs, skin pulled tightly over angular bones, it seemed impossible he could live much longer, but then she had thought that thirty years ago. Offering coins to the beggars is a necessary part of any Hindu's life. Giving to the poor and destitute would surely bring her to a better station in her next life on earth, but what was better than that which she already had? Certainly not the life of Queen Mother, the present Rani or little Krishna Bhai. No, a better next life was not her reason for giving. Just to share with this gnarled old man was as imperative to Nina as breathing. In these thirty years neither had ever spoken a word to the other.

She placed her bare feet squarely on the platform surrounding the shrine to Lord Vishnu. She had been here many times but never had really seen it. Today with starry tears in her eyes she would seek the presence of the lord in her heart, asking that he give her little family the strength to endure what lay ahead: Narendra for coping with the problems that surely amassed themselves in his absence from Jagatpur and to accept his fate whatever Akhil, his brothers and the city fathers would ordain. For Arjun she wished a grace with the wisdom of his grandfather. And for herself she wished for the inner sweetness of Krishna Bhai in dealing with her relatives. If that youngster could be so strong, Nina too should find such strength.

Staring at the stone carvings of this massive temple they represented many scenes relating to life in this world today and the world beyond. This then must be the correct place for supplication. Round the sanctuary she walked before again entering the inner sanctum to worship at the feet of the four-armed black image, reaching up to ring the black bell telling Lord Vishnu of her entrance so he could listen to her prayer.

Down the steep steps she paused briefly before mutely walking slowly through the main avenues of this charming city she prayed to see just once in her lifetime and came to know so intimately. She passed small stands of foodstuffs, tilak powders, bangles, cheap cotton tie and dye materials for head scarves or gagras. Carts roamed the wider part of the street selling their gooey orange colored jellabies and other sweetmeats. There were the stalls of the little brass water pots, larger pots for cooking rice, flat brass spoons for stirring and those for ladling. There was fresh green coriander on long stems, orange colored carrots, and aromatic spices necessary to Indian cooking, cheap cotton string ornaments to be worn in women's hair, elongated balls of brass or silver hanging from ropes to decorate the center part of women's hair, stretching down to midforehead. The whole bazaar was alive with people, some sitting cross-legged in shop doorways waiting in the quiet, patient way of the Rajasthani for a daily sale. Others chattered in high-pitched voices, still others whispering their delicate secrets.

Life bristled all around her but she was alone, alone with her thoughts of husband, son and what might be.

At the reverse side of her old palace home she stopped at the little temple where each year she joined the others of the palace in the procession to honor Sitala, the smallpox goddess. This most dreaded disease claimed the lives of many and scarred most of those who lived through it. Each year in spring the women of the kitchen dressed in their brightest and finest, accompanied by the ruler on horseback, the ladies heads laden with massive flat trays of food to be prepared later in the day for palace consumption. The local priest would in due course bless these foods and much later the procession, to the accompaniment of a brass band, would wend its way back to the palace kitchens. Nina and her child had escaped the dread disease and for this she yearly thanked the goddess. She paused now to do so again, minus the customary pomp and ceremony.

Four and a half hours had elapsed before she returned to her family under the same spreading tree. Now late in the afternoon she wanted to immediately depart, even if to cover only a very few kilometers. She had said her last goodbye to Udaipur.

A shade of wistful wonder crossed Nina's face. Irrecoverably lost were those persons of the palace she adored most. There was no satisfaction to be gained from bitterness, refusing to drain the last dregs of poisoning thoughts. Seeds of disillusionment needed to be washed from their planted furrows and Nina would not allow herself the luxury of spurious disenchantment. She would cleanly break from its shackles, to walk away with Narendra and their son, totally unencumbered.

Epilogue

is Highness Bhim Singh, 67th Maharana of Mewar, continued to rule from 1778 to 1828. His was the longest reign of any of the rulers, thus far, in this imperishably illustrious family.

Bibliography

To name every book read, every person interviewed would be to write an additional volume. Renditions of past events by ancestors with whom the writer spoke were, for the most part, identical in details, as if learned by rote.

Special thanks to the following:

Mirabai, Saint & Singer of India by Anath Nath Basu (quotation on page 178) with permission of George Allen & Unwin, London.

Meghaduta by Kalidasa (5th century A.D.) translated by late M. R. Kale. With permission of S. V. Kale.

From the Land of Princes by Gabrielle Festing. with permission of John Murray (publishers), London.

Glossary

Aachkan	long coat
Adavasi	aborigine
Bhai	(pronounced bh-eye) "sister," used as a term of endearment
Chabutra	raised platform
Chapati	a common Indian bread
Chaprasi	peasant
Charpoy	cot
Chay	(ch-eye), tea
Chhatri	gracefully curved dome
Darshan	worship service
Darwaza	door or gate
Dhai	(dh-eye) midwife
Dhobi	(dough-bee) washermen or women
Diwali	(dee-vah-lee) a brilliant and happy festival of lights
Durbar	court; meeting of the lords

Gaddi	(gah-dee) throne
Gagra	(gah-grah), very full Rajasthani skirt
Garh	fort, appended to the name of the city, for example, Chittorgarh is the fort above the city of Chittor
Ghat	steps at a water "tank" or pool
Haldi Ghat	a battle of 1576, perhaps the most famous of the Mewar kingdom
Jellabies	sticky sweet snacks
Johar	a sacred act of self-immolation, performed by throngs
Kumar	prince
Kumari	princess
Maharajkumari	any legitimate daughter of the ruler of Mewar
Maharana	(mah-hah-rah-nah), ruler of Mewar (Prior to this title they were called Rana and before that, Rawal.)
Maharani	(mah-hah-rah-nee), wife of the Maharana
Mahut	elephant's rider, usually trained together since the animal's birth
Mandapam	wedding "altar"
Maré dhost	(mah-ree dough-st), "my friend"
Mataji	"respected" or "revered" mother
Morcha	a pit dug in the dirt for hiding

Namasté	an Indian greeting: "hello" or "goodbye"
Nautch girl	dancing girl
Nullah	ravine
Paise	coin of small denomination
Puja	(poo-ja), prayer
Rani	(rah-nee), Queen
Sambar	a small deer
Sati	(sah-tee), self-immolation, especially of a widow on her husband's funeral pyre
Shamiana	tent for weddings or large functions
Shikar	(sh-car), tiger and/or leopard hunt
Sumje	(some-jee), understand
Talli	large metal flat plates with raised edges, used for dining
Tank	a pool or small lake, frequently beside a temple
Thakurs	(tah-coors), noblemen
Tiffin	afternoon snack
Toran	a wedding symbol over the door
Tulwar	curved sword of Rajasthan
Zenana	the ladies palace

Order Form

Satisfaction Guaranteed

To:

Thistle Publishing
11985 Cherokee Circle, Suite 109
Shelby Township, MI 48315

☐ I am enclosing $ _____. Please send me the following books and publications.

☐ I do not wish to order now but please **add me to your mailing list** so I will receive future offers and publishing information.

_____ *Virgin Princess: An historic novel of Mewar (Udaipur, India) — the world's oldest dynasty.* @ $15.95each
_____ *Martha.* temporarily out of print
_____ *Steadfast the Lamp.* coming in 1991

Please type or print clearly.

Name:

Address:

City, State, Zip: